P9-CQE-781

MOURNING GLORY

Warren Adler

KENSINGTON BOOKS
http://www.kensingtonbooks.com

AUG 1 4 2001

KENSINGTON BOOKS are published by

Kensington Publishing Corp.
850 Third Avenue
New York, NY 10022

All Kensington titles, imprints and distributed lines are available at special
quantity discounts for bulk purchases for sales promotion, premiums, fund
raising, educational or institutional use.

Special book excerpts or customized printings can also be created to
fit specific needs. For details, write or phone the office of Kensington
Special Sales Manager: Kensington Publishing Corp., 850 Third Avenue,
New York, NY 10022, Attn. Special Sales Department.
Phone: 1-800-221-2647.

Kensington and the K logo Reg. U.S. Pat. & TM Off.

Library of Congress Card Catalogue Number: 00-111181
ISBN 1-57566-898-X

First Printing: August, 2001
10 9 8 7 6 5 4 3 2 1

Printed in the United States of America

For Peter Lampack,
with admiration, affection,
and apologies

CHAPTER ONE

"But I can still see the wrinkles," the woman said.

Grace studied the woman's face, the dry, aged-parchment skin tight over the bone structure, pulled back taut like a slingshot. A broad smile, she speculated, would detach it from the skull and shoot it like a Halloween mask over the makeup counter. Grace bit her lip to keep herself from grinning at the bizarre image.

She knew who the woman was by reputation, Mrs. Milton-hyphen-something, a world-class champion shopper. Clerks fawned over her as if she were the Queen of Sheba dispensing largesse to the peons. For a big commission Grace, too, could fawn with the best of them, hating the process but, like the rest of the salesclerks, eager to accept the rewards.

Having never before waited on Mrs. Milton-hyphen-something, she saw the moment as pregnant with income possibilities. Besides, she needed something to take the edge off what had started out to be a very unpromising day.

"Perhaps a bit more of this," Grace said, dabbing at the spidery corner of the woman's eyes with the brush. Even in the flattering stage light of the makeup mirror, carefully wrought to wash away the telltale clues of aging, the skin ruts could not be made to disappear.

A hard and hopeless case, Grace sighed to herself, knowing it would be impossible to satisfy the woman's insistence on appearing, at least in her own mind, wrinkle free. Makeup creates an illusion, she wanted to explain, her standard lecture to women who came to her for either a new look or lessons in the art of beauty enhancement through cosmetics.

For the younger women, the lesson was easier to impart. Besides, with them, she used a more magnified and, therefore, more revealing mirror, one that enlarged the pores. These younger ones who bellied up to her counter all seemed to suffer from rampant insecurity, as if they didn't truly believe in the essential beauty of youth and needed the paints and smears to feel attractive.

Somehow it didn't jibe with the ideal of the modern woman currently in vogue, the contemporary ideal, the confident, independent, able-to-have-it-all female touted in the media. Oh, they were out there, all right, like Mrs. Burns, who managed the store. Grace saw them everywhere, admired their wonderful, cool arrogance, their I-don't-need-a-man-to-make-me-whole-and-happy attitude. She granted hopefully that such observations could be an illusion, a false positive, and that, in reality, those cool numbers prancing about were just as insecure as she was. Fat chance.

She knew in her heart exactly where she stood, one among many still barely on the sunny side of forty, an anonymous grunt in the vast army of female also-rans, the powerless majority, stuck in some weird limbo, dismissed by their more successful sisters as congenital losers, who could not, for whatever reasons, respond to the clarion of the gender's call to arms. The truth of the matter was that most of those in the ranks of these defeated battalions, like her, were unlucky, battered by inexplicable circumstances, mismanagement or, perhaps, just too dumb to find the right doors to open. Others were irrevocably stuck in yesterday's female mind-set, hopelessly old-fashioned and totally unaware of the possibilities in the new world.

Ironically, for purposes of social comment, advertising reach and political posturing, her group was statistically in demand. Not like the single females in the fifty-to-seventy category, that army of the divorced and widowed who had walked over the hill to oblivion, the cruelly cast-off, doomed by chronology, aging flesh and diminishing opportunity to a kind of loneliness and sexual limbo.

Her group was always cited as that demographic female baby boomer segment with subcategories like working poor, single mother, marginally educated and, above all, semiskilled. She was all of the above. Translated to class, she figured herself to be lower middle, very lower and, therefore, downwardly mobile, now in speedy descent. Jackie, her daughter, would undoubtedly agree, although for her sake, Grace maintained a razor-thin facade of hopefulness and optimism. By some miracle of genetics she still had her looks and figure. Small comfort since, so far, it hadn't done her much good.

Considering her status, she took some satisfaction in the irony of her occupation. Cosmetics, creating false illusions through facial paint, was, inexplicably and thankfully, exempt from prohibition by the so-called "new woman," a possibility hardly on the agenda of the woman who stood before her.

Women like Mrs. Milton-hyphen-something, well north of sixty with unlimited funds, weren't even pretending to buy the concept of cosmetic beauty enhancement. They wanted camouflage. They were dependent more on the plastic surgeon's knife than the chemist's dubious magic for their attempts to defeat or, at the least, stalemate time's relentless destruction.

"I don't think you know your business," the woman snapped, her head moving on her neck like a puppet's in a desperate attempt to find the wrinkle-smoothing reflection. To make visibility more authentic and truthful, the woman had put on her reading glasses and was squinting unhappily into the mirror.

"I am a graduate cosmetician," Grace said in defense of herself, citing her ninety-day course.

"Big deal," the woman huffed.

"And I've worked here in Palm Beach at Saks Fifth Avenue for three years," Grace countered calmly, pasting her best customer's smile on her lips, hoping to unload the crone's wagons. "I've never had a complaint." She paused, realizing she wasn't making a dent in the woman's unhappiness. "Sometimes cosmetics are designed to bring out a woman's character and tell the story of life well lived."

The woman eyed her suspiciously over her half glasses.

"What does that mean?" she sneered, her lips twisted as if she were having gas pains.

"I was merely commenting that your face shows extraordinary character. There is great beauty in character. After all, you've earned those wrinkles. Why try to hide them?"

"Are you crazy?" the woman said.

"None of these preparations are designed to hide the real you."

"Jesus. Are you trying to say that it's attractive to look like a wrinkled old fart? I don't have to come here for that, lady."

"You're misinterpreting my remark. I only meant . . ."

"I know what you meant."

Just one more nail in the coffin, Grace sighed, listing in her mind the day's toll so far, beginning with her morning battle with Jackie, sixteen years of seething anger and perceived needs. It was growing worse each day. Money for this. Money for that. It was a breakfast staple. Money! Damned money and the shortage thereof. It was the bane of her existence.

Worse, in a life of irony this one had sharp spikes. She had named her daughter after the late Jackie O, as if the name could be an inspiration for taste, gentility, elegance and fine aspirations. Now it seemed like an adolescent myth gone sour. Like her namesake, her Jackie was acquisitive, indiscriminately so. Unfortunately her taste had a split personality. She thirsted for the high end, yet seemed mesmerized by the low end, the lowest end.

"Can I help it if I like beautiful clothes, Mom? You promised that you would get me the Donna Karan when it got reduced."

The Donna Karan plaint was at the root of the latest skirmish on the clothes front. Jackie had seen the outfit one day when she had met Grace at Saks, where she often wandered through the designer clothes areas while waiting for Grace to get off from work. The slacks outfit was priced far out of line for their pocketbook, but Grace had promised that if it got to the sale stage, she would definitely buy it for her with her employee discount, which meant 40 percent off.

She had even begged the salesclerk in designer dresses to downplay it so that it would hang around unsold and be a candidate for reduction. It was on the verge, and Grace calculated that she could get it within the week, which would be a great surprise and, perhaps, a peace offering for Jackie.

This morning, in addition to the ritual of the clothes, it was the never-ending litany of the car. "A car is a must, Mom, an absolute must."

"I thought the Donna Karan was a must."

"That, too."

A "must" was condoms, Grace had countered, reiterating her own litany, which included getting good enough marks to get into Florida State, which was Jackie's only affordable option for college. Another "must," in Grace's standard lecture, which she had delivered that morning with almost hysterical passion, was realizing one's potential and developing a sense of personal responsibility. This meant, in addition to safe sex, avoiding drugs and booze, bad company and, above all, showing some respect and appreciation for her hardworking efforts to give their lives, despite the obstacles, a semblance of dignity.

Dignity, she had discovered, was a word being used by her with increasing repetitiveness. It was for Grace the ultimate fallback position, the last refuge of the working poor. It was not easy to be dignified living on twenty-five thousand dollars a year before deductions.

"I'm going to be seventeen, Mom," Jackie had reminded her, as if she were about to enter some mythological geographic environment requiring special equipment to survive. "I'm not like the other girls in school. I don't want to be a K mart person for the rest of my life. I am a Saks Fifth Avenue person, not a clerk like you, a potential customer. I am in my heart a Bendel person, a Bonwit, a Cartier and Tiffany person, with a body that craves Valentinos, Versace, Ferragamo, St. Laurent, Givenchy, not Gap, Wal-Mart or K mart. I want expensive things. Not bargain-basement shit. Is it a crime to love nice things? You should be proud of my champagne tastes. You're the one who taught me that. Remember who I was named after."

"Now you're blaming me," Grace said, troubled by her daughter's awesome yearnings and eloquence beyond her years. More and more she was feeling inadequate to Jackie's daily challenges. It was, after all, Grace who had taken her on those window-shopping forays on Worth Avenue, who had subscribed to the fashion magazines that cluttered the apartment.

"Champagne tastes are okay if you have a champagne pocketbook. Which we don't."

"And never will," Jackie snorted.

"Never say never," Grace replied.

"I hate being without," Jackie told her, which was yet another perpetual mantra that she was exposed to on a daily basis.

"We're not exactly without, Jackie," Grace sighed.

"I know, Mom. I do appreciate your twenty-five-dollar weekly allowance," Jackie said sarcastically.

"I'm happy you remembered its source."

"Daddy would if he could."

"Daddy's entire life has been based on wish fulfillment, potential events that never happen."

After six years of divorce, Jason rarely surfaced, except in periods of acute financial desperation. At times, Grace had obliged his entreaties for her daughter's sake.

"Daddy is a dreamer. The world has to make a place for people like him."

"Just as long as it's not with us," Grace shot back with barbed sarcasm. Defending Jason, her ex-husband, was an arrow in Jackie's quiver of annoyances. She had protested vehemently her mother's dropping of the Lombardi name.

"Why would he want to be here with us? Come on, Mom. We live in a dump. Nothing here but losers. And don't be so high-and-mighty about my allowance. I couldn't get by if I didn't have that job in the multiplex."

"I'm doing the best I can."

It was always Grace's last refuge.

"I know. That's what hurts the most, knowing that this is the best you can do."

Weekends Jackie worked as a ticket cashier at the multiplex. Grace had actually increased her allowance so that she could devote more of her time to schoolwork. Financially it was still not enough, and Jackie had to keep her job. Grace was absolutely paranoid about seeing her daughter get into college and, so far, Jackie had barely managed to eke out a passing average.

Grace's disintegrating relationship with her daughter, long on a downhill slide, was now accelerating rapidly. Grace's best efforts, she realized, would never be good enough, not for someone with Jackie's unrealistic expectations. Had Grace planted these ideas in her daughter? Was it wrong to point out the good things in life, to inspire a higher taste level than their pocketbook could afford? Maybe so. Whatever the reason, Grace was losing control over her daughter.

Jackie was too attractive, too sexually precocious, too manipulative and financially ambitious to accept the present condition of her life. Grace had no illusions about where it would lead. Jackie was an explosion waiting to happen, and that morning's confrontation merely reiterated that possibility.

Then, adding insult to the injury of the day, just as a pouting Jackie left for school, Jason, Jackie's father, called from parts unknown with his repetitive plea. "Help me out till I get on my feet, Grace."

She had been particularly harsh. "The only way to get on your feet is to nail them to the ground, Jay. You're a fuck-up. Never call me again. Ever."

Angry, she had slammed the receiver into its cradle.

She had had fifteen years of good looks and empty promises from this brainless mannequin who could conjure up more impossible dreams than Don Quixote. Finally she had shown him the door, shouting, literally "and take your windmills with you." In retrospect, she had come to enjoy that line, which she had heard once in a movie.

Back home in "Ballimer," they were once the golden couple. She, the cute and very popular Grace Sorentino, the barber's daughter, with the jet-black hair, soft pink skin and Wedgwood blue eyes. The movie star look. He, Jason Lombardi, a walking double for Robert Redford. Of course, one didn't make a living being a walking double for Robert Redford, as she was to find out later. And there was limited mileage in being a cute knockout with a great figure. Someone had once said she had a walk that could raise an erection on a dead man. She had taken that as an insult back then. Now, at thirty-eight, she read it as a kind of compliment, although doubtful that the description was still operative. Jason's call had brought back the hated memory of her wasted years.

Also that morning, she had learned that her bank balance, hovering somewhere around a paltry eight-hundred dollars, was frozen, lost in computer hell, and she was getting turn-off notices from the telephone and power companies. Taunting her further, she had painfully banged her big toe kicking the ATM machine, which had swallowed her bank card after the third try.

The good news, a highly exaggerated rendition, was that she had just put the monthly car payment for her three-year-old, bottom-of-the-line Volkswagen into the mail, which meant that she had merely one year to go before she owned outright what was destined at that time to be a pile of junk. She had also paid down just enough of her Visa and Master cards to restore her credit, a mixed blessing.

But these were mere details, which ignored the total State of the Union of her life, which was abysmal, not to mention the harsh fact of marching time. Her thirty-ninth birthday was just three months away, an event that promised a day of unrelenting self-pity.

She hated birthdays. Her thirty-fourth, the day she threw Jason out from her bed and board, was supposed to mark a new beginning. It did; the beginning of another phase of the downward spiral. On the horizon, on the cusp of her fortieth year, was yet another harsh reality, the onset of early menopause (she was sure of that) and a future of emotional and financial insecurity.

She'd light the birthday candle in a Twinkie and make a wish for some imagined act of deliverance to lift her out of her marginal existence. After all, she could never allow herself to abandon hope of some miraculous windfall.

"What I meant was," Grace said in a desperate effort to assuage the frowning scarecrow in her pink Armani silk pants outfit and diamond-studded clawlike fingers on the other side of the counter, ". . . that you should lead with your best shot. Play to your strength." It was a thought that barely made sense to her, but somehow, under the circumstances, it seemed appropriate.

"You mean emphasizing my wrinkles and thereby illustrating my character, right? How well I lived my life, right?" Mrs. Milton-hyphen-something said.

"Exactly," Grace said hopefully. "Present to the world an honest look."

"I don't need you for an honest look, lady. I see it every morning in the mirror. What I need you for is to find me a dishonest look, which means hiding my wrinkles."

"I've already tried the best we have to offer," Grace said. "They're too . . ." She was tempted to say "too fucking deep." Instead she added: ". . . well-established."

"Well-established. Good. I like that. Cosmetics were invented to soften and hide them, to make you look better, not worse. To do it right takes talent," the woman sneered sarcastically. "In your case, the talent is missing."

"Perhaps one of my colleagues . . ."

"Colleagues, you call them. That's a good one. Clerks, you mean."

Grace failed to find either the humor or decency in this confrontation with a seventy-plus gnome who had wandered in from creamy Palm Beach's Worth Avenue determined to either find youth in a magic vial or, barring that, validate her alleged superiority by kicking the most accessible and vulnerable unfortunate in her range of motion, which was her, Grace Sorentino, the failed daughter of the barber Carmine and the silent, fanatically devout Mama Rosa, the Sicilian papal groupie from "Ballimer," Maryland.

"You people just don't know what you're doing," the woman said, frowning at her feral image in the mirror.

"It's in the eye of the beholder," Grace said, the pasted smile faltering.

"What is that supposed to mean?" the woman snapped, her face frozen, her eyes still searching for the magic light.

"It means," Grace said, sucking in a deep breath, determined to show a patient, pleasant visage, "that you might be noticing things that others would overlook. We normally don't observe each other with reading glasses."

The woman shook her head in exasperation and looked around the store, filled now with the army of mostly middle-aged bottle blondes with considerable disposable income, relentlessly avoiding the skin's mortal enemy, the ultraviolet ray.

"Do you always insult your customers?" the woman asked. "I detest salesgirls with an attitude."

"I hadn't meant to be . . ."

"Hadn't meant. Hadn't meant. People do atrocious things and then retreat into hadn't-meants," the woman snickered. Beneath her bleached-white look, Grace could detect the hot flush of anger.

Whoa there, Sorentino, Grace cautioned herself, valiantly holding her pasted smile, although her facial muscles were beginning to hurt with the effort.

"I'm sorry," Grace whispered. "There's just so much that can be done with makeup."

"Are you calling me an old crone?" the woman snapped.

"Old is a state of mind," Grace said.

"And crone?"

"You're putting words in my mouth," Grace said, feeling her smile collapse.

The woman's eyes blazed with anger.

"Do you know how much money I spend at Saks?" the woman said. The anger had forced her face to express itself. Nests of wrinkles emerged everywhere. Her skin seemed prunelike.

"I'm not privy to such information," Grace said.

"You needn't be sarcastic," the woman said.

At that point, the woman stood up from the high stool in which she had been sitting, removed her glasses, shook her head and sneered.

"I can't let this arrogance pass," she muttered, turning abruptly and moving through the crowd.

"I need this job, you old cunt," Grace muttered, wondering if any-one had observed the confrontation. She had no idea what she had said to tick off the woman. Not that words were necessary to convey the truth of the encounter. The woman was a miserable, unhappy, frustrated bitch, determined to cause pain. Grace had been as good a target as any. Wrong place, wrong time, she sighed, preparing her-self to be figuratively taken out and shot.

She looked through the plate glass at Worth Avenue, that fantasy-land of upper-crust consumerism glistening in the late morning sun. How had she wound up here, one of the minions to the wealthy? Jason, her unmourned departed ex, had brought her and Jackie to West Palm Beach to pursue yet another of his irrational certainties, another franchise to oblivion. And so they had remained, left to rot in the tropics, along with the coconuts and seagull droppings.

She had managed to make a marginal living for her and Jackie, mostly at retailing, where she could hustle for commissions and use her personality and good looks to sell.

Unfortunately, this modest selling talent was not effective enough to secure another relationship with a man. She hadn't exactly been a passionate seeker. In this age of the independent woman such yearnings were supposed to be an insult to her gender and, for a time, she had tried to live by that caveat. It was not an attitude that had contributed to her happiness.

The fact was, she had concluded, that most people come in pairs. Wasn't that the immutable law of nature, proof positive being the anatomical construct of the human body, however it had to be rearranged to accommodate same-sex copulation. It was a subject considered every time she reached for the vibrating dildo she kept hidden in the bottom drawer under her heavy northern clothes.

But after five years, with the looming realization that Jackie would be leaving home, hopefully, for college, she had opened herself up to the possibility of another permanent round with a male of the species. The fact was that she hated the idea of preening and detested the various routines of flirtation, the small talk, the dating and mating rituals.

She had made a number of forays into that world, forcing herself to be open to such experiences. She considered herself a lusty woman, and in her years with Jason, especially the early ones, there was a cornucopia of sex.

Trying to be brutally honest on such an intimate subject, she considered herself, at least from a mechanical point of view, a reasonably efficient lay. Not that she had exposed herself to any recent reviews on that subject. Certainly not lately. Jason hadn't voiced many complaints on her performance in that department, although its frequency had diminished considerably over the fifteen years of their marriage. He had simply lost interest.

She concluded finally that the thing she dreaded most was the initial phases of the mating game, the obligatory résumé, the verbal fencing, the various elements of the seduction scenario, the anxiety of—there was no other satisfactory and honest way to describe it— the first fuck, and all initial side issues and embarrassments, the adjustment to the whole range of this new partner's sensory activities, his odors, the sound of his breathing, his body temperature, the observation and necessary inventory of his body parts, the touch of his flesh. And her own exposure to such inspection by him.

Such obligatory rituals inhibited promiscuity at her age, which was, she supposed, a blessing and certainly safe. It also threw some mental barriers in the way of flirtation as her imagination cranked out vivid scenarios of this dreaded initial phase. Strictly as a biological necessity, her vibrating dildo catered to her needs. It was a far cry from paradise, but it did the job.

She did manage one casual and lukewarm affair with her then dentist. In the age of AIDS, considering the precautions he took while she was in the dentist's chair, mask and surgical gloves, she felt reasonably safe, although she still insisted that he wear a condom. But the act had been more a validation of her femininity than a passionate experience. Most of the time she hadn't had an orgasm and was reticent about instructing him in the technicalities of her specific construct and the best method to achieve its effect.

The so-called affair lasted for exactly how long it took to put in three new crowns. He did offer a trade-out on future work, but she declined and went to another dentist, a move she had reason to regret. Despite his shortcomings in the sexual area, he was an excellent dentist.

Because of her lackluster and probably indifferent attempt to attract mating possibilities, she determined that she was "unlucky" when it came to men. Perhaps she had simply lost the skills of engagement. She felt incapable or unable to separate the shells from the peanuts. Did men perceive her as a hard case, or uppity, or too challenging or not challenging enough, or unwilling to enter into a relationship? Or all of the above and more?

Why was opportunity passing her by? Why wasn't there the slightest hint of serendipity in her life? Was the mating system itself, like a drain covered with rotting leaves, too clogged with young hard-body competitors to allow for some free flow into the pool for the nearly menopausal set. The fact was that the mating distribution system was patently unfair for a working woman heading in the wrong chronological direction? Yet she still had a good figure, and her face, with her expertise in makeup, could still appear youthful and attractive.

Men did look her way, their glance, she sensed, occasionally lingering, as she swung past. But was she perceived as a willing objective? She doubted that.

All right, she conceded, she could tell herself that little white lie that she was liberated and independent enough to do without the comfort of male companionship. But hell, she wanted to be fucked by a live instrument, caressed by manly arms, supportive and supporting. She wanted someone to bounce thoughts and decisions against, wanted someone to help her skirt the minefields, someone strong and loving and manly and loyal, someone to fuss over, who fussed over her, someone to respect, someone to share the burden. Her experience with her ex had given her insight and experience into winners and losers. She could, she believed, if given half a chance, separate the wheat from the chaff.

She considered herself intelligent, if only modestly educated with one year of junior college. Even her most stringent self-assessment gave her a sound sense of curiosity, an excellent sense of humor, a glib tongue. Everybody said she had the gift of gab. She read *The New York Times* every Sunday and was an avid reader of the *Palm Beach Post,* which gave her some passing awareness of politics, current events and the entertainment world. No one could call her a dummy. Besides, she knew more about cosmetics and fashion than most people.

People said she was a good conversationalist and men showed what seemed an interest in her, at least in a first encounter. The problem as she saw it was that she found the men she met mostly boring, which led her to wonder what had happened to the gender in the nearly twenty years that had passed since her courtship and marriage. She had concluded that her own lack of interest in them was a turnoff, which the men sensed, and rarely called her for a second date.

Comparing herself to the women who came into the store, she could not understand why she had fallen through the cracks while others of lesser looks and brains and personality had found a secure domestic haven. Something was definitely missing in her strategy. Was she sending out bad vibes? Had repeated discouragement inhibited her social skills? The fault must be hers, she decided.

It was worrisome. It wouldn't be long before the forties arrived. Then what? Would she be heading to the blue hair pastures, her glasses held around her neck by a chain, her jowls drooping lower each year, her neck wrinkling like old parchment, her tits heading downward with the force of gravity, her hips and belly thickening, her morning routine washing down her estrogen replacement pills with orange juice.

It was dangerous to let imagination run away with itself. But there were just too many examples of people left at the post in southern Florida. All it took to set her thoughts going was a trip to any mall where the army of the aging bored marched in endless battalions. It took all her willpower to keep from falling over the edge into heavy depression.

For a while she took refuge in the idea that she was too busy devoting herself to raising Jackie to have any time for a new relationship. But that was a cop-out. Jackie was reaching new levels of worrisome independence by leaps and bounds. She was losing her and knew it.

In a year or two she would consider Grace, except for a marginal financing machine, irrelevant, worthy of lip service but little else. The reality of parenthood was getting through to her hard and fast, the end result would always be the ultimate conclusion that parents loved and worried about their children far more than they could ever love and worry about their parents.

She no longer blamed other people for her failures. She had married in the midst of her first year of junior college, a mistake compounded by a mistake. During her marriage, she had been a bank teller, a secretary, had worked in boutiques and other department stores, but, because of her husband's itchy foot and quixotic view of life, she hadn't been around long enough to make much of a mark. Jason, chasing his own impossible and indefinable dreams, had taken her and Jackie to points north, west and then south. In Florida she had taken a three-month cosmetician's course, had landed this job in the makeup department at Saks Fifth Avenue Palm Beach store and had been slowly building up a modest clientele.

The telephone near the register rang and she knew instantly that it would be Pamela Burns, the store manager, on the other end of the line. The gnome had struck.

"Can you see me for a moment, Grace?"

"Of course," Grace replied, reaching unsuccessfully for an optimistic lilt to her tone. She hung up and proceeded on rubbery legs to Mrs. Burns's office.

"Mrs. Milton-Dennison told me you insulted her," Pamela Burns began directly, playing with the triple string of pearls that hung over her pink silk blouse. She was older than Grace, well-groomed, with hawk's eyes that hid behind high cheekbones and jet-black hair parted in the center and brushed straight back. Her lipstick, eye shadow and earrings glistened brightly as they caught the light beams from the staggeringly brilliant sunlight that blasted into the room from a high, round window behind her desk.

"I should have, but I didn't," Grace said. "She was rude and insufferable."

"Customers are never rude and insufferable, Grace," Pamela Burns lectured, talking slowly, enunciating clearly, illustrating her version of how a successful manager deals with anger and recalcitrant personnel, undoubtedly Grace. "Shopping at Saks is either therapy or fantasy fulfillment. But however you define it, there is only one object in mind as far as we're concerned. We check our egos and other unnecessary hubris at the employees' store entrance. We smile. We ingratiate. We flatter. We agree. Our mission, the sole objective of this enterprise, is to move merchandise."

"I move merchandise, Mrs. Burns," Grace declared with a feeble attempt at showing indignation.

"For which you are appropriately commissioned," Mrs. Burns shot back. "At the highest rate allowable in this company."

With commissions, Grace had averaged during her three years with Saks, a sum which, after deductions, barely qualified her for the working poor.

"Mrs. Milton-Dennison is a major consumer of merchandise. It is her addiction. We keep her supplied with the drug she needs."

"Merchandise?"

"Exactly."

Mrs. Burns looked at a paper on her desk and tapped it with long, polished fingernails, which also glistened in the sunbeams.

"Have you any idea what she spent with us last year, Grace?"

"She asked me the same question," Grace murmured.

"And well she should," Mrs. Burns said, lifting her eyes and studying Grace in their hot glare. "Eighty thousand a month."

"That's nearly a million dollars a year," Grace exclaimed, calculating quickly, stunned.

"A world-class movement of merchandise. That old biddy is an industry for us. We pucker on demand."

"Hard to believe ... she's such a ..." Grace checked herself. But she hoped her expression would convey her honest characterization of the woman, which was *miserable shit.*

". . . marvelous, generous, beautiful person," Mrs. Burns said, completing the comment with a sly smile of understanding.

"I gave her my best makeover advice, Mrs. Burns. Unfortunately, there is no product, except perhaps a complete face mask, that could hide her wrinkles."

"If she wants her wrinkles hidden, Grace, then you are charged with finding a way to hide them."

"Believe me, I tried," Grace said. A sob seemed to catch in her throat.

"Apparently not hard enough," Mrs. Burns told her between tight-pursed lips. "She wants you fired."

"Fired? Because I couldn't find a product to hide her wrinkles?"

"Apparently it was also the manner in which you trumpeted your failure."

"I didn't trumpet anything."

"That was your mistake. She needed trumpeting, the flattering kind. You should have trumpeted her assets."

"They escaped my notice."

"Therein lies the nub of the problem, Grace. She craved the licking of her *tuchas.* This is where she gets it. It is not for nothing that this store is named Saks."

She searched Mrs. Burns's face to find some recognition of the double *entendre* as a joke. It wasn't apparent. The woman was dead serious.

"Understand the deeper psychological implications of our role here, Grace. Mrs. Milton-Dennison gets off on shopping. This is where she comes to replace the fucking she does not get at home."

"Jesus!"

"I detest this kind of pressure, Grace. It frustrates me and I hate dealing with frustration. My only goal is to make numbers, to increase these numbers year after year. Numbers are what determines my bonus. We are not dealing here with the human equation. Numbers provide the true meaning of our existence. Mrs. Milton-Dennison represents only numbers, Grace. She is a factor here only because she puts a lot of bread into the oven. She is the soul and spirit of the capitalistic machine."

Mrs. Burns's sudden mixing of metaphors was disconcerting.

Grace wondered if she should be respectful of Pamela Burns's remarkable candor and realism. The woman was generally admired for "telling it as it is," which was exactly what she was doing now. But to whom? Grace pondered. Certainly not to Mrs. Milton-Dennison. *To me, poor impoverished servile loser me.*

"I do not like to be forced to grovel before Mammon," Mrs. Burns said, as if reading Grace's mind. She lowered her voice. "We both know what Mrs. Milton-Dennison is." Suddenly no sound came out of her mouth. "A fucking miserable cunt" were the words her lips seemed to have formed.

Grace was encouraged by the intimacy.

"A mover of merchandise," Grace said, the fear of firing suddenly diminishing as a possibility. She felt oddly relieved. "Then you're not terminating me," Grace said after a brief pause.

"What would you do if you were being threatened with a million-dollar loss of custom, Grace?"

"It would be like . . ." Grace searched her mind for an adequate image. "Like being caught between the devil and the deep blue sea."

"That represents a choice. Mrs. Milton-Dennison didn't give me such a wide range of options."

"So I am fired?"

"I hate to put it that way, Grace. It makes me feel like an instrument of cruelty. I do know your situation Grace. We have to know about our employees in these litigious days."

"Am I or am I not?" Grace said, raising her voice.

Mrs. Burns shook her head. She seemed genuinely grieved, although Grace distrusted the pose. Dissimulation was part of the stock in trade of winners like Mrs. Burns. They wore their bitchery like a badge of honor, proof that their ruthlessness was equal to men's.

"I'm going to give you a bit of advice, Grace," she said, her eyes glazing as she moved her head in the direction of the window, as if she were speaking to the pedestrians along Worth Avenue. "We are in Palm Beach, Florida, the ideal hunting ground for Mr. Big Bucks. In this wasteland, they are everywhere, like pebbles on the beach." She sucked in a deep breath and lowered her voice.

Pamela Burns paused; her nostrils flared, a tiny smile lifted her lips. "Find yourself an older wealthy man, a widower, fresh from the burial ground, someone who in his vulnerability can appreciate a good-looking woman like yourself to share his bed and his fortune.

Mostly the latter, of course, although the bed will be the conduit. You should hone your technique in that department, Grace.

"To a successful man of declining years, used to control, that part, man's best friend, is your ally. Pay it special attention. Secure your old age. No one will do it for you. Make yourself a mover of merchandise instead of a mere dispenser. It is better for your *tuchas* to be a receiver of the pucker than to be obliged to offer it. Seek out and find Mr. Big Bucks."

Grace was stunned and incredulous by the cool cynicism of Mrs. Burns's remarks. She couldn't believe her ears.

"What are you saying, Mrs. Burns?" Grace said, barely able to absorb the information presented. It seemed so out of character, so ruthless and calculating. Mrs. Burns turned her gaze from the window and focused on Grace.

"I'm simply saying find yourself a wealthy man who has just buried his wife."

"A wealthy widower?" Grace muttered, still in disbelieving mode. "A millionaire?"

"My dear girl, *millionaire* is such a passé term. It no longer connotes serious money. Learn the modern interpretation of numbers. It will open your eyes. Think in terms of a section."

"A section?"

"A hundred mil. You may not make it, but as the poet said, let your reach exceed your grasp. They are out there, believe me."

"Why are you telling me this, Mrs. Burns?"

"Because I am wracked with guilt. I hate doing this to you. I also hate Mrs. Milton-Dennison." She lowered her voice. "Lousy old cunt."

"Is there a guidebook on how one goes about accomplishing this feat?" Grace asked, hoping that Mrs. Burns would get the facetiousness and sneering sarcasm of her remark.

"Published every day," Mrs. Burns shot back without batting an eye. "The obituary columns, Grace. Make it your daily Bible reading."

"You are serious."

"Dead."

Grace, for the moment forgetting her situation, considered the irony implicit in the word.

"Are you saying that I should attend these funerals?"

"Consider it research."

"And then?"

"Assess the situation. Be sure there is money there. Survey the mourners. Evaluate their wealth and lifestyle. If possible, check beforehand. See where they come from. Look at their houses. Make a careful evaluation. Don't make the mistake of choosing a target with anything less than big money. Keep your eye on the ball, then find a way to make contact."

"But why a recent widower?" Grace asked, feeling foolish. The idea seemed preposterous, ghoulish. Here she was in the midst of a personal disaster and she was listening to what seemed like nonsense. Worse, she was asking questions.

"With a long marriage," Mrs. Burns said, expanding on the idea. "Preferably a first wife."

"Why a first wife?"

"Because men in a long marriage are more accustomed to the ministrations of women, Grace. Like horses, they have been broken, domesticated."

Is she playing with me? Grace thought. Despite her misgivings, Grace found herself bizarrely interested, as if the strange idea might divert her mind from this train wreck.

"Are there any other considerations?" Grace asked, thinking: *She wants to pull my chain. I'll pull hers.* "Is there an age requirement?"

"I'd put a cap of seventy-five on the choices, although the sixties would be better. You run into protective relatives when you go higher in age. And they need less of what a woman has to offer. They figure you are only after that person's money."

"Isn't that the purpose of the exercise?"

"I'm talking time here, Grace. Under seventy-five the lure is still there." Mrs. Burns winked.

"You sound like you've made a thorough study of the subject."

"I have. I found one."

"Mr. Burns?"

"I followed the formula. It is the best advice you will ever get in your life."

"Then why do you have to work?"

She felt compelled to keep the interrogation going. It struck her that perhaps she was not being fired at all. Perhaps Mrs. Burns had gone crazy and this interview was simply the babbling of a diseased mind.

"I don't. I need the stimulation and sense of accomplishment. Mr. Burns is very old now."

"How long have you been married?"

"Fifteen years. He was sixty-five at the time. Except for longevity, he was the perfect choice."

"How so?"

"He was Jewish. I'm an Episcopalian."

"Why Jewish?" Grace asked, mesmerized by the conversation. *Am I really buying this?* she wondered.

"Their mothers worshipped them. Because of this, they are addicted to mothering. And they are very good to their wives, particularly their second wives, especially if they are *shiksas,* like you and me . . . not Jewish. I think they see us as the forbidden fruit. That's why I'm emphasizing sex. And . . . I hope this doesn't sound anti-Semitic, but maybe their circumcisions have made them more sensitive to pleasure. Who knows? Many of them have been starved in that department by their first wives. Frankly, I don't know why this is true, but I believe it is. To them a good *shtup* is a *mitzvah,* a gift from God. These attitudes make them more vulnerable. Of course, I'm not counting out any racial or religious persuasion as a possibility. I can only give you the benefit of my own experience."

Grace was confused, not only by Mrs. Burns's advice, but by her own weird interest in it. She found herself actually contemplating the idea in the light of her own situation, her own dismal reality. How could she, a nobody from the lower classes, an obvious loser, come in contact with such people. Multimillionaires. Jews. They weren't exactly in her circle. It struck her finally that Mrs. Burns was teasing her, getting her jollies by putting a sinister spin on the act of termination.

"Am I really being fired?" Grace asked suddenly, not without optimism.

"Afraid so."

"Then this is a very strange exit interview, Mrs. Burns," Grace said. "I don't appreciate it at all. I feel as if I'm some object of ridicule and I'm pretty pissed off. Is it in lieu of severance?"

"Not in lieu of, Grace. Although the advice I offer is more precious than coin." She took a paper from a pile on her desk and slid it across to Grace.

"What is that?"

"It is a release form. Sign it and you will receive two months' severance pay based on your year's best salary. In this case . . ." She glanced at the paper. "Two thousand two hundred a month. Comes to four thousand four hundred dollars. Very generous, I must say."

"Blood money," Grace said. "To protect you from litigation."

"Your choice, dear," Mrs. Burns said. "We have lawyers on retainer."

"Do I also lose my employee discount?" Grace asked, thinking of her promise to Jackie.

"When you are no longer an employee, you no longer have an employee discount."

Furious, Grace scribbled her name on the paper, and Mrs. Burns opened a drawer and handed her a check already cut for the amount mentioned. Grace studied the check for a moment, as if to illustrate her distrust, then stood up.

"It's an unfair world, Grace," Mrs. Burns said. "Nevertheless, if Mrs. Milton-Dennison should take her business elsewhere or die, believe me I can make a firm commitment at this moment to give you back your job."

"You are one cold-blooded bitch, Mrs. Burns," Grace said. They exchanged glances, and after a moment of staring each other down, Mrs. Burns nodded.

"I pride myself on that perception," she said.

Grace turned and started toward the door, stopping suddenly when she heard her name called. She turned again and faced the woman behind the desk.

"In the enterprise I suggest, Grace, there is one more caveat. It is fundamental."

Grace looked at the woman, a commanding presence behind her desk. Mrs. Burns lifted her left hand. At first Grace wondered if she was giving her the traditional gesture of contempt.

"Ring around your finger," Mrs. Burns said cheerily. She directed Grace's attention to the glittering diamond marriage band on the finger of her left hand. "This is essential. And beware the prenup, the deal before you get it."

"You make it sound like a sales agreement."

"Now you're getting to the heart of the deal. Especially if he's got kids. They'll guilt him into a tough prenup. Fight it. My advice . . . get him while he's hottest."

"Is this stuff relevant to me? Really, Mrs. Burns. Never."

"Never say never."

Speechless, Grace turned to the door with a heavy heart.

"Last word of wisdom, Grace," Mrs. Burns said. "Never move in before . . ."

"Before what?"

She lifted her left hand again.

"This," Mrs. Burns said. "Ring around your finger."

"Screw you," Grace muttered.

This woman is off the wall, she thought, slamming the door after her.

CHAPTER TWO

Her daily routine disturbed by these incredible experiences, Grace felt disoriented and rootless. She had no idea how she was going to spend the rest of the day, no less the rest of her life. She headed back to her apartment for no apparent reason except that that was the only destination that offered a haven.

She lived in Palm Tropics, a small garden apartment community a few blocks south of the Tamiami Trail built sometime during the bucolic fifties. She shared a one-bedroom apartment with Jackie, who slept on a studio couch in the living room.

It wasn't exactly what she preferred as the perfect living environment for raising a teenage daughter, but she lived with the sense, despite her daughter's daily harangues, that all this hardship was merely a passing phase. Unfortunately, after five years of living in this place, the hope of imminent escape had become a cruel illusion. Jackie was exactly right: The place was a dump.

The management company prided itself on its maintenance performance, the result being that the plumbing and kitchen fixtures were very workable and, as a consequence, very unmodern, and the vomit-green-painted stucco made the building rows look like World War I army barracks.

Grace referred to the project as "shabby genteel," which took the sting out of the inescapable fact that this was a place for the downwardly mobile, of which she was a fellow traveler. Especially now. Still, she refused to allow herself to brood, fearful that overanalyzing her present condition would lead to depression in all its many facets.

Call it lousy luck, she told herself, which sounded a lot better than a squandered life. Besides, thirty-eight was still young in this land of the blue hair, Social Security checks and Medicare. Maybe it was time to go back to Baltimore. It was a thought that called her to attention. She hated Baltimore and the rigid little lives her father and mother had lived. Besides, there was nothing in Baltimore for her now or ever again. The image of her father, Carmine the barber, still living there as a widower in the rooms above the shop, completed the circle of dread. Baltimore was dead. She had escaped along with many of her childhood friends. Escaped to where?

She brushed off her long-term problem and concentrated on her immediate dilemma, which was to fill up that time normally devoted to her job. She ticked off possibilities. There was always a movie, but they didn't open until later. Or the beach, but that meant exposure to the enemy, the sun.

An errant fantasy of hitting South Beach in Miami and picking up a young hard body surfaced, but briefly. The risk of humiliation or worse, rejection, would be too much to bear. There were bars, some probably just opening, but the prospect of both lonely drinking and the possibility of small talk and flirtatious innuendo made her nauseous. There was always the comfort of food, but events had demolished her appetite, and she had no desire to threaten one of her last remaining assets, her figure.

She pulled into her parking space and sat for a moment in the car, unable to gather the energy to emerge. On a weekday, with most of the residents off to work, the area seemed desolate. Most of the cars were gone. She noted a motorcycle parked nearby that she had never seen before. At least on Sundays, she had the sense that she was not alone, that others shared her fate.

Fighting off a wave of self-pity, she got out of the car and let herself into her apartment. But she had barely shut the door behind her when she heard odd sounds emanating from her bedroom. Frightened, she held herself still, feeling the pounding of her heart against her rib cage.

But fear quickly turned to shock and anger as she observed what was happening. Jackie was strenuously engaged in a pretzel-like sexual escapade with a young hard body with a shiny shaved head. Their clothes were strewn about the room, testifying to their abandon.

They were so focused on their activity that they did not respond to her presence, and since she was too stunned to announce herself she was forced to witness more of this sexual theater than she might have wished.

"Oh, no!"

It was Jackie herself who sounded the alarm and began a panicky extrication of the young man's firm embrace. The sight of a glistening naked male penis emerging from the sex of her daughter finally broke the spell of paralysis, and Grace sprung into action.

She grabbed the young man by his ear and pulled him screeching from the bed as Jackie escaped into the bathroom. In an effort to free himself, the young man punched her in the stomach, blasting the air out of her. She doubled up in pain and fell to her knees.

"You were killin' me, lady," he cried. "Bet you're her mama, right?"

Grace nodded, unable to find her voice. She looked up at him, suffering the indignity of watching him pull on his pants.

"Hell, we was only balling."

Grace's breath came back finally, but she could only shake her head in despair. On her knees, barely able to accept the reality of what she had witnessed, she felt a profound loss of dignity, a sense of acute degradation.

"Where's the harm in that?" the young man continued, tightening his belt. She noted that his large silver belt buckle sported a raised black swastika. Only when he turned slightly did she see the leather sheath that hung on the belt. In it she could see the handle of a knife, also emblazoned with a swastika. He must have seen her look of fear. Apparently to enjoy it further, he pulled the monster out of its sheath, brandishing it, making circles in the air.

She was too angry for tears, and the image of the young man who stood above her playing with this terrible weapon only increased her desolation. He was scruffy, unkempt, with recently shaved head scarred with razor nicks. His body was tightly muscled and slender, and he observed her through small, intense, angry eyes, half hidden behind high cheekbones. He was hardly from the world Jackie claimed to aspire to enter. Smiling crookedly, he grabbed his crotch, a conspicuous bundle in his tight jeans.

"Got some left, Mama. Want some?"

"Get the hell out of here," she cried to the young man, staggering to her feet, finally finding her strength. As she watched him, she

noted an odd tattoo crawling across a muscled arm, a dagger, not unlike the one that hung from his belt, complete with swastika and encircled by a coiled snake and the words DEATH BEFORE DISHONOR. The
illustration seemed even more intimidating than the real thing, and
she felt a shiver of fear ratchet up her spine.

She watched him slide into a torn T-shirt, over which he put on a
black leather jacket festooned with metal rings on which hung silver
swastikas. He clumped around in high-heeled white lizard-skin cowboy boots.

"I could send you right to heaven, Mama. Just like Jackie. Man, you
got the hottest little lady in South Florida."

"Get out of here, you pig," Grace shouted shakily, trying to stare
down the arrogant expression of disdain on the young man's face.
Dressed now, his lips formed in a cocky smile.

"Pig you say," the young man said, turning to the closed bathroom
door. "Hey, Jackie, your mama thinks I'm a pig." He turned again to
Grace. "Hell, you got that right. I been porkin' your daughter." He
let out a high-pitched laugh.

"Just leave, please," Grace snapped.

The young man shrugged, then opened his hands palm upward.

"Not like I raped her. Other way around, Mama. Little girl of yours
goes for the meat." He cupped his crotch again.

"You know how old she is?" Grace sneered.

"I don't ask for no birth certificates."

"She's sixteen," Grace blurted, shocked by his sudden hateful references.

"Nothin' tighter than that, Mama."

"You could be in big trouble," Grace said.

The young man moved closer to Grace. His nose was almost touching hers.

"Come on, Mama," the young man said. "Cool out. You wouldn't
want to make no trouble, would you, Mama? Not for your hot little
baby there." He tucked her under the chin.

"No," Grace conceded. "I don't need more trouble."

"Smart Mama."

The young man winked.

"Maybe if you're a good little Mama, I give you a ride on my hog.
Got a bitch pad with a golf ball. Wrap your legs around that, Mama,
and you'll know what high is."

The young man turned and walked to the window, opening the
blinds.

"See that beauty, Mama?" He pointed to a black Harley-Davidson motorcycle, glistening brightly in the sun. His eyes, she noted, were glazed with pride and admiration, as if it were a religious icon. He moved closer to Grace again and whispered, "Ain't that somethin', Mama? Better than pussy. Rigid frame Evo with a kicker, look at them pulled back buckhorns, two hot cylinders, thirteen-forty CC. Go for a put on that hog, Mama, you gonna be in heaven." He laughed his high-pitched laugh again, then knocked three times on the bathroom door. From inside came the sound of a shower.

"See you, baby. Me and your mama's been makin' it up. I promised her a ride on my Evo," he shouted.

He looked toward Grace, who was only partially confused by his biker's talk, which had evolved for his generation. Jason had had a bike when they were going together. He winked again, cupped his crotch, then made a good-bye gesture with two fingers.

"You didn't use a condom," Grace said, suddenly frightened by what she had observed.

"Looked like nice, clean meat to me," the young man said, punching Grace lightly on the arm. Shaking his head, he swaggered out of the front door. Moments later, she heard him gun the motorcycle and roar away.

Grace sat down at the table and tried to calm down. The young man was positively awful. She shivered with fright. Her hands shook. The sense of her parenting failure was overwhelming. She wished she could cry, but she couldn't. After awhile, the bathroom door opened and Jackie, wearing a robe, a towel wrapped around her head and looking remarkably fresh and unruffled, came out. There was not a sign of contrition on her face.

"You weren't supposed to be home," Jackie said.

Grace looked up. Jackie without makeup was radiant, a vision of the unspoiled, virginal, hardly the image of the wanton sexpot she had just seen squirming on her bed.

"I can't believe this, Jackie," Grace said, shaking her head.

"Mom. It happened, okay? Maybe if I had a car . . ."

"Good God!"

"Darryl's been taking me to school on his hog for the past month. So I cut Phys Ed this morning. He was going to take me back for afternoon classes. What's the big deal?"

"The boy's a horror. Did you see that knife he carries, and those swastikas? He's what they call a skinhead." She was choking with anger. It was bad enough to have witnessed her daughter's sexual es-

capade with this man, not to have it compounded by what she perceived as the dark ugliness of his character.

"So what? He knows what he's doing."

"You're jailbait, Jackie. Do you understand what I'm saying?"

"Perfectly. And I had better not hear it again."

Grace could see that she had gone too far. But the implied threat
was ominous.

"This is not the way you've been brought up, Jackie."

"Stop that crap, Mom. I don't think we want to talk about the way I
was brought up. Hell, I'm the daughter of two losers."

"And you seem to be heading in that direction yourself," Grace
said, fighting to remain calm.

"Monkey sees, monkey does," Jackie muttered.

"He seems . . . subhuman." Grace sucked in a deep breath. Her
frustration was acute as she searched her mind for ways to admonish
her daughter that wouldn't make things worse than they already
were. "You keep talking about your champagne tastes. It's sickening,
trading your body for a lousy ride to school. And with that . . . that
Nazi."

"All right, Mother, you've made your point," Jackie sneered, pouting with typical adolescent indignation. "At least he has the courage
of his convictions. He's making a statement."

"A statement? It's a curse. The Nazis were worse than devils,"
Grace cried.

"Come on, Mom. Cool out," Jackie said, resorting to her usual ploy
when the argument between them grew too heated. "Don't be so old-
fashioned. I think he's cute is all. It's all for effect. And riding his hog
is a lot better than the school bus. Besides, I get a lot of respect from
the kids. . . ."

"Respect!"

"Have you forgotten what it is to be young?"

Always that, Grace thought. Emphasizing the generational disparity, throwing it up to her as the root of their misunderstanding.

"I haven't forgotten what it means to be a parent, Jackie. You're
sixteen. That's still a kid in my book. And legally you're still under
my jurisdiction."

"Again, legally! Jesus, Mom. What are you gonna do, hire a lawyer?"

"Well, it's obvious we need some kind of help here. Maybe a coun-
selor. Really, Jackie, things are getting out of hand. You're my only
child. I love you and I hate what you're doing to yourself."

"You sure are making a big deal out of nothing, Mom."

Jackie shrugged, but Grace could see that her burst of rebellious-
ness had softened.

"Please, Mom. I love you. I really do. Don't force me to say things
that are hurtful."

"Hurtful? What I just witnessed was hurtful."

"Mom. I haven't been a virgin since I was thirteen. You knew that.
I'm on the Pill. You knew that, too. I felt horny. Darryl is not anyone
I'd choose for a serious relationship. He's got a good body and is
good in the sack and I like him a lot. I know he seems weird, but he
serves my needs."

"He scares the shit out of me, Jackie. That shaved head, that ugly
knife and those Nazi things. . . ."

"Turns me on, Mom," Jackie quipped. "Just don't worry so much. I
can handle him."

"Handle him? You shouldn't even go near him," Grace sighed,
feeling suddenly nauseous. She did know about Jackie's sexual pro-
clivities but had never brought herself to picture her doing it, actually having sex. Except for dire warnings, they had never discussed it
in intimate or graphic terms. She supposed it was a form of denial.
Or acceptance. She wasn't sure which. What made it even more terrible was that it was being done in her bed, her own private place. It
added to her sense of violation.

"He's a low-life slob, Jackie. White trash," she managed to say.

"That's Darryl's biker image, Mom. Macho man. So he's a skinhead, but don't let his macho talk fool you. He's smart."

"I forbid you to see him," Grace said.

"Forbid? Now you're my jailer."

Grace sighed in despair.

"This isn't fair, Jackie," Grace said. "It's a worry we don't need.
Why can't you size up this situation . . . ?"

"Worry about yourself, Mom. I'm perfectly capable of watching
out for myself. Haven't you always taught me the value of self-
reliance? Hell, last year you got me the *Book of Virtues,* remember?"

On a whim, Grace had picked it up at a secondhand bookstand.
She thought the title apt but hadn't read it herself.

"I thought you might learn something." She shrugged.

Jackie harrumphed with mocking humor, unwrapping the turban
and starting to towel dry her hair.

"This is serious, Jackie."

"That's the problem." Jackie moved the towel vigorously.

"I don't want to see this ever again," Grace said, recognizing the weakness and futility of her warning, deliberately shifting the focus of the argument. She knew in her heart that Jackie would defy her admonition. "And I don't want to come home to this. Do you read me? In my bed, no less?"

"You know what it means to open the studio couch, Mom. It's a hassle." She smiled ruefully. "Okay. I didn't know you would come home. I mean, I do see your point. It must have shocked the shit out of you. Believe me, I understand. I mean, seeing your daughter balling a guy. Mom, I may be sixteen, but I'm a woman, and I have needs and emotions."

"What about self-control? Morals?"

"Morals? Really, Mom. What's wrong with getting laid? It's a normal thing. And it feels good. I mean, do you really believe I don't know about that dildo in your drawer? I never asked. But why don't you look for the real thing? Believe me, I'll respect your privacy."

"It's . . . it's dangerous . . ." Grace cried, her face flushing, hating the idea of her little secret revealed. She felt she was floundering somewhere in a time warp. "He wasn't wearing a condom. Haven't you heard about AIDS?"

"Mom, he's not diseased. He's very clean. Don't you think I look first?"

The image that statement summoned up was the last straw.

"Are you totally ignorant, Jackie?" Grace shouted. "You can't see a virus. It's terminal."

"He's not gay, Mom. And I never let him . . ."

"Enough," Grace said, standing up. She felt herself on the other side of anger, something akin to disbelief. She was not a prude or a fool. Yes, she had known that an older boy had deflowered Jackie at a beachside party. She had cried then, more out of her sense of powerlessness over her daughter's life and the realization that her child's girlhood had ended. She was, by biological definition, a woman, or so the act seemed to herald. But the fact was, it was a false positive. It was obvious that Jackie's emotional maturity hadn't yet caught up with her hormonal development. Would it ever? Grace wondered, dreading her daughter's future.

Jackie hadn't mourned the end of her virgin state. She reveled in it. She had been positively celebratory, just as she had been when she had her first period. Grace, being an enlightened mother, not like her own, had whisked her to a gynecologist. The doctor prescribed birth control pills, along with dire warnings about the dangers of promiscuity, all of which Jackie had apparently ignored.

"You just can't bed down with anyone who asks," Grace said, searching for some common ground.

"I don't, Mom. What do you think I am? I told you. The reason I ball Darryl is he's good at it."

"Jesus, Jackie," Grace sighed. "Will pregnancy be next?"

"Don't be ridiculous. I'm very religious about taking my pills."

Grace shook her head, feeling the total loss of all parental authority. She supposed it was partially her fault, acknowledging that concerned parenting had taken a backseat to sheer economic survival. Surely Jackie could not doubt that her mother loved her. That was a given. As a single mother, she had tried her best to shelter her daughter from the dangers of living on the edge of economic disaster. Hadn't she been dutiful, concerned and protective during the early years, before the hormonal rush had diluted her control over her daughter's life?

It was all coping now, dealing with issues of parenting only when they arrived on her doorstep. It was almost impossible to make the right decisions every time one was required. The best she could do was to live in hope that mother and daughter could surmount the problems of the teen years and look forward to a better future for both of them. The shock of observing her daughter in this shameless exhibition had exposed Grace's failure as a role model and a mother.

All right, she conceded, she did have sex with Jason before they were married. It felt normal, just as long as it was exclusive and private. Her mother, the papal groupie, would never believe such a thing could happen. She would be the last person on earth for her to confide in. The woman would have spent overtime in the confessional and doubled her prayers for her daughter's soul. Her father, the barber, would have been oblivious, disbelieving and indifferent. The act of sex, after years of deprivation, would not be in his frame of reference.

The image of the little man with the thick Italian accent appeared in her mind. A decent, compassionate man, he had endured the woman who was her mother until her death. More fanatical than a nun, Mama Sorentino's life revolved around the Church and the confessional. She had believed that somehow Grace, her only child, had been responsible for killing the fertility of her womb. Such an attitude did not make for a particularly joyous maternal relationship.

Yet she did love her father, the long-suffering, inarticulate Carmine, who had been liberated at last when his wife had gone to her great reward. Could anyone have known that Grace had shed tears of joy at her graveside, celebrating the little man's freedom? He still cut hair, played checkers with his cronies, smoked ropy Italian cigars and lived above his little shop in Baltimore.

She called him once a week. The conversation was always stilted, the communication sparse. But somehow she sensed that he took comfort in just hearing her voice. The words hardly mattered.

"Maybe we should confide more in each other," Grace said to Jackie, choosing the path of placation rather than confrontation.

"Mom, we do confide."

"Not enough."

"Mom, I can't tell you everything. Not everything."

Grace sucked in a deep breath. What more could she be hiding?

"You don't tell me everything, Mom," Jackie said, planting a kiss on her mother's cheek. Grace felt suddenly grateful that her daughter had not accused her of being jealous of her pleasure. Such an accusation would be unnerving, hateful, although it was a real possibility. It had to be in Jackie's thoughts, Grace was certain, grateful for the repression. Perhaps, after all, she had raised a daughter with some character. Or were such thoughts on her part merely a form of denial?

"I better get dressed, Mom. Phys Ed I can miss, not math. Lose one day and it's worse the next."

"I'll drive you," Grace said, welcoming this chance at repairing her relationship with her daughter.

"Great, Mom. Just great."

Again she kissed her on the cheek, then bounced into the bathroom.

In a few minutes, Jackie was dressed, looking every bit the prim high school junior. It was hard to reconcile this image of the wide-eyed teenager with the girl wrapped around the naked form of the young man.

They got into Grace's Volkswagen.

"It's not—what did he call it?— an Evo something, but it will have to do," she said, suddenly remembering Jason's motorcycle, which he had taught Grace to operate. It wasn't a Harley-Davidson, but it had its share of bells and whistles and, for a while, it was Jason's pride and joy. Perhaps there was some truth in Jackie's remark. Maybe she had forgotten what it was to be young. But that didn't negate her dark feelings about Darryl and the danger he posed for Jackie.

"Darryl doesn't ask everyone, Mom. He says it's a privilege."

"I wish you wouldn't," Grace said, starting the car and backing it out of the parking space.

"Wish I wouldn't what?"

"Go near him."

Jackie shook her head, falling into silence.

"We're like two ships passing in the night," Grace said when they were heading toward Jackie's school.

"All in all, I think we do okay for a mother and daughter," Jackie said. "I know girls who tell their parents nothing. And I mean, there's lots to tell."

"I worry about you, Jackie."

"And I worry about you, Mom. Really I do. I would love it if you found a guy." Jackie turned to Grace and smiled, showing her glistening white teeth. "Like today. Maybe if we could devise a kind of signal that the apartment was in use, we could avoid the . . . you know . . . anyway, you wouldn't have been that upset."

"On top of everything, your stud socked me in the stomach," Grace blurted.

"That's because he was frustrated. Don't you know about men, Mom? Because of your interruption, he didn't get off. That's a sure road to male hostility. They get real nasty when they get to a certain point and don't get it off."

"I appreciate the insight," Grace muttered, astonished, wondering how her child had acquired such knowledge.

Up to then, Grace thought she had heard everything.

"It happens to women, too. I already came two or three times. I was just about to finish him."

"Jesus, Jackie. Where do you get all this?"

"From life's experiences, Mom. But this I can tell you honestly: I don't drink and I don't do drugs. There, doesn't that put your mind at ease?"

Did it really? She wasn't sure. But she did wonder who was the mother and who was the daughter in this relationship. The fact was that she felt inept and an abysmal failure as a parent.

"Maybe I'm naive," Grace sighed, half to herself.

The school loomed into view, and Jackie checked her makeup in the visor mirror. But as the car slowed, Jackie turned to her suddenly.

"Why were you home so early?"

"I was fired," Grace said, actually enjoying the revelation. She watched her daughter frown and shake her head.

"Are you serious?" Jackie asked, studying her face.

"I was rude to one of their best customers."

"You were? That wasn't smart."

"I know. It was dumb."

"So what will we do now?"

Grace shrugged.

"I'm entitled to unemployment. That will give me some breathing room."

"Breathing room? We've never had that."

"Don't worry, darling. I have plans."

"I guess that means the Donna Karan is out," Jackie said, pouting.

"Afraid so," Grace said.

"Not to mention the possibility of a car."

"It was never a possibility, Jackie."

"Shit, Mom. How could you be so stupid?"

"It's inherited."

"From who?"

"From you, Jackie. I inherited it from you."

It was supposed to elicit a laugh from Jackie. It didn't. She had stopped the car in front of the school entrance. Jackie started to get out, then scrutinized her mother's face.

"Sometimes I worry about you, Mom," Jackie said, shaking her head. She kissed her mother on the cheek and bounced out of the car. Grace watched her until her eyes filled with tears and Jackie became a blur in the distance.

She drove west on the Tamiami Trail, in the opposite direction of her apartment. That was the last place she wanted to be. Her sense of failure was acute. The events of the morning had been a massive blow to her self-esteem.

Her eyes surveyed the ugly clutter of stores, fast-food franchises, furniture and car dealers, TV shops and shopping centers that serviced the army of what was euphemistically referred to as the middle class. Lower, she muttered, knowing exactly where she stood on the income continuum, despite the forty-two-hundred-dollar check in her pocketbook, feeling the full and stifling weight of her despair.

Her thoughts, though depressing, managed to trigger her instinct for survival. She would have to remember to register at the state unemployment office and go through the usual processing to obtain her check. She had done that before, and it never failed to fill her with a massive sense of humiliation. Just standing in line with the rest of the losers was a horrifying prospect.

The midday traffic crawled slowly as she squinted into the bright sunlight. Then she noticed an enterprise that her mind either had rejected or ignored in the past. BRODSKY'S MEMORIAL CHAPEL. On either side of the name was a Star of David.

Mrs. Burns's advice suddenly replayed in her mind, bringing a smile to her lips. She felt a kind of hysterical giggle build in her chest. The advice, even the ethnic specificity, was one of the more enduring and amusing spoken clichés of the mating game. Under ordinary circumstances it would be taken as a joke. But Mrs. Burns did not have a shred of humor in her bones. Her advice was neither satire nor trivia. She meant it with all the force of her convictions.

Nevertheless, it was unthinkable and ghoulish, a long way from her own frame of reference. But it did set her to wondering if she could ever be so cold-blooded, so calculating and amoral, to pursue this bizarre course of action. And if she did, would she have the resourcefulness, the acting ability, the blatant insincerity required to make a success out of such a strategy? She doubted it. And yet, despite its outlandishness, it did suggest a tantalizing opportunity.

It surprised her that she didn't reject the possibility out of hand. Did it mean she would have to suspend her own sense of herself, her so-called dignity, a quality growing more and more illusory with each passing moment? And would the expenditure of energy be worth the candle? She imagined platoons of desperate single women of uncertain age with the same idea.

Almost as if she were driving in a trance, she pulled into the parking lot of the Brodsky Memorial Chapel. It was totally filled and she was forced to exit the lot, which meant, in her present suggestive state, that fate had solved the problem for her. But when she reached the exit, a man wearing a Star of David armband waved the car to the left and another also wearing an armband gestured insistently that she park in the space he was designating.

Choices were being made for her, she decided. Destiny was intervening, she thought foolishly, guiding her actions. She got out of the car hesitantly, not knowing what to do next.

"This way," another man said. He, too, wore the official armband, and she found herself going with the flow. People were mostly silent and appropriately somber. A man at the door asked whether she was here for the Farber or the Schwartz funeral. The couple ahead of her said Farber and she nodded and followed the couple up a flight of heavily carpeted stairs to a darkened chapel crowded with silent, respectful mourners.

Still following the couple, she moved to a seat on a long polished bench and sat down next to the woman. Gloomy organ music played in the background.

"Molly was a wonderful person," the woman whispered to her.

"The best," Grace said, afflicted with an accelerating desire to escape. Unfortunately, she was seated in the center of the row and there was no way to leave now without attracting attention. Instead, she resigned herself to the situation, as if she were watching a documentary entitled *Jewish Funeral.*

She observed that the people did look different than she had seen at her mother's funeral in Baltimore, although many of their faces bore the familiar stamp of Mediterranean origin under their suntans. There were, of course, the regional differences of more colorful clothing and the absence of drab female papal groupies in somber black. The mourners, too, were better groomed than their Baltimore counterparts, which reflected both income and geographical disparity.

There were, of course, vague similarities of ritual, although the Catholics hands-down offered more ornate spectacle, costuming, mystery and audiovisual effects than this grim, unadorned auditorium. Catholics, she told herself, gave great funerals. But then, wasn't their ceremony more of a bon voyage to a glorious heavenly resort reached through a corridor lined with angels with white wings playing long trumpets, which led to golden gates manned by St. Peter himself? Where, after all, did the spirit of dead Jews go? Was there a Jerusalem station in heaven accepting arrivals?

In front of the auditorium was a closed coffin and on a small stage behind it was a lectern. The men wore funny little black hats stamped with the name of the funeral parlor. In the first row, she noted a group of sniffling and red-eyed mourners of both sexes, who, she assumed, were the immediate family.

Was this what Mrs. Burns had meant when she advised her to read the obituaries? Somehow Grace had interpreted this to mean that one made the initial "contact" at the funeral parlor, simply appearing, becoming visible to the . . . she hesitated as her mind searched for an appropriate definition. Target? Pigeon? Victim? Mark?

Studying the group in the front row, she could not pick out anyone who might fit the profile suggested by Mrs. Burns of a distinguished, very rich Jewish gentleman. She felt a hysterical giggle crawl up her chest and knew she did not have the restraint to hold it back. Pressing her hand to her mouth, she felt the sound emerge despite her valiant effort to stifle it.

"I know. I know," the woman next to her whispered. "Molly Farber was the salt of the earth. Charitable? Nobody was more charitable. She will be sorely missed by all of us."

Grace nodded, her hands hiding much of her face, making sounds that were open to the woman's interpretation of stifled sobbing. She took deep breaths to get herself under control. It was, she knew, less a giggle of humor than a kind of hysterical comment on the events transpiring before her eyes.

Again, she surveyed the all-important first row. Still, she couldn't find anyone who might fill the bill according to Mrs. Burns's suggestion, although she could sense the logic in what, on the surface, was a serviceable but bizarre idea.

If one bought into Mrs. Burns's weird premise—and, so far, Grace was still eons away from a true believer—the ritual of the funeral offered a kind of preview, an opportunity for observation that was a lot more efficient than a blind date. She could get a good look at the prospect, study him under fire, even, if the size of the funeral was any measure, assess his standing in the community and, perhaps, his financial status. Was it not logical to assume that the more the widower grieved, the more compelling his need to assuage his loss?

Mrs. Burns hadn't invented the idea. It was a generally accepted pop-psychology hypothesis that a widower who was happily married was more likely to seek to replicate such a situation. Now, how had she come to such knowledge? Television talk shows, newspapers, comments on the radio, bits and pieces of trivia from somewhere out there in the glutted information firmament? Was this insight or bullshit, she wondered, suddenly questioning the powerful desperation that had driven her to this place.

When the gloomy musical background sound ceased, a man rose to the lectern. He was youngish, wearing one of those funny black hats, and he spoke in what seemed like a carefully practiced, mournful cadence, offering the assemblage a picture of a woman who had devoted her life to husband and children and who had managed to live to the ripe old age of ninety.

Wrong place, wrong range, Grace realized suddenly. Perhaps she should have chosen the Schwartz funeral. She felt the hysterical giggle begin again. This time, she fished quickly for a tissue and used it to press against her lips and muffle the sound.

She could never do this, she told herself. It would be impossible for her to be so calculating and cynical. How could she live with herself? She wished she could get up and leave. The words of the man behind the lectern lost all meaning as she delved deeper into her thoughts, rebuking herself for giving in to such cynicism.

But as she debated the question in her mind, she realized how detached she really was from these proceedings. *I am not here to do evil,* she assured herself as the logic of the idea began to grow in her mind. It wasn't as if she would be causing the death of a spouse. She would simply be taking advantage of an opportunity to bring joy, affection and rejuvenation, perhaps even love, to a grieving man, filling the void caused by a profound loss. Where was the harm in that? She could be the silver lining in the dark cloud.

On the practical side, at least she would be trolling where the fish were. That, too, was not a crime. All right, so she had a hidden agenda in the pursuit, and the means might be considered blatantly cynical and parasitic, but the end result, if it occurred, would be beneficial to both parties.

At least she would have a well-defined objective, and the fact was that she considered herself a good person, a well-brought-up woman from a traditional Catholic, rigidly moral and religious Italian family. Certainly she would be closer in generational mores to such a man than she was to her own daughter. She would be an asset to a good man, especially a kindly, decent and generous man, a very generous man. To whom, she vowed, she would be exceedingly grateful, body and soul.

Yes, she decided, she would repay a man dearly for such kindness and generosity. Images of herself engaged in the required sexual gymnastics stimulated another rising giggling hysteric. She would practice giving great head with a banana and encourage the use of Viagra. Stop this, she urged herself, remembering with a hot, angry blush the scene with her daughter and her disgusting copulation a mere couple of hours before.

Marrying rich would certainly offer expanding opportunities for Jackie. She would meet a better class of people the higher up they went on the economic ladder. She'd be driving a great car, a Porsche maybe, and buy her clothes at Saks or Bonwit's or Bergdorf's, clothes of her favorite designers.

Perhaps, too, the boost in fortune might get her into a good Ivy League college like Harvard or Yale, which would give her opportunities for success unimaginable in her present status. She would be able to network, meet the offspring of America's elite, connect with the people who made the big decisions and meet well-bred young men and women. God knows she needed that. Especially young men who respected her. No more skinhead idiots brandishing swastikas, white trash animals on motorcycles who forced her into unsafe sex. Money attracts money and a better class of people, she decided; the more money the better.

It comforted her to daydream about a brighter future for her daughter. Of course, this did not detract from the benefits that would accrue to her. She supposed she was not without her material needs. She could envision her own closets full of designer clothes and velvet-covered boxes filled with jewelry, the real thing, and a regimen of exercise and massage to keep her figure tight and, when the time came, a tuck or two here or there. Were these crass aspirations? Perhaps. But her man might want her to obey the conventions of the class, and she would be a willing participant.

Then there were the house or houses they would live in. She would read *Architectural Digest* with a specific purpose in mind. After all, she wouldn't be expected to live in the same house where he had lived with his late wife. No way. She would have to put her own stamp on things. Create her own individualized world for his new life. Indeed, it would be her house that would be a candidate to appear in *Architectural Digest,* and she would be featured in those photos entering some posh ball in Palm Beach or New York or Paris, London, Venice. God, it was wonderful to think about.

Such thoughts convinced her that there was, indeed, a point to Mrs. Burns's suggestion, once one got beyond the bold idiocy of the idea and the necessary subterfuge that would be entailed. That was the hard part. The initial phase, the acting, the dissimulation. And, calling a spade a spade, the lying, the outright lying. But if her intentions were basically honest and good, not evil or sinister or selfish, where was the harm?

It was certainly a better course of action than living on empty dreams and surrendering to the inevitable life in the lower depths, the slow lane, the bottom of the barrel. Time for a little realism here, she rebuked herself. Better to try for the roses than settle for the weeds. Her optimistic speculation was exciting her.

She thought about possible ages in her target range. The fifties, of course, would be ideal. But rich men widowed at that age, she had observed, seemed to look for girls in their twenties, trophy wives. Sixty to seventy would probably be the logical range for her. Even a young over-seventy might fill the bill.

Mrs. Burns had suggested a Jewish widower and had given her reasons, which had at first seemed shallow, stereotypical and comical. She had heard that oft-repeated cliché, reiterated by Mrs. Burns, that Jewish men were supposed to be steady family types. They also did not drink, like non-Jews. Their loving over-possessive mothers were supposed to have instilled in them gobs of guilt, and when they fooled around they compensated by being even more generous to their wives, as she had learned by observing them at Saks. Of course, that wasn't the life she wanted. She would much prefer a faithful husband who was satisfied with her in every respect.

Certainly, from her observations and experience, Jewish men seemed to treat their wives a lot better than Italian men, who preferred the company of other Italian men to their spouses. In her mother's case, she couldn't blame her father. To her mother every man was a perpetrator of sinful acts. In fact, most things, especially thoughts, were sinful to her and required weekly and sometimes daily exorcism by the priests. Grace considered it a minor miracle, coming from that background, that she had, defying the devil, ever summoned up the courage to get laid.

It occurred to her suddenly that she was really ignorant about the aging process of men, especially their sexual capacity. Her experience with Jason and the dentist had validated Mrs. Burns's assertion that man's best friend was, indeed, their penis, and getting it up was a matter of utmost importance to them. They were proud of their erections, especially their endurance and capacity for orgasms. When that diminished Grace assumed that their self-worth would be negatively affected. *Viva Viagra,* she thought.

Thinking about this brought on another hot blush that crawled up her back. She had never gone to bed with anyone over sixty, but the dentist did have episodes when his erection had abruptly collapsed. The thing had just deflated, as if someone had put a pin in a balloon, and no amount of ministering brought it immediately back to life. The dentist was initially depressed by the episode, although luckily, after a brief nap, he was able to rise to the occasion, not that it performed any great feats that gave her any pleasure.

But the experience had taught her that an erect penis was a very delicate and important instrument and meant more to a man than was commonly thought among women. She suspected that men over sixty required a great deal more sexual inspiration than younger men, and she would, of course, be fully committed to providing that ingredient. Why was she dwelling on this aspect? Had what she had witnessed with Jackie aroused such thoughts?

She had heard many jokes about Jewish women and their disinterest in sex, which might or might not be true. Certainly, she was prepared to provide a marked contrast to that supposition.

Depending on the man, she would show an aggressive interest and an adventurous spirit in the sex act and whatever special desires the man might have, especially at the beginning. She would encourage him to confide his sexual preferences to her and would be enthusiastically open to everything for his pleasure and appreciation. If the man would offer the same service for her, so much the better.

Nor was she a stranger to a circumcised penis, which had not been the case with Jason. The dentist, who had not been Jewish, was circumcised. As for her penile preference, it was a toss-up, although she did have a brief experience with a bent erection, which had been a definite turnoff. But that would be the luck of the draw.

A healthy interest in sex, of course, feigned or real, would be an essential part of the package she would bring with her, aside from companionship, devotion and faithfulness, a sense of humor and, of course, keeping herself as attractive, well-groomed and as interesting as possible, presenting herself in a way that would make the man proud of her. She would be cooperative but not servile. Above all, her dignity must remain intact. In every way, she would try to remake herself into a trophy wife. In public she would present herself as an elegant, enviable asset. In private a great lay.

She would subscribe to the daily *New York Times* and the news magazines, become conversant with the computer and the Internet, watch *Lehrer* and PBS, keep up with politics, read all the best-sellers, see all the latest plays, concerts and movies and generally enhance her knowledge of the world around her and thereby increase her ability to discuss things of importance. She would learn how to be a great hostess, take courses in art, learn French, take up golf or tennis, support every appropriate philanthropy and participate in all activities in which her mate required her presence.

She was surprised at the absolute candor and raw honesty of her thoughts. There was no point in self-delusion. If she were to take this road, she had to be fully provisioned for the journey, without cant or wishful distortion. Was she ready for such a commitment? And if so, did she have the courage and equipment to pursue it?

When she returned to her sense of place, the coffin was being wheeled down the aisle toward the exit, followed by the grieving relatives. She realized that in reading the obituary notices she would have to pay particular attention to the age of the spouse. Eighties and nineties would have to be screened out, even if it required some telephone calls or advance visits to the funeral parlors.

"What a wonderful person," the woman next to her said as Grace filed out and followed the flow of the crowd to the back of the chapel.

As research, Grace decided, this was a very profitable experience. Not that she had fully decided to pursue this course of action. She would hate to be beholden to Mrs. Burns on any matter. Besides, such a course would take a massive effort of time, total focus and commitment. And if she put all her energy and resources behind the process there would be no assurance of success. In fact, this would have to be her full-time job.

The check that Mrs. Burns had given her coupled with the unemployment proceeds would barely be enough to carry her forward for more than a few months. She would come up short week after week, which would mean she would be under the pressure of time, under the gun. It might mean, too, that she would have to take a job and pursue this enterprise on the side.

The prospect was certainly daunting. Did she have what it took? She went over in her mind the qualities that she would have to muster: cunning, courage, restraint and discipline. Then there was the matter of hypocrisy, craft and the various arts of dissimulation and the telling of outright lies, which might be required to present a proper facade and inspire an emotional connection in the man.

These later qualities were those that she had never considered possessing or even developing. They were not part of her frame of reference. She had never been a good liar. Ironically, she was encouraged by this new way of thinking. For the first time in her life, she was actually setting goals for herself, plotting the tactics and strategies to reach them, like a general preparing to make the crucial assault and take the objective.

She waited in the shade of the building while the men with the armbands assembled the automobile procession behind the hearse,

and soon the cars rolled out of the lot off to the cemetery. A few minutes later the group from the other funeral passed out of the building and were efficiently dispatched by the monitors in the direction
of the burial ground.

   She stood there in the empty lot for a long time, debating her future course of action. She felt the devil's advocate inside of her surrender. It was time to gird for action, take control of her own destiny,
muster her weapons and prepare for battle. Suddenly, she felt ener-
gized and ready.

CHAPTER THREE

The process became a daily round. She concentrated on the obituary columns of the *Palm Beach Post* and, after attending a number of funerals for "beloved wives of," she began to narrow down the possibilities by assessing the relative cost of both the memorial sites and the cemeteries where the internment was to take place. Naturally, she used the most expensive places on which to concentrate her attention.

After a few weeks, she embellished her research by searching out the homes of the deceased and making her funeral attendance judgments on the size and location of the residences. She had quickly learned that it was pointless to waste her time on what was not economically viable and attended only those funerals of bona-fide wealthy ladies whose husbands had outlived them.

She hadn't told Jackie about her campaign, reasoning that if her daughter had been more aware and attuned to her mother's activities, she would have noticed her unusual interest in the obituary columns. Nevertheless, her effort and its daily routine had all the earmarks of job hunting, and she would often return home in a state of obvious disappointment. By then, she had gone through the processing routine at the unemployment office, and they had promised that her first check would be coming in a few weeks.

"No luck, Mom?" Jackie would ask.

"Nope."

The fact was that the operation had more hope and promise in theory than in practice. Opportunity was not as Mrs. Burns had characterized it. Real prospects were difficult to find. She was, in fact, a fortune hunter, and anyone with a fortune was by nature cagey and illusive. A male in this enterprise would have a much easier time of it finding his mark. There was, after all, no equality in the chronology of death. Statistics cited men overwhelmingly as dying before women.

In three weeks, she had managed to attend several funerals, none of which offered a truly viable candidate. Most were for older ladies in their seventies and eighties whose husbands were out of her range. Some were in wheelchairs; the others seemed comatose. Even so, she did consider the possibility, but the price seemed far too high.

There were, however, moments of optimism. She attended one for a woman in her fifties with a husband who was attractive and remarkably stoic and appeared at first blush to be a perfect candidate. She had checked out their home and had learned that the man was a well-known banker from Broward County.

Dressing carefully for this one, she arrived at the service full of great expectations until she noted that the man sat in a row behind his three grieving children and their spouses, which seemed unusual, until she learned, as they were filing out, that the couple was in the midst of a bitter divorce and the woman had died suddenly from an embolism that might have been brought on by the tension.

"There's a relief," she overheard one of the female attendees say as they filed out. "Now he can marry his *nafka.*" Days later at a funeral she overheard both the word and its translation. *Nafka* meant whore in Yiddish.

One funeral of a woman in her early sixties did seem to suggest a hopeful possibility. Her research informed her that the couple had lived in a lovely old mansion off Banyan Road, one of the most expensive areas of Palm Beach. The woman, Rebecca Horowitz, had been very social. Her husband was reputed to have made a fortune in oil. He was handsome, apparently healthy and reasonably well preserved for a man in his late sixties.

She attended the funeral in the most prestigious synagogue in the area. Shiny Rolls Royces and stretch Mercedes limousines filled the parking lot. The women who attended were appropriately solemn but dressed to the nines and the men all looked prosperous and successful.

The prospect was exciting, although she had no illusions. This would require all her resources. The woman got raves from the rabbi and various other participants, who lauded her many good deeds. There were numerous mourners in the first row. She assumed a number were the couple's children. The widower was tall and good-looking, with a dignified, gracious way of accepting condolences.

During the service she had fantasized over the various ploys she would use to make contact with the man and the manner in which she would conduct herself. She joined the funeral procession, managing to get a lift from one of the well-groomed couples who had room in their big cream-colored Cadillac.

By then, experience had taught her that a wonderful repast was served by the grieving family after the return from the cemetery, like an Irish wake, except that the guest of honor was not laid out in the house. On occasion, depending on the state of her hunger, she would join the procession in her own car or, if it was convenient, solicit a lift from one of the party.

She gave her real name and offered a cover story that she had struck up an acquaintance with the dead woman after meeting her at Saks.

"We became friends and confidantes," Grace told the couple, who introduced themselves as the Saypols.

"That must have been before she got worse."

"Yes," Grace said. "Before."

"Too bad the way she went," the man said. "Up to me, I'd go poof myself." He motioned with his hands to emphasize the point.

Still, it wasn't very decent of him to start dating while she was still alive," his wife said.

"He was lonely, for crissake. His wife was in a damned nursing home with Alzheimer's. She didn't even know who he was."

"She was still his wife," the woman said.

"He had needs," the husband grumped.

The wife looked toward Grace.

"Men and their needs," she said with disdain.

"What do you women know about those kind of needs?" the man said, with a sudden burst of anger.

"He didn't have to flaunt it," the woman said, turning to Grace. "He's already made plans to marry some bimbo. Everybody knows it. I think it's disgusting."

"Betty is not a bimbo."

"She's not even thirty."

"That's not bimbo, that's just young. Are you jealous?"

"Me? Don't be ridiculous. He's more than thirty years older than her and he won't be able to keep up." She shot her husband a knowing glance. "No way. And, in the end, she'll get all his money and the kids won't get a dime."

"He's already worked out a prenup."

"Very wise," Grace said, remembering Mrs. Burns's reference.

"Sure it's a smart move," the man explained, "It lays out the boundaries."

"For the moment," the woman pointed out. "Wait'll she gets her hooks in," she said. "Women like those know what they're about. The day will come when he'll tear up the agreement or else."

"Or else what?"

"You know what."

"What? You mean she'll cut him off?"

"You got that right."

"You just said he couldn't keep up, meaning you know what. What would it matter if she cut him off? Cut off from what?"

"Men are stupid," the woman said with another quick glance at her husband. "That's all they think about."

"What do women think about?" He turned to Grace.

"I'm not sure how you mean that," Grace replied, uncomfortable at being thrust into this situation. Thankfully, the man provided the answer to his own question.

"It's all about money, possessions, hair, clothes, face-lifts, security, shopping, gossip, the children. Nothing about the man, the essence of the man they call husband. We're just here to make the dough while they figure out ways to spend it, mostly on themselves."

"What would you do without us?" the woman said, offering a mocking laugh.

"Plenty," the man said.

After that, they both seemed to crawl into themselves and remained silent and morose until they got to the cemetery.

Under a canopy at the cemetery she sat next to a woman who could not contain her contempt for the man, who looked appropriately mournful and teary-eyed.

"Look at him, the lousy bastard, making like he's gonna miss her."

The rabbi said a prayer and the mourners watched as the coffin was lowered into the ground. Having seen so many funerals lately, Grace was beginning to view death with less fear and to consider "time" with a lot more appreciation. Funerals certainly gave living people a moment to reflect, not only on the worthiness or lack thereof of the life being dispatched but on the conduct and finite nature of their own lives. So far, hers hadn't been so hot.

What was it all about, she wondered, if this was the way it ended, a bag of bones in a box? It did teach that human beings, despite all the differences of religion, race, gender, intelligence and talent, came ultimately to the same place at the end of the line. This was small comfort for someone like her, who had, barring a catastrophe, about half her allotted time to fill. But the reflection did act as a spur for her to get on with her project before it was too late. At that point, of course, she had already written off this man as a possibility. He had his bimbo.

After the burial, the couple she had come with drove her to the mansion of the widower.

"You gonna cry at my funeral, George?" the woman asked.

"I won't be there," the man said. "Just look at the statistics."

"You'll be there."

"No, I won't."

"Maybe you'll both get lucky and die together in a plane crash," Grace suddenly blurted. They looked at her, not knowing whether it was meant as a joke or not.

"Who'll cry then?" the man said.

"Not my daughters-in-law," the woman huffed. "They'll be dancing on our graves."

At the widower's home, a huge spread was laid on, and Grace spent most of the time inspecting the rooms, the magnificent artwork and antiques and other expensive appointments. She wondered if the new woman, the bimbo, had given up her claim to them in their prenuptial agreement.

She would have to be wary of men like that, Grace decided after inspecting the widower at close range. What she would strive for was parity with the first wife, she decided, despite the growing remoteness of the possibility.

She treated this after-burial ritual as a learning experience. The food, she had noted, was invariably catered and beautifully displayed. There was often champagne. It was more than a repast. It was a feast. She wondered whether these people were celebrating death or life.

After a dozen or so funerals, she began to recognize familiar faces, both men and women, who nodded knowingly to her, and she soon realized that these were the "regulars," who apparently attended funerals solely for the after-cemetery feast. Few questioned them, but when they did they had, like her, a ready story to account for their appearance. So far, no one had questioned her except for the Horowitz funeral, and she had actually told the truth; well, a half-truth. Thankfully, she saw no regular that might offer her any real competition.

One of them, an oldish woman of indeterminate age with a solemn face and hair done in an old-fashioned gray bun, seemed to appear most often. Grace noted that she ate sparingly and always managed to find an opportunity to offer what appeared to be heart-felt words of condolence to the grieving spouse. Once Grace had gotten close enough to overhear the conversation.

"Parting with her personal worldly goods can be traumatic," the woman said. "I knew her well enough to know that she was a woman of deep compassion. I'm sure that after the children have made their selection, she would have been honored to have her clothes given to the homeless and various welfare services and charities."

"I'm sure," the grieving husband had retorted.

"And you can avoid the trauma of going through her things. I can tell you, it hurts. I had that experience with my own dear Sidney. It was awful. All those memories. It's too painful a process. I can spare you that. Why not let us take care of everything? We'll make sure that they go to her favorite charities. We owe her that. Can we do that for you? Take the burden and pain away?"

The grieving man looked at his hands and shook his head in despair.

"I'd appreciate that very much. Yes, it would be very painful. That is so kind of you, relieving me of that. She had such wonderful taste. Yes, please. That's a wonderful idea."

The conversation made an impression on Grace. She hadn't thought about that aspect of death, the disposal of the deceased's intimate possessions, particularly clothes. She had often wondered where on earth those compulsive shoppers at Saks had stored their mountains of clothes. In these big homes, she supposed there were acres of closets holding long lines of designer clothes.

Of course, she did allow herself a twinge of cynicism. This woman did, indeed, look like one of the funeral party. Everything about her seemed appropriate to the occasion, including the way in which she approached the grieving spouse. Did she really give the deceased's clothes to charity, or would she sell them to secondhand clothes stores, which were in abundance in southern Florida? A brilliant scam, Grace concluded. It certainly showed flair and imagination.

Once or twice she had come home tipsy from the wine or champagne, causing Jackie to remark that she hoped that Grace was not hanging out in bars and heading toward alcoholism.

"Why can't you get yourself a nice guy, Mom, then you wouldn't have to resort to drink?"

"I'm trying, darling. Really I am."

"Not very hard," her daughter would harrumph. "And you're always dressed so . . . so gloomy. You really look lousy in black, Mom."

"I want to look conservative, Jackie."

"That I can understand. But you don't have to look like you're going to a funeral."

It was getting discouraging. Time was running out. Not that she felt ghoulish about going to funerals. The events seemed so commonplace, banal. There was the body in the coffin, the first row occupied with visibly distraught mourners, the others filling the sequential rows in order of their emotional stake in the proceedings.

Then there were the various eulogies, all of them sounding alike. Why did people wait until death to say such nice things about each other? She wondered if people would say nice things about her when she died. Except for the priest, she doubted it. There would probably be less than a handful of mourners present. Maybe Jackie would attend on Darryl's motorcycle. Her father, she supposed, would be long gone, and Jason, by then, would have forgotten who she was.

Of course, if her consciousness were still alive to observe it, she was sure she, or it, would feel humiliated by the low turnout. She began to contemplate cremation. Quick and clean. No fuss, no muss, no bother. She'd have her ashes flushed down the toilet of Saks Fifth Avenue's employee rest room.

It occurred to her that attending these funerals was encouraging a macabre sense of humor, or was it masking a growing feeling of personal depression and frustration? So far the only thing she seemed to have gained was a modicum of insight into the finite nature of time and the inevitability of death.

Unfortunately, it hadn't put her one step closer to finding her quarry.

Until the Goodwin funeral.

By then, not wishing to waste her time on marginal opportunities, she had taken more care with her research and had, as best she could in a short time, checked out Sam Goodwin's situation. She had learned that he was a successful businessman, meaning rich, that he was sixty-four years old and that his wife had died of cancer.

He had a large house on the north side of Palm Beach, the only place on the island where the houses were directly on the beach, an excellent measure of his net worth, which had to be considerable. The house was close to the former Kennedy compound, as well as other homes reputed to be the property of old moneyed families. She had actually toured the area the evening before the day of the funeral, stopping to get a better look at the house.

By chance, as she observed the area, a man came out of the house with a golden retriever who relieved himself on the manicured front lawn. The man was tall, slender and handsome, with steel gray hair and a strong chin. She wondered if this was "the" Sam Goodwin, the grieving widower. She hoped he was, and she observed him with more than proprietary interest until he went back into the house.

The sight of the man and the property she wished he was inhabiting did set off her fantasies. The house was lovely, designed in a Tudor style. She sat in the car as the sun went down and the house lights came on. From her vantage, with the blinds only half drawn, it appeared to be tastefully furnished.

She contemplated summoning the courage to get out of the car and closer to the house, where she could peek through the windows and inspect the inside more thoroughly. It seemed too risky. Besides, other people suddenly appeared, leaving through the front door. They were well dressed and, from experience, she suspected that they were heading to the funeral parlor.

So far she had only visited funeral parlors the night before a couple of times. There, the body, carefully groomed, was displayed and visitors viewed it in hushed silence. At times, depending on the wishes of the relatives, the coffin remained closed.

Jews, she had learned, buried their dead quickly, usually the day after the death, unless their Sabbath intervened. She was getting to be an expert on such matters.

She found such a visitation far more depressing than the funeral itself and hadn't made it a regular practice. Besides, she hadn't wanted to expose herself too blatantly to the mourning family members or court embarrassment by being asked questions about her relationship to the corpse.

But this time her earlier observation of the prospect was encouraging and she felt that, despite the risk, he deserved a closer look. She was not disappointed. The open coffin, with lighted candles in elaborate candelabra on either side, displayed what could be described as the vestiges of a once pretty woman.

The dead woman had bleached blonde hair, was appropriately made-up and laid out in an elaborate coffin dressed in what appeared to be an expensive designer gown. If she had to guess, Grace would say the gown was a Galanos. A diamond brooch, which looked like the real thing, was pinned to the gown. She looked vaguely familiar; but then, on the Saks floor, many of the customers looked as if they were stamped out by the same plastic surgeon, hair colorist and beautician.

The grieving husband, Sam Goodwin, was, indeed, the man she had seen the night before. He wore a dark pinstriped suit and sat on a velvet-upholstered chair along one side of the room. Seated beside him, each holding one of his hands, were a man and a woman, obviously, from the resemblance, his grown children. Their eyes were puffy and red.

At this close range she noted that the man's steel-gray hair was full and curly. His face was square, rugged and tanned. He might normally have appeared handsome and virile, but under these conditions he looked whipped, broken and grieving. The son was a younger version of his father. Grace estimated him as late thirties, the daughter younger. She wore round steel-rimmed glasses and her black hair was brushed back severely off her face, which was smoothly white and sharply contrasted against her hair. She wore no makeup. With the right makeup, Grace observed, she could be quite startling.

The room was filled with people, some of whom lingered respectfully over the body in the coffin, then moved to pay their respects to the three grieving people, who acknowledged them by a nod, a touch or a handshake. It was obvious that they were in a kind of mourning trance, barely able to be communicative. People spoke in whispers, offering condolences in the time-honored ritual.

Grace stood in a corner trying to appear equally concerned and respectful, while peripherally focusing her attention on Sam Goodwin. She did not want to stay too long or appear conspicuous. At one point the man's eyes rose and scanned the room. His gaze fell upon her briefly and she imagined he nodded in her direction, then passed on to others.

"Will you sign the book, Mrs. . . . ?" a tall man said. He was standing behind her, near a lectern on which was a visitors' book.

"Sorentino," she said. "I was a friend . . ." Her voice trailed off. The man had started a conversation with another person.

Grace signed the book and noted the various names on the list above her. She vaguely recognized some of them as names she had seen in the social pages of the *Palm Beach Post*. The name Goodwin seemed familiar. She noted, too, that the names in the book were not only Jewish names, but seemed to cover a broader spectrum. Also, the people in the room seemed more anglicized than those she had seen clustered together in other Jewish funerals.

To Grace, who had learned something about the social makeup of Palm Beach from her Saks experience, this meant that the man had crossed the rigid lines of social status and was equally acceptable to gentiles in the various social enclaves of the wealthy where money, at times, could cover a multitude of prejudices, at least partially.

A man she recognized as a former senator from Florida came in and immediately sought out the grieving trio, who rose in tandem. The man embraced the widower, who towered above him, and then embraced the children in turn.

"I'm so sorry, Sam," the former senator said. Sam Goodwin nodded and dabbed his eyes with a handkerchief.

She took one last look around the room, impressed by the people in attendance, the atmosphere and especially with the grieving man, who was distinguished-looking and definitely in the age range that she had set for herself. Unfortunately, she felt unworthy and remote, far below the man in social status and sophistication, definitely a class or two apart.

Contemplating her inferiority depressed her and made her feel clumsy and undeserving. She was ashamed of this cynical caper borne out of desperation and, probably, naïveté. Was she any better than Jason, chasing rainbows and impossible dreams? Where did she get the idea that she could simply snap her fingers and insinuate herself into the life of such a man, even in his present vulnerable state? She slinked out of the room feeling defeated and remote, woefully inadequate to the mad task she had assigned herself.

But as she drove farther from the funeral home, she made a valiant attempt to retrieve her courage. She did have assets, she insisted to herself. All right, she was not very educated or sophisticated, had not traveled in the same circles and was definitely not the traditionally glitzy trophy-wife type. Nevertheless, she was certainly ready and willing to fulfill all the obligations of being an exemplary, dedicated,

sexy, loyal and supportive wife. She was a catch, she told herself, feeling slightly giddy.

But then she began to project herself into reality. This handsome
widower would be a magnet for battalions of single, attractive ladies
with extraordinary trophy-wife potential, divisions of accomplished
and athletic widows who would fling themselves in his path, women
from his own class who knew him and did not have to contrive sub-
terfuges to meet him, who would park their shoes under his bed at
the lift of his eyebrow. How could she possibly compete against
them?

Her courage dwindled further as she got closer to her apartment.
It wouldn't take him five minutes to discover what she really was,
a lowly, out-of-work cosmetician, a fancy name for makeup sales-
person, with no prospects or money, who had, so far, made a mess of
her life.

It was all right for Mrs. Burns to suggest this course of action. She
was educated, polished, articulate, self-confident, a born leader and
executive with a proven track record and a great job. She could attract men like moths around a candle. Any man would be proud to
have her on his arm.

She took a realistic inventory of her present position, and it offered a dreary prospect. People should stay within their own circle,
she decided, as she let herself in the door of the apartment. Jackie
wasn't home yet from her job in the movie theater.

She went into her bedroom, took off her clothes and lay on the
bed. Often in this state of uncertainty and despair she had turned to
her dildo for comfort. She got up, fished in her lower drawer and
took it out. But when she lay back in the bed, activated the device
and began the process she felt nothing. She shut off the motor and
put it aside. Sex, in this artificial manner, struck her now as repug-
nant, humiliating in its implications. Her mind continued to dwell
on the crazy premise that had dominated her life for the past few
weeks.

She had been a fool to consider such a patently cynical and stupid
idea. It was time, instead, to deal with real alternatives, like a job.
Suddenly her life seemed to have stopped on a dime. Yet, in an odd
way, she likened her present state to that of Sam Goodwin. His life,
too, at least temporarily, had also stopped on a dime.

He was probably, at this very same moment, considering his future
without his beloved wife. The manner in which he was grieving, she

assumed, attested to his devotion to her. She admired that kind of devotion.

It was the curse of her early Catholicism that made it impossible for her to be morally neutral. She was, after all, engaging in a cynical, dissimulating, hypocritical act, building her future prospects on a tissue of lies. She could not escape the clearly defined sense of right and wrong promulgated by the Church. According to those strictures, she was doing wrong, something sinful. At times such ironclad, uncompromising definitions seemed more powerful than the act of survival itself. Wasn't that what she was pursuing in these funeral capers? Survival. Deliberately, she pushed aside the concept of *sin* as presenting far too rigid a barrier and began to rationalize her intent.

Was it really sinful to want to replace a man's loving departed wife, to bring him joy and rejuvenation? She pictured him as she had seen him earlier that evening, looking after his dog. He was graceful and elegant, handsome.

In her mind, she imagined him coming closer to where she was observing him in her car. He smiled at her and offered his hand, which she took. It was strong, yet gentle. He eased her out of the car and, hand in hand, moved with her into the house. Inside, he turned to her and they embraced. He kissed her deeply, his tongue caressed hers, as he enveloped her in his arms. She responded, felt all the wonderful sensations of his embrace.

A sudden thrill charged through her and she reached for the dildo again, activating it, placing the tip on her clitoris, picturing him now naked, erect, entering her. She felt open, moist, accepting, as he moved deeply inside her, speeding his strokes. After awhile she felt the first signs of an oncoming orgasm. Finally the spasm came, and it seemed more intense than usual.

She calmed slowly, surprised how strongly Sam Goodwin had entered her fantasy life. *Hold that thought, Grace,* she told herself as she dropped into a dreamless sleep.

She awoke in a turmoil. It was still dark. Her body was hot and moist and her heart was racing. By some miracle, she had held the thought, and she remembered the fantasy that had stimulated her. But, she discovered, there seemed a lot more to the fantasy than the sexual component, and she gave it full reign as she remained in bed waiting for daylight.

She saw herself as the chatelaine of his big Tudor house on the beach, the new Mrs. Goodwin. It was morning and she imagined herself locked in his arms as she awoke, the sun peeking through the blinds, lighting the room, dancing along the walls bedecked with works of art and ornate ormolu-trimmed mirrors and antiques. The sunlight would awaken the colors of the gorgeous Oriental rugs on the floor.

She would stretch and observe the silken lining of the canopied bed, and soon he would stir beside her and they would make love, a long, lingering episode of foreplay and glorious orgasms for both of them, then the delicious time of leisurely afterglow.

Later there would be breakfast on the terrace. She would be wearing a long, silk, embroidered morning gown enhanced by a delicate gold necklace around her neck. The maid would serve them, cold orange juice in stemmed glasses, eggs, over light the way she liked them, and crisp bacon, toasted bagels, strawberry jam and wonderful coffee, the aroma complementing the sea air.

They would read *The New York Times* and occasionally comment about various events in the news, lock eyes at times and purse lips in a mimed kiss. Before them would stretch the white sands of the beach and beyond, the glistening sea, twinkling in the sunlight.

Sam would enter his study and do his various business chores, perhaps overseeing his investments, calling his brokers. He was still in action, of course, a captain of industry, offering suggestions to his colleagues and underlings in the business community in which he operated.

She would be involved in her many activities, running the house, meeting with the staff to plan the evening dinner party. The governor would be coming, of course, along with his lovely wife and two or three other couples, perhaps a famous movie actress and her industrialist husband and, for extra excitement, a duke and duchess from Great Britain laden with the latest gossip of the royal family. A cozy little dinner for eight by candlelight. On the good china, of course, the set that had previously belonged to the czar of Russia.

Later there would be tennis doubles at the club . . . what club . . . perhaps the Everglades, which was, she knew, notoriously anti-Semitic. In this fantasy, Sam had been chosen their first Jewish member. Initially, he had refused, but the club president had persuaded him after a long private dinner that it was time that class, not religion, should dominate the selection process. She, his new wife, had been mentioned, of course. A distinct asset, the president had said, a wise and glorious match.

After tennis, an exquisite lunch, overlooking the eighteenth hole with the retired chairman of AT&T, after which they would be driven back to their home, still a little tipsy from the Dom Perignon that they had imbibed a bit too freely.

Back home they would have a brief swim in the pool, then retreat to the beach house and have a delicious sexual episode before falling off into a delightful nap, rising with just enough time to dress, supervise the table settings and discuss the final arrangements with the cook and the couple who would be serving.

Dinner would go off without a hitch and they would linger over the brandy, while the men smoked their Havanas and the talk waxed eloquent about the current state of affairs in Washington and the world. They would listen with rapt attention to her views as she outlined the prospects of monetary reform based on her assessment of the latest conference of the World Bank.

Before the guests said good-bye, Jackie, coming home from the dance at the club, looking radiant in the latest Oscar—by then she would be referring to all designers by their first names—would introduce them to her date, the son of the owner of the largest cruise company in the world, and they would remark on Jackie's beauty and poise and her date's good looks and sophistication.

Just past midnight they would bid their guests good-bye with effusive two-cheek kisses, and she and Sam would be alone for one last nightcap and, before going upstairs, they would take off their shoes and walk to the water's edge and kiss in the moonlight, finally going to bed, but not before one last slow turn at lovemaking to cap off the day as they fell asleep in each other's arms.

Then, suddenly, the first beams of the rising sun revealed the truth of her present reality, her dreary bedroom, the sounds of the early morning army of drab working people setting off to their dead-end jobs, all of them two paychecks from oblivion and the unemployment lines. The long fall from fantasy to reality had taken merely seconds, and she was back to the decisions, anxieties and poverty of the present.

She heard Jackie in the shower, put on her quilted, much-abused robe and went into the kitchenette to make coffee, pour the juice and make toast. It was certainly a long cry from the breakfast she had created in her imagined world.

"Sleep well, Jackie?" she asked when Jackie came out of the bathroom, her skin pink with youthful health, her teeth glistening in a broad smile. She bent down and kissed her mother's cheek.

"You were asleep when I came in, Mom. I didn't have heart to wake you."

Grace reached up and caressed her daughter's cheek, wary of showing too much demonstrative affection, fearful that it might be interpreted as phony or manipulative. She loved this child with every fiber of her being, but guiding her through this crucial period of her life was both baffling and extremely worrisome.

"That's my girl," Grace said.

Jackie threw off her robe, revealing her nakedness. Her figure was perfect: high, beautiful breasts with round pink nipples, flat stomach, a patch of rich black curly pubic hair, the finely rounded rump, the long legs, tight thighs, shapely calves. This was a beauty. And the face—gorgeous, long curling black lashes shading light brown eyes, a curving Italian nose chiseled into high cheekbones and angel lips over a cleft chin. She knew that Jackie could feel her inspection.

"You think I'm pretty, Mom?"

"A knockout."

"Lot of good it does me," Jackie pouted.

"Just have patience, Jackie. Things are beginning to turn around. I can feel it. You'll see."

"Sure, Mom." Jackie sighed, stepping into her panties and bra, then fastening a beige skirt around her slim waist and slipping into a cream-colored blouse. Yes, Grace thought, she was bright and beautiful, with enormous potential to make the jump into the best circles. She was aware of her sexiness, too aware. She needed to learn how to use her allure for her own advantage, not to dispense her favors indiscriminately.

"Really, Jackie. Something's in the wind."

"Like what?"

"I can't say."

"Are you keeping something from me, Mom?" Jackie asked.

"Not really," Grace replied, thinking of Sam Goodwin. "But I do believe I have possibilities." It was, of course, pure fantasy at that point, but she felt she needed to offer something to keep hope alive.

"Possibilities?" Jackie sighed. "Sure, Mom, possibilities."

"And if I latch on to something good, first thing we do is get you that car."

"I've heard that before, Mom."

"I mean it. Maybe even . . ." She recalled her fantasy. "Lots of things."

She sat down at the table and sipped her coffee and delicately buttered her toast.

"It's nice thinking about."

"Yes, it is," Grace agreed. "Very nice."

"Things just can't stay like this."

"No, they can't."

"It's the pits."

"We have to make good things happen," Grace said suddenly. "Take the bull by the horns."

She knew she was giving herself a pep talk, trying to work herself up to continuing her quest, despite the odds against it ever being fulfilled.

"You're right, Mom. We can't just let things happen to us."

"We've got to *make* them happen. We've just hit a bad patch is all."

"To put it mildly," Jackie said.

"I'll find a better way for us Jackie. I promise."

"Sure, Mom," Jackie agreed, studying her mother's face with a wry smile.

"What are you looking at, darling?" Grace asked.

"I do think about you a lot, Mom."

"You do?"

"Darryl is probably right."

"Not him again," Grace snapped, her mood changing. "I thought we had an understanding."

"No. You did. I didn't."

"He's trouble, Jackie. Dangerous and mean-minded."

"Shows how much you know."

"We both know where his brains are," Grace said, remembering his swollen genitals. Jackie sneered.

"He has convictions. And he's smart. He knows what's really going on. He's against the government and he thinks there's a conspiracy to make us all slaves to the Jews."

Grace felt her stomach tighten.

"Oh, my God. Not one of those."

"One of what?"

"A troublemaking bigot, a Nazi creep from one of those militias."

"He's not a creep either."

"He's a menace, Jackie. He's just using you for his own gratification. Can't you find someone decent?"

"Can't you?"

"People like that are scary, Jackie. Just look at that ugly knife he carries. Gave me the shivers, and he's probably got guns all over the place."

"That's his business."

Grace felt a shiver of fear roll through her.

"He does have guns, doesn't he?"

"Considering what's going on in the world, it's not such a bad idea."

"Jackie . . . I . . . I don't think he's a good influence on you. Can't you see how awful . . . how can I put this? You really have got to stop seeing him. For your own sake. No good can come of it."

She feared making her suggestion seem like an absolute command, which, so far, hadn't done much good and would only push her closer to Darryl.

"You never like my boyfriends anyway."

"He's trouble, Jackie. I'm your mother and I'm just thinking of your welfare. You're still young, sweetheart. I'm just trying to keep you from making a terrible mistake. Men like that are . . . well, just no good. Why look for trouble? Haven't we got enough on our plate without that?"

"You're still angry because you caught us in bed together and he hit you."

"Two very good reasons . . . among others," Grace muttered, her patience ebbing. The joy of her morning fantasy had disappeared. "Besides, you're under age. How old is he, anyway?"

"That's dangerous talk, Mom. Very threatening." Jackie paused and clicked her teeth. "It's no joke."

"I just asked how old he was."

"I wouldn't advise your finding out, Mom."

"Now who's threatening?"

"It's you who's looking for trouble, Mom. If you're thinking of turning him in, don't."

"It wouldn't be a bad idea."

"You'd be making a big mistake."

"What are you now, a gun moll?"

"Very funny." She began to pace the room like a caged tiger. "I'll see who I want to see. I want to see Darryl. And I'd advise you not to make threats. You don't know him. He's exciting and smart and sexy. And he likes me."

"Big deal. He likes you. Ho ho," Grace mocked, her anger bursting through her self-imposed barrier. "Why shouldn't he like you? Sweet jailbait flesh."

"That was out of line, Mom." She paced for a few moments more, then turned to Grace. Her look seemed softer.

"Not to me."

"What is it with you? Every time I mention Darryl you go up the wall."

"Not at the mention. It's because of the reality. I can't believe you can't see what he is."

"I know what he is, Mom. You don't." Jackie clicked her tongue. "Here we go again. Let's both cool it. Okay?" She came close to Grace and kissed her forehead, but it struck her as mechanical, more like a dismissal.

"Tell you the truth, he likes you, Mom. Maybe I'm jealous."

"Of me?"

"He said he thought you were sexier than I was."

"Is that supposed to be a compliment to me or an insult to you? He did make an obscene offer, if I recall. It was disgusting."

"He also said that you really didn't look like a mom. That you seemed to be hiding your light under a bushel."

"I can't believe you're repeating this . . . making this asshole's words seem profound."

Jackie smiled and shook her head, as if Grace was the errant child.

"You just don't know about men, Mom. That's why you haven't got any. You need to tune in more to your real self. Give your desires more room to breathe."

"Where is this shit coming from?"

"I know you think I'm a stupid teenager. But I think I know more about the opposite sex than you do."

"Is this your big talent, Jackie?"

"I know this: If I put my mind to it, I can really manipulate the opposite sex. I know my assets in that regard."

"You're sixteen, Jackie. Going on fifty." Grace stood up, the last vestiges of restraint collapsing. "And this is the most ridiculous and eccentric mother-daughter conversation we've ever engaged in. You're recycling his bullshit as true wisdom. He's a dangerous wacko with all his brains in his dick."

"Mind your tongue, young lady," Jackie mimicked, laughing. She reached out, took her mother's hand and kissed it.

At that moment, she heard the raucous sound of a motorcycle as it stopped nearby.

"Stop diddling me, Jackie."

"I'm not going to stop seeing him. Get that through your head."

She ran out of the door before Grace could respond. Looking out the window, she watched Jackie put on a helmet and straddle the bike behind Darryl as they roared away. The sound was ominous, like distant thunder warning of an impending storm.

She closed the door behind her and leaned against it for a long moment. Somehow she felt chastised, as if her daughter and she had reversed roles. But as she thought about it, she felt more challenged than rebuked, and the image of Sam Goodwin refocused itself in her mind. Suddenly, all options seemed closed. Except one.

When you're drowning, she thought, *you grab anything that floats.* Then she rushed into the bathroom, removed her quilted robe and jumped into the shower.

CHAPTER FOUR

She deliberately took a seat up front, behind the first row of mourners, where she could observe them more clearly. The scene was familiar. The coffin was open, with the upper part of the body exposed for viewing.

The synagogue was packed. She had noted the lines of Mercedeses, BMWs and Cadillacs lining up to get into the parking lot. Judging by outward appearances, everything about this funeral said *money* and *upper class*. It fit in very well with her fantasy.

The organ music boomed out its solemn dirge. She was sitting a few feet away from the grieving Sam Goodwin. Sam! She called him Sam now, having fantasized her familiarity. She noted his handsome face in profile, dignified, calm, the eyes moist. Occasionally he looked back at the assemblage and smiled thinly at various people. He wore a dark pinstriped suit and a creamy white shirt. His hair, she noted, was carefully barbered with just the right amount of steel-gray hair falling over the high collar.

On either side of him were the man and woman she had seen the night before, obviously his children. She recalled other familiar faces from the funeral parlor.

Suddenly the music trailed off and a man in a black robe and yarmulke—by then she had learned the names of the various ritual trappings of these people—entered. The man, she knew, was Rabbi Seltzer, and he made the usual remarks about the late Anne Goodwin. Anne, Grace thought. A classy name.

Apparently Anne Goodwin was very charitable, loving, compassionate and well regarded. This was not just lip service. The rabbi was specific about various organizations she had supported, both Jewish and non-Jewish. She made a note of them in her mind. His eulogy was exactly the appropriate length and to the point. Then he said a prayer in Hebrew. Some of the words she had come to recognize.

At the end of the prayer, the rabbi announced that there would be one speaker, and he introduced Sam Goodwin, who rose solemnly. Patting the yarmulke on his head, he pulled himself up to his full height and smoothed the creases from his jacket, which fell beautifully on his slim frame. His children touched him as he moved past them, walking solemnly and ramrod straight to the lectern. He stood behind it for a long moment, scanning the room, obviously gathering the strength to control his emotions.

"Friends," he began, his voice deep, mellow, wonderfully resonant. Grace felt thrilled by its sound. Her pounding heart beat heavily in her chest.

"Anne would have been delighted by the turnout." He stopped abruptly, and Grace knew he was reaching for control with all his resources. "She had this uncanny ability to relate to people. It was a phenomena I observed the moment I met her at a sorority dance at Wellesley College. She was a magnet for people. They clustered around her, sought her out. Like me. I remember how I, too, sought her out, basking in the light of her lovely face, her beautiful eyes that radiated wonder and beckoned me, a rather shy, stumbling and bumbling young man. I was captivated by her, charmed, and passionately committed to this rare human being for forty years. For me it was forty years of sheer joy and happiness. We enjoyed every moment we were together. She was my pillar of strength, my lover, my confidante, my best friend. She thought I was hopelessly disorganized and I probably was, because she took on the job of organizing me from the day we met. She was beautiful, vivacious, giving, a loyal and faithful wife, a cherished pal. . . ." He paused and studied the assemblage through a long pause. Grace could not hold back her tears. Sobs echoed through the auditorium, and she suspected that there wasn't a dry eye in the house.

It was not just the words he spoke. It was the way he said them, the wonderful resonance of his voice, its solemn lilt, the sincerity of his meaning. Oh God, Grace thought, would anyone ever say such words about me?

"Good-bye, sweet Anne, my love. You are too soon gone. I should have preceded you."

The sounds of grief, the sobs and coughing, accelerated as he left the lectern and returned slowly to his seat.

Grace felt the urge suddenly to rise and embrace him. He looked, to her Catholic-conditioned eye, positively saintly, a man to love. Was he, Sam Goodwin, her destiny?

After the ceremony, she asked one of the men organizing the ride to the cemetery if he might find her room in one of the cars in the procession.

The man arranged for her to ride with two couples in a Lincoln Town Car. In the front seat were the McDermotts, Sally and Mike, people in their sixties, and in the rear were the Hales, Bob and Clara, slightly younger.

"Did you know Anne long?" Clara Hale asked as the car moved along in the line of the long procession. She was a bleached blonde with thin parchment skin and the pale, mottled look of a woman who received most of her calories from alcohol. Her husband Bob had a complementary appearance, and Grace had the impression that tippling was their principal common bond and the basis of their marriage.

"About five years. I was involved with one of her charities."

"She was a helluva lady," Mike McDermott said as he drove.

"A little imperious," his wife Sally said, realizing suddenly that the remark seemed inappropriate under the circumstances. "But giving. Very giving."

"Jewish people are very charitable," Grace said. "I'm Italian. Most of our charity goes to the Church."

"They do give," Clara said. "But you've got to admit, they are different from us."

Grace wondered about that remark. They did seem different, but she attributed that more to the difference in economic status than to their being Jewish. Were they different? It was hard for her to know.

"How did you know her?" Grace asked.

"Mike was the contractor for their house," Bob said. "Have you seen it?"

"Yes," Grace said.

"She was one tough lady, that Anne. Jewed us down to rock bottom."

"Be careful about your remarks, Mike," Sally said, looking around her reflexively.

"I'm among friends, aren't I?"

Grace felt him eyeing her through the rear-view mirror.

"She ran the roost," Sally said. "Never met a man so pussy-whipped in my life."

"Except me," Mike chuckled.

"Not me," Bob interjected. "I'm the absolute master of my home and hearth."

"Bullshit," Clara said, poking Grace in the ribs.

"I would think," Grace said, "from the way he spoke about her, it was so beautiful, he must have adored her."

"Yes, he did," Sally said. "He gave her anything she wanted."

"He was scared shitless of her," Mike said.

"Scared," Sally said. "No way. Sam Goodwin is not afraid of anything. Frightened people don't get that rich."

"He respected her," Clara said. "That's a lot more than I can say for the way you two treat us. Right, Sally?"

"I'll take this bastard. Warts and all."

"They say that Jewish men are good to their wives," Grace said, hoping it sounded more like a question.

"These bozos could sure learn a lot from Sam about how to treat a wife," Sally said. "Say what you want, Anne led a charmed life. And I don't think he ever fooled around."

"How the hell would you know?" Mike snapped.

"Women know."

"Women know shit," Mike said.

"They know," Sally said, as if she was determined for her own reasons to have the last word. Grace noted the sudden tension between them.

"If he did," Clara said, "Anne would never know it. He'd never embarrass her. Not Sam. But then, you never know what goes on behind the bedroom door."

"Nothing goes on behind ours," Mike said, lifting his hand in mock self-protection.

"Your definition of *nothing* leaves much to be desired," Sally said. She turned to those in the backseat. "To him nothing means never enough."

They were silent for a long time while each, Grace supposed, contemplated their own relationship. She wished she had one to contemplate.

"Anne was tough," Bob said, turning to Grace. "But she did have great taste. I did their landscaping. You had to be real alert when you dealt with her. Tell you the truth, I liked her a lot. Poor woman. I'll say this for Sam: He stood by her to the end. She suffered like hell."

"I guess I liked her, too," Mike agreed. "Once I got past my anger, she was okay. I think she knew just how far she could go. I'll say this for old Sam: He was a good soldier. He went along."

"He seems to have a lot of class," Grace interjected. "And he's quite distinguished-looking."

"And available. Are you married, Grace?" Sally asked.

"Divorced."

"Well, there's your big chance," Mike chuckled.

"They'll be crawling over him like flies on honey," Sally said. She looked at her husband and poked him in the ribs. "Stop thinking what you're thinking."

"How do you know what I'm thinking?" Mike protested good-naturedly.

"I know where your thoughts come from," Sally said.

"I hope he finds what he wants," Grace said.

"He will," Bob said. "Men like Sam always find what they want."

It was an observation that did not augur well for Grace's ambitions. The competition alone would be daunting. How could she possibly get a man like that to notice her?

The mourners gathered under a green-and-white-striped tent in front of a freshly dug hole. On the side of the hole was Anne Goodwin's coffin, on a specially built contraption used for lowering it into the grave. Grace took a seat next to the couples who had brought her.

There were about a hundred seats, which were quickly filled. An overflow crowd clustered in a semicircle around the seats. The coffin was lowered into the grave as the rabbi read from a Hebrew prayer book. Grace never took her eyes off Sam Goodwin, all her thoughts concentrated on how she could possibly open up a dialogue with him. This was now the central question in her mind.

She watched him stand up, then reach down into the mound of earth. He picked up a handful of dirt and threw it into the hole. It made a hollow sound as it landed on the coffin, triggering in Sam a brief sobbing fit. His pain transmitted itself to Grace, and she, too, began to sob. Again, she wished she could take him in her arms and comfort him.

Recovering himself, he wiped his eyes and returned to the tent. At one point he lifted his eyes, which seemed to meet hers, lock into them for a brief moment, then pass on. She wondered if it had been her imagination or merely a response to her own intense staring. But she could not deny the thrill that had gone through her.

"One thing we'll get at Sam's house is a good feed," Mike said when they were back in the car. The procession was looser now and no longer had the luxury of being able to pass through lighted intersections in a single group.

"I'm starving," Sally said.

"I could use a drink," Bob said.

"Likewise," Clara said. "These events tend to make one thirsty." She turned to Grace. "What about you, Grace?"

"Maybe a drink would do me good," she said, surprised at her candor. To approach Sam Goodwin she would need a drink, maybe more than one. What troubled her now was that she might not be able to muster the courage to open a dialogue with the grieving man. She felt this moment of opportunity swiftly approaching and all it did was inspire fear. She could not think of a single opening line.

"You suppose he'll keep the house?" Sally asked.

"No way of knowing," Mike said. "He certainly doesn't need it. One person thrashing around in all that space."

"He won't be one person for long," Clara said.

Grace felt suddenly in touch with her own inadequacy. It was panicking her.

"It'll be tough trying to determine the real thing. He'll wonder if they're after him for his money or his character," Sally said.

"Character shmarachter," Mike said. "Bottom line: his shekels are the big lure."

"Were the two people beside him, his children?" Grace asked, suddenly feeling the need to glean more and more information about Sam and his life.

"The son is a fancy lawyer in San Francisco, a real tightass. The daughter lives in New York with some weirdo. Sam has been very good to his kids."

"Lucky bastards," Clara said.

"Chose the right pop," Mike chuckled.

"Jewish daddies are very good to their kids," Sally said.

"Guess you have to be circumcised to be a good daddy," Mike said.

"I don't think you should personalize this," Sally said, barely repressing a giggle.

"Very funny," Mike snickered. "But the fact is, Jews think their shit don't stink."

"Come on, Mike, cool it," Sally said. "We're going to Sam's wife's funeral, for crying out loud."

"It's all propaganda. They create it, then everybody's got to think it," Mike said. "Isn't that right?" He looked sharply in Grace's direction.

"I don't think I'm qualified to be a judge of that," Grace said, stumbling over her words, surprised at his outburst.

"I'm not anti-Semitic," Mike said. "It's just sometimes they act so fucking superior. Good husbands. Good daddies. Hell, why not? They got all the goddamned money in the world."

"He gets that way when he's hungry," Sally said, embarrassed for him. Clara and Bob exchanged glances.

"They treat me okay. That's all I care about," Bob muttered.

"I need a drink," Clara said.

They had to park a good distance from the Goodwin residence. It looked like the entire funeral group had arrived.

The house was large but deceptively cozy. It was as if one entered a colonial home in Virginia. Walls were rich, dark, polished panels, floors were heavy oak. American antiques were everywhere, accentuated by oil paintings depicting early Americana, except for those painted of the deceased Anne in various stages of her life.

Grace counted three oil paintings, one in the den showing Anne Goodwin as a young woman beside a horse, a smaller one in the dining room showing Anne Goodwin as a younger woman, pensive and serene against a woodsy background and one large vertical in the living room above the fireplace depicting the departed Anne as a middle-aged woman of means, her demeanor regal and elegant, dressed in a gorgeous blue gown, wearing a magnificent diamond necklace. Grace was stunned by the beauty of the woman, even allowing for the painting's embellishment.

Crowds clustered around the dining-room table, groaning with food. A bartender dispensed drinks behind a dark-paneled bar. It seemed, like the others she had attended, more like a cocktail party and buffet than an after-the-cemetery repast.

By then, Grace had learned the difference between reformed, conservative and orthodox Jewish rituals. She knew the custom of *shiva*, where the immediate relatives sat on low wooden benches and wore black crepe pinned to their clothes while they received a steady stream of guests. Someone had explained that the custom was ancient and symbolic, a mark of respect for the departed and a sign of deep mourning for the irrevocable loss of a loved one.

There were no wooden benches visible, but the principal mourners did sit in the large living room receiving their guests. The visitation was also part of the ritual. Grieving was intended as a gathering of people to keep the mourners company, share their loss and comfort them.

Sam Goodwin sat on a straight-backed chair in the living room, receiving the condolences of the company. He wore slippers, had removed his jacket and taken off his tie. She watched him greet his guests, chat briefly, thank them for their condolences and urge them to partake in the repast.

Grace hung back, not knowing what to say. She was too nervous to eat. Between bouts of staring at Sam, she observed the house, its richness of detail and the scale of its rooms. She roamed into the kitchen, with its gleaming center island and its ultramodern appliances. She had never been in a kitchen so beautiful.

She toured the bathrooms, each one different, wallpapered with varied colonial scenes. Others, too, seemed to be touring the house as if they were inspecting it prior to a purchase. She went up the back stairs to the bedrooms, which, eerily, seemed the way she had pictured them in her fantasy, especially the master bedroom with its canopied king-size bed and high mattress which one apparently reached with a wooden step sitting beside the bed. The bedroom was huge, taking up the entire rear of the house.

Across the room from the bed was a nest of photographs in silver frames, depicting, what she assumed were past generations. There were many pictures of Anne: Anne with two children, Anne in a tennis costume, Anne and Sam in Venice, Anne with Pyramids in the background, Anne at the railing of a ship . . . Anne everywhere.

She was struck by the vast plethora of images of Anne scattered throughout the house, as if it were a kind of shrine to the woman. It filled her with envy to contemplate someone so worshipped and adored by her husband. It also emphasized the daunting task ahead for any female who attempted to fill the spousal void in Sam Goodwin's life. Grace knew she wasn't equal to the challenge, but the

idea did stir her competitive spirit. Why not? Looking at the monumental task from her vantage at rock bottom, she could see nowhere
to go but up.

There was a telescope facing out to sea, and beyond the picture
windows was a terrace with a table over which stood a colorful umbrella. There were two chairs, indicating that this was a place where
they had cocktails in the evening or morning coffee, just as she had
pictured it. The accuracy frightened her. Was this destiny playing
with her subconscious?

Along one wall of the bedroom was a sliding closet with floor-to-
ceiling doors. Opening one door, she took a peek inside. It was more
than just a closet. One could walk into it. Racks of women's clothes,
which she recognized as products of famous designers, hung on two
rows circling around the carpeted space. Above them on a shelf were
what looked like endless pairs of shoes. She had never seen or even
imagined a closet this big. It looked like a dry-cleaning establish-
ment.

Hearing footsteps approaching, she closed the door instantly and
passed into the upper hallway. Moving through other rooms that
opened off the corridor, obviously guest rooms, she noted that each
room and bath was individually designed. Wherever she looked oil
paintings hung on the walls and the furniture seemed genuine antiques.

Yes, she could be the chatelaine of this house. She had even gone
one step farther than her fantasy, choosing one of the rooms for
Jackie and hoping, foolishly, she would agree with her choice.

She started down the front stairs, which led to the main hall, now
crammed with people. Suddenly she spied the woman with the bun,
the clothes lady. Seeing her milling in the crowd, waiting for exactly
the right moment to spring, gave her the answer she had been looking for, her opening gambit. Of course. Why hadn't she thought of it
before? The lady with the bun represented a goading challenge. She
would beat her to the punch.

She moved quickly down the stairs and headed for the living room,
where Sam Goodwin was sitting. She stopped only briefly to take a
glass of champagne off a silver tray, which she swallowed in one gulp,
then took another. Girded for action, she inspected the arena. Men
shook Sam Goodwin's hand and women bent to kiss him on the
cheek. His son and daughter sat on the other side of the room,
guests crowded about them in clusters.

From the corner of her eye she saw the woman with the gray bun approaching. She felt the adrenaline rise in her body, sparked by her intake of Dutch courage, urging her forward, filling her with determination and a sense of mission. Opportunity was knocking loudly. This, she decided, was her last shot at the good life for her and her daughter.

An older man and woman were just offering their condolences. Behind them were another couple, and not far behind was the lady with the bun. Then, suddenly, she was facing him, her eyes staring into his. She noted that his were bright blue, still glistening with tears of loss and grief. He looked up at her and smiled, took her hand and held it between both of his. His touch was electric. Her knees shook.

"I haven't had the pleasure, Mr. Goodwin. I'm Grace Sorentino. I was a friend of Anne's. She was wonderful. One of the truly great ladies."

"Thank you so much," he said, his voice slightly hoarse. "I'll miss her."

"We worked together . . . on her various charities. The homeless especially. We focused on that."

"That was her mission," Sam Goodwin said, still holding her hand. "To help others."

"I don't know if this is the appropriate moment . . ." Grace began. She felt her voice waver, cleared her throat, then managed to speak again. He must have taken this action as the beginning of a good cry, because he patted her hand in a comforting gesture.

"I know how you feel, Grace." *He remembered my name,* she thought joyfully. "People loved Anne."

"She may have mentioned it, Mr. Goodwin."

"Please. Call me Sam."

"Sam."

"What had she mentioned?"

"The business of the clothes," Grace blurted. "She said that she wanted to make a donation of her clothes to charity. It was a kind of verbal promise. I don't know if she put it in writing, but . . ."

"Of course, Grace," he said. "What use would I have for them? The children will go through them and take what they want. Frankly, Grace, I don't think I could bear to look at them again, ever. Yes, by all means, keep her promise."

"I know how you feel . . . Sam. But I assure you that we'll take care of it with the least amount of pain to you . . ."

"I suppose time will take care of the memories." Sam sighed, still holding Grace's hand. "We had great times together."

"She was the best there was," Grace said. "Wonderfully compassionate. Believe me, I'll see to it that her clothes go to those who are the neediest, which is what she wanted."

"I know you will, Grace."

He finally released her hand.

"You're so sweet to come," he said.

She turned slightly and saw the woman with the bun, patiently waiting her turn.

"Can I count on that as a commitment Sam? The clothes?"

"You have my word on that, Grace," Sam said, his eyes roving now to the couple moving toward him.

"Thank you so much, Sam. I'm sure Anne will be very pleased. I'll . . . I'll stop by in a few days."

"The sooner the better, Grace."

She moved away, then posted herself at a spot where she could view his coming encounter with the lady with the bun. She noted that he did not spend as much time with the couple behind her as he'd spent with her. And he hadn't forgotten her name. He had called her Grace six or seven times, which meant he was likely to remember her when she called. The sooner the better, he had said. She decided she would wait two days.

She watched the lady with the bun begin her spiel and wondered if he would be true to his commitment. Hearing her out, he smiled benignly and shook her hand. Grace was too far away to hear what he was saying, but she could tell from the woman's expression that she had not gotten her usual positive answer.

Satisfied and elated, she roamed through the house again. A new sense of proprietary interest seemed to have made subtle changes in her attitude toward the house. It bothered her suddenly to see some of the guests abusing the various possessions.

Someone had toppled a Waterford crystal glass, cracking it. A group of Dresden figures on an antique table had been toppled, breaking the arm of one. Someone had leaned against a framed Catlin print, moving it awry. She quickly straightened it. In the dining room, cakes had fallen to the oak floor, and people were stepping on it, making a mess. She noted a small Oriental rug stained with red sauce.

Someone had used a beautiful china cup as an ashtray. It occurred to her that she was taking too much of an interest in the house, as if her wishes had transcended her fantasy. She decided finally that the damage was not being done deliberately but because vast numbers of people were moving through the house. She felt certain that Sam was indifferent to any violation of his property. His loss, after all, had not been material. The crowd had increased since she had arrived, and it seemed to be getting more and more difficult to get to the buffet table.

Despite the solemnity of the occasion the din of conversation rose naturally into a high-pitched crescendo. She threaded her way through the crowd to the patio that led to the beachside pool. At the far end of the pool was an ornate fountain, which directed its waters into a spill that fed into the turquoise pool.

She surveyed the house from the rear, noting the details of the stonework and how it complemented the dark timbers of the Tudor styling. How could anyone want anything more than this? she thought. What an unfair stroke of fate for Anne to have left all this behind. She sighed at the absurdity of the thought, then moved back into the house, heading for the living room and another look at Sam Goodwin. Perhaps they might make eye contact. He might nod, mime her name from a distance.

She saw him sitting in the same chair as before, his legs crossed, his head tilted upward to meet the gaze of the people still coming forward to pay their condolences. She stared at him for a long time, willing him to turn his eyes toward her. *Notice me,* she cried silently. *Notice me.* Then, miraculously, he did. She sensed a moment of connection, as if they were physically touching. Fate was doing its mysterious work, she told herself, feeling a trill of joy jump up her spine.

"Grace," a voice said from behind her. It was Mike McDermott, holding a plate piled high with food in one hand and a beer in the other. "Thought we had lost you."

"Here I am," she answered lightly, almost gaily.

He bent over her and whispered in her ear. "Party like this makes you kind of wish for more dead Jews."

She felt the anger rise from the depths of her, as if the insulting remark was directed at her personally.

"You are a bigoted prick," she snapped, conscious of the heat of her response.

"Hey, cool out," Mike said, blushing scarlet. "I thought you were Italian. It's a joke."

"Not to me."

She felt an overwhelming sense of kinship with the occupant of this house and, for the most part, his visitors. She turned away and looked toward Sam again, wishing he had overheard the conversation. It would have illustrated the extent of her commitment to him.

He was locked in conversation with an older man. Obviously, he had missed the confrontation. Nevertheless, she sensed that she had made the right impression on him, and in her reaction to Mike McDermott, she had passed some test and put herself squarely in a new and once alien place.

CHAPTER FIVE

Sam Goodwin sat on the chair of the bedroom terrace and stared out to sea in the waning hours of the afternoon. Mostly he thought about his life with Anne and he cried, sobbing quietly to himself. A week had passed since Anne had died.

For the past three days, since his children had left to resume their own lives, he had spent most of his days sitting in this chair, rising only to change the direction of the umbrella to escape the burning rays of the sun. Often, he had sat here with Anne, hearing her lilting voice in conversation as they contemplated the white beach and the spangled ocean beyond.

He hadn't shaved. He hadn't even gotten out of his terry-cloth robe, now gamy with the odor of his dried perspiration. Normally, at least when Anne was alive, he was fastidious about his personal hygiene, showering twice on most days.

Carmen, the Salvadoran maid, brought up a tray at mealtimes, but he barely touched the food, much to her dismay.

"You no eat?" she would admonish when she came to reclaim the tray.

"I'm fine, Carmen," he told her, waving her away. She shrugged and nodded, and he knew she was concerned, but he just couldn't

find the motivation to do anything beyond sitting on this chair on
the terrace and looking out to the glistening, infinite sea, as if await-
ing Anne's return from some mythical voyage.

In the first few days after Anne's funeral, he had kept himself open
to people, had answered his telephone calls and accepted the condolences of relatives, friends and business associates. He had fielded all
attempts, especially by his children, Bruce and Carol, to seriously
consider his future and the consequences of Anne's death.

They thought they were so wise and caring, these children of his.
They had been demonstratively affectionate throughout the ordeal
of the funeral. During Anne's illness they had been concerned and
attentive. They had called often, Bruce from San Francisco, Carol
from Manhattan, although never to the point where they had interrupted their own lives to be at her side.

That could, of course, be his fault. He had always been willing to
accept blame for the conduct of his children. He had engaged
nurses around the clock and had not encouraged them to come, and
Anne seemed to have been content with talking to them at length on
the telephone.

Now, beyond his depression and grief, he needed Anne to help
him sort out the future relationship with his children. He supposed
he loved them, but he was no longer as certain about that as he was
before they had become adults. In fact, he was beginning to suspect
that, as they pursued their own lives, they would provide little comfort for his present or his future. Nor did he understand how that
comfort could be defined. He supposed that was the way of the
world.

With Anne alive, he had not dwelt on the subject, as if it were hers
alone to contemplate. With Anne gone, he found himself ruminat-
ing upon it more than he wished.

Bruce had gone to Harvard Law School, where he had graduated
near the top of his class. He had done, mostly at Anne's urging, an
obligatory stint as a storefront do-good attorney for the poor and
powerless and had been a public defender.

In those years, he was resentful and guilty about the income from
his trust fund and extremely critical of the way his father earned his
money. Sam's specialty was buying ailing businesses, cutting costs,
building them up and selling them off at a profit.

He and Bruce had had their share of arguments about the way
Sam conducted his business. Bruce was extremely critical of what he
believed was the ruthless way Sam behaved when he took over a busi-

ness, accusing him of ignoring the human equation, throwing people out of work, looking only at the bottom line.

"It's the American way," Sam had argued. "By preserving a business I serve the greater good. In the end more jobs are created and people and communities prosper."

Sam had accepted the schism as the traditional rich father/idealistic son confrontation. If he had had a rich father, he would have acted in exactly that manner.

Bruce in those days had been adamant in his position. Of course, he had no real experience of where Sam Goodwin had come from, a child of the Depression, the son of a father sporadically unemployed, his spirit and self-esteem broken by defeat and failure. Sam had been working since he was twelve years old. He had graduated from Brooklyn College; setting off on a path that he knew was a reaction to his father's experience.

He was certain that his drive to acquire wealth was a form of vindication for his father's failure.

Yet, he had learned that such acquisition was not an end in itself. Money, for its own sake, was simply money, a commodity to keep the wolf far from the door.

But the real value of money, he had discovered, was its ability to grease the skids to power, to the power of status, prestige and social acceptance, to the power that inspired respect and admiration. Money without power was superficial. His marriage to Anne, without his consciously realizing it at the time, had provided the catalyst to achieve such power. Anne, with her WASP background and breeding, knew instinctively how to realize that potential. Without Anne, he felt that he had lost his rudder and was floundering without direction. Without her, the power had lost its allure.

His son, Bruce, had married Harriet Stone, who now taught psychology at Berkeley and was on her way to becoming a tenured full professor there.

Harriet came from a family of intellectuals who, on principle, looked down their noses on people with lots of money, like Sam, although much of their conversation with him revolved around the price of real estate and the stock market. Ironically, since Bruce married Harriet, his lifestyle had become far more material. He had joined one of the most prestigious and buttoned-down law firms in San Francisco and was fast becoming one of that city's most ardent champions of liberal causes, the classic limousine liberal.

Anne, who might also be characterized as such, approved of her son's political leanings but could not abide his wife and her superior attitude. Harriet believed that her own judgment about people was infallible, especially about Sam and Anne. To Sam, his son's wife was the quintessential hypocrite, a compassion groupie and money addict who resented and at the same time hungered for the lifestyle that Sam's head start had provided for her and Bruce.

Sam shrugged off the resentment. His son had married this woman and he was determined not to mar his son's happiness with contention.

"I think she's a shit," Anne had concluded.

"She's our shit," Sam told her.

Harriet had become pregnant about the time of the onset of Anne's illness and was now into her seventh month. She attributed the conception to the miracle of the subconscious, which was providing genetic continuity, meaning that the child would be a replacement for Anne. Sam tolerated her ridiculous remarks on the subject for Bruce's sake.

Bruce, now the officious, self-important corporate lawyer, was not shy about his thoughts on the disposition of his parents' estate. In fact, Sam detected that this might be their only future connection. Harriet, too, seemed unduly interested in the subject.

"We have to protect the future generations, Dad," Bruce had told him more than once, with appropriate apologies, during the funeral visitation, which had lasted four days. For his part, Sam avoided the discussion, not entirely puzzled by his son's urgency. Sam always prided himself on having a good nose for greed.

Carol, his daughter, who was three years younger than Bruce, was less concerned with the finer points regarding the welfare of future generations. She had been divorced twice and was now living with a man whom she had characterized as a serious artist with a promising future. She had made such judgments before. Invariably they were wrong.

"With the right backing, he can make it big," Carol insisted. He knew, of course, where the backing was supposed to come from.

He had long ago given up on providing any sensible guidance to Carol's life. She was a wild card, had always been a wild card and, as far as her future was concerned, she would be a perpetual dependent. He was resigned to the fact that she would be a conduit for his largesse, which eventually would end up in the hands of the men she coveted.

He had also given up confronting her with this supposition. Anne had coped with her by assuming she was evidence of her parents' romantic side, an analysis that had elements of truth.

But Carol's concern these days was that her shrewd sibling would somehow be able to inveigle more treasure out of her father than she did. Her plaint was that she was really in need, while Bruce, with his and his wife's income and prospects, had little need for more. Sam, of course, knew that *more* was a black tunnel to infinity. Only a lucky few had ever found the light at the end of it.

While Anne had rationalized their children's faults, Sam had acknowledged his disappointment. He had concluded that parents loved their children far more than children could ever love their parents. This was a form of life's vengeance. Yet he knew he would always be there as a safety net for his children, regardless of their attitude toward him. It didn't mean he had to like them or trust them.

In fact, he was well aware of their wishes, which were for him to divest himself of most of his estate in his lifetime and pass it on to his children before it could be heavily taxed and dissipated by fortune hunters and bad judgment. He girded himself for that pressure to accelerate.

On the third day after the funeral, Bruce began to prod him about the disposition of Anne's personal property. Carol was present when the subject was broached, which meant that they had already decided on a joint strategy. They needn't have bothered to approach it so cautiously. He had already made the decision to give them what they wanted, the division to be decided between them.

"She's got a closet full of clothes," Sam said. "Take what you want."

"I don't think the clothes would interest Harriet," Bruce said. "Wouldn't fit with her lifestyle."

"I'll look through them, Dad. Chances are I wouldn't take much." Besides, she was two or three sizes larger than her mother.

"Go through her drawers and the safe and take what you want," Sam told them. He didn't want to think about it.

"We'll do that, Dad," Bruce said.

Sam knew what they were really after and said so. "I guess you mean the jewelry?"

Anne had loved jewelry, almost as much as she loved clothes, and there were many expensive pieces in the safe.

"For starters, yes," Bruce acknowledged.

"Only if it suits you to do it, Dad," Carol said, exchanging glances with her brother.

The fact was that Anne and he had discussed it, and it was her wish that it be passed on to the children. But he had not thought the matter would come up so soon after her death.

"Good idea," Sam told them. "She wanted you kids to have the pieces, said that they would make great heirlooms." He suspected that such a fate was highly unlikely. Both Carol and Harriet were not much interested in jewelry for its own sake.

He led them into the master bedroom and moved aside one of the pictures to reveal the safe, which he opened. The jewelry pieces were in velvet-covered sacks and boxes. They helped him carry them downstairs into the dining room, where they were laid out on the table. A number of trips had to be made. There was also a sheaf of papers covering the appraisals.

"Divide it between you," he told them. "Just be fair with each other."

"Have you a calculator, Daddy?" Carol suggested.

"Don't you trust me?" Bruce asked.

Carol had looked at him and smiled.

"No, Bruce, I don't."

"Your share is only going to go down a rat hole," Bruce snapped. "You're only going to waste it on your new stud."

"What I do with my share is none of your business."

"I think we should dispense with the sibling rivalry here," Harriet had intoned. She had come into the room to participate in the proceedings and monitor the sharing process.

"This is none of your business, Harriet," Carol had snapped.

"Sorry, Carol. I'm afraid it is."

"Mother couldn't stand you, Harriet," Carol had cried.

"That's beside the point," Harriet had replied calmly. "I'm not suggesting a three-way split."

"Good," Carol had replied, "because Mother wouldn't have wanted it that way."

Bruce began to read through the appraisal sheets, searching for the jewelry it described. Separated and unwrapped, the glistening pieces took up the entire length and breadth of the table. Every precious gem was represented in a variety of configurations.

"Some of it is a little too gaudy for my taste," Harriet said, looking over the selection.

"I have no intention of wearing any," Carol had pointed out.

"Then let's do it strictly by value."

"You think that's fair?" Carol had asked, looking at her father.

"Keep me out of it, children," Sam had protested, remembering with what care each piece had been selected by Anne. The bickering was almost too painful for him to observe.

"How will we know what's fair?" Carol whined.

"Bruce is your brother, Carol," Harriet had intoned angrily. "Why would he want to cheat you?"

"He wouldn't need a reason," Carol sneered.

"That was uncalled for," Bruce had replied.

Sam had been both offended and depressed by the antagonistic byplay between them.

"Just work it out," he told them, leaving the room before they could see his tears flow.

Bruce had come by later and assured him that, to keep the peace, he had made sure that Carol had received more than her share and that it was all right as far as he and Harriet was concerned.

"Is it too early to talk about the artwork, Dad?" Bruce asked.

Sam repressed his anger.

"Not yet, Bruce."

"Sure, Dad. I understand. I assume it depends on whether you intend to keep the house."

"I haven't thought about that," Sam sighed.

"Might be a good idea to sell it. For one person it seems . . . well . . . very large."

"Where else would I go?"

"I don't know. Maybe a smaller place. A condo, perhaps. Someplace you wouldn't have to think about. In that case you wouldn't really need all this artwork and furniture."

"I'll have to sort that out," Sam had said. He really hadn't wanted to discuss his future with his son.

"You're vulnerable, Dad. I just don't want you to do anything foolish."

"Vulnerable to what?" Sam asked.

"I don't know. There are a lot of predatory females around."

"At this moment, it's the furthest thing from my mind."

"You're a rich widower, Dad."

"Thank you, Bruce, for the observation."

"I'm only thinking about your interest, Dad. Your future. I want you to be happy."

"You'd make me really happy if you'd drop this subject for awhile. I'm in no mood to discuss changes."

"Whatever you say, Dad," Bruce said. "I just want you to understand your vulnerability."

"I appreciate your concern, Bruce."

"I'm your son, Dad. Also a lawyer. In fact, I think I should be executor of the estate."

"Do you?"

Sam had given that assignment to David Berkowitz, a lawyer friend in New York with whom he had grown up.

"I'm many years younger than David. I'm a damned good lawyer and I'm your son. I think you owe me this, Dad."

"I'm not planning to check out just yet, and David is in very good shape."

"Dad, I'm only discussing this as a precaution. I hope you live a long time. You know I do. I just worry about you and want to do the best by everybody."

"I'll think about that, Bruce."

"And you know that I'll be fair to Carol."

"I wouldn't think otherwise."

"As you know, there are lots of tax consequences to an estate your size," Bruce pointed out. "You should really start thinking of lifetime disposition."

"I have been, Bruce. I've discussed this with David."

"And made provisions?"

"Is this really the time to discuss it, Bruce?"

"I'm afraid it is. Sad to say. I assume Mom was insured."

"Yes. I have a last-survivor policy, which should take care of a chunk of the estate taxes."

"You see, as an heir, I should know about those things."

"I've just told you."

"Before the fact. Not after."

"Well, I *am* the last survivor."

"Is the insurance enough to carry the tax burden?"

Sam noted the lawyerly talk and intonation. Sadly, he had no illusions about Bruce's motives, which were control over the estate and an excuse to discuss ways to hand parts of it over in Sam's lifetime.

It was, Sam knew, awful for him to ascribe such maneuvering to his son. Despite the lawyerly and logical way in which Bruce approached the subject, it struck Sam as unsavory, not what he would have expected from a loving son. Sam had loved his own father, who had not been able to leave anything of material value behind. To this day, he continued to love and revere him. Such affection seemed so natural, so fitting, so comforting. If only he could sense the same deep feeling he held for his father in his own children. Instead, he felt a widening irrelevance, an ever-opening chasm growing between them, a relentless separation.

In Bruce, beneath the reasonable language, the heartfelt expressions and protestations of sincerity, he sensed a disturbing hint of greed. He hoped he was wrong, but he felt such acute disappointment in both of his children that he couldn't bear to continue the conversation. He wished they would leave.

"I'm sure there'll come an appropriate time to discuss the future, Dad," Bruce said, hoping, Sam supposed, to plant such a thought in his mind. "It's a subject that can't be avoided."

He felt considerably relieved when they finally said their appropriate good-byes and left to return to their respective homes.

For the last few days, he let the answering machine take his calls, responding only when it was absolutely necessary. So far he had eschewed the computer on the grounds of it being a kind of generational protest. He had his private unlisted number for the children to use when anything important came up. Important or not, they both called him daily, but the conversations with them were getting repetitive and further assailed him with feelings of guilt as he continued to distrust their sincerity.

Mostly, Bruce gave him dire warnings about his current vulnerability, especially when it came to designing women. Carol, allied with her brother for her own obvious self-interest, echoed the warning. The fact was, as he reiterated to them ad infinitum, the very last thing on his mind at this moment was consorting with other women.

The fact was, he could barely contemplate a future without Anne. She had been integral to his life, his friend and companion. In many ways she had run his life, organizing the business of living, administering the smooth running of their household, tending to all the little details of personal and material maintenance, their social life, a roundelay of charity events, of big and little dinners, of cocktail parties, of travel, tennis games, bridge, gift-giving, shopping, directing his health concerns, supervising his diet, choosing his clothes. She was the planner, the scheduler, the arranger of his time.

Now he was adrift on a sea of ennui, ignoring all forms of organization. Her absence collapsed all routine. Even in the throes of her illness, despite her pain, Anne had continued to direct the minutia of their daily existence. It had by necessity run at a reduced pace, but it had been as efficient as ever.

Out of habit, he continued to make some business calls. Most of his efforts these days were to monitor his investments, which he had entrusted to a varied group of money managers. He hadn't been involved in acquiring businesses in many years. He had made his fortune, and all his efforts now were involved in preserving it. For what? he often wondered.

Anne's illness had complicated things considerably. All of his financial planning was based on the statistical premise that he would be the first to die. Actually, he was still considering the possibility up to the moment she had expired, hoping for the miracle that would reverse the situation. It hadn't happened.

It was ironic now that he had spent the last few years simplifying their existence. He had given up their London flat and their New York apartment, had sold their log ski chalet in Aspen. Anne had centered their life in Palm Beach, had established her circle and had found time to participate in her various charities.

Aside from the efficient organization of his life, he missed her presence, her voice, her movement, the aroma of her perfume. Not having her around was eerie. He hadn't yet accepted her absence. He actually felt that she was still moving around in the house. At times he was sure he heard her voice calling his name.

He missed her jokes, wisecracks, put-downs, laughter. He missed her quiet breathing next to him at night, another sound he continued to hear or sense or feel. When he awoke, it surprised him that she was not sleeping beside him.

Reminders of her were everywhere, of course. It pained him to see her things around the house and he could not open the huge closet they had built to house her considerable wardrobe without his eyes filling with tears. It was unbearable.

She had always been a beauty, with a natural elegance and taste that had been embellished by her being able to afford the best of everything that money could buy, especially things that she wore. Her wardrobe of designer clothes was monumental. She possessed extraordinary self-confidence and assurance, as well as impeccable societal instincts. She could mix with anyone, of any persuasion, social position, race or religion. Instinctively, she knew when to be imperious, when to be soft, when to flaunt, when to demand, when to surrender.

Despite their wealth, she had died a liberal, although the way they lived seemed a mockery of that ideal. Their circle, mostly ultra-conservative, tolerated their politics on the grounds of their consid-

erable wealth. Because of this, too, they were able to cross the fault
line that still existed in Palm Beach between Jew and gentile, a much-
denied hypocrisy that remained a persistent reality.

Although they lived a life of evasion and isolation from the
poverty, danger and turmoil of the inner city, Anne never lost her
compassion for the unfortunate, and her charity work was evidence
of this continued interest. Of course, she understood that her
lifestyle, her passion for expensive, tasteful possessions was an example of her own liberal hypocrisy and, at times, she allowed such feelings to agitate her. But those episodes were rare. She thought of
herself, as he did, as a good, decent, loving and caring person.

He made no apologies for his wealth and never felt the slightest
guilt about the fortune he had acquired. She was in charge of charity
giving and he gave her carte blanche, although he would have preferred to keep his name out of it. His ego simply did not need the
stroking.

In the past week he had relived their courtship, marriage and life
together so many times that his mind finally refused to recycle the
memories. Mysteriously, they had become different people from the
days of their youth, or so it seemed. At this moment he wasn't so
sure. He felt more like Sammy Goodwin, only son of Gladys and
Seymour. "My Sammy," Gladys had called him. My Sammy got all *As*,
she would tell the girls, her cronies at their mah-jongg games. To her,
Sammy could do no wrong.

Her "my Sammys" had become a litany. They made my Sammy a
partner, she had boasted. Then, a series of "Can you imagine my
Sammy? He bought us a place in Florida." He was hardly a *What
Makes Sammy Run?* Nor did he ever consider himself anything more
than lucky, with a flair for numbers. He was always good at arithmetic, a talent inherited from poor, luckless Seymour, who had zero
talent for making money or even holding a job.

In fact, when he analyzed his so-called success, his accumulation of
wealth, he characterized it as a kind of poetic justice for the treat-
ment his father had received at the hands of the bosses. Never once
after he graduated from college as an economics major had he even
considered spending a lifetime working for other people, being subject to the whims and foibles of bosses. The first chance he got, he
went into his own business, then businesses, then big businesses. It
didn't matter what kind of businesses, except that they had to make
money.

If he had a talent, it was in picking good people. He made money on their labor, their ingenuity and their creativity, and he rewarded them handsomely. So he had made money, lots of money. At this stage it was somewhere between fifty and sixty million, a pittance in comparison to the dot-comers and computer zillonaires, but more than enough for two or three lifetimes. What did it matter now? Once it had seemed to be a goal, his passion; now it struck him as quite meaningless and of lesser and lesser importance as he grew older. In fact, it was becoming more of a burden than a comfort.

To Gladys and Seymour, Sammy's "success" was as natural as his daily bowel movement. He had never given them a moment's worry and their expectations of his success was simply the natural order of things, Sammy's destiny. The odd thing about his parents was that they never craved the creature comforts he was easily able to give them, preferring to live modestly, more on the scale of their friends, ordinary people who still counted their pennies.

Sitting now on the terrace outside his bedroom, he contemplated his destiny. Life, at the moment, was shit. All his money was so much garbage. In fact, he had been feeling this for years, even when Anne was alive. He pushed such thoughts from his mind. It wouldn't be fair to her memory.

It was simply inappropriate to contemplate the other life he had lived, his secret life. Not once had he given Anne a hint of this secret life, the yearnings, the secret longings and the numerous culmina-tions among the vast worldwide army of prostitutes he had fre-quented. He had been crafty and cautious and secretive and had never let this other world interfere with his mainstream life, the life that Anne had constructed for him.

There was a moment when she lay dying that he wanted to tell her, to explain the drives and compulsions that led to this other life. But he could not summon the courage. He would never dare the risk.

He had justified this secret life on the grounds of personal neces-sity, and he had been clever and lucky enough to avoid it biting back and embarrassing Anne by its revelation. He could never abide the thought of hurting Anne in any way. There had been guilt in it and justification and torturous remorse, but he had miraculously escaped any emotional involvement and, also miraculously, any disease. Nor had he blamed Anne for his resorting to such habits.

Actually, he had reasoned, the sheer excess of this secret life had probably increased the tranquility and happiness of his life with Anne. They had never really argued, although at times he had expressed himself forcefully, if only for appearances' sake. When, in his present state, thoughts about this other life surfaced, he pushed them from his mind as he had always done.

Was this simply a testament to his cleverness, or his hypocrisy? Remorse was eating at him and, at the moment, he was defenseless against it.

If he had paid for this secret life in any tangible way it had been through the repetitive dream of Anne's infidelity with a young stranger whose face was impossible to recall when he was awake, although the dream remained vivid. In the dream Anne insulted and reviled him as she made love to the stranger. It was an odd and sometimes horrific dream, perhaps a subconscious transference of guilt. It came frequently when she was alive but, so far, had been dormant since her death, although he did expect its return. He wondered if it would be as terrible and nightmarish as it was when she was alive.

As he sat on the terrace, hoping that his mind would empty itself of his thoughts, he heard the door chimes. Carmen would answer it, ask the caller to wait, then come upstairs to tell him who it was. If it was something about the house, he had instructed Carmen to handle it by herself. Invariably he told her to send the caller away.

After awhile he heard her heavy tread on the stairs, and a moment later she was on the terrace.

"Woman say she come about madame's clothes," she said.

"Clothes?"

It took him a few moments to absorb the information.

"Say to tell you her name was Grace Tino-something. You know a Grace?"

"Grace. Grace," he repeated, trying to retrieve the vague memory. "Tell her to call next week. No, next month. Maybe never. Send her away."

Carmen turned and started moving to the door. Then he remembered.

"That Grace! About the clothes. She's going to dispose of madame's clothes."

He mulled it over quickly. Perhaps eliminating Anne's clothes would hasten him through this debilitating grief. He had told the children to take what they wanted. He assumed that they had. He remembered what the woman had said about Anne promising the clothes to the charity. The needy in designer clothes? He chuckled at the idea. Anne, too, would have had a good laugh over that one. Why not? Without the labels, they were simply clothes. Wasn't it the labels that gave them cachet and made them expensive? God, would he be open to argument over that one.

Once he had been in that business. It was all smoke and mirrors. All public relations bullshit. The designers had become franchises, products of the celebrity mill selling everything from perfume to T-shirts. Next would come toilet paper, designer toilet paper for tender, pampered assholes, or was it already out there?

The clothes were contracted out to sweatshops in Third-World countries where wages were a fraction of what they were in the countries where the finished goods were bought. But when the magic labels were sewed in, abracadabra, the price went through the roof. Celebrity consumers, he thought bitterly. Someday there might be a market for death masks, fingerprints, maybe even the bodily wastes of the worshipped ones. Or the body parts. He was getting morbid and was thankful for Carmen's interruption.

"What should I say, mister?" She always called him mister. He often wondered whether she could pronounce his name. She had waited patiently for his decision.

"Tell her to come on up."

"Me make some coffee?"

He shook his head. He merely wanted to show her where the clothes were hung. He wasn't interested in conversation, especially with someone he could barely remember.

"What was her name again, Carmen?"

"Grace."

"Right. Grace. Send her up."

Carmen shrugged and went out of the room.

He got up from the chair and went into his bedroom, glancing at himself in the mirror. He looked awful. His hair was awry, dirty-looking, and he had a three-day growth of beard. So what? he shrugged.

There was a knock on his bedroom door.

"It's open," he called.

He recognized her instantly and gave her a very cursory inspection. Black-haired, well-groomed. He registered the observation casually.

"You said I should wait a few days before I called."

"Did I?"

"I tried to telephone a number of times. All I got was a message. I didn't leave any. At first I thought you had gone away. Then I decided to stop by today."

He sensed that her eyes were studying him. He knew he was in a sorry state. As a reflex, he pulled his robe tight around his chest.

"Very resourceful, Grace," Sam said. Did he detect a note of sarcasm in his tone? He hadn't meant it that way. He led the way to the closet and slid open one of the doors.

"Help yourself."

"I'll inventory everything," Grace said, "and give you a receipt."

"It's all right. You needn't bother."

"No bother. I believe you get an income-tax deduction."

"How thoughtful," he muttered. "But please don't. It would be just one more complication."

She hesitated, continuing to study him.

"Pretty messy, aren't I?"

"Considering what you've been through . . . and I did barge in here."

She had good bones, he noticed. The lowering late-afternoon sun caught the glint of hazel eyes, or were they green?

"I'm going to make sure that her clothes go to the right charities. That was a condition of her promise."

"Was it?"

"She lived for helping others," Grace said. She stood through a long silence but made no move to begin work on the clothes.

"I know," he said.

"How are you managing?" Grace asked.

"Can't you see?"

"From here, not very well."

She put her hands on her hips. She was wearing a silk blouse and a single strand of pearls around her neck. Her skirt was dark and tight-fitting, short, slightly above her knees. It occurred to him, more as a reflex than an observation, that she was reasonably attractive, pleasant.

"You'll find lots of designer clothes. Anne was always impeccable in her taste. But I doubt if the homeless will have occasion to wear her gowns."

The woman hesitated a moment. A nerve began to palpitate in her cheek and she looked uncomfortable. She turned away for a moment, then looked at him again.

"Perhaps we'll find a way of converting the gowns to cash and use the money for other things."

"I'll say this," Sam said, "you people sure are dedicated. Anne was like that. Very dedicated."

He walked toward the door to the terrace. When he got there, he turned and looked at her again. It felt odd seeing this strange woman in his bedroom. Except for Carmen there had not been a strange woman in his bedroom since Anne died, not alone with him as she was now. He was suddenly reminded of his grief and shook his head.

"She . . . she, ah . . . died here," he said. Providing this information seemed inexplicable. "Three weeks she lay here. I had nurses around the clock. She told me she didn't want to die in the hospital. I agreed and took her home. I think being here actually extended her life." He shrugged and chuckled dryly. "A week maybe. But there were no life supports. Neither of us wanted that."

"Nor would I," Grace said. "At that point, I'd want nature to take its course."

"Anyway, we had a good life together. What more can you ask?"

Sam turned and looked out of the window at the sea. Listening for a moment, he could hear its rhythm, the splash of the curling waves against the sand. He started to open the door to the terrace. In one sense, he thought suddenly, it had been a life of compromise, a negotiated life, but satisfactory in every way. She had been his anchor, his underpinning, his home base. The unfaithful part of him belonged to another life, another compartment, another plane, perhaps even another person.

"I guess you were luckier than most," Grace said. When he turned, he noted that she had changed her position in the room. She seemed to be standing in a puddle of light, glowing slightly orange from the lowering sun, which came obliquely through a side window.

"You say that as if you've had a bad experience with marriage."

When the woman had arrived in his bedroom, he didn't want to talk. Suddenly he felt himself becoming inexplicably loquacious. It surprised him. Maybe it was the situation of having this strange woman in his bedroom. He felt no desire, no interest. This would not be the place. Not here, where Anne had died. Even in his secret life he had avoided such proximity. Indeed, the entire state of Florida was verboten.

"I'm divorced," the woman said. "Not very pleasant, I can tell you."

"So you're not sorry."

"No way."

"Does he give you alimony?"

It seemed, even from him, an oddly inappropriate question, and he detested himself for asking it. Always money, he thought. He was immersed in money, drowning in the idea of money.

The woman hesitated, and he noted that she turned briefly, as if to avoid his glance. He saw her in profile now, face and body, noting that she had a fine womanly figure. Again, he shunted the thought away. Was he so conditioned by his secret life that he could not control a knee-jerk reaction? He felt foolish and disgusted. Worse, guilty. Not here, he admonished himself. But the woman insisted on answering.

"I get more than enough to keep my daughter and myself," Grace said. "We don't live lavishly, but we live very, very well." She seemed to have added the last remark as a necessary qualifier, offering him her indifference to his wealth.

"Good. Then he's doing the right thing by you."

She smiled and nodded.

"Here I am babbling and you have work to do."

He moved across the room and passed by her, close enough to smell the aroma of her perfume. Was the scent familiar? He wasn't sure. When he got to the closet, he flicked a switch and the light came on.

"I couldn't bear to give you the grand tour of my late wife's closet, but it goes well back." He shook his head and sighed. "In order to get it big enough we had to build a room below it. We call it a sun room. Actually it's redundant. It was only built to support the closet. You will note, too, a double moving rack. There is a switch to operate it just to the right of the door. Tell you the truth, I've never really been inside it, except at the beginning, before it was stocked with her clothes. I've always considered it Anne's private place."

"I understand," Grace said. "I wouldn't want someone else poking around in my closet, especially a husband."

"She loved clothes. It was her grand passion."

"Yes," the woman said. "It was apparent to everyone who knew her. She was always magnificently dressed."

"Did you ever see her wear the same outfit twice? She had personal shoppers in New York, Paris and Milan who sent her clothes. She was always sending stuff back and forth."

He moved away from the closet and went back to the terrace door and again prepared to open it. Then he turned once again.

"I'd like to know how you're going to cart this stuff out of here. You'll need a truck."

"I haven't got a truck. I guess I'll have to do it in stages. Do you mind? It might be inconvenient."

"Inconvenient?" He paused. "I don't think so. Actually, I suppose I should get off my ass and start moving around. I've been holed up here for more than a week."

He rubbed his chin. "I've got the whiskers to prove it."

"I guess it's not easy to get yourself going again. . . . I mean . . . you know what I mean. Your life has been so radically . . . changed."

"Very much so," he said, shrugging. "I never had to think about what came next down here. Anne took care of everything. I don't know which end is up. She programmed me. She was my scheduler. Now, hell, I'm way off schedule. Nights melt into days. I haven't even read the papers or watched television. Everything seems totally irrelevant." He felt some dike breaking inside of him. "Shall I tell you something? I wished it was me who went first. She would be able to handle things better than I can. I think basically that women are more organized. At least she was." He paused, studied her, then asked, "Are you organized?"

"I try to be."

"You look organized," Sam said. "I had a secretary who was very organized. But a few years ago I gave all that up. I didn't want anyone organizing my business life except me. I use a computer now to keep track. . . ." He chuckled wryly. "I haven't kept track for a few weeks. For all I know, all my investments have gone down the drain. Fact is, I don't really care."

"I suppose it's all part of the grieving process," Grace said.

"Have you ever lost anyone . . . Grace . . . what is your last name?"

"Sorentino."

"Sorentino? Italian?"

"Italian descent. From Baltimore. Both parents died recently."

"Mine are gone as well. Hell, nobody lives forever, do they? They're buried in West Palm Beach, just across the inland waterway. Kind of a very . . . well . . . unfancy cemetery. Not that it matters. You saw where Anne is buried. That's the fancy place. I thought she'd be more comfortable there." He shook his head. "This grieving thing makes you crazy. You don't accept the idea that they're dead and gone forever. Not right away. To tell you the truth, my folks still seem alive to me as well. I think of them a great deal. Did you know, Grace, that as you grow older you think more about your parents than when you were younger? At least that's the way it is with me. I keep remembering my early life, sometimes with such emotion that I actually tear up over the terrible loss of it. I guess I'm getting old."

"You don't look old," Grace said.

"Sixty-four. I'm eligible for early Social Security and I can get senior-citizen airline coupons, both of which, as you can see, I don't need. But I do like the idea of it. Not to mention the movies, where I get in at a discount. That doesn't bother me as much. Most of the films they're making today are hardly worth paying for . . . at least from the perspective of an old fart like me. Anne used to be too embarrassed to get me the discount ticket. She just missed being a senior citizen. She would have been sixty-two in July."

He was speaking to her still standing near the terrace door. She, too, had stood stock still at the closet's entrance, her feet at right angles in a kind of a model pose, as if she were exhibiting herself.

"Hey, I'm talking your ear off and keeping you from your work."

"I don't mind," Grace said.

"Probably good for me. Maybe it will help stop the brooding."

"I've always been a good listener."

"And I've always been a good talker." He was surprised at the sudden compulsion to run from the mouth, but he had no wish to stop himself. "Maybe we should sit down."

There was a grouping of upholstered chairs in one corner of the room. A couch, an easy chair and a chaise longue.

"Take your pick."

She sat on the easy chair and crossed her legs primly. He sat on the chaise longue, stretching his slippered feet, which reached over the longue's edge.

"This was made for her. My legs were always too long for it."

"Would you prefer this chair?"

"No. It's all right." He shook his head. "Sometimes, when she was sick . . . in those last days . . . I carried her from the bed to this chair to give her a change of scenery." He grew silent. The shadows were lengthening in the room. "It's an awful thing to watch someone you love waste away. She was down under a hundred pounds when she died. You feel so helpless . . ." He raised his voice. "So damned helpless."

"I can imagine."

"Can you? I wonder. I don't mean to be insulting, and forgive me if I am. But this is something you can't know until you know. Do you understand?"

"I'm not insulted and I understand."

He observed a nerve palpitating in her cheek and hoped he hadn't upset her.

"It's something you can't escape from. Like being in a prison cell."

"I'm not looking forward to the experience," Grace said. She crossed her long legs and her dress hiked up. He noted that she pulled it down quickly. Suddenly he realized how she must feel, a strange woman in what was now a single man's bedroom. He pulled his mind away from such thoughts.

"It's so nice of you to listen to the ravings of an old man."

"I don't mind."

"You're being very tolerant. You don't have to be, you know." He shook his head again and felt his lips curl in a smile. "I look like hell, don't I?"

"It doesn't matter."

"Are you always so tolerant?"

He was sounding arrogant.

"I'm sorry," he added quickly.

"For what?"

"I sometimes get testy and arrogant. It's a side of me I don't like."

"These are special circumstances," Grace said.

He wished suddenly that she wouldn't be so understanding.

"Forgive me, I'm a grumpy old fart."

"Would you like me to leave?"

He shook his head.

"Just make allowances."

"I have."

"I'm old and grieving and bereft. Indulge me.

The woman remained silent.

"Do I seem old?" he asked suddenly.

"Do you seem old to yourself?"

"Questions with questions." He lifted his hand limply and waved it. "Sorry."

He was being obnoxious, he thought. The woman did not respond.

"Actually, I've had my satchels removed," he said, pointing to his eyes. "Anne called them that. She was always joking about something. One-liners. Lots of wisecracks. She kept me laughing." He looked up at her. "Maybe that's the secret of a long marriage. Humor. A sense of humor. That's it. I haven't laughed, really laughed, for days. Weeks, maybe."

"I'm not so hot at jokes."

He looked out of the window again. The sea was taking on the orange glow of dusk.

"It's getting dark and here I am keeping you from your work. So tell me, who will most likely be wearing my wife's clothes?"

"You'd be surprised how many women are desperate for clothing."

"Homeless women?"

"All kinds of women."

"I'll tell you this: They're going to look good in those clothes. Especially if they have the figure for it. She was . . . a six . . . I think. Yes, a six. Funny, I'm not sure. In an odd way size is a very private thing. Above all, I respected her privacy. What size are you?"

"At the moment, nearly an eight. At times I can fit in a six. Depends on the cut."

He inspected her figure, noting that she was larger-boned than Anne, taller and fuller.

"She watched her diet like a hawk. And worked out like crazy. We have a gym in the basement. I used to work out on the treadmill, but it's too damned boring. Instead, I take walks along the beach with my dog. He's been in the kennel since she died. I suppose I should take him out of there. I don't get aerobic, but who cares? Anne had a trainer come in three times a week. A lot of good it did her." He sighed. "Life's unfair."

"Yes, it is."

"Has it been unfair to you, Grace?"

He watched her grow thoughtful. The nerve that had palpitated in her cheek began again. She seemed to be searching for an answer.

"I try not to analyze things so closely."

"Ah, that means you think it's unfair."

"You go on and do the best you can. Period.

"You start at the beginning and go on until the end." He chuckled, finding the sensation illogically pleasant. "Alice in Wonderland."

Grace smiled.

"An interesting way to think about things."

At that moment there was a knock at the door, then Carmen's voice.

"Mister, you want supper?"

"Is it that late?" Sam said. "I really have kept you from what you came here for."

Carmen opened the door and inspected the two of them sitting in the bedroom. She seemed annoyed.

"I think I'm going to clean up and go downstairs," Sam said. "I can't stay up here forever. Life goes on."

"Good attitude, Mr. Goodwin," Grace said.

"Sam."

"Sam."

"Thanks for talking to me, was it Grace?" Sam said. She nodded. "Although apparently I did most of the talking."

"Probably a good thing for you."

"Probably."

He watched her uncross her legs and stand up. Carmen, too, watched her. She seemed none too happy.

"Make for Grace," Sam said

"No. I can't stay, Sam. I've got an appointment."

"I seem to have used up your time. Well, the clothes won't go away. Start when you can."

"What days would be convenient? Actually, it will probably take me awhile. Give me a time when I won't be intruding."

"Anytime, really. I'm not scheduled for anything. Not for awhile. Besides, you won't need me around."

"Can I start tomorrow?"

"If that's convenient for you. If I'm not around, which is unlikely, Carmen knows where everything is."

"I'll make for one," Carmen said, having listened to the conversation with interest. She shuffled out of the room, shaking her head. Sam smiled.

"She was very devoted to Ann," Sam said. "Everybody was very devoted to Anne."

"She was worthy of that devotion, Sam," Grace said.

"Yes."

He came closer and took her hand. It felt cool to his touch.

"Tomorrow, then."

"Tomorrow."

CHAPTER SIX

She played the conversation over and over in her mind, trying to see herself as he saw her. From her point of view it was nothing short of a miracle, surpassing her wildest speculations. Once again, destiny had spoken.

She had spent the entire week planning for this event, thinking about it, staging it in her head, agonizing over her strategy, reacting to imaginary conversations, wondering if she would even be allowed into the house.

It had been, she supposed, like girding for battle, treating Sam like an objective, high ground to be captured. She decided that she needed to engage him in an unthreatening way, appearing low-key, a dedicated volunteer, sincere and, above all, someone who would look the part, dress the part, even talk the part and pass as his wife's social equal. That was essential.

She knew the physical image she needed to emulate. She had seen plenty of examples at Saks. Expensively attired, pampered women whose self-esteem was buttressed by their pocketbooks, women who could afford to maximize their best attributes by emphasizing them with clothes, grooming and cosmetics. Her job at Saks was part of that system, enhancing the customer's best features and, more importantly, hiding their flaws.

She was far more confident about presenting the physical, the external view of herself, than the internal view. It was impossible to script in advance what she could say to him.

Certainly, she had to be cautious in her words, wary in her responses. She had to seem intelligent and strike just the right note of sincere sympathy. In effect, she had to tap all her resources and convey to him the first faint hint that she was someone worthy of his notice.

It was, she knew, a long shot motivated by desperation. It was one thing to plan and fantasize, quite another to make something happen that was far beyond her ability to manipulate and control. In fact, it was, by the laws of logic and reason, a ridiculous undertaking, a form of madness. What she needed most in this enterprise was blind luck.

Luck, she supposed, was a matter of timing, fate, Karma, the fickleness of the gods, being in the right place at the right time, saying the correct thing, placed in exactly the right atmosphere at the precisely perfect moment and striking exactly the right chord. If such conditions were the stuff of luck, she had never been blessed with it. She had never won a contest, had never come close in a lottery, had never been lucky at any form of gambling. The few times Jason had taken her to Atlantic City or to the local jai-alai games, she had always lost. Her horoscopes were never on target. Even her fortune cookies made only hapless predictions. Lady Luck had never given her a tumble.

She was a Sagittarius but had few of the vaunted attributes of that position in the Zodiac. Although she had been a committed Catholic, at least to the age of twelve, none of her prayers for her future had ever come true. She had prayed for a loving and prosperous husband and had gotten Jason. She had prayed for a boy and gotten a girl. She had prayed for good jobs, good wages, a nice home. *Nada.*

None of her wishes, hopes or ambitions had ever panned out. In truth, although she loved her, she was disappointed in her daughter: her performance in school, her values, her priorities, her aspirations, her morals, her choice of friends, especially that Nazi lover of hers. Worse, she blamed herself.

This was not to say that she felt totally luckless and devoid of hope and optimism. She was very healthy, almost never sick with colds or flu, had a good metabolism, white strong teeth, good posture, good skin and high energy.

The potential of a relationship with Sam Goodwin, although still in its embryonic phase, had forced her into a brutally honest self-evaluation. While her mental and emotional state might be considered shaky, her body, thankfully, was in excellent shape for a woman approaching her fortieth year.

Her figure, although fuller than when she was twenty years younger, was still reasonably muscular and youthful. She went sporadically to aerobics classes and rarely drank or overate. Her stomach hadn't pooched, her buttocks hadn't fallen, her breasts hadn't yielded to gravity and her gynecologist had commented that her vagina still held good tone and tightness. She was also quick to orgasm. Even Jason, at his worst, before he lost interest, could make her come.

Nevertheless, she believed that destiny required a bit of outside help to move it along the preordained track, which is why she took the long drive to North Miami to search out secondhand clothing stores that recycled designer clothes. It proved to be hard work, but she did find a silk blouse designed by Versace for fifty bucks, along with a complementary skirt designed by Donna Karan for another fifty. It took awhile, but she lucked out with a pair of shoes by Ferragamo, a bit pricey at seventy-five dollars but in fairly good condition.

With optimistic intent, and not without guilt, she went so far as to purchase a set of sexy underwear on sale at Victoria's Secret, in styles not quite Frederick's of Hollywood but close enough. Satiny and beautiful underwear, as every woman knew, gave one a sense of security in case of either accident or whatever unpredictable situation came up. Armored in this costume she felt comfortable, confident and strong enough to make her first sally into the alien territory of Sam Goodwin.

It was an agonizing decision, probably a wild gamble. She rationalized her expenditures by considering them an investment in her future. Besides, it helped keep her optimism in high gear. Her actions, she supposed, were like gambling, and she allowed herself to believe that perhaps her number, at last, was coming up in the big roulette wheel in the sky. Thinking about this made her giddy with enthusiasm and assuaged her guilt, at least for the moment. Would Jackie understand? She doubted that, although she assured herself that she was taking these steps for both of them.

What had actually happened in her first encounter with Sam Goodwin had exceeded her wildest expectations. He had even re-

membered her name. Not at first, but by the time she had left. And
he asked her to call him Sam. At the beginning he had been indifferent to her presence. Then he had become a bit on the rude side,
for which he apologized like a true gentleman. Then he seemed to
have warmed up and, she thought, actually paid her some notice.
She had been nervous at first, but then she had calmed down considerably and believed she had struck just the right note in conversation and demeanor.

She had no preconceived expectations, except to engage his interest in her as a woman. Beyond that she dared not speculate, except
to wonder if Mrs. Burns would have approved of her technique.

She had certainly tried to display her wares in the best possible
light, and apparently her choice of clothes was a grand success. Not
that she wanted to remind him of the ill-fated Anne, but merely to illustrate that she came from the same high-class environment.

Sam did look awful, hardly the beautifully groomed, handsome
man who appeared at the lectern to eulogize his dead wife. He
needed a shave and his robe was creased and stained, as if he had
slept in it. But she considered that allowing her to see him in this
state had a sense of intimacy about it. Perhaps it even provided a
bonding mechanism. She couldn't be certain.

She had been conscious of maintaining a certain level of propriety.
Although her skirt was deliberately on the short side, she was demure
in displaying much above the knee. If he had come on to her, despite
her preparation, she had no idea how she would handle it. She dismissed the thought. Not so soon after his wife had died. She would
definitely lose all respect for him if he had. She chuckled at the
thought. Here she was, playing a role, a true hypocrite. What had respect got to do with it?

After awhile, her nervousness had receded and they had had a
pleasant conversation about matters that were certainly not trivial.
She could tell that the maid was not overjoyed at her presence and
would probably be an obstacle. For that reason she had declined his
invitation to dine. Above all, she didn't want to appear too pushy.

Nevertheless, despite the apparent success of this first encounter,
she was uncomfortable about the lies she had told him. This business
with Jason and the alimony, not to mention the original lie, that
Anne had personally promised the gift of her clothing. One might
argue that since the entire episode was one big lie, what did more lies
matter? Call it desperate measures, the means justifying the ends.
But then, her cause, she told herself, was just.

The visit itself was a charade. She had portrayed herself as some-one she was not. Well not exactly that, she had conceded. But she had falsified her history. If he became attracted to her and they did form a relationship, would she ever be able to find the path back to truth? Probably not. She would have to pile on lie after lie and hope that he would be too involved emotionally with her to care. Or, if he did find out, she would hope that it would be too late for him to take any action, whatever that might be.

Anyway, she told herself, she'd cross that bridge when she came to it. If she ever came to it. Honesty and expedience often conflicted. Didn't they? She was definitely jumping the gun on possibilities. Go with the flow, she admonished herself. Ignore all false hopes.

On her way back to her apartment, she decided to work out some of the finer points of tomorrow's visit. She couldn't possibly wear the outfit that she had worn today. Nor could she avoid the task of be-ginning to remove Anne Goodwin's clothes. Tomorrow, she decided, she would take a chance on tight jeans and high heels and a blouse open at the throat, showing just enough décolletage to broadly hint at the reality of her good tits.

She had done some preliminary research on what charities Anne Goodwin worked for and inquired which of them recycled clothes for the poor. The Jewish Welfare Society, the Salvation Army and the League for Homeless Women were three of them. Her objective, considering the sheer volume of Anne's clothes, was to make a major project out of it, slow things down, keep it going.

She decided that she would remove the clothes from Anne's closet in increments, pile them in the backseat of her car and bring them back to her apartment, which would be the site of the pickup by the various charities. There was no way of knowing how long it would take to empty the closet. It was huge, and she hoped it would take many trips and give Sam a chance to get to know her better and, she hoped, get used to her presence at the house.

Back at her apartment, she realized how much tension had built up inside her. To relieve it, she stepped into a hot bath and tried to calm herself. Her mind spun with scenarios. Above all, she needed to be brutally frank with herself.

She was, after all, one of many predatory females bent on Sam Goodwin. At least, she hoped, she might have gotten her oar in first. Obviously he was having a hard time accepting his wife's demise. She considered that a good sign. The more grieving the merrier.

She giggled suddenly. Perhaps that, too, was a reaction from the

forced solemnity of the day. She was certain that, at least initially, if
their conversations continued, she would have to hear long and
loving recitations about his life with Anne—Anne the fabulous,
Anne the wonderful, Anne the sainted, dear, beloved departed. She
would force herself not to be resentful or jealous or mean-spirited
about Anne. If necessary she would worship at the same shrine, pay
tribute to the icon of recent memory. It would be one tough competition.

Lying in the bathtub with the warm water doing its work of relax-
ing her, her mind drifted into sexual fantasies about Sam. He was
sixty-four, he told her, although there was no way of knowing the
power of his libido or if he even had normal desires in that department. She had always felt that these desires were an essential factor
of her plan. But until they got down to business, there was no way of
knowing.

She pictured him naked, trying to imagine his penis in its aroused
state. It was making her horny, and after awhile she got out of the
tub, dried herself, went back to her bedroom, removed the dildo
from the bottom drawer, then lay down spread-eagled on the bed
and pressed the button that started the vibrating action.

It took her only a few moments to get going. She raised her hips
and manipulated the dildo to bring herself to a long, shivery orgasm.
It took her a while to calm down, and when she did, she got up from
the bed and replaced it under the folded clothes in her bottom
drawer.

Masturbation, she suspected, was a secret shared by most human
beings. Long ago she had considered it a sin. Her early Catholic upbringing had made it out to be an act against God, the devil's work, a
ticket to hell, as well as being unhealthy, crippling and preventing
conception. What disturbed her most was the fact that she was using
it as a desperate substitute for the live article, as if the use of this mechanical toy was evidence of her inadequacy, her inability to attract a
viable living partner.

She also worried that she might be developing a dependency that
might make it impossible for her to climax when and if she did become involved with a man. Brushing such negative thoughts aside,
she allowed to herself that the use of the dildo was an emergency
measure. Besides, it felt good, it relieved tension and hang the consequences.

She was just getting into her dressing gown when Jackie came into
the apartment.

"That you, dear?" Grace called from the bedroom.

"Yeah."

From her tone, Grace detected her mood, which was not good. She came into the living room, where she confronted Jackie's pouting, clearly belligerent expression.

"What is it, Jackie?"

"Leave me alone."

"You got it," Grace said. She went to the kitchenette and put up water for pasta, then opened a can of sauce and put it in the saucepan to heat.

She watched as Jackie got up and paced the room. She picked up her books and flung them angrily onto the studio couch.

"Don't break anything, baby," Grace said calmly.

"If I broke anything it would be over your head," Jackie said.

"Well, well," Grace said. "I must have done something that didn't meet with her highness's plans and perceptions."

"Screw you, Mom."

"So we're being respectful now," Grace said, noting that the water had not yet reached a boil.

"If you hadn't gotten fired, you could have got me that Donna Karan outfit with your employee discount."

"It was out of my control," she said, knowing that this reference was only one in a long line of Jackie's complaints.

"It didn't stop you from getting what you wanted."

"What are you talking about?"

"I saw the clothes you bought, fancy designer stuff. Versace, Donna Karan, Ferragamo shoes. I know what these things cost, and you couldn't see your way to spending a few hundred dollars on your own daughter. Not to mention the car. You know a car is a necessity in this area. You know. How could you?"

"So that's it."

"Pretty selfish, don't you think? All that bullshit about sacrificing for dear Jackie. Goes to show."

"Goes to show what?"

"Money talks and bullshit walks."

"I hate to say it, but it was secondhand. Worn by others before."

Jackie contemplated the explanation, then paused for a moment, as if searching her mind for an alternative argument.

"How tacky," she said after a long pause.

"Tacky?" Grace shrugged. "I'm working on something and I need to look the part."

"Like what?" Jackie said with contempt.

"When it happens, you'll be the first to know."

"When what happens?"

"When what I'm working on happens."

"A big job?"

"Yes," Grace said with an air of finality.

She was determined not to tell Jackie what she had been doing with her time. What kind of a role model would she be if she revealed how she had followed the obituaries and haunted funerals, how she had set about, with dogged singleness of purpose and probably malice aforethought, to mount this mad campaign to find Mr. Big Bucks. Someday, if and when, by some miracle, she succeeded in this enterprise, when Jackie was mature enough to accept her explanation, she would reveal a much-edited version of what she had done. Not now.

"I have something in play that requires an expensive look," Grace embellished, hoping to evade the truth rather than confront it.

"What's the big secret?" Jackie asked.

"Like a real good job, one that pays very, very well. I have to look the part."

She detested the idea of lying to Jackie. It negated the concept of complete candor between them and underlined her own hypocrisy. *It's for your good, darling,* she explained silently. And her own, she added.

"With whom?"

"I can't say. You just have to be patient. It might not work out."

"Probably won't," Jackie said, shaking her head.

"It will be very good for you as well, Jackie," she said, putting a voice to her rationalization. "Trust me."

"'Trust me.' I hate those words. I'm beginning to learn that you can't trust nobody."

"Anybody."

"What?"

"You can't trust anybody," Grace said.

"Oh, shit. You know what I mean."

"You should polish up your language."

"Why?"

"You might be meeting a better class of people someday. You can tell a lot from the way a person speaks."

She put the pasta in the now boiling water and stirred the sauce. While not mollified, Jackie had calmed down.

They did not speak again until Grace put the pasta on the table and they began to eat.

"I'll never meet a better class of people, Mom," Jackie said. "The fact is, we're stuck at the bottom and always will be."

"We'll see about that, Jackie," Grace said. She refused to accept any hint of defeatism, thinking it might jinx her destiny.

CHAPTER SEVEN

Carmen let her into the Goodwin house the next morning. Her expression was sour and unwelcoming and she said very little.

"Mister not home," she said.

"It's all right, Carmen," Grace said pleasantly. "I'm here about the clothes. I know the way."

She did not let Carmen see her disappointment. In the bedroom, she looked out toward the beach. In the distance she saw a man walking a dog along the water's edge but could not be certain it was Sam.

Sliding open the closet door, she put on the light and went in. It felt like a giant cave. There were rows and rows of dresses, skirts, blouses, all hung neatly like soldiers. She pressed a button on the wall and the rack moved, which made it possible to stand in one place and watch the clothes roll by.

What she at first thought were shelves for shoes was actually a moving belt which operated from a separate button. She pressed it and the shoes rolled past. She had never in her life seen a collection of clothes like this. Apparently Anne, who was a bleached blonde, was partial to beige. She noted, too, that there were a lot of dresses with colors compatible to green, assuming, then, that Anne had green eyes.

The closet seemed to have a separate cooling system and smelled vaguely of cedar. It was exclusively for female clothes, so presumably Sam had his own closet.

Apparently Anne took great pains with the organizing of her wardrobe. Gowns were carefully separated by length, and she seemed to favor Galenos in that category, although there were a few Valentinos and Bill Blasses mixed in. She recognized sportswear by Donna Karan, Sonia Rykiel, Calvin Klein, dresses by Yves St. Laurent, Lacroix, Cerrano, Karl Lagerfeld and Versace, shoes and pocketbooks by Ferragamo, Gucci, Manola Blahnik and Paloma Picasso.

There were some gaps in the racks, and she assumed that the children had already made their selections. She contemplated the time and money required for a woman to collect such a wardrobe. There was no telling how many outfits there were, but she could tell by the styles that Anne was a pack rat and had accumulated a great deal of clothing that she had not worn for years.

She declined to characterize Anne as a clotheshorse, which connoted something superficial and flawed in a woman's character and would be untrue to the portrait of the saintly woman Sam had painted in his eulogy. She was determined not to verbally denigrate the woman in any way and to guard against any chance remark that would inadvertently diminish her sacred memory in Sam's mind.

Grace decided to start by categories—skirts, blouses, slacks, jeans and obvious sports clothes first—reasoning that they would be easy to dispose of to those charities set up to aid the homeless. Despite her dissimulation, she was determined to be true to her stated purpose and not expose herself to be unmasked as the cheat she was.

It did cross her mind that she might sell the clothes to secondhand dealers, but she rejected the idea on principle. Considering the subterfuge she was employing, she had convinced herself that she was, win or lose, doing something charitable and morally correct. To sell the clothes would put the mark of sleaze on her effort, as well as open her up to charges of stealing and other consequences, which could backfire and interfere with her plan. No, she decided, she would do exactly what had been promised. She would resist the temptation to profit from this enterprise and give Anne's clothes to charity. If discovered, she reasoned, her act might be forgiven.

She pressed the button and carefully reviewed the passing parade of clothing, made her selections, then took them off the rack one by one and laid them carefully on the bed and the furniture. Her initial removal hardly made a dent in the amount of clothing left in the closet, and she realized happily that this job would be a full-time chore, probably taking weeks.

Since merely disposing of the clothes was not the real reason for the exercise, it would serve no purpose if she were to arrive and find Sam gone. She needed to know his schedule, if he had one. She looked out of the window and noted with pleasure that it was indeed Sam and his dog walking along the beach.

They were obviously heading homeward, which gave her an excuse to slow down her effort. She sat on the edge of the couch and looked out of the window, watching Sam come closer. Looking at her watch, she estimated that it would take him a good half hour at his present pace, which was more like a stroll, to get him back to the house.

"I help you bring down to your car," Carmen's voice said from somewhere behind her. Grace didn't know how long she had been watching her. She had not heard her come up, which was unusual for such a heavyset woman.

"Thank you, Carmen."

Carmen did not respond. Instead she took a large batch of the clothes and started to make her way out of the bedroom. The load looked very unsteady in Carmen's arms.

"You needn't carry so much, Carmen," she said. It seemed blatantly obvious to Grace that Carmen was trying to hurry her out of the house as soon as possible, certainly before Sam was due to arrive.

"You take some," Carmen said.

She heard Carmen's heavy tread on the stairs, then a sudden thud, which, she assumed, meant that the clothes had fallen from her grasp. Grace smiled knowingly and watched Carmen struggle to get the clothes in some kind of order for hauling. She watched for a moment, making no effort to help, then returned to the bedroom, observing Sam and his dog as they came closer. Nor did she make any effort to gather up the remaining piles of clothes.

As she watched, she saw Sam break into a run, followed by the dog, a large one with a rust coat. They headed for the ocean. Sam dived into the surf. The dog followed. She saw him disappear for a moment, then surface, swimming with strong strokes, heading for the calm beyond the breaking waves. He swam for a few minutes, the dog swimming behind him, then headed back to shore, riding in on the waves. At that distance, he seemed young and strong, emerging out of the water, the dog by his side, both jogging toward the house.

"You bring more?" Carmen shouted from the floor below.

"I'll be along when I'm ready, Carmen," she answered pleasantly but firmly. "And I'll need to go over my plans with Mr. Goodwin."

Carmen did not respond. Nor had Grace any intention of letting herself be intimidated.

A few moments later Sam, still dripping, came into the room. Having seen the evidence of her appearance as he came up the stairs, he was not surprised to find her.

"Don't let me interrupt," he said as he moved across the bedroom to the bathroom. She noted that his body was hard and slender, further belying his age.

"Looks like you've enlisted Carmen," he said as he grabbed a towel and slipped it around his shoulder. Then he closed the bathroom door, and she could hear the shower going. Sometime later he emerged. He had shaven and his silver gray hair, still moist, was carefully combed. He was barefoot and wore jeans and a blue and white T-shirt with horizontal stripes.

"Back to my routine," he said. "I swim every morning. Me and Marilyn. She's a golden retriever, loves the water."

"It's a good sign," she said.

"Makes it hurt less," he sighed.

They exchanged awkward glances.

"It's going to be quite a chore, Sam," she said. "I hadn't realized how much clothing was in there."

"Take all the time you need."

"I don't want to be a bother to you."

"Won't bother me. Besides, I have my own closet. Won't be much of a job when I check out for good. Mine is a lot more humble. I detest shopping. Wouldn't even go with Anne. My suits are made on Regent Street in London. I haven't ordered any new ones for three years. Anne, on the other hand, loved the whole process of buying clothes . . . as you can see."

"They are quite beautiful, Sam."

"Yes, they are. And they looked great on her," he said, his eyes moistening as he turned his gaze toward the sea.

She found herself searching for things to say. He seemed less willing to engage in conversation than he was yesterday. After awhile he turned toward her.

"If you need any more help, just holler."

"Not from you, Sam," Grace said. "Our deal is that I take this off your mind."

"And a deal's a deal. Besides, I'm not sure I could hack it without falling to pieces."

"Carmen will help." Grace cleared her throat. She had no illusions about Carmen's attitude toward her. "She's been very cooperative."

"Good."

She started to gather up some clothes. As she did so, she felt him observing her.

"You're right. I couldn't face it. Getting rid of those things."

"I'm glad I could help."

"They were part of her."

"Yes, they were."

"Funny thing about possessions. It's the wrong word, *possessions*. Nobody really possesses anything. It's all temporary. We use them like rented goods, then poof." He shook his head sadly. "She loved those clothes. So what? They're of no use to her now . . . wherever she is. "

"It does make you think," Grace said. From his vantage of abundance, he was right, of course. From hers, the vantage of deprivation, it did not have the same meaning. Possessions made life a little easier, and that was no small thing.

She saw his eyes moisten. He turned away and looked out of the window. She felt compelled to speak.

"I saw you coming from way out there," she said. "Looks like a great place to walk."

He continued to look outside. Then he cleared his throat.

"I like walking beaches. It can be sunny, cloudy, rainy or foggy. I always jump into the sea for a quick swim," he said. "That's why we built on this spot. One of the reasons, anyway. I've walked a lot of beaches in my life."

"Anne must have enjoyed that a lot."

"Hated it. Anne wasn't a walker and stayed out of the sun as much as possible. I told you she took her exercise in a gym we have in the basement. I would have liked her to come along."

Grace saw it as a good point for an opening.

"I love to walk beaches and swim," she said, hoping she wouldn't seem too obvious.

"Do you?"

"I do. I like the feel of the sand and the sound of the surf."

"So do I. Has a soothing effect."

Her heart was pounding. But she sensed that this was the one moment that she had to seem casual and only mildly enthusiastic.

"I try to start the walk around nine. It's kind of late, but I make some calls, read the paper, have a cup of coffee, then take off."

He looked at his watch.

"I give it a couple of hours. Marilyn loves it. Speak of the devil."

The dog, muzzle still dripping, came up to Sam, who rubbed her behind his head.

"Marilyn. Doesn't sound much like a dog's name."

"She's not a dog. She's a bitch. Officially. Actually, even that's a misnomer. She's a person. Since Anne . . . well, it's sort of strange for her. Last night she slept with me."

She wondered if that was meant to be another opening, but she ignored it. A sixth sense nagged at her to avoid any hint of a double entendre or even the most innocuous reference to sex.

"Even though Anne adored her, she never let her sleep in the bed with us. Not even in the bedroom. Slept right outside the door. I had her boarded since Anne died. Took her out last night. Did I tell you that yesterday? She's been over the house a hundred times, looking for Anne." He paused for a moment and sighed deeply. "So have I, for that matter."

Marilyn came over to her and sniffed, but when Grace bent down to pet her, the dog snarled and growled, baring her teeth in a threatening manner. Grace jumped back, genuinely frightened. In her panic she dropped the clothes on the floor.

"Stop that," Sam shouted, tapping Marilyn on her muzzle. He kneeled and pointed a finger at her. "Bad girl. Bad girl." He looked up at Grace. "Never did this before. Probably confused about Anne not being here."

"Am I so threatening?" Grace asked, instantly sorry. She did not want to put such a thought in his head.

"Down, girl," Sam shouted, displaying a hand signal. Marilyn calmed, then, obeying Sam's command, lay down on the floor on her paws.

"I hope she didn't frighten you."

"Not really," Grace lied.

"Good."

She started to pick up the clothes from the floor, and he bent down beside her to help. He had never been this close to her and she smelled the salt tang of his skin. She wondered if he could smell her perfume.

"Please, Sam, I can handle it," Grace said.

He stood up and nodded.

"Considering the circumstances, Marilyn's reaction is perfectly understandable," Grace said.

"For this annoyance you deserve lunch. I eat early," he said, smiling. Was it a flirtatious smile, she wondered, or merely a manifestation of politeness? "What do you say?"

Grace hesitated, then nodded her consent.

"Good."

He went out of the bedroom and called down to Carmen.

"Yes, mister," Carmen responded from the stairwell. "Two for lunch." He turned to Grace. "Tuna fish okay?" Grace nodded. "Two tuna fish sandwiches." He turned to Grace again. "Coffee?"

"Sounds fine to me."

Grace tried to look busy as she arranged the clothes on the bed. The telephone rang. Sam answered it, and she could hear him talking on the phone next to his bed. She left the room and passed down the stairs with her arms full of clothes.

Outside, she opened the trunk of the car and placed the clothes inside. Then she discovered that Carmen had thrown her load helter-skelter in the backseat. It confirmed what she had already suspected: Carmen viewed her as the enemy. It took Grace some time to rearrange the clothes.

As she came back into the house and passed by the kitchen, she felt Carmen observing her. Looking up, she caught her sneer. Grace hadn't expected this kind of opposition. She shrugged it off. There was no point in setting up a reason to be paranoid.

She reviewed various options of behavior. Above all, she must act nonchalant, interested but standoffish. She rejected voicing any criticism of Carmen's attitude.

On another level, she observed that she liked this man. He was gracious, self-effacing, polite and pleasant. He was quite good-looking, too. His maturity was an asset, and he carried himself with confidence, despite his grieving. She hoped that she had engaged his interest. It seemed so, but she was afraid to trust her own instincts. Perhaps he was simply lonely, looking for human contact, and she was merely there.

Carmen had set the table in a room off the kitchen.

"This is the breakfast room, but it's okay for us to have lunch here."

It wasn't much of a joke, but she chuckled anyway.

Carmen came in and put a carafe of coffee on the table. Her manner was surly and the way she set down the carafe seemed a provocation. If Sam noticed, he ignored it.

"I hate to eat alone," Sam said. "Normally I would lunch at the club after a few sets of tennis, but I haven't been feeling like going back to it just yet. Do you like tennis?"

She was tempted to say yes, but the lie would have little chance of sustaining itself. She had never played tennis.

"Never touched a racket," she said, feeling good about her honesty.

"You'd like it," Sam said, biting into his sandwich. "Anne was a great tennis player. Used to beat me at singles. She was very focused. More so than me. I play at it." He put down his sandwich and studied her.

"I suppose you're a golfer."

"No, I'm not."

"Bridge player, right?"

"Sorry."

"Me, too. I'm not much for games."

She wondered if her honesty was making her less and less interesting. But if she told blatant lies that could be confirmed by action, sooner or later they would be found out and her motive would become obvious, as obvious as it was to Carmen. She didn't want to set any traps for herself.

"So what interests you . . . I mean, aside from your charity work?" Sam asked.

"There's my daughter, of course. She'll be seventeen in a few months," Grace said, searching her mind for answers that would enhance, not diminish her chances. She knew what that meant: lies.

"Tough age," Sam said. "Parenting doesn't come with a handbook. Gets worse as they get older."

"That's not very encouraging."

"Unfortunately, it's a fact."

"My Jackie's a wonderful girl," Grace said. His taking on the frustrating obligation of helping to raise a teenage girl, especially one with Jackie's propensities, was a consideration she had not thought about. Quickly, she erased the idea from her mind. It was blind, stupid optimism, reminding her suddenly of Jason and his foolish dreams.

"One more year and she'll be off to college," Grace said, unable to quite banish the idea, as if she were hoping to minimize Jackie's involvement as an issue between them, another stupidly hopeful premise.

"What college are you thinking of?"

She grew thoughtful for a moment, watching his face as he waited for an answer. In too deep now, she decided, searching her imagination for more fictional signposts. Was this reinventing of herself a form of madness?

"She's at the top of her class. Ivy League definitely. Princeton is her first choice. That's where Brooke Shields went. You know how teenagers like to emulate," Grace said, moaning in her soul.

"Really . . . that's where Bruce . . . my son . . . went as an undergraduate. Maybe I can be of some help."

"I don't think she'll have any trouble getting in," Grace said, panicked now, conscious of her clumsiness, feeling like a criminal bungling a burglary. Plunging ahead, she knew she was painting herself into a corner. "She's a very dedicated student. Her marks are excellent. Quite a young lady."

"What is she considering studying?"

"Medicine, probably. She has expressed an interest in being a doctor."

In her mind's eye she crossed herself and heard the words whispered in her own voice, "Forgive me, Father, I know not what I am doing."

"Wonderful," Sam's voice intruded.

"Yes. I'm quite proud of her," she said without missing a beat.

"I went to Brooklyn College," he told her. "Damned fine school. But my real education was out in the jungle. I became a businessman." He took a bite of sandwich and washed it down with coffee. "And you, Grace, where did you go?"

"Johns Hopkins," she said after a moment's hesitation.

It was a reflex reaction. But it was a logical lie. After all, she was, like Johns Hopkins, from a place called Baltimore. She was well aware that she was puffing herself up beyond all possible validation. *Please,* she begged herself, *put on the brakes.* She needed to bring her background down a peg. It was totally unsustainable at this level. She felt lost in a labyrinth, not quite Alice in Wonderland, more like Gretel, who with Hansel, was thrown into an oven by the wicked witch.

"We lived in Baltimore, you see. My parents didn't want to send me out of town. I'm an only child. They were very protective."

"What did your father do?"

"An engineer," Grace replied. It had been the first thing that popped into her mind. She knew she was beyond saving now. "Mom was a piano teacher."

"Too bad they're both gone."

"That's life." She giggled nervously.

Forgive me, Pop, she told herself, feeling the quicksand crowd in around her.

"A great school, Hopkins. What did you study there?"

Oh, Jesus, she thought. This man is relentless. Damned if she does, damned if she doesn't. Her mind was reeling with the effort of invention. Of course, she had to answer his question.

"Political science," she replied.

"Did you work in politics after graduation?"

"I did. I worked in Washington for awhile."

"I was an economics major, with a minor in English," he said.

Actually, she remembered, she hadn't been a bad student, but there was never a chance that her parents could find the money to send her to a good college, and she wasn't scholarship material. Average and ordinary, she sighed.

"Where did Anne go?" she asked, hoping to change the focus from herself.

"Wellesley," Sam said. "She started out as a biologist. Phi Beta Kappa. She was on to her doctorate at Columbia when we married. She never did finish."

Grace's heart jumped into her throat. With barely a year at Baltimore Junior College, the comparison was embarrassingly awful. How could she possibly fill Anne's shoes? Despite her misgivings, she smiled at the reference, remembering suddenly the rows upon rows of shoes on rotating display in the woman's closet. The humor somehow relieved the sudden pain, but it totally excised her appetite.

"We met on a blind date. Friends fixed us up. The moment we were introduced we knew." He sighed and shook his head. "It was a great forty-year run."

"And she had no regrets? I mean . . . not finishing her doctorate?"

"Who knows?"

His mind appeared to wander, and he sucked in a deep breath. It seemed an odd response. He was silent for a long time and his eyes glazed over. She left him to his silence, sipping her coffee, which had become lukewarm. She wondered if he was tiring of her presence.

"And your husband? What did he do?"

"Lawyer," she said, again without thinking but hoping she showed no hesitancy.

"Poor woman. We have too many lawyers as it is. What was his specialty?"

He was like a finger persisting in worrying a scab, and she was growing agitated.

"No specialty. General law," she said, groping to keep the explanation logical.

"Too bad it didn't work out."

"I have no regrets," she said. It was the first really honest remark of their exchange.

"Here I am, prying into your personal life. Forgive me."

"It's all right," Grace lied. She wished he had been less curious, so she'd had more time to think things out. They were silent for a while, and at what seemed to be a proper interval she spoke.

"I think I'd better get going."

"I expect I've been taking up too much of your time. I hope you haven't been bored," he said.

His comment seemed incongruous, and she wondered if she was approaching this correctly.

"Not at all," she said.

"At least I'm not crying as much as I was. One of my doctor friends diagnosed it as a manifestation of senile depression brought on by the loss of one's spouse. He had a Latin name for it, but I told him to spare me."

"You seem to be holding up very well," she said.

"Compared to what?"

"To yesterday."

"God. I was a mess, wasn't I?"

She felt him looking at her.

"You helped, Grace."

"I did?"

"Suddenly there you were. A breath of fresh air, and I was forced to crack open the shell."

"I had nothing to do with it," she said, feigning modesty. The panic of the earlier course of the conversation had receded. She knew it was a temporary respite.

"I like the idea of your fulfilling Anne's wishes about the clothes. I'm sort of hung up on things like keeping one's word. It's a caveat of the way I do business. I believe in the concept of the handshake. It underlines the bond of honesty."

"You're saying you're a man of your word."

"Bottom line," he said. "It may sound corny, but I have found in business that honesty and integrity always wins. It has stood me in good stead. I'm not saying that I don't believe in contracts that outline conditions, but essentially, with me, it is that sense of trust when I look the person in the eye. I think the secret of my success in business is the ability to quickly size up what a person really is. Sometimes it happens almost instantly in the first few seconds of contact."

She felt heartburn begin in her chest. Here she had fed this man a pack of lies and he was going on about the virtues of honesty and being able to tell what a person really was instantly. She felt diminished, as if his words were some kind of a warning. Had he sized her up? Was this business between them a cat-and-mouse game, merely a diversion from his tragedy?

"Would you like more coffee?" he asked. "Look, you've hardly touched your sandwich."

"I'm fine," she said. "I . . . I really have to get going."

"Carmen," he called. "Pour me some more coffee."

Carmen came in with the carafe and poured some coffee in his cup. She seemed to deliberately ignore Grace's presence, but he didn't notice and she didn't care.

"Where do you live, Grace?" Sam asked suddenly.

"Oh . . ." His question caught her by surprise. "Over in West Palm Beach."

"One of those beautiful new high-rises?"

Grace nodded, thankful for the much-needed help.

"Great views, I understand."

"Glorious."

"Used to be the place where wealthy Palm Beach residents housed their servants."

"Did they?"

"Was lily white here in Palm Beach, meaning no Jews. It still has its boundaries, but its not half as bad as it was. *Meshugana goyem.*"

The last words seemed to be in Yiddish, which she didn't understand. Nevertheless, she nodded as if she did.

"They weren't so hot on Catholics either. Blacks weren't even a factor. The joke is that we Jews think we've won the battle. Wrong. They captured us. We've become like them. White bread and mayonnaise. Joke's on us."

She was confused by his explanation, having never heard the term "white bread and mayonnaise" used in this context.

"Anne used to hate it when I said things like that. She was very political, a real knee-jerk liberal. It caused some lively discussions, I can
tell you. I loved it. The give-and-take. Anne was very passionate in her
views. You must know that, of course. As a political science major, you
must be very interested in politics."

He was leading her to more shaky ground. She was vaguely interested in politics, but she wished she were better informed. Also, she
hadn't quite expected their conversation to take such a sudden turn
in that direction. She reviewed in her mind the names of the state's
important politicians. She knew the name of the governor and only
one senator and searched her mind in vain for the name of the other
senator and the congressman who represented her district.

"Yes," she said, not embellishing the point, fearful of both retreat-
ing from the subject and being exposed as ignorant.

"She hated the idea that I became a Republican twenty years ago. I
guess it's because I understand business, and government is running
a lousy business. But don't get me wrong, I'm not exactly a fanatic."
He looked at her. "And you, Grace?"

"I'm an independent," she said quickly, satisfied that she had responded well to his query. "I vote the man . . . or woman, not the
party."

"I kind of expected your answer, Grace. You strike me as someone
who is her own woman, not doctrinaire."

She wondered what that meant, but he came to her rescue, as if he
knew she didn't know.

"You know what I mean, somebody too damned rigid. You strike
me as someone who would rather keep an open mind. Go with the
flow. Am I right?"

"More or less," she replied. The fact was, the flow she always went
with moved downward. She silently contradicted his view of her as
having an open mind. If she really did, he would see how empty it really was. At that moment she felt very self-deprecating.

He looked at her, and for a brief moment she had the sensation
that their eyes had locked.

"Have we ever met before, Grace? At the club? A charity ball
maybe? Some party somewhere?"

"I don't think so," Grace said.

He was probably confused, having seen her briefly at the funeral
parlor the night before the funeral. They had exchanged glances.
But her mind explored other possibilities. Perhaps he had seen her
behind the counter at Saks. It was a possibility she dreaded. For her

part, she had no memory of him or his wife. How could she? They had lived on different planets.

"Do I know any of your beaus?"

"I don't go out that much. Remember, I have a teenage daughter to keep an eye on."

"No significant other on the horizon?"

"I date. But no, nothing serious. Which is fine with me."

"You're a very attractive woman. I'm sure someone will sweep you up and carry you off on his white steed."

"I'm not holding my breath."

"I'll bet your standards are quite high."

"So I've been told."

"Why compromise? You're an independent woman, obviously financially secure. Why settle?"

"I agree."

He studied her again, shrugged, smiled and was silent for a while as he sipped his coffee.

"Anne was a passionate feminist," Sam said suddenly, apropos of nothing. Perhaps the fact that he was having a discussion with a woman had triggered the idea. "We had some knock-down-drag-outs over that one. I consider myself a supporter of women's rights, but some of those ladies seem to be going too far. Am I out of line, Grace? What do you think?"

"I have mixed feelings," she said. Better to be noncommittal and avoid a discussion in which she would reveal the shallowness of her knowledge.

The fact was that she had thought about that subject, but from her perspective the woman's movement hadn't done much for her. They were always shouting about the expansion of opportunities for women and how great it was that women's voices were being heard. She wondered where all the opportunities were for women like her, and it didn't seem much like her voice was being heard or ever had been.

Oh, it did make her feel some pride in seeing women break into all those places once forbidden to them, and she was genuinely inspired when she saw women rise to the top in fiercely competitive corporate America and in the military. But what of her class, the underachievers, the bottom-of-the-barrel broads, the down-on-their-luck ladies? Wasn't only glass ceilings. There were also glass walls and she was trapped, boxed in by them on all sides, closed in on top and bottom.

Was she trying to justify her motives in going after a guy with big bucks to solve her problems? Damned straight she was. In spades. Okay, she was a throwback. Her activist sisters out there would see her as a Neanderthal female, a kind of prostitute, a lying, designing bitch, a male-dependent sell-out, a cynical gold digger on a campaign to snare a wealthy man at his most vulnerable moment.

Let she who was without sin cast the first stone. What she really was, was a hunter stalking filthy lucre, out there armed only with a tight pussy, a lying heart and an educated tongue in more ways than one. Survival was a helluva lot more important than maintaining idealogical certitude and sisterhood loyalty.

How could she fully argue that point without outlining all the true, dreary facts of her own life? It was becoming increasingly obvious that this man was far above her in knowledge and intellect. He had also lived with a woman for four decades who was certainly equal to him in brainpower. A Phi Beta Kappa, no less.

She was hardly a match for this man. What had she to offer that would fill the gap of his beloved Anne? Her own inventory of her charms had been shallow indeed. She had been depending on her sexuality, as if she would provide a gift from God for an aging man. What a stupid idea she was pursuing. All right, she had cleverly insinuated herself into this man's company, but eventually he would find her out, would discover that she was a shallow, lying, grasping, phony bitch whose first priority was to putter in his money pot.

Was she too hard on herself? Was she really the woman she had just described? Did she really have such evil intentions? Yes, she did. It troubled her to see herself in this light.

She realized suddenly that she had become lost in her own thoughts. Her attention had drifted and she had been silent for a long time.

"You seemed far away," Sam said. Apparently, he had been studying her.

"I was just thinking of all the things I still have to do today," she said. Another lie.

"You've been very polite, Grace."

"Polite?"

"Taking the time to keep me company. You've helped, too, I might add."

He looked at her and smiled. She averted her eyes, as if they would reveal her shame. She had no business in this place.

At that moment, she heard a telephone ring in the kitchen, then Carmen's voice.

"Bruce," she said.

"My son the lawyer. I suppose I'll have to take that."

He stood up and held out his hand. She took it and noted that it felt smooth and strong. Had it lingered more than was expected? She wasn't sure.

"I've kept you long enough," he said, then started to leave the room. Suddenly he turned, looked at her and waved his finger. "If you have the time . . . tomorrow you can walk the beach with me. Bring a suit. And Marilyn better behave."

CHAPTER EIGHT

As she drove home, she became increasingly depressed. How could she possibly survive in this tangle of lies? The image she had projected was a long way from what she really was. A graduate of Johns Hopkins, a daughter who wanted to go to Princeton and study medicine, a resident of a swanky condominium, a friend and peer of his late wife. And worst of all, making Jason a lawyer. Jason had barely gotten through high school.

She had been tense and uncomfortable all through lunch, and the effort of keeping her wits about herself and concocting logical answers, mostly lies, had exhausted her. Her optimism about pulling this off was fading.

She was also finding it difficult keeping her eye on the ball, which, in this case, was Sam's money. There was no escaping that motive. Certainly, money was at the root of most, if not all, her problems. There was no point in lying to herself. This ploy was about money. Money, money, money. But the human factor kept intruding, shifting her focus, revealing her own vulnerabilities.

Reaching the goals outlined by Mrs. Burns, at this juncture, seemed impossible. Ring around your finger! No way. She had better step back and look for a more modest possibility, ratchet her goals downward where they belonged.

Sam would be a fool to marry her. At best, he might offer her a brief affair, and even that was a dicey possibility. If he knew the truth about her, he would quickly show her the door. And yet he was an attractive man. She held that thought for a moment, then, sensing its danger, she brushed it aside. Such ideas were counterproductive. Why settle when you could go for the whole enchilada? She would have to guard herself against defeatism.

Hadn't she succeeded, through lies and subterfuge, in worming her way, ever so slightly, into his life? Nevertheless she felt uncertain. It was scary, and she was uneasy about going on with this effort, convinced that she was getting way over her head.

She had no doubt that Anne's friends were waiting for the appropriate moment to throw a woman Sam's way as a possible mate. They would be dipping into an entirely different gene pool. Widows would be the meat of choice, some Jewish, some, like Anne, not, bejeweled and dressed to the nines, with the experience and expertise to handle this multimillionaire who was used to living with a beautiful woman with a great education and a fine mind.

They would fuck him blind, even if they had never got off in their lives. Squirm and scream and swallow and lie like hell. *Sam, oh Sam, the earth is going to move for you whether you like it or not.* She felt suddenly jealous. She was there first, she told herself.

By the time she got back to her apartment, she was nursing the wounds of her inadequacy. Those other women understood his lifestyle, his mind, his psyche and his world. Perhaps even his sexual needs, which could be far different than what she had assumed. She would be no competition. Maybe it was time to back off. The idea of retreat and surrender was beginning to take hold in her mind.

She unloaded the car and carried armfuls of clothing into the apartment. It was unsafe to leave such valuable things outside all night.

It took her three trips to carry the clothes inside. There she sorted the various items and prepared them for a pickup. She stored some in what little space was left in her and Jackie's closets. The rest was scattered in batches around the place.

She called the Jewish Welfare League and told the nice lady who answered that she had clothing to donate that she wanted picked up first thing tomorrow morning. The nice lady thanked her and confirmed that a truck would be by early the next day.

Despite the doubts she held about the possibilities of snaring Sam Goodwin as a husband, she did feel good about disposing of Anne Goodwin's clothes for charitable purposes. There was something cleansing in the act. She was doing a good deed.

Jackie had come home early and left her a note telling her that she was going to stay on in school for tutoring, after which she would go on to her movie cashier's job.

Don't wait supper for me, Mom, the note read. Although they were going through a rocky time together, Jackie was still considerate about not worrying her mother when there was a blip in her schedule. And the scrawled message had ended on a positive note: *Love, Jackie.*

She slapped a frozen dinner into the microwave and put on the television set. She cycled through the remote without finding anything of interest, finally shutting the TV off. Her thoughts seemed uprooted, her concentration unfocused. When the food was done she discovered she had no appetite. She knew she was losing her courage and it agitated her. Unable to sleep, she paced the small apartment, tried the television again, then sat uncomprehending through some sitcoms.

Jackie came in around ten. As expected, she was startled by the sight of the clothes.

"I'm doing charity work," Grace explained. "There'll be a pickup tomorrow morning." She hadn't expected it to end there but hadn't adequately prepared a response.

Jackie opened the closet. "You'd think you were opening a store. Where did they come from?"

"From the relatives of people who died."

It wasn't quite the truth, Grace realized, but it was close enough.

"You mean these clothes belong to dead people?" Jackie asked, cocking her head, waiting for an answer.

"The point is that they don't belong to them anymore and the relatives want them disposed of. Giving them to charity is a wonderful gesture."

Jackie began to go through the clothes with rising interest.

"This is expensive stuff, Mom. Look at these labels. Bill Blass, Geoffrey Beane, Sonia Rykiel. You know what these are worth?"

"I hadn't noticed," Grace said. "Besides, it doesn't matter. They're for people who are poor."

"The poor are getting this? You're kidding?"

She hadn't calculated on Jackie's intense interest. She continued to look through the clothes, holding up particular outfits against her body and studying them in the mirror.

Why don't you just put them down, dear? They're not for you."

"Are you getting paid to do this, Mom?"

"Not exactly."

"What does that mean? Are you or aren't you?"

At that moment she knew she had to bend the truth even further.

"It's something to do while I'm looking for a job. Maybe if I did something for other people . . . well, it might come back to us. Give us some luck."

Jackie shook her head and stared at her, perplexed.

"You just go into the houses of dead people and collect their old clothes?" Jackie asked. "I never heard of such a thing."

"Whatever the family doesn't want is usually given away. I'm facilitating that. Sometimes it's too painful for a loved one to get rid of."

Grace sensed that her explanation was floundering. As she spoke, Jackie removed her outer garments and, wearing her panties and brassiere, began to try on outfits she fancied.

"I told you, they're not for you, Jackie. They're for charity."

"I'm just trying them on, Mom."

"Well, don't get too attached to them."

"Six," she said. "That's exactly my size."

She had put on a Sonia Rykiel skirt and an Yves St. Laurent blouse. She looked great in the outfit.

"Too old for you, Jackie," she said, noting her daughter's expression of admiration as she modeled in front of the mirror.

"You think so? This is great stuff. Look at the designers— Lagerfeld, Valentino, Givenchy. Mom, this is a gold mine."

"I don't think you understand, young lady. These aren't for us. They're for charity. Why must I keep repeating myself?"

"Are they counted? I mean, does somebody check on it?"

"That's not an issue, Jackie. They're earmarked for poor people. And that's where they're going."

"We're poor, Mom," Jackie said, snickering.

"You know what I mean."

"Is there more where this came from?"

"That's beside the point."

"That *is* the point, Mom."

Jackie took off the outfit she was wearing and tried on another. "I look great in these, Mom."

"Don't even think it," Grace said.

"Who's gonna know?" Jackie said, studying her mother's face.

"I will."

"Don't be an idiot, Mom. If nobody but you knows . . . I have an even better idea. You know those places where you buy secondhand clothes? Heck, you just bought stuff there. Mostly they take them on consignment. These are all designer clothes. I'll bet they buy them outright. They'll go like hotcakes. Why don't . . ."

"I won't listen to this," Grace cried.

"Be practical, Mom. You're out of work. We need the extra money. I'm sick and tired of doing without."

"So am I. But the answer is no. I've made a commitment and have given my word, and I intend to do the honorable thing."

"Honorable?"

Jackie shook her head.

"You're as dumb as Dad," she sneered. "Here we are with the money shorts. Your unemployment checks will probably barely cover us. Stop living in a dream world. This family is broke. It's time you faced reality, Mom. Nobody gives a shit about us."

"I don't intend to stand here and be lectured to by a greedy adolescent. I'm your mother, Jackie."

"Dammit. And there I was begging you to buy me that Donna Karan outfit. Some of this stuff is great, Mom. What I don't wear, you can sell. Maybe some of these will fit you if you take them out. Use your head, Mom." Jackie pouted into the mirror. "Sometimes I feel like I'm the mother and you're the daughter."

"It's stealing."

"You're making me want to barf. Who from? Dead people. How will they know?"

"It's wrong. I won't have it."

"You know what I think?" Jackie said. "You're too scared, too afraid to take risks. Mom, this is money for us. Who do you think we are, Mom? We're the working poor, the people at the bottom. We're the ones who always get shafted. Here's a golden opportunity to do something for ourselves for a change."

Grace's stomach knotted as she watched her daughter studying her face in the mirror, waiting for a reaction.

"What am I bringing up here?" Grace said, her anger churning inside her.

"Get real, Mom. Stop being a loser."

"Bringing this stuff here was definitely not a very good idea," Grace muttered, thinking that maybe this business with Sam

Goodwin was not a very good idea either. This was a bad sign. Her destiny seemed to be taking a permanent detour.

"I can't believe this," Jackie said. She turned and looked directly into Grace's face. "You're an idiot, Mom," she shouted. "That's why you'll never make it. Never. You'll always be nothing."

"That's it. Take those things off immediately. They do not belong to you. I gave him . . . gave them my word." She forced herself to remain calm. Pausing for a moment, she cleared her throat. "The Jewish League is picking up these clothes early tomorrow."

"The Jewish League?" Jackie exploded. "This stuff is for Jews?"

"I promised . . ."

"Shit, Mom," Jackie persisted. "Most Jews are filthy rich. They don't need these clothes. Don't you get it? They've got so much they're giving them away."

"Case closed," Grace said, trying to regain some authority over her daughter.

"If I know Jews, they'll probably be selling them anyway."

Grace shook her head in despair. She had always taught tolerance for others, live and let live. It was one of the reasons she had left Baltimore and its tribal ways, its ghetto mentality. Italians stuck with Italians. Poles with Poles. Jews with Jews. Blacks with blacks. Not to think like that was a measure of her inner esteem. She was not a prejudiced person, not a bigot. Suddenly, a wave of fear engulfed her. Would Jackie's attitude be another obstacle to face with Sam Goodwin, Sam the Jew?

"Where do you pick up this stuff?" she sighed.

"I'm stating facts."

"Facts?" Revelation came suddenly. This time it was Grace who exploded. "Its that idiot horror with the motorcycle. He's brainwashing you, teaching you to hate. You're becoming a bigot like that moron, that's what's happening to you. I think it's disgusting."

Staring her down, Jackie looked at her as an adult mocking a child.

"What's disgusting is that you don't face reality. I don't care what you say, Jews are pigs. As for us, we're at the bottom of the barrel, Mom. So what if we rip off some rich kikes. Who will know?"

"I refuse to be that hateful. What's got into you? Don't you have a mind of your own?"

"Damned straight I have. Where the hell is *your* mind? You haven't got a clue. Look around you. See the way you live. Then take a look at how the Jews live. . . ."

"Stop lecturing me," Grace cried. "This is for charity. Period."

"You're so naive, Mom."

"Maybe so. But I gave my word. . . ."

"Your word?"

"People do that. People who still have a shred of integrity. Some of us are still . . . honorable."

"Honorable. Holy shit. Like you, huh, Mom? Well, I have a question to ask: Where has all that honorable stuff got you so far? I'll tell you where: in the toilet."

Grace was too infuriated to continue. She decided to retreat, end the confrontation, which was getting ugly. "Just take those damned things off and hang them up again. The charity people are coming early to collect them."

Mother and daughter exchanged angry glances; then Grace turned, went into the bedroom and slammed the door. Fuming with frustration and anger, she lay down on her bed and stared at the ceiling. Jackie was getting increasingly difficult to handle, and Grace's role as mentor and mother was slipping away.

Worse, aside from this business about Jewish people, which was awful, she had stated a partial truth. Perhaps it was naive to have integrity, to be honorable. It stood for honesty and decency and keeping one's word and doing the right thing. Unfortunately, Jackie's argument was compelling. Being honorable had, indeed, gotten her nowhere. Besides, wasn't she lacking integrity in lying to Sam? What was one more packet of lies?

She knew she was living a paradox, being honorable on the one hand and being dishonorable on the other. The fact was that she was a goddamned hypocrite. Certainly she wasn't being honorable with Sam Goodwin. Who was she kidding? If she knew about Sam, Jackie would see right through her. All Grace's high-minded preaching would explode in her face.

It was a subject she wished she could exorcise from her mind. She opened the drawer in the end table next to her bed and took out the bottle of sleeping pills she kept for emergencies. Shaking two into her hand, she gulped them down without water, then lay down and waited for their effect to begin.

CHAPTER NINE

She was awakened by a persistent ringing of the front door-buzzer, which pulled her out of a dreamless void. Stumbling to the door, she opened it a crack, surprised that the chain lock had been unlatched. A young black man stood in front of her.

"Pickup for Jewish Welfare Services," the man said.

"Oh, yes," she mumbled, still groggy. "Just a moment."

She returned to the bedroom and put on her terry-cloth robe, then opened the door and let the man inside.

"Over there . . . " she began, then stopped abruptly. The pile of clothes on the couch was gone. She looked in the closet. With the exception of two outfits that Jackie had tried on last night, the others were gone as well.

"I don't know what to say," she muttered, looking at the young man. Her head had cleared instantly and she needed no mental prompting to know what had happened.

"Is there some mistake?" he asked.

"Gone. All gone."

The young man shrugged.

"Guess there was some mistake."

"I'm so sorry."

He seemed puzzled, shrugged again and left the apartment. Seething with anger, she sat down on the couch. Then she spied the note that Jackie had left her on the Formica counter. Grace rose and ripped open a sealed envelope.

> *Mom,*
>
> *Somebody has got to take charge here. We have to think of our-selves first. If you can't, I'll have to think for both of us. This doesn't mean I don't love you. In fact, I'm doing this because I love you and I hope you'll understand. I'm taking the car and bringing the clothes to a secondhand consignment shop. I'll bring the car back. Darryl is meeting me in front of the apart-ment. He'll take me to school. I know you think I'm being terrible and disobedient, but sometimes I believe I have to save you from yourself. Please don't yell at me when I come home tonight. I still love you.*
>
> *Jackie*

Grace read the letter again, then let it float to the floor. It was obvious by now that she had little influence over her daughter, and this letter, she supposed, represented the end of parenthood for her. She felt utterly helpless and discouraged.

For a long time she sat on the couch and contemplated how she should react. It was, she knew, pointless to get hysterical. No one was actually hurt by her act, except perhaps the poor and homeless or others who might have needed the clothing. And it was true that these expensive designer clothes were incongruous to their situation.

Of course, she was concerned that somehow this might get to Sam's attention, which would be a disaster. She would lose all credibility. Worse, aside from being unmasked as a liar, a hypocrite and a cheat, he could bring charges against her for theft. She tried softening the anxiety with logic. Yes, it was worrisome. Yes, there was a risk of exposure. Jackie's disobedience would be of little value as an alibi. The fact was, that revelation itself would explode Grace's plot to snare Sam Goodwin as a husband with all its ludicrous scheming and weird duplicity.

She could adopt a less pessimistic notion, she decided after a bout of serious rumination. After all, the clothing's ownership was theoretically anonymous. She had made no representations to Sam that she was going to reveal the true donor. Not really. And Jackie didn't have a clue as to the clothing's owner. It did occur to her that, perhaps, she should have gone through the pockets for any identifying items. There was always a chance that the storeowner might question where the clothing had come from, but somehow she felt certain that Jackie was resourceful enough to provide the owner with a logical cover story.

Whatever the consequences, she decided not to brood over the issue. Moreover, she also decided to heed the voice of destiny. This plan of hers was having side effects she hadn't banked on. Her clothes ploy had backfired. In fact, the entire process was getting too complicated for her to continue. Hypocrisy, she was learning, with all the associated baggage of dissimulation and invention, was much too stressful for her.

Her eye drifted to the clock. It was past eleven. Sam had already returned from his walk along the beach. Destiny was shifting gears, driving her life in another direction. Should she turn back, retreat?

Perhaps it was time for this caper with Sam Goodwin to end. She was getting in over her head. *Mrs. Burns,* she screamed inside of herself, *go to hell.*

CHAPTER TEN

"Okay, okay," Sam said to Marilyn, who was pawing his leg with impatience. He looked at his watch. It was nearly nine-thirty. It was a beautiful, sunny day. He had waited long enough.

Not that she had actually said that she would meet him. He had merely suggested it. For some reason, he had felt that she would jump at the chance. Why? He had disobeyed one of his prime caveats: never assume. And he had assumed. Vague assumptions almost always resulted in disappointment.

He stepped out on the beach. The sand was still cool as he walked to where the water hit the beach. Marilyn had shot out ahead of him and was sniffing the edges of the wire rubbish baskets placed at intervals along the beach, safe from the tide.

Perhaps he had talked too much about Anne. Maybe the heaviness of his grief had put her off. Unfortunately, there was no way to hide it or avoid thinking about Anne. He supposed that time would soften the terrible sense of loss.

Last night he had awakened at three A.M. He hadn't had a complete night's sleep since Anne had come back from the hospital. Declared terminal, she had wanted to die in her own bed. She had gotten her wish.

He had felt Marilyn's weight at the foot of the bed. She hadn't stirred. Then he had reached out and patted Anne's side of the bed. The emptiness was palpable, instantly recalling the pain of his grief, the terrible reality of his loss.

Yet, there was no alternative to accepting the fact of her death. Death was final, the end of life, but far from the end of memory. Memory survived in the living. Anne was still alive in his memory. Not only the memory of his visible life with her, but also the memory of his invisible life, his secret life. It was odd that he was more troubled about this secret life now that she was gone than when she was alive.

The fact was that he had been a liar and a cheat, a fraud. He wished that he hadn't been so successful in keeping his dirty little secrets. Perhaps that would have eased his current pain. He had let her go into oblivion with this unfinished business hanging in his mind and conscience.

The only bright spot in his nocturnal thoughts was that Grace might be walking with him along the beach in the morning. Grace was pleasant and attractive, easy to talk with, unthreatening, a tonic. He sensed no hidden agenda on her part, no wish to get involved. She seemed open and honest. Getting emotionally involved with another woman was, at this stage in his grieving, the furthest thing from his thoughts.

He dreaded what was coming up in that regard. Even in those few calls that he took from old friends and from his children, their concerns were ominous. When the appropriate time came, if it ever did, he supposed that their warnings might have some validity. He could understand their protectiveness and tried to be tolerant of their cautionary views.

He was, in fact, a rich widower and ambitious, fortune-hunting ladies would be expected to swarm around him, like hyenas around carrion. Examples abounded among his circle of foolish older men getting involved with younger women whose eyes were more on the money than the man. Did his children think he was stupid enough to fall for that?

Nevertheless, both he and his children would have to accept the risk of his single state. Perhaps he would be vulnerable, although he doubted it. And if he was, so what? It was his business, not theirs. He felt a growing belligerence rise to the surface of his thoughts.

He had no intention of cutting himself off from life, although he wondered if he would still be comfortable in the world in which he had lived with Anne, the world of country clubs, golf and tennis, dinner parties and charity balls, the world at the so-called pinnacle, where the old, moneyed WASP aristocracy mixed on occasion with the new, rich, super-achievers of the meritocracy, even if they were Jews. Big money was a great leveler, allying the old aristocrats of Palm Beach with the new money, providing they greased the skids of their favorite charities. Indeed, the fuddy-duddy, bigoted old guard had let some of the barbarians, like him, through their guarded gates for a glimpse of their restricted strongholds.

Anne had been his guide and mentor in this world. Without her it would not be the same. Not being Jewish, she knew the turf and made him acceptable, or made him behave in ways that assured his acceptability. Actually, he had learned to tolerate many of the people in that social world, overlooking their narrow focus and overblown sense of entitlement. They were different enough from what he had come from to appear exotic. Often they struck him as some alien species lost in a time warp. They were often amusing, if one didn't take them seriously. Some were even comical.

He picked up a piece of driftwood and flung it into the foaming surf. Marilyn dived in after it and brought it home clutched in her jaws. He patted her wet muzzle and pulled her ears, then moved on, leaving Marilyn temporarily nonplussed. Marilyn would never tire of the repetition of retrieval.

God, he missed Anne. He sat on the sand, pulled his knees to his chin and looked out to sea, rippling and glistening out toward the horizon. Seagulls floated gracefully overhead and little sandpipers strutted along the ocean's edge. Marilyn came up and sat down beside him.

Without Anne, he knew he was adrift. She had been the Pied Piper who had led him into the social web of wealth and privilege. She had an unerring instinct about what having money really meant. She knew how it was done; her sense of direction was flawless as she led them through the minefields into the privileged oasis.

She had known how to dress and how to dress him, what to say, what not to say. She knew the chitchat and the nomenclature, the various procedures and protocol, how to walk into a room with memorable dignity and flair and, equally important, how to walk out of a room toting your aura with you.

He marveled at her uncanny talent to magnetize people and capture them as loyal friends. Indeed, he had the sense that he was more than simply her husband but an honored member of her coterie. Without her, he knew, he was lost in that world.

And the other? With an extreme effort of will, he pushed it out of his mind. His life with Anne, he knew, was really half a life. But he had participated in that half joyously, obediently, and he had kept it totally segregated, a world apart from the other half.

He got up, patted away the sand, then continued his walk, Marilyn beside him. Even dogs, he thought suddenly. Even dogs, like Marilyn, seemed to have pledged their fealty to Anne.

It was one of the great ironies of fate that she went first. All of his planning for the future was dependent on him being the first to die. She was the one who was supposed to be the survivor, to deal with the details of passing their fortune to the next generation.

While Bruce portrayed himself as the loving son, which he might very well have been, he couched his concerns in lawyerly ways, concocting scenarios that would move "the fortune" into his generation with the least tax impact. Apparently, he had consulted a number of his peers, who had provided numerous methods to make such a transfer possible.

Carol was more emotional and less subtle, but the bare bones of her motives were clearly evident through her skein of daughterly love. Her various peccadilloes had already cost him a small fortune. She seemed to specialize in liaisons with artistic types with profound appetites for extravagance. Her present lover seemed to be world class in that persuasion.

If Anne had been the last survivor, Sam knew that she would not have been able to stand up to their relentless pressure. She would have capitulated early and gone along with their various allegedly unselfish scenarios. A streak of strong guilt ran in Anne, far more than he was able to muster.

These days he almost dreaded Bruce's calls. Sometime during the call he would profess to have an "expert" on estate planning waiting in the wings, by which he probably meant the wing chair that faced his desk. Each step of this strategy, he knew, had been gone over with his wife, whose covetousness was far more transparent than Bruce's, if that was possible.

He handled Carol differently, offering relatively small donations to the cause periodically, not quite enough to keep her off his back but to keep the spaces of her entreaties at longer intervals.

He had never confessed to Anne how terribly disappointed he was in the way their children had turned out. He would have wished for more loving children, more devoted, more demonstrative of their love and respect. He would have liked his son to have joined him in business and would have preferred his daughter to have stuck to some single enterprise instead of fishing all over the lot for so-called "fulfillment" and consorting with men who used and abused her.

Yes, he decided, as far as Bruce and Carol were concerned, Anne's death before his own was an awful blow in more ways than one. She would have been a lot easier to deal with.

He had no illusions about his children. He no longer had any confidence in their attachment to him as a loving father figure, another fantasy destroyed by life's experiences. If this was the ultimate reward of money, he wanted no part of it.

He doubted that either his son or his daughter would be there for him in his hour of need. His exit, he knew in his heart, would, if left to them, be lonely and forlorn. He would leave this earth unloved, in pain and despair, suffering their lip service and hypocrisy. It was, of course, a painful idea, horrific in many ways, but he was convinced it was the truth.

What had he expected? He wasn't sure. Certainly not gratitude. It was a paradox. He had loved his parents to the end and beyond, and he had never once doubted their love and admiration for him, their respect and encouragement. He supposed that in many ways he had failed his children, but he wasn't sure how. Perhaps he was exaggerating his disappointment or developing a case of galloping paranoia.

He would have liked Grace Sorentino's company. Perhaps it had been impossible for her to get going that early, he thought hopefully, although it was more likely that he had offended her in some way.

She wasn't at the house when he returned. But then, no specific time had been imposed on her, and he had no reason to believe that she had abandoned the project of disposing of Anne's clothes. Yet his disappointment at her absence surprised him.

He showered, dressed, went off to the club, where he was greeted by the regulars with handshakes, pats on the back and whispered condolences. Somehow, he knew, the calibration had changed. Anne knew better than he how to mix and maneuver in this world. Without her, he felt unsure and uncomfortable, less secure about his place in that world.

When Anne was alive, he actually enjoyed, or allowed himself to believe that he enjoyed, the country club life. Or, more to the heart of the truth, he tolerated the life because of her. Please, he urged himself, no more heart-of-the-truth personal confessions. Not yet. Not now.

CHAPTER ELEVEN

When Grace did not show up the next day either, or the day after that, he began to speculate on possibilities. Had he insulted her in some way? He continued to recycle their conversations in his memory, but nothing he said seemed untoward or offensive.

On the other hand, he was also annoyed. She had made a commitment to him to dispose of Anne's clothes. A deal was a deal, and he had turned down other offers. Such thoughts gave his concern another dimension, anger. At himself, for not sensing her unreliability. At her, for not having the courtesy to call and give him the status of her situation. She owed him that.

By the fourth day of her absence he worked up a full head of steam. She had not kept her word. She had let him down. She had betrayed him. In his business dealings he would write off anyone who behaved in that manner. He was especially put out by his own lack of insight into her personality. A sixth sense was at the heart of his business acumen, his one great talent. Was he losing it?

He tried to analyze why something about this woman engaged him. He eschewed any idea of a sexual motive. He hadn't even thought in those terms, as if such ideas would be a betrayal of Anne's memory. Not that his life with Anne would have provided anything that could induce a sexual memory. The fact was, her interest in sex was, to be kind, tepid. Yet never had he blamed her for his own transgressions.

By the evening of the fourth day he had decided that he had better call someone else in to dispose of Anne's clothing. But before he could reach for the phone, he decided that he owed her one last opportunity to explain herself. Perhaps she was ill, or worse.

It was a simple matter to find her telephone number. She had told him that she lived in West Palm Beach and that her name was Grace Sorentino. He dialed. A voice answered that seemed much younger. He assumed it was Grace's daughter.

"This is Mr. Goodwin," he said. "May I speak to your mother?"

"I'm sorry," the voice said. "She's not home from work yet."

"Work?" She hadn't mentioned work to Sam. But then, he had not asked her directly. Besides, it could mean charity work.

"Is this her daughter?" he asked.

"Yes."

"Would you give her a message that Sam Goodwin called?"

"Can I tell her what's it's about?" the girl asked.

"Just tell her it's Mr. Goodwin and to please call me back."

He hung up, wondering if he should have probed more. In his business dealings he would have done just that.

When she didn't return his call that evening he was beginning to feel that he had, indeed, said or done something that had been offensive to her, but he couldn't remember what that was. When he awoke the next morning he began to dwell on the idea that he had wronged her in some way. He felt pummeled by a terrible wave of contrition. He called her number again. It was a little after eight; too early, but he wanted to be sure to catch her in.

"Yes?" a sleepy voice said hoarsely.

"Grace?"

He heard a sigh and a long silence.

"Don't hang up please. It's Sam."

Again a long silence.

"Yes, Sam?"

"Did I wake you?"

"Sort of."

"I'm sorry. But I felt obliged to call."

"Obliged?"

"I just wanted to be sure you got my message."

"You left a message?"

"With a woman. I think it was your daughter. She must have forgotten. Children are like that."

"You can say that again."

There was a moment of silence.

"It's been five days," Sam said hesitantly. "I was going to call someone else to do the job. Should I? I mean, have you abandoned it?"

"I guess you might call it that," Grace said hesitantly.

"Was there something . . . something I might have done or said that . . . ?"

"Oh, no," Grace said hurriedly. She seemed awake now, more alert to the conversation. "My fault . . . really." She seemed suddenly flustered.

"Your fault?"

"I guess I let you down, Sam," Grace sighed. "It hadn't been my intention to do that."

"I'm relieved, Grace," Sam said. "It was really giving me a fit . . . the thought that I had inadvertently said something . . ."

"I'm sorry that such a thought jumped into your head."

"So am I."

There was a long pause. Finally Sam spoke. "I guess it was your daughter I spoke with last night. She said you were at work . . ."

"Oh, yes. I had made this commitment . . ."

"Are you still . . . committed?"

"Actually, no. Not anymore."

She was emphatic, which surprised him. As if she was glad that this commitment was over.

"Well, then . . ." Sam said. "There shouldn't be any reason why you can't come on over and finish the job. I'm . . . I'm about to go on my walk. I can wait if . . ." For some reason he was stumbling. He cleared his throat. Now, why did he mention that?

"Well, I . . ."

"If you decided against it, then that's all right, too. I'd just like to have the matter settled."

"Yes. I imagine you would."

"Well, then . . ."

He heard her suck in a deep breath.

"It doesn't have to be today. I just would like to know something definitive. If you're not going to do it, then perhaps I should get someone else."

"I . . . I don't know what to say."

"Perhaps you can call me back later. Or, if you decide that you want

to start again, then . . . just show up when you can. If I'm out on my
walk, Carmen will be there. In any event, call me before the day is out
so I know where I stand. Okay, Grace?"

"Okay, Sam . . ."

He sensed her hesitation. More like an awkwardness, which was
the way he actually felt.

Then he heard the click of the phone as she hung up. It left him
confused.

CHAPTER TWELVE

At first she thought he had called to tell her that he had found out about Anne's clothes. She had lived in dread of that phone call. How could she possibly explain the truth about what had happened? If he discovered the truth she would not have the courage to face him.

Jackie had, despite her prohibition, given the clothes to one of those new, upscale secondhand stores in North Miami. Grace had waited all day for her to return, and when Jackie had finally come back in the afternoon and admitted the circumstances of the transaction she had gone through the roof.

She was too ashamed to call Sam. Of course she would have liked to join him for a swim and a walk on the beach, and to continue the "project" of disposing of Anne's clothes. Obviously he enjoyed her company, which had encouraged her. Now this! Instead she spent the day staring at the door, simmering with anger, waiting for Jackie to return.

She heard a car come to a stop outside their apartment door. Then she heard the key turn in the lock and Jackie came in, smiling and excited

"The lady flipped over them," Jackie said, as if the confrontation of the night before had never taken place.

Grace came closer and slapped her daughter across the face.

"How dare you?" she cried, feeling instant remorse when she saw the outline of her fingers on her daughter's cheek. But Jackie stood her ground, unflinching.

"I dare. So what?" Jackie said, rubbing her cheek. "That hurt, Mom."

"You left me no choice," Grace said, the fires inside of her banking. She had slapped her daughter before, but usually on the posterior. This was the first time she had ever slapped her across her face, and it bothered her.

"Feel better now?" Jackie muttered.

"I feel like shit," Grace said. "Is there no controlling you? And since when do you take my car without permission?"

"How the hell was I going to move the clothes?"

"You had no right."

"Dead people have no right either."

"I made it perfectly clear what I intended to do with those clothes. You disobeyed me."

"You should be glad I did," Jackie said. "They flipped over the clothes. Absolutely flipped."

"You're evading the issue here."

Grace felt totally impotent. Worse, she felt that she had broken a pact with Sam Goodwin. It had been the only shred of integrity that she could hang on to. Everything else concerning her strange relationship with Sam had been a tissue of lies. How could she possibly face him now?

"They wanted to know the source, so I made up some story about their being yours and because of certain problems you needed cash, and they paid up immediately."

She held up a pile of twenties and started to count them out on the Formica counter.

"I don't believe this," Grace said.

"Five hundred dollars," Jackie said. "Mom, I was right. These clothes are valuable. The lady wanted to know where I could get more. She said that she could turn this stuff over in a minute. That's why she paid up in advance. Just as I told you."

Grace felt sick to her stomach.

"How could you do this, Jackie?" she asked.

"How? Easy. And you were going to give them away to charity. Mom, charity begins at home. We need it here."

She smiled at her mother and kissed her on both cheeks, then told her to hold out her palm, which she did. Jackie picked up the pile of bills and put them in Grace's palm. Grace looked at the money, then flung it across the room.

"Are you crazy, Mom?" Jackie shouted.

"I gave my word," Grace said, shuddering.

"Who to?"

Grace shook her head in despair.

"The point is that you had no right to do this. In fact, I forbade it. There's a principle here."

"What principle is that, Mom?" Jackie said, defiant, hands on her hips.

Again she felt the sting of her own hypocrisy. It was better, she decided, to drop the subject, drop the whole thing. Her instincts told her it would end in disaster.

She watched as her daughter knelt on the floor and began to pick up the twenties. Seeing her do this made Grace think of herself. Stooping for dollars. That was exactly what she was doing with Sam Goodwin.

Moment of truth, she told herself. Destiny was sending another message. She declared the Goodwin venture over.

Instead, she had decided, she would seriously pursue a job, a real job. There were plenty of stores in the area who could use a good cosmetician who knew makeup. Get real, Jackie had said. She was right. Reality demanded that she get a job and support herself and her daughter. Mrs. Burns had sent her on a wild journey for which she was not equipped. She wasn't tough enough, smart enough, duplicitous enough.

"Where are you going, Mom?" Jackie asked when she came out of the bedroom dressed in her secondhand designer blouse-and-skirt outfit.

"To get a job," she said, taking the car keys from the Formica counter where Jackie had left them.

"What shall I do with the money?"

"Keep it, Jackie. It's yours."

"Come on, Mom, don't play with me."

"I'm not. Besides, you don't play by the rules."

"M-o-m."

"See you, little girl."

It was midafternoon, still time to look for a job. By now Sam would

152   Warren Adler

be very confused by her nonappearance. She shrugged it off. *Get real,* she thought again. *You, too, Sam. Don't be so vulnerable a target for any little hustler come off the street looking for your bucks.*

Again destiny intruded, and she got a job at the first place she applied. It was a swank beauty parlor two blocks north of Worth Avenue. She simply walked in the door, asked for the owner and made her pitch. Funny, she thought, how determination and singleness of purpose drowns your shyness. Like with Sam. She had better push that little caper out of her mind, she thought in tough-guy talk.

She introduced herself and outlined her experience with cosmetics to the owner, a glossy lady named Mary, dressed in a pink jumper.

"Just the person I'm looking for," Mary said. "We're putting in a line of our own cosmetics. We need someone to sell it for us."

"Right up my alley," Grace said, overjoyed, more convinced than ever that destiny wanted her to take this turn.

"Maybe you got a following from Saks you can bring in here," Mary said.

"I can try," she said hopefully, doubting the prospect and adding, "I haven't signed a noncompete with Saks."

She was hired on the spot, only the catch was that she was to get commissions only and no advance. She looked over the product line. The products were named for the owner, Mary Jones.

"Not very original, but it's my real name, what can I tell you?" the woman said. "It's pretty good stuff."

Grace looked over the line and tested the products on herself. They were inferior to what she sold at Saks, although in this business, marketing and illusion were the watchwords, not necessarily quality.

"Good stuff, huh?" Mary Jones said. "You look like a million."

"Great," Grace acknowledged, wondering if there would ever come a time in her life when she could call it as it was and not suffer the consequences. She doubted it.

The first day on the job she sold four-hundred-dollars' worth of cosmetics and made sixty dollars. Grace calculated that she might gross about twenty-five to thirty thousand a year, although there were no health insurance benefits, which meant she would have to pay for that herself.

It was back to the working poor again, although it seemed a pleasant place to work, with Mary Jones making a gossipy running commentary on her customers. She had bought the business from a woman who had founded the shop forty years earlier. As a consequence, most of her clientele were connected with the old rich elite of Palm Beach.

Mary herself specialized in doing the hair of the older women, who insisted that their styles be done in the fashions of another era. But there were plenty of younger customers: daughters, grand-daughters, mistresses of the moneyed members of the posh Everglades Club, which still maintained the antiquated restrictions of the old WASP culture.

"They think they piss blue and shit gold," Mary Jones whispered as she finished the hair of a woman whose last name was a national product. "And they still tip in small change." She held out her palm, showing two quarters. "So I just figure in twenty percent."

After her third day, Grace felt more relaxed about Sam Goodwin. So far there hadn't been any repercussions about the clothes, and Sam had probably found someone else to get rid of Anne's wardrobe, probably the woman with the bun.

But she did have mixed feelings about what might have been her missed opportunity, although she dismissed the entire venture as an act of foolishness. In her mind she called it her ghoulish period. Sam, she knew, would eventually stop grieving for his beloved Anne and would begin dating the available women introduced by her friends, upscale ladies with similar credentials.

Thinking about this gave her an odd sensation. She wasn't sure whether it was resentment or jealousy.

On the fourth day a youngish woman came into the shop wearing tight black tights and a man's shirt with the tails out. Under it she wore a T-shirt two sizes too small, which displayed the awesome out-line of a pair of mammoth breasts.

"Silicone before it was banned," Mary whispered. It was still early, and the older customers hadn't shown up yet. Only one younger woman was having her hair done.

"I'm free, free at last," the woman announced as she sat in the chair, where another operator, Maggie, a Japanese girl, worked. A squeal of well-wishing came from the customers and operators.

"That's Millicent Farmer," Mary whispered to Grace. "Married to George Farmer, former chairman of the board of General Marathon."

"Ten mil, ladies," Millicent Farmer said, crossing her legs and smil-ing broadly. "I broke his prenup. Got me a mean ball cutter for a lawyer. Held the blade to the scrotum and nailed the bastard to the wall. I'm here for the works, girls—hands, face, hair. Send me out in the world to look for new fish to fry."

"You're something, Mrs. Farmer," Maggie said as the operators moved their equipment into place around the loquacious woman. Grace figured her for about forty, with a well-tended face and body. Mary whispered her own running commentary.

"She's had a tuck here, there and everywhere."

"Ten million," Maggie squealed. "Fantastic."

"I put in three years with that alky. That figures out at three million, three hundred odd thousand a year. Not bad for a kid from West Virginia whose old man made moonshine and who never even graduated high school."

"Hell," the woman who was having her hair done in an adjacent chair said, "I've got a masters in psychology and all I could get was a dentist."

"Come on, Barb," Mary Jones said. "Tell it like it is. He's a dental surgeon who does implants in Palm Beach, the land of the implants."

"That's what old Georgo needed, only not his teeth."

The women screamed with laughter.

"Tell you the secret, ladies," Millicent said. She really loved the attention. She looked around the shop, as if to be sure there wasn't anyone around who might be offended by what she had to say. Her eyes rested for a moment on Grace.

"That's Grace Sorentino. She's the makeup lady," Mary Jones said, vouching for Grace as a safe member of the group.

Millicent Farmer lowered her voice.

"Free advice for all you greedy pussies." Millicent laughed. "Find yourself a very rich, divorced golfing drunk. George Farmer, case in point. Distinguished career, captain of industry. Good looks, power, charisma. Living on his laurels. A golden parachutist who made a soft landing on the nineteenth hole of the Everglades Club."

"There are only eighteen, Mrs. Farmer," Maggie said.

"Ah, you're forgetting the watering hole. Think strategically, ladies. He's off to the club before the heat sets in. Eighteen holes, then three martinis, maybe four with his buddies for lunch. Then he comes back for a siesta. You're gone by then, doing your daily dozen, whatever turns you on. When the sun's over the yardarm, the bastard's up for a batch of homemade cocktails, then we're both out to cocktails and dinner. My job, ladies, lookin' good. Lookin' good. Always lookin' good. He sucks his bottle. You keep lookin' good.

Day's end, he comes home for a little nightcap and stumbles off to beddy-bye."

"Who could keep up with that?" Maggie said.

"That's the point. Four, five glasses of Dom is all you need to get you through the day and night. He takes his snoot full to bed . . ." She lowered her voice. ". . . along with his limp dick. Doctor keeps him off Viagra. Too much booze for that. Besides, all you have to do is cuddle his face between your tits for a few minutes, make a few weird noises and he thinks he's made the earth vibrate for you, then he slips away into the drunken fog. That's half the secret, ladies. The other half is picking right." She tapped her temple. "Keep your eye out for the double dippers."

"Double dippers?" Maggie asked.

"Been through it. Knows the ropes. Number one is usually a twenty-year-old airhead he met in high school, the mother of his children, whose fucking is one note, the missionary position performed with frozen pelvis. No class. No social graces. He makes money and tosses her into the sewer. Number two is a cry for respectability. She's used to the upscale life. Country Club Connie. Has her regular foursome with the ladies, thinks her shit is perfume, works the charity circuit, never says fuck, likes to be on top in the dark, but really gets off on her finger in the tub."

Along with the others, Grace listened, spellbound.

"And now comes Miss West Virginia. Little me." She grabbed her breasts. "Big tits, brassy, barrel of laughs. All his buddies get a big kick out of her. Talks dirty. Keeps his mind on that thing he loves the most. Easy on the booze during the courtship, shows him a thing or two about working his libido and he thinks he's the star of the sheets. Hell, I could give classes on faking orgasms. It's all in the squeal and the body moves. You've got to keep your eye on the ring. Never let your eyes stray from the ring. It's the ring, dummy." She held her hand out, lifting the third finger of her left hand, where a huge rock embellished an engagement ring under which was a diamond-studded wedding ring. "Too valuable to take the fucker off. Forget this significant-other shit. Everything is in the expectation. Show him the best product you got. Make him think he's found Nirvana and that the best is yet to come."

Grace watched the faces of the other women as they listened, mesmerized and awestruck, to Millicent's story. She looked like royalty, a queen on her throne, being pampered, administered to by three women at once, smug and satisfied that she had bilked some poor bastard out of ten million dollars.

Once she got past the humor inherent in Millicent Farmer's narrative, she felt a wave of sadness sweep over her. In a number of ways, her story resonated with what had been going through Grace's mind when she went looking for her own Mr. Big Bucks. She tried to imagine what it would be like married to the drunken Mr. Farmer, a never-ending saga of fooling a very sad alcoholic basket case. Weren't there limits to what one did for money?

"But how did you manage to get out of the marriage, Mrs. Farmer?" Maggie asked. It was, Grace knew, the question on everybody's mind.

"Never go into a deal unless you've got an exit strategy. Suddenly Madame Sweetness and Light got to be Dame Big Bitch. By then you know which buttons to push. You also know he's hung up on his drunken lifestyle. It's a no-brainer to pick a fight with a drunk. We became incompatible. I began to sleep separately. No more nose-between-the-tits sex. But it was a symbol, you see. Hell, he was a fucking chairman of the board. Thousands kissed his fat butt. He fantasized that he was Mr. Swinging Dick. I took the swing out of it and got ten million to take a hike. Hell, it won't make a dent in his lifestyle, and ten minutes after I was gone the groupies started to gather."

"Did you ever tell him you loved him?" the woman doing her pedicure asked.

"Ten million times. Hell, the first words he heard in the morning and the last words he heard at night were 'I love you, Georgie.'"

"What would have happened if he had died?" the woman doing her nails asked.

"The prenup had it at two and a half mil. Old George wasn't better off dead, let me tell you. That's another reason why I bailed out while he was still kicking."

"Sounds like your marriage was like serving time," the woman having her hair done in the other chair said.

"Soft time, as the convicts say, in more ways than one." She enjoyed her joke and laughed uproariously.

"It should only happen to me," Maggie sighed. "The man I married is a driver for UPS."

"It's not for everyone, dear," Millicent Farmer said. "Be content. Your husband loves you."

"Loves me? If he loves me so much, why does he carry condoms around in his back pocket? I found them and confronted him."

"What did he say, Maggie?" the woman in the next chair asked.

"He said he's a driver and sees lots of strangers in a day. Says he's vulnerable to all kinds of savage attacks, including rape. Says the condoms are his protection against AIDS, which proves how much he loves me and the kids."

"And you believe that crap?" the woman doing the nails asked.

"Believe him? You think I'm stupid? But I told him I believed him and thought he had a good idea. I said I was going to carry them, too. Just in case."

"And do you?" the woman doing the pedicure asked.

"Always," Maggie said. "A half dozen. My husband counts them sometimes."

"What if he finds one missing?" the woman in the next chair asked. "He did."

"And what did you tell him?"

"I told him I was attacked and had to protect myself," Maggie said, giggling.

"And he believed you?"

"He had to. It supported his story."

The woman squealed with laughter.

"Basically, men are idiots," Millicent Farmer said. "All their brains are in their dicks."

"So what are your plans now, Mrs. Farmer?" Mary Jones asked.

"I'll probably stay in Palm. Hell, I got the name, the club memberships . . . oh, that was part of the deal. Mrs. George Farmer, that's me. I've been dating like mad, strictly sport trolling. I haven't found my next fish yet. But I will. Can't be too rich or too thin."

Grace searched deep inside herself for the truth of her reaction to this woman. Did she envy her? Studying her, sitting there, reveling in her importance, satisfied that she was making an enormous impression on every woman in the room, Grace marveled at her cool amorality. What did the means matter? She had ten million dollars in her smooth, polished little mitts.

This woman had no qualms, no second thoughts, no regrets. She reveled in her dishonesty, enjoyed the lies, the conspiring, the whole squalid routine. Grace felt sickened by the idea that she had entertained doing a variation of pretty much the same thing. Was she that crass, that unfeeling?

It struck her, too, that she might have subconsciously used Jackie to force the issue, tempted her so that Grace could terminate her effort to capture Mr. Big Bucks on the grounds that it would further corrupt her daughter. But even that theory didn't erase the idea that she had gone into battle ill equipped materially and psychologically.

She observed Millicent Farmer sitting on her throne, being ministered to by sycophants who laughed uproariously in the expected places, their attitude and demeanor geared to their tip expectations. *It's the tips, dummy.*

Was Grace any better than any of them? At least Millicent had been amply rewarded for her dishonesty. And she probably had left Georgie none the worse for wear. Grace wished there was more Millicent in her; more brashness, more boldness, more shrewdness, more hypocrisy, more cynicism. Her talents were paltry in this regard, Grace acknowledged. Maybe she was genetically programmed to wither away on the bottom rung of the ladder.

Or she was powerless to rise up against the ingrained, old-fashioned value system of her upbringing, a system bounded by Jesus, God, catechism, confessions, heaven and hell. However uneducated her parents were, they did convey to her the difference between right and wrong, good and evil, lies and truth. Under that system virtue and honesty earned their rewards in life, no less than the hereafter. Maybe such conditioning was impossible to get rid of, like a second skin.

She watched the dynamic of power, the women sucking up to Millicent Farmer perched on her throne, dispensing wisdom and the favor of her witty confidences, while the impotent Grace Sorentino stood by, a silent, powerless observer, unable to control anything in her life, anything, not even her own daughter.

"I have a question, Mrs. Farmer," Grace said suddenly. She felt a hot flush cover her neck and her chest.

"Shoot," Millicent said. "I'm an open book."

"How did you feel . . . I mean . . ." She looked toward Mary Jones, who was smiling amiably. "Living with this guy. All that time, knowing you were out to . . . you know."

She felt herself faltering, losing courage. Again she looked toward Mary Jones. Her smile of amiability had disappeared. She looked downright hostile.

"Fuck him over, right?" Millicent said.

"You look at it from that point of view . . . it's like . . . I mean, you had no feelings for the guy. . . ."

"Feelings?" She emitted a high, cackling laugh. "Feelings? That'll fuck you up every time. You can't have feelings. This is business. Business and feelings just don't go together."

"But doesn't that make you like a . . . like a . . ." She paused, swallowing hard. "A high-priced hooker?" Grace said, instantly regretting the remark.

"Hey, Mary," Millicent said, her tone dripping with sarcasm, "who is this little Miss Goody Two-shoes you got there?" She turned to Grace.

"I'm sure she didn't mean it like it sounded," Mary Jones said, shooting an angry look at Grace.

"Hookers never get the ring, asshole," Millicent said, directing her remark to Grace. She studied her from head to toe. "I see you're not wearing one. Problem with you, lady, you aim your cunt too low. But then, that's where it probably belongs."

"I guess that's an insult," Grace said, shrugging, knowing, at that moment, that her job with Mary Jones was over.

"You got that right, puss. I got enough fuck-you money to say it. Which I do to you. Fuck you." She turned to Mary Jones. "What do you need this little shit around for anyway?"

Mary Jones pursed her lips, shrugged and said nothing.

After Millicent Farmer, properly and expensively coiffured and stroked, left the store, Grace turned to Mary Jones.

"I guess I'm over."

"You pissed her off. You should have kept your lip buttoned. You're right, you blew it."

"She's still no better than a hooker, Mary," Grace said.

"Maybe so. Not for us peons to judge. Hookers or not, they're good customers, Grace. They know how to spend it and they tip good. They come here to be butt-kissed and worshipped, never contradicted. Get it?"

"I got it."

"Nice knowing you."

That night, lying in bed, she realized how much it bothered her to be bereft, to be a loser in the game of life. She felt herself gliding into a swamp of self-pity. Somehow, hours into the night, she slipped into a deep sleep. But not before she made a fervent wish that she would miraculously awake a changed woman, devoid of conscience and guilt, dancing beside the flaming pyre of that old value system.

Even after she had hung up from Sam's call she could not be sure she had the guts to carry the ploy forward, but she knew that blind fate had miraculously given her one more chance to find out.

CHAPTER THIRTEEN

From the indifference he detected in her voice on the telephone, Sam concluded that Grace Sorentino, for whatever reason, had abandoned the idea of disposing of Anne's clothing. He decided not to brood about it. He would make other arrangements.

He was already beginning to feel the first faint signs of the healing process. He still dwelled on Anne's absence in his life. The spirit of her presence still permeated the house. His mind had not quite accepted the idea that her voice was forever silent, and there were moments when he was certain he had heard her speak, heard her laughter or the sound of her footsteps walking through the room or coming up the stairs.

Even Marilyn's sudden inexplicable bark, sometimes in the middle of the night, told him that she, too, sensed her presence and might have believed she heard Anne's voice.

His other senses also reacted in odd ways. There were moments when he was absolutely certain he had just seen her turn a corner, not a full-bodied view, but the vision of a tiny wisp of her skirt or dressing gown. Reaching that place, he was certain he could smell the familiar scent of her perfume.

At night, asleep, he was awakened abruptly on more than one

occasion by her touch. That, too, was familiar, since she often touched him if he snored too loud at night, a gentle prod to break the rhythm of his breathing.

He supposed that such experiences were common to people who had lost a loved one, and he did not think of them as manifestations of the supernatural. He was too logical, pragmatic and earthbound to believe in ghosts, reincarnation, out-of-body experiences or any-thing remotely connected with the so-called occult.

He was hardly surprised that the old nightmare of her infidelity had returned, although it came less frequently than it had when Anne was alive. It was a bizarre, repetitive scenario in which she was blatantly insulting and cursing him while having sex with a young stranger. The sense of intimidation was so intense after these dreams that, at times, he would awaken in a state of terrible anger, thirsting for revenge, his heart pounding, his body soaked with perspiration.

He had never told Anne about this dream, except to say that he had hysterical anxiety dreams in which she was prominently fea-tured.

"I thought I was losing you," he explained when she had inquired about the dream.

"Well, here I am," she would reply, kissing him on the forehead.

He had been walking for an hour, his usual halfway point. Marilyn loped along beside him, occasionally dashing off course in a futile at-tempt to catch a sandpiper whose survival skills were based on the speed of its tiny toothpick legs.

He started the return journey heading toward his house. The sun had risen to an angle that gave him a clearer view into the distance, where he saw a moving figure heading in his direction.

Grace!

There was nothing to indicate that it was she except his intuition. He stepped up his pace, almost to a jog. Marilyn surged ahead, as if the sudden change of pace was a signal for rough play.

As he drew closer, he saw the outlines of a woman, but it wasn't enough to validate his intuition. Then he saw her clearly, and his ex-pectations were not disappointed. She was barefoot, wearing a long T-shirt over what he assumed was a bathing suit. Her black hair, which she wore long, was braided in the rear. She wore eyeliner, which seemed to frame her hazel eyes, greener now, enhanced by the sunlight and the color of the ocean. It surprised him that he noticed these details.

She smiled as she came closer, showing even white teeth. Marilyn started to jump on, but Sam called her back. The dog hesitated, then turned and came back to him. He grabbed her collar and held her.

"It seemed like a nice day for a walk and a swim," she said, with a glance at Marilyn.

He released her and gave her the "sit" command. Marilyn, none too happy, obeyed.

"Yes, it is," Sam said, surprised at his sense of elation at seeing her. "I had just about decided you weren't going to show."

"I wasn't sure myself," Grace said.

"You sounded . . . not very interested."

"Well, here I am."

They headed back toward the house, walking slowly. Sam snapped his fingers and Marilyn shot forward; then, looking back, slowed her pace and began chasing the sandpipers along the shore.

"I suppose it was because I had just gotten up. I'm always foggy in the morning."

"Are you?" He felt his mind drifting, then coming back. "Anne was a little like that in the morning. She was more of an evening person than a morning person."

"Yes. Apparently so . . . I mean, I could tell from her clothes. Lots of gowns and cocktail dresses. I figured her for a night person."

"She sure loved a party."

"And you, Sam? Did you?"

"Most were interesting. A few were boring. It was like playing roulette. We lucked out more than most. Anne saw to that. She had great instincts when it came to people, and she protected me from the idiots, of which there are many in this town. Among other things, I'll miss the way she organized my life."

"I wish someone would organize mine," Grace said. It struck him as an incongruous remark, but he let it pass.

"Anyway," he said, "I'm glad you came. I wanted to call earlier. It bugged me that I might have said something that put you off."

"I should have contacted you," Grace said. "I'm sorry. Anyway, I've finished my commitment. Now I'll be able to devote my time to tackling the job of disposing of Anne's clothes. . . . That is, if you haven't made other arrangements."

"Nearly did," Sam said.

"I'm glad you didn't. It would have bothered me . . . not keeping that promise to Anne."

"Well, then, I'm glad I took the bull by the horns and called you."

"So am I."

Somehow, he felt that he required more of an explanation for her
absence, but he let it pass. They walked for a while, then Sam
stopped, looked out to sea and contemplated the horizon.

"Looking out there gives you the illusion that life is unending, an
infinity. It's a damned lie, of course."

"Would you want to live forever, Sam?"

"Maybe. If everyone else did. I'd hate to have to do it by myself.
Contemplating an endless life of been-there, done-that. Watching
friends and loved ones expire. I don't think I could cope with this
kind of grief over and over again."

"Who knows?" Grace said. "You might get used to it. Discover that
people are interchangeable."

"I doubt it and they're not."

"You're probably right. I guess I'm being insensitive, considering
what you're going through."

"I'm afraid it's not exclusive to me, Grace. When you get right
down to it, loss is a pain in the butt. And it can really discombobulate
your sense of reality."

"I don't understand."

"It was a sort of ritual for me to bring Anne a cup of coffee in the
morning. I usually got up before her. Carmen would make me breakfast, then I would take a cup of coffee upstairs for Anne, put it on the
table beside the bed." He shook his head. "Do you know, I actually
did that two days ago? Habits sure die hard."

"My husband never did that for me. I envy you your great marriage, Sam."

"We had that. Oh, I traveled a great deal for business, although not
in the last few years. Maybe absence is good for a marriage. Puts you
on your mettle."

They were standing at the water's edge, the foam lapping around
their toes.

"You were trusted, Sam. That's part of it."

He felt an inner gulp, imagining he heard the sucking sound. So
she, too, had bought the concept of his being the faithful husband.
He wished he could tell her the truth. *I cheated,* he wanted to say, *enjoyed it, reveled in it, but, above all, I loved Anne and was faithful to her in
my heart. Good God,* he thought, *what skewered reasoning.* And yet he
knew it to be the truth.

"Did you trust your husband, Grace?"

"Afraid not."

"Too bad. I trusted Anne. And she trusted me," Sam said. He grew reflective, and in the long silence he pondered the idea of trust. It was an irony that in business he was above reproach. His word was his bond. In his marriage, trust had a different definition. He had been scrupulously evasive, which meant that honesty was selective. Dishonesty evaded was, he had once decided in a convoluted definition, a form of honesty.

"So you didn't trust your husband?" he asked suddenly, realizing that his ruminations had caused him to be silent for a longer period of time than seemed polite. "Why not?"

"My husband was a man in the wrong situation, and therefore his entire life with me was a lie. I don't think he could help himself."

"Was he unfaithful?" Sam asked, confused by her answer. He watched her purse her lips.

She grew hesitant, then turned away for a moment. Finally she spoke. "Always. My husband was a homosexual."

"Actively unfaithful?" Sam asked.

"I never knew for sure. But I assume so. He tried, I think, to be straight. Managed to fake it. In the end, he left me for a man."

"That must have been a shocker."

Again, she hesitated.

"It was devastating. Made even worse by the fact that I never had a clue."

"He must have been very good at keeping his secret."

"A master."

"How long since you were . . . well . . . since you split?"

"Twelve years. Imagine that. Jackie, my daughter, was four."

"At least he did the right thing by you, left you financially independent."

"Did I mention that? Oh, yes. He did the right thing. We've managed very well."

"From just a short time knowing you, I'd say that was pretty predictable," Sam said.

It wasn't flattery. He attributed it to insight. His business insight had always been acute. His greatest gift, he had discovered, was accurately reading other people.

"And since your divorce . . ."

She looked at him, smiled and caught his meaning.

"Slim pickings, Sam. No hits. No runs. Lots of errors."

His eyes roamed over her face and what he could see of her figure under the T-shirt.

"That's hard to believe."

"Believe it."

"Am I out of line, asking you these questions?" His own curiosity surprised him.

"I'm an open book, Sam. Ask me anything."

Her candor amazed him. "Don't you hold anything back?" he asked, looking at her archly.

"So far you haven't asked me any hard questions."

"Like what, for example?"

"Now there is a hard question, Sam."

There was another long silence between them, until Sam said, "You haven't asked me many questions, Grace, soft or hard. Or maybe you don't think I'm that interesting, someone not worth asking about."

"Now you're fishing for compliments."

"From you, I am."

"From me? Do you really need compliments from me, Sam?"

"Now there's an easy question. Yes, I do. That would be very nice."

"Okay, then. I think you're quite a guy."

"Damning with faint praise," Sam chuckled. He was enjoying the banter. She was keeping him on his toes.

"I practically just met you, Sam. It takes a while to know how a person really is."

"Sometimes it's quick." He snapped his fingers. "A feeling, a gut reaction. That feeling can never be captured in a résumé. I've hired people based on that feeling, ignoring references and experience. And so far I haven't been disappointed."

"And I hope you never will be," Grace said.

Not in your case, he wanted to say, but held off. Was that a sign that he was still unsure about her?

"You're a very nice person, Grace," he said, meaning it, maybe meaning more. Her presence was, above all, comforting.

"Swim?"

"Why not?"

He jumped into the water, Marilyn following. She removed her T-shirt and jumped into a wave. Looking back as she dived, he observed her figure, remarking to himself that she was in mighty good shape. He decided that she was somewhere in the middle thirties. Her bathing suit, he noted, was a modified bikini.

The water was calmer and they cavorted like porpoises for a while.

"Feels great," Sam said. He hadn't felt so good for months. Not since before Anne was first diagnosed. For a moment he felt a stab of guilt. *Should I be feeling like this?* he asked himself.

"Wonderful," Grace shouted, swimming parallel to the beach. She lifted her hand and waved. He waved back.

Then he signaled her to come in and they walked together back to the water's edge, then headed again on the beach toward the house. Grace's black hair glistened, catching the rays of the sun. Her body was tight and athletic, he noted, forcing himself, with difficulty, to be indifferent. His sensory perceptions surprised him. After all, he was in mourning.

As they moved toward the house, he looked at his wristwatch.

"I hadn't realized. It's nearly time for lunch. I hope you'll join me."

"Sure," she agreed. "I brought a change. And, remember, I've still got work to do."

He was very pleased. They walked in silence for awhile, getting closer to the house.

"Was the charity pleased with Anne's clothes?" he asked suddenly.

"Oh, yes," Grace answered, hesitating momentarily. "Very much so. It was something of a bonanza for them."

"Anne would have loved that. She took great pleasure in spreading happiness."

"Yes, she did."

They came close to the house. Grace picked up her sandals, which she had left sitting in the sand just outside the beachfront entrance, and followed him into the house. She hadn't rung the front door and Carmen seemed startled to see her come in with her boss.

"Two for lunch, Carmen."

He turned toward Grace. "How about omelets? Carmen makes great omelets."

Carmen scowled. Grace nodded, and she shuffled back to the kitchen.

"You can shower and change in Anne's bathroom," he said.

"Thank you. I know the way."

Sam went upstairs, took a shower and was quickly dressed. When he came down again, Grace was still upstairs. Carmen had set the table on the back patio, overlooking the beach and the ocean.

"How lovely," Grace said, coming out to the patio wearing white slacks and a pink blouse. Through the material he could see the outlines of her breasts and her nipples. She must have seen his glance and quickly crossed her arms over her chest.

"I'll be right back," Sam said as he went into the house, got a bottle of Dom Perignon from the refrigerator and two fluted glasses and brought them back to the patio.

"Remember, Sam," Grace said, "I still have work to do."

He wondered if she thought it inappropriate for him to be drinking champagne with a strange woman just weeks after his wife had died.

"Anne only drank Dom Perignon, Grace."

"Good. Then we'll drink to her."

He uncorked the bottle with a pop and carefully poured the two glasses. He noted that his fingers shook and realized he was uncommonly nervous. When he had finished pouring he lifted his glass and tapped hers.

"To Anne," Grace said.

"To Anne," Sam said. He felt a sudden sob rise in his chest. "The best of the best."

They drank. The champagne felt cool and tart on the tongue. He studied Grace as she drank.

"Lovely, isn't it, Grace?"

"I'm afraid so."

"Why afraid?" Sam asked.

"I feel . . . well . . . a little guilty. Sitting here in her place."

"Actually, we rarely ate out here," Sam said.

"Drinking her favorite drink."

"I'd like to feel that maybe she would approve," Sam said. He took a deep sip of the champagne. "We were very sensitive to each other's comfort levels. We were careful to provide each other with the things that made us happy. I think that Anne would be happy to see that I was not alone and brooding."

"With a strange woman," Grace said.

"Anne was not a jealous person."

They drank in silence for a few moments. Sam was attentive to his guest's glass and poured her another.

Carmen came out with the omelets. One of them was of lesser quality than the other. She placed that one in front of Grace.

"No, Carmen. Give this one to Mrs. Sorentino," Sam said.

None too happy, Carmen switched plates.

"I think she resents me being here," Grace said after the woman had gone back to the kitchen.

"Perfectly understandable," Sam said. "She'll get over it."

"Are your children taking it well?" Grace asked.

"Yes. Very well. But then, they live far from here. It's been years since we all lived under one roof. Oh, I'm sure they all miss the telephone calls, the family holidays, although even those had petered out. Grown children have a different agenda." He thought of those agendas. "It's money now. The estate. This is not to say they didn't love Anne. I suppose they think they did, in their way. They might even think they love me, a sort of obligatory love, an expected love. Nothing really compelling. Rooted in nostalgia. But then, what would they be expected to do?"

He sensed that he had said too much, but looking at her interest in it, he felt comfortable.

"I'm sure you love your daughter, Grace. Do you think she loves you as much?"

Grace sipped her champagne and seemed to be contemplating the question.

"As you say, perhaps obligatory love."

"It's an odd thing how money becomes paramount. They want to be sure that my arrangements maximize their personal inheritances. They seem to be worried that I'll make some stupid moves and fritter away my fortune."

"Will you?"

He wanted to tell her what Bruce really thought, that he would be vulnerable to some bimbo who would find a way to get his money, but he held back.

"Maybe." He laughed, pouring the remnants of the champagne into both their glasses.

"But then," he said, "why should I have to think about that? I'm sixty-four years old. I've made mostly good judgments in my life. Why should I make bad ones now? It's too ingrained in my psyche. Maybe they think I'm a doddering, senile idiot. To them, sixty-four might seem ancient."

"It doesn't seem so from here, Sam," Grace said.

"I appreciate your diplomacy, Grace. I'll bet I've got thirty years on you," Sam said.

"You're close."

"I'm not afraid of dying," Sam confessed. "It's the constant noise about the estate that bugs me. My son Bruce, the lawyer, that's all he seems to care about. As for Carol, that's a hopeless case."

He upended his glass.

"Look at me," he said. "I'm whining about my problems with my children. When Anne was alive, she was the one who bore the brunt of it. She was supposed to be the survivor and deal with this. Now I'm stuck with the job and I hate it."

"Don't dwell on it, Sam," Grace said.

"You're right, Grace. Little children, little problems. Big children, big problems."

They finished their omelets and Carmen, still scowling, took the plates away.

"Here I am," Sam said, "monopolizing your time."

"Well, I should get on with the clothes."

"The clothes. Yes."

He watched as she rose from the table and brushed bread crumbs from her slacks. He liked her looks and, despite himself, admitted the beginnings of sexual stirrings. Yet he did not want her to think that was his motive for extending the hand of friendship. It had nothing to do with that, he assured himself. Nothing.

"I'll be upstairs, Sam," Grace said.

Sam watched her rise on the stairway. It felt good to watch the sway of her hips, the graceful movement of her legs. She had good legs, a wonderfully proportioned rump. But when she was out of sight, he turned suddenly and saw Carmen watching him as if he were committing some great crime.

"I'm still alive, Carmen," he muttered.

He went into his study and made a series of phone calls to his various money managers. The acquisition of more wealth seemed a pointless endeavor, and, considering the pressure he was getting from his children, a needless burden. Nevertheless he continued his routine by rote.

Up until Anne became ill, he had traveled throughout the world, liquidating those businesses that required his personal attention. Earlier, he had deliberately set up various businesses in other parts of the country and in Europe and Asia, not only considering profit potential but also to ply his secret life, his carnal game. He had even lost interest in that.

He came out of his study and moved upstairs to his bedroom. The doors to Anne's closet were open and the bed was already piled high with Anne's clothes. He heard Grace rustling about in the closet's interior. She appeared with another handful of clothes and piled them on the bed.

"It seems endless," Grace said. "It's the sorting that takes the time. I want to be sure the various charities get their fair share."

"With your good efforts, I'm sure they will, Grace."

"What they'll probably do with the gowns and more expensive clothes is sell them." She paused and looked at him. "Do you mind?"

"Not at all," Sam said. "I wouldn't even mind if you took some for yourself."

"For me?" Grace said. "That would be unthinkable."

"It wouldn't matter," Sam said. "In fact, I wouldn't even mind if you tried some on. I'd like to see how you look in them."

"In your wife's clothes?"

"Does it sound ghoulish?"

"No. Just surprising. Wouldn't it depress you?"

"You've got a point. Maybe it would."

He looked at some of the clothes she had put on the bed. There was a beige dress on the pile. He picked it up and handed it to her.

"This might be nice. Hold it up."

She lifted the hanger with the garment on it, got the dress in position and pressed it against herself.

"It could be too small," she said, looking into the mirror. "I'm larger, almost a seven."

"Looks perfect to me," Sam said.

She held the dress at arm's length and inspected it, noting the label. Geoffrey Beane.

"It is lovely." She shook her head. "But I wouldn't feel comfortable wearing it, knowing that it was Anne's."

"Why? It's an inanimate object," Sam said, surprised at his own remark, remembering that the reason this woman was here was to take the sting out of the process of disposing of Anne's clothes.

"No, it's not, Sam," Grace said. "It's a reflection of Anne. A lot went into such a purchase, not just money. A wardrobe like this was not just about clothing. It was a way of life."

"I know that," Sam said. "Still, when you think about it, clothes are made to be worn. Really, Grace, try it on. I'd like to see it on you."

"To remind you of her?"

"Maybe. Go on. Try it on."

She hesitated, studying the dress.

"It's lovely, but it doesn't feel right somehow."

"Your call, Grace. Am I being awful to ask?"

"This is embarrassing, Sam," Grace said, scanning the room. "Is it that important to you?"

"Maybe it was a crazy idea," he said. "If it makes you uncomfortable, just forget about it. I might be out of line."

"You did suggest it," Grace said. "That's one clue to its importance." She paused for a moment. "Why not, Sam? What's the harm?"

"You think I'm being weird?"

Grace shrugged. She held the dress in front of her.

"I suppose you can change in Anne's dressing room," Sam said,
pointing to a door that led to her dressing room and bathroom. "I'm
sure you'll find everything you need there."

"Are you sure about this, Sam?"

"I'm not sure about anything, Grace," he said. "It might stir up
memories that I don't want to deal with. Your call."

"If it doesn't fit, I won't show it to you."

"Fair enough."

She seemed to be studying him; then she shrugged and went off
into the dressing room carrying the beige dress.

Sam was surprised at the course this was taking. It was as if, for the
first time in months, perhaps years, his body was awakening from a
long slumber. He felt a quickening in his crotch and discovered he
had a steel-hard erection. It was an odd sensation, since he had rarely
had any sexual stirring in this room.

Although he enjoyed being with his wife here, enjoyed being with
her everywhere, for that matter, he had discovered early on that she
had little interest in sex. It was an anomaly, since Anne had a sexy
look. Others had commented on this, telling him how lucky he was
to have such a sexy and attractive wife.

It was the one missing link in his marriage, perhaps the primary
factor that propelled him into his secret life. Early on, he had given
up any idea that she might change.

When they were young, in the first few months of their marriage,
Sam had noted Anne's sexual unresponsiveness. She performed du-
tifully but without passion or interest. Before their marriage, while
they did not, in the mores of the day, "go all the way," they masturbated each other to mutual orgasm. But when they married, it
seemed that desire had simply disappeared from Anne's life.

Sam found it a difficult subject to think about, and he and Anne
had rarely discussed it. Even his most oblique references to her sexuality always brought the same smiling answer.

"I intend to be a good and dutiful wife always," she would tell him.
"Always available."

"But you don't seem to get a kick out of doing it."

"I love you being close to me."

"But it's the feedback . . ."

"Don't be ridiculous, Sam. You always seem to enjoy it immensely."
"I do, but . . ."

"No buts. It shouldn't be so important to our happiness."

He loved her and there seemed no point in making either of them uncomfortable. Nevertheless, he tried to be both patient and imaginative in his lovemaking, but except for some minor variations of the missionary position, sex between them became boring and routine. He acknowledged that perhaps it was his fault, something inside him that froze her desire, or some fault in his technique that could not overcome her natural reluctance.

Sexual activity between them dwindled. It became the accepted condition of their marriage. He did not let it become a bone of contention between them.

He would often grapple with the question and wonder why he had not pursued the matter further. He did consider the possibility of therapy for both of them, had agonized over it, then rejected it, deciding that he did not wish to bring to her attention what she might consider a serious flaw in herself, a flaw she neither understood nor recognized. Or perhaps he lacked the courage to risk discovering some missing link in himself, some mysterious biological inability to arouse her, despite the usual patient textbook ministrations.

He knew, of course, that this issue flew in the face of marital intimacy and the common idea that total communication, body and soul, was necessary for a strong marriage. Weighing the pros and cons of keeping this subject dormant between them, he chose evasion and conscious repression and, from the evidence of their life together, the strategy had been reasonably successful.

But it became apparent to Sam that he could never have a totally rounded relationship with his wife. They had sex less and less as time went on, and apparently both of them got used to the idea of less sex, which eventually became no sex. Neither questioned the other about this phenomenon. They both enjoyed each other's company and they had many things in common. Except sex.

As time went on, he felt certain that she had interpreted his lack of sexual ardor as merely the inevitable result of familiarity and, possibly, the aging process, a highly unlikely idea, unless she believed that the sex drive diminished in men as they reached their thirties. Actually, he hoped she thought so. The fact was that, because she showed no interest in sex, she became less interesting as a sexual partner. He began to prefer secret masturbation and took some solace in an enriched fantasy life.

Frequency dwindled considerably, then became abstinence. It was as if that part of their lives together had been placed in cold storage in a locked compartment. What it meant, too, was that their lines of communication to each other were subject to a great deal of detouring. They avoided any reference to that side of their natures and, as a consequence, he knew that his relationship with Anne would be subject to much editing and evasion. Perhaps she thought him impotent. What did it matter?

As a businessman, Sam had learned the value of pragmatism and compromise. Always, he knew, something had to be left on the table for the other person. No one was supposed to have it all. Under those conditions no deal could be consummated. Perhaps it wasn't an ideal way to conduct a marriage, but it became workable and did not inhibit their respect for each other, their friendship or their general pursuit of happiness. They liked each other and, as time went on, they grew used to having each other around. It was comfortable. They had created a life together without rancor and with mutual respect.

Where was it written that communication between married couples, or between anyone, needed to be total? People, he supposed, were like icebergs, with most of what was really inside them hidden. He gave her that part of himself that she could accept without pain. Apparently, she gave him that part of herself as well. Other couples, he had noted, had fared much worse.

Anne had never, not once in their long marriage, confronted him with any suspicions about his fidelity. He had concluded that it just wasn't in her frame of reference, as if she thought the state of their sex life was somehow normal.

Respecting that and not wishing to agitate her or interfere with the tranquility of their relationship, he chose, after fathering two children a slow retreat from the act until total sexual withdrawal in their marriage, and his own resort to masturbation, had become a permanent part of their married life.

Her reaction to this retreat was, at first, inexplicable, leading him finally to conclude that she had neither insight nor knowledge of the power of the male sex drive. She made no comment about it, nor did it interfere with their outward show of affection and the other mostly positive aspects of their marriage. They still kissed, hugged, held hands and participated in all the obvious touching rituals of any devoted couple. Not long after his discovery of her condition, he began to seek sexual gratification elsewhere, choosing what to him seemed the least dangerous path, mostly paying for the privilege.

These activities were confined to places he visited on business or, when he was home, assignations in other towns like Fort Lauderdale or Miami. Eventually it became a way of life for him, and he accepted her lack of suspicion as evidence that either she was equally uninterested in sex or she had accepted the idea that he went elsewhere for his sexual gratification. He had never been certain, nor did he ever raise the subject.

He followed a routine of complete caution and secrecy. Never would he put Anne in a position that would embarrass her or cause her the slightest twinge of pain. During all their life together, he had been extraordinarily lucky. Not a single one of the dozens of women he had bedded outside of the marriage bond had caused trouble.

Of course, he had taken extreme precautions. He did wonder how she might have reacted to a discovery of his affairs, even one of the many, but he always aborted the prospect in his imagination. It was too painful to contemplate, both as to her disappointment in him and his own sense of humiliation.

He would never, ever, compromise himself with someone in their circle or in the geographical proximity. He had had women everywhere that he traveled, wherever he had businesses. With some he had become infatuated, always a sign of danger requiring immediate extraction. Money usually accomplished his purpose. He had also made a point of making it clear that he was married irrevocably, that there was no chance of anything but a transitory relationship.

The fact was that the more his libido was repressed at home, the more it exploded outside. He pursued whatever fantasy seized his imagination and found no end of participants for every variation that might satisfy his starving libido.

With the onset of the AIDS epidemic, he became more cautious, more selective and, eventually, too frightened to be promiscuous. So far he had been lucky about contracting a venereal disease. Now it was different. Not only did he fear for his life, but, by then, his fear of exposure, which meant discovery by Anne, had reached a level of morbidity that bordered on paranoia. It wasn't guilt. He had never felt guilt. Necessity, he assured himself, had given him permission to live this secret life. He wasn't proud of it.

Despite this deviation, he devoted his life to building his credibility and portraying himself to her as a person of the highest moral standards, faithful to a fault, a dedicated and loving husband, helpmate and father, a man of sterling principles. Indeed, he had often thought, he had accomplished the impossible. He had compartmentalized his life, mind and body.

The onset of Anne's illness, a form of bone cancer, forced him to temper his desires, although he once again took up his practice of secret therapeutic masturbation. It was more occasional than it had been early in his marriage.

Once or twice, as he sat beside Anne's bed, he had contemplated the idea of confession, but he had decided finally that what he had done, his secret life, had hardly touched her. Why contribute to her pain? he decided.

It was a revelation to him that her death did not elicit any feeling of regret for what he had done. His secret life had remained just that, secret, and irrelevant to his marriage. He grieved sincerely for her loss and missed her terribly. Despite the withholding and his lack of total honesty, she had been, undeniably and irrevocably, the anchor of his life. Her death had set him adrift.

Grace came out of the dressing room in Anne's beige dress and stepped immediately into Anne's closet. When she came out she was wearing high heels. She had also applied some makeup.

"You look lovely," Sam said.

"Do I?"

"May I watch you walk around a bit?" Sam asked. "You know, like a model."

Grace laughed.

"Really, Sam. It's sort of embarrassing."

"Go on. Walk across the room."

She did as he asked, moving with a self-conscious swagger, exaggerating her walk like a model.

"It gives me great pleasure to see you walk," Sam said.

"I suppose I remind you of Anne."

"In a way."

"I hope it doesn't make you feel too sad," Grace said.

"A little," he admitted. "But I do appreciate this, Grace." He sighed. "Go on. Walk some more."

She walked across the room and back. He felt his erection throb against his pants and crossed his legs to hide it from her. He noted that her legs were not bare.

"I guess you found her panty hose," Sam said.

"It wouldn't have looked very well with bare legs."

"I believe she had drawers full of underwear, lingerie and panty hose."

"Yes, she did."

He felt an odd sense of elation rising along his spine. Looking at his crotch, he saw the telltale signs of arousal. He moved in his chair in such a way so that she would not see what was happening.

"Tell me, Grace, do you feel uncomfortable in that dress?"

"Honestly?"

"Of course, honestly."

She put a hand on her hip in a kind of pose.

"Good. I feel good." She smiled, and they exchanged glances. "Honestly."

"I'd like you to keep it, Grace. It becomes you."

"Sam, I told you before, I don't think it would be . . . well . . . appropriate."

"Who will know?" He looked around the room. "It's just between us."

"I couldn't."

He wanted to argue the point, but he feared that she might misread his motives, although, at this stage, he wasn't quite sure what they were. Above all, he didn't want to scare her away. In fact, what he really wanted was for her to try on more of Anne's clothes.

"I'll tell you what, Grace," he said. It was a sentence he used commonly in his business dealings. "Let's not rush this. Look through the closet. There must be certain types of clothes, like jeans, T-shirts, sneakers. Things that might look ordinary to the charity folks. Easily disposed of things. Why not get rid of those first?" He was being the dealmaker now, engaging his negotiating skills.

She grew thoughtful for a moment, studying him. He noted her hesitancy and suspected that her decision might seem as if she was crossing some kind of a line. It was not unlike the feeling he was having.

"It's certainly a practical idea," she admitted. "But it doesn't mean I will accept any of her clothing."

"I wouldn't think of pressuring you about that . . . although . . ." He hesitated, still cautious about going too far, now that he had gained a point.

"You won't think I'm being ridiculous, Grace?"

He knew what he wanted to say, but this time he grew hesitant and, for a time, he was silent.

"You've been through a traumatic experience, losing someone you cared about so much. How can I possibly think you could be ridiculous?"

"The fact is, it gives me pleasure to see you, someone alive, living and breathing, wearing her clothes."

"That doesn't sound ridiculous to me."

"Thank you, Grace. For your understanding. The truth is, I do feel slightly foolish. Above all, I don't want you to feel you have to do this."

She studied his face and smiled.

"Would you like me to continue?" she asked.

"Please."

She walked back and forth across the room, again with the model's swagger, as if to underline her comment. Her walk seemed more exaggerated than before, and he wondered if she knew what was going on inside him.

He had no illusions about what was happening to him. It was startling. He was turned on, his libido fully awakened.

He tried to keep his reaction hidden as she continued to strut the length of the room. Thankfully, she hadn't seemed to notice. If she had, she might think he was perverted in some way, or kinky, a dirty old man, which might strike her as far worse than appearing ridiculous. He hadn't expected this to happen and he was embarrassed.

"I appreciate this, Grace," he said, crossing his legs to hide the evidence as she stopped her model's walk and approached him.

"I've got a confession to make, Sam. I'm enjoying this."

Then she ducked into Anne's dressing room. He wondered what she meant, what degree of pleasure she was indicating. Was it possible that she was having a similar reaction?

CHAPTER FOURTEEN

She looked at herself in the mirror. Her face was flushed, and when she removed Anne's dress she noted that the flush had spread all the way to her chest. Removing Anne's panty hose, she noted the profusion of moisture in the crotch. Letting the water run in the sink, she dropped the panty hose in and let them soak.

She felt giggly, slightly high and sexually charged. She was completely surprised by her own reaction, and she knew that the slightest help from herself would bring her to a climax, but she repressed the urge. She might get too carried away by the process, make noises that he would hear. She had expected the world of the rich to be different, but not this different.

She certainly had not banked on events taking this turn. In fact, she couldn't believe what had occurred. It was hardly in her lexicon of possibilities. And it did further expand her knowledge about the sexuality of older men. She had indeed seen the telltale signs of his arousal, despite his attempt at hiding his condition. It certainly seemed at odds with his grieving, and it confused her.

She slipped back into her slacks and T-shirt and wondered if it was she who had turned him on or some imagined fantasy about Anne for which she was a sort of substitute. Did he see her as herself, or as

Anne? However he saw her, he was obviously engaged in a sexual way by her presence in Anne's clothes. Nevertheless, it did amaze her. But if that's what it took, she told herself, then she would be a willing participant. If that was his turn-on, so be it.

Grace was further confused about how to conduct herself now. Would he attempt to seduce her? Not that she needed much prodding. Above all, she didn't want to be perceived as an easy lay. On the other hand, she didn't want to appear standoffish and unavailable or merely a sex object, a role in which she had never seen herself. Actually, she had enjoyed modeling Anne's clothes for Sam, wiggling her fanny as she walked across the room, feeling his hot eyes watching her, getting a sexual charge out of it herself.

She had consented willingly. Had it been too willingly? She still needed to maintain her dignity. Sam, at least outwardly, seemed a dignified man. He had a distinguished presence and appeared kind and gentle, a man of caring and feeling. With such an attitude, she was surprised that he had accumulated a fortune. Captains of industry, entrepreneurs, bosses in general, were supposed to be ruthless, unfeeling, concerned only with the bottom line. Mrs. Burns was the embodiment of that attitude. *We are here, Grace, to move merchandise,* she remembered her saying.

Admittedly, she had never confronted a man like Sam Goodwin, a multimillionaire and a Jew, at such an intimate level. Nor had she ever had much contact with men over sixty. For that matter, she had never tasted Dom Perignon. The beige dress was a Geoffrey Beane, easily costing in the thousands. She had never worn such an expensive dress in her life. This barrage of "firsts" was heady stuff. She felt suddenly misplaced and contrived. Yet it was not unpleasant. Yes, she told herself, she could get used to this life.

She squeezed out the panty hose, hung it from a towel rack, then came out of the dressing room. Sam was nowhere to be seen, a good thing, since she was still flushed. She decided to concentrate on her original plan, the disposal of Anne's clothes. She mustn't lose sight of that chore. It was the umbilical cord of her relationship to Sam.

In keeping with his wishes to give away the so-called ordinary clothes, jeans, T-shirts and sneakers, she stopped the mechanical rack at that section of the closet reserved for them. She had never ceased to marvel at the way Anne had organized her clothes. Of course, the ordinary clothes were hardly ordinary—jeans by Calvin Klein, Ralph Lauren and Tommy Hilfiger. T-shirts were also expensive designer products. Sneakers as well.

She removed them from the rack and replaced the expensive dresses, skirts and blouses that she had collected earlier. She was determined to keep within the boundaries of the deal he had set. Considering how she had lied her way into his presence, and continued to lie about her history and background, especially that extraordinary bit about her ex-husband being a homosexual, she did not want to compound the danger by showing him any sign of acquisitiveness.

Nor would she be tempted to do what Jackie had done, despite the fact that she was increasingly doubtful that the act would ever be discovered. She was not Millicent Farmer, she insisted to herself, although the commonality of their objectives was too similar for comfort.

She studied the bedroom, as if seeing it for the first time, the Goodwins' king-sized canopied bed, the thick carpeting, the antique mirrors and lovely oil paintings, the furniture, elegantly French provincial, the wonderful appointments and expensive knickknacks. This, too, seemed to reflect with amazing accuracy her earlier fantasies, although she had definitely not pictured the photographs of Anne in various poses and ages scattered around the room. Yet she felt no inhibition about speculating what changes she would make if she, by some miracle, would become the next Mrs. Goodwin.

While she admired Anne's taste, she knew she would have to put her own stamp on things. Her experience in design was rudimentary. Having never been exposed to such choices, she was not even sure what she liked in terms of period or furnishings. Baltimore's Italian ghetto was eons away from this. Naturally, she would have to hire the best decorators and designers. Thinking about that brought her to a new level of anxiety. She had no idea what she meant by her own stamp.

From her vantage everything in the area, including all of Anne's clothes in the closet, as well as the undergarments, panty hose and nightgowns that filled the cabinets in the dressing room, were excessive, beyond the needs of any individual. She supposed that this was what wealth meant: the ability to acquire more of everything, regardless of the waste.

Apparently Sam couldn't care less about what Anne had spent on all this. It boggled her mind to think of the money he must have. Was such generosity a manifestation of his love for her, his abject and unjudgmental devotion? God, how wonderful it must have been for Anne to revel in such worship.

She picked up an armful of jeans and started down the stairs. Carmen came out of the kitchen to peer up at her and scowl, but she said nothing and offered little help. *You'd be history if I ever ran this house,* Grace said to herself, annoyed at the woman's obvious rudeness.

It took two trips to put the jeans and other sports clothing in her car. In retrospect, she was satisfied that the day had gone very well. Perhaps she had needed the respite, needed the time away to assess the situation. Besides, destiny had intervened. His phoning her proved that.

When she came back into the house Carmen stood at the door, looking belligerent, as if she were guarding the entrance.

"Would you get Mr. Goodwin, Carmen? I'd like to say good-bye."

"I not know where he is," Carmen answered grudgingly.

"Has he left?"

"I tole you. I not know."

She started to move through the ground-floor level of the house.

"You can't do this," Carmen said, following her. She heard Sam's voice in the distance and started to follow it.

"I tole you," Carmen cried, stepping in front of her.

"Carmen, get the hell out of my way. I'm here at the invitation of Mr. Goodwin and you have no right to be rude to me."

"You got big eyes, woman. I see." She pointed a finger at her eyes to emphasize the point.

"Is that you, Grace?"

Sam came out of his den. He was wearing half-glasses, which he slipped off when he saw her.

"I'm going, Sam," Grace said. "As you suggested, jeans and sports stuff first. I'll drop them off today."

"Good," he said, hesitating. He looked toward the hallway, where Carmen was still standing, watching them. Meeting his glance, Grace noted, Carmen turned away indignantly and moved back to the kitchen. Freed from her surveillance, he seemed to loosen up. Smiling, he looked into her eyes, and she forced herself to meet his gaze.

"I hope you'll be here tomorrow," he said.

"There's still lots to do."

He nodded. She sensed a silent understanding between them. Would there be more of Anne's clothes to model for him tomorrow?

"We could take a walk first, go for a swim. Up for it?"

"I'll try, Sam. It was fun."

For the first time she was conscious of studying the details of his face. He had Wedgwood blue eyes, full lips, his square chin was slightly cleft. As a cosmetician, she knew faces. His face was well boned, tightly fleshed for his age, although it was impossible to hide the aging skin on his neck, around his Adam's apple.

At this distance she could see his teeth, which were even, too even, and glistening white. Implants, she decided, which brought her gaze back to his eyes, looking for the telltale signs of the surgeon's knife. In her line of work she had seen enough plastic surgery to tell at a glance. He had admitted that he'd had an eye job, but there were no signs of a face-lift. His steel-gray hair was razor cut and colored naturally. He was obviously vain about his appearance and had taken steps to hold back the disintegrating aging process as best he could. As a younger man, he might have been characterized as handsome, and age had made him distinguished in a very sexy way.

She knew his age. He did not look it, although she had no real frame of reference or comparison. Sixty-four, he had told her. She remembered the Beatles song about being sixty-four. In terms of chronology and by comparison with her own age, he was certainly old, although there was a proud aura about him of virility and strength.

Realizing that she was studying him too intently, she averted her eyes. Did he sense the intensity of her scrutiny? She wondered what was going through his mind. What did he see in her face? Did he see the insecure Italian girl from Baltimore who, with her life at least half over, had made a mess of it? Could he see through her deception?

Did he see what she saw in her mirror, the first tiny signs of sag, the little wrinkling around her eyes and neck, the minute sprigs of gray sprouting beneath the black?

Could she stand up to his scrutiny? Could he detect her meager education, her limited experience, her lack of class and knowledge of the so-called finer things? Carmen had immediately seen through the false facade. Would he eventually? Of course he would.

Suddenly he touched her bare arm and smiled at her. His skin on her flesh sent a shockwave through her. Recovering quickly, she realized it was a gesture of camaraderie. He was merely accompanying her to the door.

"I'm expecting you," he mock scolded. "Don't let me down."

"I'll be here. I promise."

He moved toward her and kissed her on the cheek, a polite little gesture. She felt the skin burn where his lips had touched. It was only a courteous good-bye kiss, she assured herself, part of the ritual of his class. She hoped he hadn't seen her turn her face, then check its motion. He wasn't aiming for her lips. And here she was obligingly puckering to receive his.

As she moved toward her car, she felt her knees wobble. What was going on here? she wondered.

Driving toward the Palm Beach bridges, she realized suddenly that she was carting home a backseat full of clothes, providing more temptation for Jackie's budding entrepreneurial talents. Thinking of her act in those terms seemed to take the sting out of it.

Perhaps she was being too hard on her daughter, Grace thought. Jackie's survival skills were apparently better honed than hers. Where had they come from? Where had Jackie learned to tempt fate and take wild risks? And spite her by continuing to see that monster Darryl. The unpleasant image of Jackie having unsafe sex crossed her mind. These traits must have come from Jason, she concluded, the idiot risk-taker, he of the impossible dream. The acorn did not fall far from the tree.

Looking back, she realized that she had foolishly bought Jason's dreams, had followed him as a dutiful and faithful wife to the scene of every failure. She had long ceased to analyze her actions. At first she had blamed it on the blindness of love. To her youthful, inexperienced, love-shrouded eye, beauty had counted for wisdom. When that veil was pierced, not long after their marriage, beauty died and wisdom fled, leaving the ashes of dead dreams.

When you are young, she had come to realize, it was fun to dream, glorious to imagine the future and believe in the treasure that lay in wait just down the road, the pot of gold at the end of the rainbow. For her the rainbow had dissolved and the pot became the old saw about not having one to pee in.

She speculated what life might have been if they had found that illusive treasure. Would it have mattered? Would Jason have been, like Sam Goodwin, the devoted, generous, loving and monogamous husband? Either way, rich or poor, her marriage was doomed to failure. Beyond Jason's beauty was a hallucinating fantasizer. When he felt optimistic about a deal he fed his optimism by acquiring things he couldn't pay for, as if the wish would soon become the reality. It never did and, always, the acquisitions either had to be returned or they had to push on, pursued by process servers and lawyers.

Eventually it had become a way of life—the failed dream, the wild flight and the inevitable pursuit, winding up, finally, in the dustbin of West Palm Beach, well short of Nirvana.

She gave him more than a decade of her life, and the accident of Jackie hastened the demise. It had, indeed, been an accident. She had forgotten to put in her diaphragm. Actually, it had lain neglected and unused in its case for months. The act of conception itself was more in the nature of an obligation than consensual lovemaking. Her motive had been pity. Another of his many deals had ended in failure, and she sensed that he might need this to validate his manhood, or whatever it was inside him that needed validation. As for Grace, Jackie's birth had motivated her, given her a profound reason to separate herself further from her failed husband.

Had Jason unwittingly placed a genetic depth bomb in their daughter? It frightened her to see the similarities in their makeup, the same flaws and miscalculations. Perhaps, she thought hopefully, sudden wealth, the ability to acquire without consequences, would abort or repress the genetic curse.

With Jason she had experienced weakness, sloth, stupidity, naïveté and ignorance. In contrast, Sam was strong, clever, intelligent, successful and, above all, rich. In her mind he represented her last chance to save herself and her daughter from the wasting disease of material deprivation. She feared such thoughts, knowing they encouraged desperation, and desperation was not an emotion compatible with her plan. Wild, unrealistic, wishful speculations of success always invited a letdown.

Was she merely an interim diversion for Sam? Was Sam using her to help chase away his grief, ease the pain of loss? Or was it simply sexual deprivation urging him on, the starving gonads needing sustenance? She had certainly succeeded beyond her wildest dreams to achieve the first stage in her original plan, the initial engagement. Now she was heading into more complicated and dangerous territory. She would need all her courage now, all her resources. There was no turning back. She was committed to the enterprise, body and soul, beyond all hesitation, beyond any second thoughts or ethical or moral considerations.

CHAPTER FIFTEEN

By the time she got to her apartment it was getting dark. She suddenly remembered that she had made no plans for disposing of the clothing in the backseat of her car. Tomorrow, she decided, she would bring it to the Salvation Army drop-off place, wherever that might be.

Not wanting Jackie to see the clothes, she parked a distance away from her unit, noting that another car, a small yellow Honda, was parked in her usual place. Since there was no reserved parking, seeing another car in her usual space was not an uncommon occurrence.

Jackie jumped up and embraced her when she opened the door of her apartment. Enthusiastically, she returned the embrace. It seemed like a long-awaited reconciliation.

"What's that for?" Grace asked.

"Did you see it, Mom?" Jackie cried excitedly.

"See what?"

"The car, silly. The little yellow Honda."

Grace's heart thumped suddenly.

"Yes. I saw it."

She extracted herself from her daughter's embrace.

"It's mine. I made a fantastic deal. I used the five hundred dollars for a down payment."

"You bought it for five hundred dollars?"

"Two thousand. It's fantastic. I bought it from Darryl, who was selling it for a friend. He went over it with a fine-tooth comb. Even though it's ten years old, it's clean as a whistle, Mom. Only a hundred thousand miles on it."

"You can't do that. In the first place you're a minor. In the second you have to buy car insurance. Then there's sales tax and who knows what else."

"I know all that. Darryl says he'll take care of it."

"Take care of it? What does that mean? Have you any documentation, registration, bill of sale, minor little legalities like that?"

"I told you, Mom, Darryl is taking care of it."

Jackie was starting to pout. The euphoria of a few moments ago had dissipated.

"You don't have paperwork?"

"Just a handshake. We did it on a handshake. I gave him five hundred dollars and will pay him a hundred and twenty five a month until it's paid off in a year."

"I don't believe this. One accident and your license is over and God knows what else. Are you crazy? Do you believe that Nazi bastard?"

Grace's temper was rising. She was livid with rage, trying valiantly to keep a lid on her temper.

"Your attitude stinks, Mom. I know you hate Darryl, but he's made this great deal for me. The fact is, Mom, I can't live without a car. And you can't buy me one. I can't worry about buses all the time. I'm trapped without a car. Hell, I'm nearly seventeen years old. Please, Mom, let's not argue about it. It's a done deal."

"No, it's not. Just give it back and tell that stupid skinhead to give you back the five hundred. And, by the way, you're not seventeen yet."

"In three months I will be."

"And you'll be just as stupid," she blurted, regretting it instantly.

"You don't have to be insulting." Jackie pouted.

"Well, then, tell me how to get your attention. You have just done a ridiculous transaction. You're right, Darryl isn't as dumb as he looks. The car's probably stolen. Maybe he even stabbed the owner with that ugly weapon he carries. Look, I'm still legally in charge. You have got to give it back."

"I can't do that. We shook hands on it."

"Shook hands? With that moron. You don't buy a car like a pig in a poke."

"Okay, then. I'll talk to Darryl about it. I'm sure it's not stolen. Darryl says he's selling it for a buddy and I believe him. But if you want, I'll talk to him and give you more details, okay?"

In the initial excitement of her rage, Grace had neglected to consider the arithmetic. She tried to calm herself, hoping reason and logic might prevail.

"Let's consider the details you already gave me. You said you were charged two thousand. You gave him five hundred. That means that you still owe fifteen hundred on the car."

"A hundred and twenty five a month for twelve months. I give it to Darryl. He gives it to his buddy."

"No interest?"

Jackie looked at her blankly.

"Never mind. Where is the hundred and twenty-five supposed to come from?"

"I've already taken care of that, Mom. I got a job at McDonald's, mornings, before I go to school. And I'll ask Mr. Barlow for a raise at the movie theater."

She tried to do a quick calculation, but it eluded her.

"Aside from the murkiness of the transaction itself, I don't see how you can do it."

"You have absolutely no faith in me, Mom."

"Your judgment leaves much to be desired, Jackie, and don't ask me for help. I just quit my new job."

"So who's stupid now? You can't even hold a job."

"It was my choice, Jackie. I told you, I quit."

"And you criticize my judgment," Jackie sneered. "How could you quit when we need the money?"

Jackie paced the room now, pouting, deep in thought. Suddenly she turned and faced her mother. She looked exactly like Jason, with the same defensive anger, the same sense of false calculation, the same hopeless grasp of the way things worked in the real world. At the same time, Grace knew she couldn't evade criticism of herself. Her best efforts had come to naught as well. So far, she thought, allowing herself the tiniest sliver of optimism.

But, even if she were successful with Sam, a vague hope, would her rescue attempt come in time to save Jackie? Grace had a sudden vision of her daughter years from now, uneducated, waiting tables in some lowly dive, boozing, promiscuous, permanently trapped at the bottom of the economic ladder.

Such a vision hardly jibed with the false snapshot of her daughter that she had given Sam, the brilliant honor student, top of her class, on her way to Princeton, determined to become a doctor. A mother could be proud of that. She looked at Jackie and shook her head in despair.

"All I'm saying, Jackie," Grace said, forcing herself calm, reaching for logic, hoping it might penetrate her daughter's ignorance of the real world, "is that it's a deal that is both legally and financially stupid."

"I wish you would stop with all the name calling."

"You don't see it, do you?"

Jackie muttered an obvious curse under her breath, looking at her mother archly, with snarling contempt. "Mind if I ask a question, Mom?"

"That depends," Grace countered, fearful about what was coming.

"Where did you get those clothes?"

"So the best defense is an offense," Grace snapped, hoping to evade the question with her own defensive ploy.

"Something very weird is going on here," Jackie said, searching her mother's face. "You suddenly show up with all that expensive stuff and say you promised to donate it to charity. Sorry, Mom, it doesn't add up. Darryl says you probably had a shady source and intended to keep the money for yourself. And who is this mysterious Mr. Goodwin who called last week?"

"Hardly mysterious. Probably calling about some unpaid bill," Grace said, dismissing the reference to Sam's call. Above all, she was determined not to tell her daughter what she was doing. At this early stage of her relationship with Sam, the revelation of Jackie, the real Jackie, could spoil everything. And Jackie wasn't one to repress her curiosity.

"I'm not so sure about that, Mom," Jackie sneered. "You're into something that you don't want me to know about. Bet I have that right."

"Another Darryl deduction?"

"He's smart, Mom. He can figure out the truth of things."

"God help the truth."

"Its pretty obvious, Mom. Something stinks here. Doesn't it? Don't think you can hide it forever. You're up to something and you're keeping it a secret. We'll find out. No matter what, Darryl and I will find out."

The ominous threat frightened Grace. But she was determined not to show her daughter any anxiety.

"Darryl is on my case?"

"I told you, Darryl has a sixth sense about things."

"We'll see how brilliant you'll rate him when you get pulled over for speeding and are asked by some cop to see your registration. Or if you get into an accident and the guy whose car you bashed wants to see your insurance papers. We'll see how smart Darryl is at that point. And don't think I'm going to stand still on the other issue either. You're underage and he's vulnerable."

"I told you before, Mom, Darryl doesn't like threats," Jackie snapped. "I'd be very careful if I were you." A picture of Darryl's ugly knife surfaced in Grace's mind, but she tried to will it away.

"I'm not afraid of him, Jackie," she said, knowing it was bravado. She was scared, for Jackie as well as herself.

"You should be."

"There are rules, Jackie. Legalities. With all his macho posturing, he still can't escape them."

"You've played by the rules, Mom. Where did it get you?"

She had a point, Grace thought. From her daughter's perspective at that moment she probably did look like a loser. Yet, remembering her day with Sam and thinking about the prospects for tomorrow, she didn't feel like a loser.

"It's only over when it's over."

"Now isn't that profound, Mom," Jackie said, her sarcasm blatant. "I know you think I'm a stupid, immature idiot. But I'm gonna show you I can do it on my own, without your help. You'll see. It's about time I stopped depending on you for everything. And I'm sure Darryl will take care of things about the car. He's a lot smarter than you are."

"Smarter?" Grace paused, trying to assemble her thoughts and control her anger simultaneously. It crossed her mind that maybe the thing to do would be to call the police. "I think the man's a dangerous bigot who's heading for trouble and taking you with him. I hate to think of where that car might have come from. He's got you in some kind of a mental hammerlock and I've got to figure out a way to stop it, even if it means calling in the cops."

"If he was here, I don't think he'd appreciate that threat, Mom. You'd be in deep shit."

"You're already there, Jackie."

She looked at her mother, shook her head and offered a pitying stare. But to Grace she looked like a frightened waif, whistling in the cemetery. With a gesture of disgust, Jackie turned and headed for the door.

"I'm outta here."

"Where are you going?"

"I told you . . . outta here."

"To where?"

"I've got my own transportation now, Mommie dearest. I can move around when I need to. And I need to now."

She walked out and slammed the door. In a few moments Grace heard the cough of the yellow Honda's motor. It didn't sound very clean at all.

CHAPTER SIXTEEN

In the morning she awoke very early, put on her bathing suit and, over it, slacks and a T-shirt. She packed a change of clothes, put on her makeup, then slipped out of the apartment before Jackie was awake. She had brooded over the confrontation with her daughter the night before. It was very worrisome. She made an effort to tuck it into the back of her mind as she looked forward to her next meeting with Sam. Nothing must spoil that. Nothing.

Parked in front of the apartment was the little yellow Honda, quite cute really, but obviously old, and she was certain on further inspection that it was painted over. She looked inside, saw the wear of the years and tried to glimpse the odometer, which she couldn't see, although she was certain it had been moved back.

Last night, before she fell asleep, she had tried to imagine how it was possible that Jackie could claim ownership of the car based on the manner in which she had taken physical possession of it. Darryl was obviously exercising a sinister influence over her. He was scary and dangerous, but Grace knew there was no point in trying to talk Jackie out of her relationship with him. She was brainwashed. Protesting would only drive her closer to him, perhaps even out of the apartment. The prospect was frightening, and she suddenly felt weak with worry.

Maybe it was best to let this thing with the car play itself out. Although there was a risk in the process, it might illustrate to Jackie the truth about Darryl.

The hard reality, considering the wonderful snapshot she had created of Jackie for Sam Goodwin's benefit, depressed her. Not to mention the résumé she had created for herself, a tissue of lies, one false fact piled on another. How could she, if she were found out, possibly explain away such blatant, self-serving, outrageous lies? Worse, how could she explain the manner in which she had expressed them, so cool and smooth, with such absolute surety and confidence.

There was no point in dwelling on it, she decided. It was too late. The lies were stitched irrevocably into her false history. How could she justify them? She could charge that a mysterious force had inserted these ideas into her mind, that she had been merely the medium, an evil conduit. Hardly a logical excuse, she concluded, pushing such absurdities out of her thoughts. Her more immediate worry was getting the facts straight when they were needed again.

Stopping at McDonald's, she had an Egg McMuffin and a cup of coffee. It was a long way from her terrace meal with Sam Goodwin. She smiled at the memory, recalling the cold tang of the Dom Perignon on her tongue, the view of the white beach melding into the azure sea, Sam's eyes searching her face.

Lingering over the coffee, she also recalled yesterday's modeling experience. Was she replicating Anne for him, recreating in his imagination some sexual episode with her? The idea encouraged her. After all, she was exploring ways to replace Anne. So was he, for that matter. And she hadn't felt demeaned or cheapened or even insulted by participating in this fantasy of a reincarnated Anne. And it had excited him. She smiled at the memory. It was exciting and sexually stirring for her as well.

When she left McDonald's she headed for the supermarket and bought a package of large plastic garden bags. In the parking lot, she emptied her car of Anne's clothes and stuffed them into the bags. The process brought back the memory of Jackie's suspicions about the source of the clothes and her wild accusations about Grace's motives.

It angered her to believe that her own daughter could practically characterize her mother as a scheming, greedy thief. Yet Grace knew that she was partly to blame, keeping the real situation a secret. From

a phone booth she called the Salvation Army, where someone instructed her to bring the offering to a collection station in downtown
West Palm Beach. At this point, considering how she had bungled
the pickup at her own apartment, she was too embarrassed to call the
Jewish Welfare League.

A middle-aged lady at the collection station looked into the plastic
bags and nodded her head in gratitude.

"Bless you," she said. "We really appreciate these. This is exactly
the kind of clothing we need."

Grace smiled in acknowledgment and, in response to the woman's
request, gave her name and telephone number and was given a receipt.

"There's a place where you can fill in the value of the contribution
and get an income tax deduction."

"Thank you," Grace said, having no intention of claiming the deduction, as if that too would be a violation of her promise, a betrayal
of the private pact with Sam Goodwin and, of course, her own integrity. Besides, her income tax obligation at this moment was nil.
She tossed the receipt into a trash can, got into her car and headed
over the bridge to Palm Beach, then north on Ocean Drive to Sam's
house.

She was surprised when Sam himself opened the door before she
could ring the bell. Marilyn shot out of the door, but instead of
growling and bearing her teeth she came forward and licked Grace's
hand.

"Now there's a welcome for you," Sam said, chuckling. "I guess she
likes you after all."

"And I like her," Grace said, tickling Marilyn behind the ears.
"Where's . . ."

"Carmen? I gave her the day off. She was working too hard."

"With only one person to take care of?"

"All right, then," Sam said. "She was having an attitude problem."

"About me?"

"I didn't inquire," Sam said, leading her through the house to the
beachside door.

The wind was up along the beach, making the surf pound and
foam in angry bursts. To hear each other, they walked closer together
than they had yesterday. Marilyn bounded beside them.

"I had one of those eerie experiences last night," Sam said.
"Anne's voice awakened me. I thought I heard her call my name. I
woke up, then answered her. Of course, when I put my arm out to

her side of the bed there was nothing but empty space. It's happened before, but this time it took awhile for me to orient myself. I tell you, Grace, it was very real to me."

"Maybe there is something to this ghost business," Grace said.

"Do you believe in ghosts?"

Grace hadn't expected the question. But she considered it carefully.

"I don't think I do," she said tentatively.

"That means your mind isn't closed to the idea," Sam said.

"Maybe not," she said, wondering where he was going with this.

"Okay, suppose it is true. Anne's ghostly spirit, watching. Watching us right now, walking the beach side by side."

"And yesterday. Watching me trying on her clothes."

"You think that would bother her?" Sam asked.

"Do you?"

He shook his head.

"No. Actually, I think she would be delighted to see a lovely person like you wearing her clothes. You know that Anne was a very magnanimous person. You saw that yourself. Open and honest." He paused. "Like you."

"Me?" Grace said, her voice rising, as if in protest.

He nodded; then, in a surprise gesture, he took her hand, and she made no effort to pull away. They continued to walk in silence. Marilyn played tag with the breaking waves.

"I'm not what I seem," he said suddenly. She wondered if the ocean's din had garbled his speech.

"I don't understand."

She shot him a mock skeptical look.

"I'm not what I seem," he said. It was what she'd thought he'd said, and it confused her.

"You mean to me?" Grace asked.

"To you . . . and, when she was alive, to Anne."

Grace was puzzled by his assertion, especially since she was the one who had falsified her history, while his seemed an open book. It was impossible for her to believe that he was something other than he appeared to be.

From the evidence based on her own observation, he could not deny his wealth or the respect shown him by others, and especially the sincerity of his devotion to his late wife. As for the details of his inner life, she admitted that she was not clairvoyant, but he certainly appeared to be a decent, honest man. Certainly, like everyone he had problems specific to his situation. He was a businessman, which, by definition meant that he had to be shrewd, cunning, disciplined, perhaps somewhat ruthless, but not blatantly deceptive.

Was it inconceivable that he was not what he seemed? Because of her own culpability she pushed it out of her mind. It was a subject she chose not to pursue.

"Feel like a run," he shouted, pulling her along as they jogged on the water's edge for a short distance. It relieved her to know that he, too, was inclined to drop the subject.

Marilyn shot forward, then chased a sandpiper. A high wave broke and she scurried back. Sam slowed down to a walk. Grace felt her heart pounding in her rib cage.

"I'm not in great shape," Grace said breathlessly.

"That's debatable," Sam said, winking at her. He seemed mildly flirtatious, and she reacted with a smile and shrug.

"You are," Grace said, her breathing subsiding.

"Not bad for an old man, right?"

"There you go, fishing for compliments again," Grace said, chuckling.

"Just as long as you don't give me that you're-as-young-as-you-feel baloney."

"Well, aren't you?"

"Today I feel a lot younger than yesterday."

"That's an encouraging sign."

"Keep young company, stay young."

"You think I'm young? That's a laugh. Sometimes I think of myself as being over the hill."

"Which makes me over the mountain. Hell, I was over twenty-one when you were born. I could drive, drink and vote." She had given him her real age, perhaps concerned that he might take a peek at her driver's license.

"I'm catching up fast, Sam."

"When you're my age, I'll be eighty-nine. If I make it."

"You seem to be hung up on the subject, Sam."

"Maybe so. I guess I'm just resentful."

"About what?"

"Getting to this point, confronting my disappointments, knowing it might not get any better than it was."

For her this was a troubling attitude.

"Does this mean you're foreclosing on any future possibilities?"

She wondered if her remark was really as transparent as it sounded.

"'Grow old along with me, the best is yet to be,'" he snickered. "I remember that from school. I'm inclined to believe it's bullshit."

"I wouldn't bet on that. There might be lots of surprises still to come."

She was conscious of her own flirtatious reaction. He smiled and continued on their walk. When they reached the halfway point, they turned and headed back toward the house. Sam was silent for a long time, as if reflecting on something deep within his mind.

As they walked, he continued to hold her hand, squeezing it at times to acknowledge her. She assumed it meant that he was enjoying her company. She returned the squeeze, feeling much the same way.

At his customary swimming location, he stopped.

"Too rough for you?" he asked.

It was, but she refused to admit it, slipping off her slacks and T-shirt. He took her hand and they ran into the water. He released her only when they had to dive into a breaker. The agitated water was both scary and exciting. Suddenly a wave knocked her over and she was upended, went down, then fought her way to the surface. Suddenly, she felt his hard body against hers.

"It can get hairy," he shouted above the din of the waves.

"Not when I have my private lifeguard."

She let him hold her for a few moments, then they coasted in on a wave, Marilyn beside them. She noted that Marilyn kept a watchful eye over her.

"That was fun," she said, proud that she was able to keep up with him and had conquered her fear.

"Anne hated the water," Sam said.

"Everybody's different," she said. She wished she could be more profound.

Sam helped her up and, hand in hand, they walked toward the house.

As she had done yesterday, she went into Anne's bathroom, showered and changed, while Sam showered and dressed in his bathroom. It was odd, but in one short day it already seemed like a routine.

"Hungry?" Sam asked.

"Not really. I stopped at McDonald's. I got up early. I dropped yesterday's batch at the Salvation Army."

It seemed important to tell him that she was on the job, doing what she had set out to do.

"Great," Sam said. "Now I've got a job to do."

"And I'll start the day's work," she said.

Sam went downstairs and she entered Anne's closet. She had determined that it was essential to continue her work with Anne's clothes. She pressed the activating button and watched the racks pass by her in what seemed like an endless parade. It was hard to decide what clothes to dispose of next.

After awhile, she heard Sam call her name from the bedroom, and she came out of the closet. Beside him on a table was an opened bottle of Dom Perignon in an ice bucket and two fluted glasses.

"Now that's a real surprise, Sam," Grace said as he poured her a glassful, then filled his own. Against the sunlight in the room she saw the bubbles rise from the top of the glass. He handed her a glass and took his own, raising it.

"What should we drink to?" he asked.

She thought of saying "To Anne," but wondered whether she might be overdoing it. Hadn't they drunk to her yesterday?

"How about . . . let's not brood about the past or worry about the future," Sam said, "which leaves the present."

"Yes, I like that. To the present, then. This moment."

They clinked glasses and sipped. She couldn't believe how delicious it tasted. The bubbles tickled her nose. When she looked up at him, his eyes seemed to be scanning the room. He shook his head.

"There is so much of Anne here in this room," he sighed.

"Ghosts again?" she asked, more as a rhetorical question. Anne again, she sighed. She supposed there was no escape from her, not ever.

"I always felt . . . well . . . more like a guest in this room."

"A guest!" Grace exclaimed. "This is your bedroom. Once shared with Anne. Now yours. Surely you can't think of yourself as a guest here. How long did you live here?"

He grew thoughtful, as if he were calculating.

"Nineteen years. Yes, nineteen years. That's when we moved in. Before that we lived in Westchester, outside of New York City."

"How could you feel like a guest if you lived here for nineteen years? This is your home," Grace said, reluctantly accepting the fact that the present, which included her, would always be haunted by his past. For her part, she would be ready and willing to scuttle her past, her reality-based past.

She sipped again and, as he had done before, scanned the lovely bedroom. By her standards it was huge, spanning the entire rear of the large house. In comparison, her little bedroom seemed no bigger than the bed on its pedestal.

"Yes," he sighed. "My home."

"Home is where the heart is," Grace said.

They exchanged glances in silence for a long moment, then emptied their glasses. Sam poured two more.

"I enjoy your company, Grace."

"I'm glad, Sam. I enjoy yours."

He studied her, then shook his head.

"I hope you do, Grace."

"I wouldn't say it if I didn't mean it."

It surprised her that he needed such reassurance.

"I feel very comfortable around you, Sam," Grace said, reiterating her honest feeling.

"I enjoyed seeing you model Anne's clothes," Sam said. "You were very kind to do that."

"Kindness had nothing to do with it. It was fun, Sam. I felt like a little girl trying on Mommy's clothes." She hesitated for a moment. "I suppose I reminded you of Anne."

"Yes, you did." He paused. "In a way."

"In a way? How so? I'm sure she looked a lot better in them than I did."

"Now who's fishing for compliments?" He chuckled. "Of course she always looked great. But so do you."

"Different, maybe. Great is debatable."

"Yes," he acknowledged. "Different . . . and great."

She felt his eyes inspecting her.

"Yesterday," he said, "you didn't think I was being, you know . . . kinky. Asking you to do that?"

"We've been there, Sam. I did it because I wanted to do it. And, as I told you, I enjoyed it. It gave me great pleasure." She felt a hot blush rise to her face.

"Really?"

"That was the truth, Sam," Grace said, suddenly wary. Did her reply hint that she wasn't telling the truth in other matters?

Suddenly she grew silent, not knowing how to proceed. Considering all the lies she had fed him, she felt an increasing uneasiness. Did he think she was pandering to him? Blatantly ingratiating herself? She felt uncertain about her reactions, psychologically clumsy. She wished she had the intelligence and inner resources to be surer of herself, like Mrs. Burns.

He lifted his eyes and seemed to study her intently. Then he smiled.

"You looked great in her clothes, Grace," he said. Instinctively she knew what he was getting at.

"Thank you, kind sir. I'm flattered. And Anne's taste in clothes was wonderful."

"Yes, it was."

He upended his glass and poured another, refilling hers. Their eyes met. She felt the heat of their contact and knew what was coming next.

"Would it be imposing, Grace, if . . ."

"Model again?" She giggled, feeling the effects of the champagne.

"You don't think I'm a bit sick in the head about this?"

"Not at all. It was fun for me. When you think about it, it could be characterized as a tangible way to memorialize Anne."

"I suppose you have a point. You don't think it's an indulgence?"

She stood up. Then, in a gesture of mock decision-making, she tapped her teeth. If this was to be their common ground at the moment, she thought, so be it.

"Maybe you're being too analytical, Sam. It was an indulgence for me, too. What harm is there? Why not? What's your pleasure?"

"How about . . ." He paused for a moment, considering. "Something flowing, wispy."

"Flowing and wispy. Coming right up."

She ducked into the closet. Earlier she had noted a cinnamon-colored cocktail dress by Geoffrey Beane. Taking it off the rack, she came out of the closet, stood before him and pressed it to her body.

"What do you think?"

"Perfect," he said.

"Do you remember Anne wearing it?"

"Funny, but I was never able to remember what Anne had worn on a given occasion. But the dress does look vaguely familiar."

"Give me a few minutes. I need to accessorize it."

"Take your time."

She noted that his face was flushed. Little red circles had popped out on his cheekbones.

She went into the dressing room, searching through drawers filled with underthings. In one drawer she found, to her surprise, a number of suspenders and stockings, the kind she had often seen advertised as products from Frederick's of Hollywood. Eschewing panties, she put on the suspenders, attached the stockings, looked at herself in the mirror, declared herself provocative, then put on high heels and posed as if she were a model for *Playboy*, feeling her own heightened sexual tension. Did Anne do this? she wondered, feeling moist and hot.

She put on the dress, which was a hairsbreadth tighter than she would have purchased if it were her decision to make. But it suited this event admirably. Then she found appropriate cocktail jewelry, quickly made up her face and hair to fit, piling it up like a Gibson Girl, then surveyed herself in the mirror. She loved the way she looked. Would he think she was sexy? She hoped so. To heighten the effect, she removed her brassiere. Her nipples pressed against the material, erect with excitement and clearly visible.

"Go for it," she whispered, taking a last look at herself in the mirror. She was high from the champagne and knew it.

His face lit up with a broad, appreciative smile when he saw her. She walked with exaggerated, hip-swinging movements a number of times across the length of the room and back, so that the dress lifted with the breeze of her walk and her bare breasts bounced under the flimsy silk.

"Do you like it, Sam?"

"Very much."

She noted the outline of his erection in his pants. Imagining it, its size, shape and bulk, made her body react accordingly. He crossed his legs and bent over slightly to hide it."

"Why don't you take it as a gift? You look fantastic in it."

"We've been through that, Sam."

"I'm sure Anne wouldn't mind."

"It's me who would mind. It's just not appropriate and would make me uncomfortable."

She wondered if he appreciated her gesture, seeing it, hopefully, as a measure of her independence and integrity.

"Whatever you say," Sam said.

She again walked the length of the room, then back again.

"It's a pleasure to watch you, Grace."

"Would you like to see me in another?"

"Yes, please."

She moved toward him, but only to pick up her glass and drain it. Proffering her empty glass, he poured champagne to the brim and she carried it with her to the closet. Heated and flushed by the champagne, she felt a growing sexual excitement. She removed the silk dress, re-hung it on the rack and walked along the huge closet in suspenders and high heels, bare-breasted. She looked for something . . . she groped for the words . . . dashing, sexy and dangerous.

She found a slinky, long black gown with a low bodice and a high cut to the thigh. Givenchy, she noted, putting it on. Moving again to the dressing room, she studied herself in the large three-way mirror.

She was astonished at her transformation, marveling at how the gown molded to her body. It's low cut and bra infrastructure pushed up her breasts and made them seem larger. She felt wonderful, exciting. She removed her previous makeup and redid herself in more severe tones, without lipstick but with more eye shadow, parting her hair in the middle, hoping the outfit made her look like a woman of mystery, a seductress, which was exactly what she wanted to be. She giggled at her image in the mirror. She was drunk, deliciously drunk, devil-may-care drunk.

When she came out she saw him sitting in the chair, legs crossed. He had replaced the empty bottle of Dom Perignon with another and was starting to pour again. But when she came out and slinked across the room he stopped pouring and stared at her, mesmerized.

"Fantastic," he said.

"Thank you, dahling," she whispered throatily as she moved around the room, loving the feeling and his attention.

She stopped suddenly and posed, draping herself against the wall.

His face, like hers, was flushed, and his eyes glistened. She sensed that she was giving him pleasure and enjoyed the idea of it. It struck her suddenly that they could spend days like this, weeks and months. Her modeling Anne's endless wardrobe.

She wasn't much of a drinker and knew that the champagne had made her feel high and uninhibited. Although she loved the sensation, she worried that she might cross over some imaginary line and dampen his interest by appearing whorish and undignified. Was she moving too fast, becoming too brazen? This scene, her actions, was so far from anything she had ever experienced or fantasized before.

She was hot, turned on.

Still, despite her uncommon surge of lust, she held back from making that first crucial move, fearing the aftermath, revealing herself as wanton and without modesty. What came next was up to him, she decided, wishing it. *Come and get it,* she cried within herself, yearning for him to act.

Despite her body's hunger, her mind would not let her be careless.

This was all part of the orchestration, she told herself. She had to be, most of all, indispensable to his every need. A complete replacement for Anne. *Help me, Anne,* she pleaded within herself. *Make him want me.*

What she lacked in intellect or style she would compensate for in other ways, she vowed. She was open to learning Anne's ways. Above all, she did not want to suffer in comparison. She would be all things to this man, as Anne had been, a lively companion, a good friend, a passionate, uninhibited lover and a wife. *Give me that chance,* she begged Sam in her heart.

"More?" he asked, lifting the champagne bottle as she swaggered past him. He poured the amber liquid into her glass and handed it to her. Bending low to receive it, she felt the weight of her breasts against the material of the dress. She saw his eyes watching them and felt her nipples harden and react to his inspection.

Still he did not make any untoward move. Perhaps he was not giving himself permission, as if Anne really would care that he would be fornicating with another woman so soon after her death. She sensed he was holding back, wanting but waiting. For what?

It struck her that what was happening might be a re-creation of sex games he had played with Anne. *Am I doing it the way she would?* Grace wondered. Setting the spark, the way she did? Was there such a thing as a clothes fetish? She had heard of men being turned on by high-heel shoes or cross-dressing or kinky things like that. She hoped she had found the path to his libido. She was prepared to play whatever role was necessary.

They exchanged glances as she drank off the champagne in one gulp. She felt oddly empowered, as if it was necessary for her to seduce him now, before the moment passed, knowing it was her need as well. This was one bridge that had to be crossed and crossed now. An idea popped into her head.

"Just a sec," she said, ducking into the closet again. She removed the gown and searched through the closet, where she had seen the fur coats. Pulling a white ermine off the rack, she put it on. Underneath she wore only the suspenders, stockings and high heels. The feel of the coat on her body tingled her skin and covered her with goose bumps.

She went into the dressing room, found a lipstick and painted her aureoles. She had never done such a thing in her life. In fact, she had never experienced anything like what was happening to her now. It was like an internal earthquake, unstoppable.

"Did Anne do this?" she wondered as she pulled the collar of her coat up and walked out into the bedroom. She walked directly in front of him.

"Do you like this, Sam?" she asked. "Am I like her?"

He had been holding his champagne glass. Watching her, he slowly put it down on the table beside him. She noted that his hand shook and he spilled some of the champagne on the table's surface.

"Did she look like this?"

She opened the coat. Her body, she knew, simmered with lustful sensations. *So he's leaving the first move to me,* she thought.

"May I?" she asked.

He nodded his head, and she knelt before him and unzipped him, pulling his pants and shorts down to below his knees. He let her. Then she straddled him, letting herself gently down on his erect penis, then kissed him deeply on the mouth, her tongue caressing his.

"Was it like this with Anne?" she whispered, feeling her heartbeat accelerate as she swiveled her hips in a rotating motion. He did not answer.

"And this?" she said, increasing the tempo of her rotations, feeling her orgasm gathering strength deep inside her. Waves of pleasure exploded inside her.

"Oh, yes," he said repeatedly, indicating his own pleasure. Then his lips found hers.

She straddled limply over him for a long moment as they calmed. Slowly, her mind found its reason again and she was able to reflect on her actions.

She had never done anything with such compulsion in her life. It worried her that somehow she might have crossed the line, destroyed her credibility, blown any chance of a permanent relationship. Had she acted too soon, gone too far? And more to the point, did he believe that her pleasure was real?

They stayed together in a tight embrace until she lifted herself off him. He held her for a moment, then edged her forward so that he could kiss her again on the lips.

"Back in a minute," she said, going to the dressing room.

She looked at herself in the mirror, hardly recognizing her face, blotchy and flushed, the obvious result of excitement and passion. Then she washed and came back into the bedroom. He had drawn the blinds in such a way that the light in the room was muted, but not dark. He was lying in the big bed, obviously waiting for her return.

When she came into the room, he lifted the thin coverlet and beckoned her to join him.

She hesitated briefly, unsure, but knowing that there could be no turning back. Besides, she wanted to be in his embrace.

"I'm not Anne," she whispered as his arms folded around her.

"I know," he whispered.

CHAPTER SEVENTEEN

He sat in the chair of the bedroom patio, watching the rising sun spangle the water. She had left sometime in the night, probably just after he dozed off. They had made love repeatedly and he had reveled in it. He felt more charged with erotic lust and sexual endurance than he had ever felt before, even with those others he had coupled with. It made him doubt the ravages of age. Perhaps aging was a state of mind, he thought, knowing it was a fool's wish.

It was as if he had come to an oasis after a long journey in the desert. Never had this bed, this room, seen such passion. He felt transformed, renewed, and his sexual acrobatics apparently came as a surprise to Grace as well.

"You're like a man of twenty, Sam," Grace told him.

"You've inspired me," he had replied, but he was thinking beyond the sex, believing that this attraction was more than that, something mystical. Or was he romanticizing a perfectly natural event? He had, after all, emerged from months of physical deprivation and years of psychic hunger.

"Am I as good as Anne?" she had asked.

"I've told you. Different."

At that moment he knew that he must bring himself to offer the full truth of himself, that he could not go forward with Grace without her hearing his full confession, the complete revelation of his stunted life, the final reckoning of his endless chain of lies. His marriage, he knew, had been a compromise, however he had rationalized it. With death closing in, he had determined that he could not, would not, go through such a gauntlet again. It was too late for lies.

Such had been his silent vow as he sat beside Anne in her final moments. His regret had been too painful and profound. Never could he be less than scrupulously honest, less than forthright. No more lies, white or black. Only truth, pure, pristine, unblemished truth. The soul must be purged.

Nor did he dare believe that he had had the blind luck to find in Grace the whole woman he had looked for all his life. It was, of course, still too early to tell. He was mystified by his powerful attraction to her, especially coming so close on the heels of Anne's death, and when she was away from him, like now, he longed for her, craved her. Was it his vanity talking, his apparent rediscovery of his youthful libido, a kind of last hurrah? The boys in the locker room would call it pussy fever. Surely it was more than that.

To the structured world of accepted standards of propriety in which he lived, such an event as this so soon after Anne's death would be looked upon by his peers and certainly his children as a betrayal, a callous and disrespectful act, an insult to her memory.

It was too complex to understand, no less unravel. He had betrayed Anne years ago, had continued to betray her. Their marriage, if one dwelled on the sexual component, was one long betrayal, and yet he had adored and respected her as a friend, a companion and, in all aspects but one, a wife. He missed her and grieved for her. He had silently vowed at her deathbed that, in the future, there would be no more lies, no more dissimulation, whatever the circumstances there would be truth, only truth. He needed to believe that her death would have some meaning, some impact on his future. His vow had been his gesture of repentance.

"What you see is what you get," he had told Grace as they lay in the afterglow of their lovemaking, knowing she would be confused by the assertion. "What I say is the truth as I conceive and believe it. No more sham. No more lies. No more manipulation. No more playacting. These are the conditions."

He observed her puzzled look.

"The conditions of what?" Grace had asked. By then, in just a few short hours, their intimacy, at least in his mind, had accelerated to another dimension. She had lain crosswise, her head resting on his upper thighs.

"Of us," Sam said, stroking her hair. "If we're going to continue to be . . . lovers." He had difficulty expelling the word, fearful that it would signal a note of possession for which neither of them was quite prepared and, as yet, were unwilling to accept.

"Lovers?"

"It's my line in the sand," he emphasized, remembering all the years he had held back the truth of himself from Anne.

"Who can argue with that?" Grace said.

"Truth validates everything," he said, his fingers caressing her. "Nothing is complete without that."

She had nodded but remained silent.

"You must think I'm paranoid about this. Grace, it's a terrible thing, living with secrets. Believe me, I know."

He wasn't sure that she was getting the whole import of what he was telling her, but he was certain he was conveying what was most important to him. He had the sense that she was giving him breathing room, letting him dig deep down into himself.

"My life with Anne . . ." he began, pausing, feeling some psychic dike inside of him begin to give way.

"Yes," she said. He felt her stiffen, poised to listen.

"All in all, my life with Anne was a good life," he said, but did not go further. She waited. He continued to explore the tunnel inside of him. "But the truth of it was that we did not live as man and wife."

"You can't be serious," she said, raising herself on her elbow and looking into his eyes.

"I am," he replied.

"Then I was wrong about . . ."

"About that part, yes."

"I thought I was doing what Anne did," Grace said. "I thought that maybe I was imitating her."

"No," he said. "We were totally estranged in that way."

His hand moved over the nipple of her breast, which he caressed briefly, then dropped his hand to her genitals.

"She refused you?"

"Not exactly. She ceased and I desisted."

In the semidarkness, he saw her eyelids flutter. Then she stared upward at the ceiling, frowning.

"Was she ill in any way?"

"Not in a physical sense."

"You mean she was frigid."

"I assumed so."

"You never went to, you know, psychologists, professional people?"

"No. In fact we never discussed it. That part of our life simply disappeared."

"But how could it? For how long?"

"From the beginning. Almost."

"How did you live with it?"

"I . . . I found other women. Many other women."

Grace was stunned.

"And she never knew?"

"Never."

"Not even suspected?"

"I can't be sure of that. It simply was not part of our lives. It was a subject never discussed between us. I suppose you might say we lived like brother and sister."

"Did she think you couldn't do it, that you were impotent?"

As if to emphasize the point she kissed his penis briefly, then caressed him until he was hard again.

"You wouldn't know it from this angle," Grace said.

"She never explored the possibility. She just wasn't interested."

"Do you think she masturbated?"

"I doubt it. I certainly never saw her at it."

"And you?"

"Considering the frequency, I should be blind. That's what they used to tell young boys. Masturbation could make you blind."

She giggled at the explanation.

"You poor man," Grace said.

"I never allowed the deprivation to get in the way of our marriage."

"I always thought it was part of it."

"You never refused your husband?"

"Never. Not that he was exactly an athlete in that respect. I did what a married woman was supposed to do."

After this remark Grace fell into a long silence, while he reflected on his life with Anne. Never had he shared this revelation with anyone.

"I guess Anne didn't see it that way." Sam shrugged. He had long ago made peace with this part of her nature. At first, he remembered, he had been angry, disappointed, self-pitying. Didn't she know what it meant to be a man, to have this compelling biological need for sexual satisfaction? It tortured him, forced him into unnatural repression. He was not a priest, had not made a vow of chastity to some imagined God, who, if He did exist, would be revolted by the penance of distorting his creation. In the end, following the old adage that necessity was the mother of invention, he had concluded that his only choice was to seek satisfaction elsewhere.

But the burden of keeping Anne from the truth of himself, his real feelings, his sensual nature, his searching need for sexual experience, had been almost too great to bear. In the end he had accepted her frigidity as a kind of genetic fault. Hell, he had his fun outside the house, like eating out from time to time.

All his married life he was tortured with the possibility that this lack in Anne was really his fault, something in his aura or persona, some mysterious force that could not light the spark of her sexuality. Perhaps it was his own cowardice, his fear of confrontation that prevented a resolution of what might have been simply a physical or psychological problem of sexual dysfunction.

Or he might have backed away deliberately from any further exploration of this phenomenon for his own subconsciously nefarious reasons. Under his facade of respectability, his real agenda might be that of a satyr, a voluptuary, a sex addict who needed a varied menu of such activity.

Quite often in his life, he considered that he might be using Anne's indifference toward him sexually as an excuse for his own secret excess. He had even fantasized what it might be like if his secret life was exposed, if Anne knew he had betrayed her, was betraying her. He feared that the most, not only the embarrassment of discovery, not only the humiliation and acknowledgment of his own failure, but the devastation she would have felt about her inability to function as a complete wife, and how that would affect the good things between them.

But it meant living forever with a missing link, because he loved everything else about Anne, loved her surety and confidence and social skills, loved her good taste and the life she had made for him.

Suddenly it seemed necessary to, once and for all, let it out of himself, as if he needed the comfort of confession and he had discovered just the right moment and a willing ear. Even as he spoke, he wondered if he could ever fully explain or ever understand the complexity of his relationship with Anne. Indeed, his characterization of Anne and her attitude was filtered through his own perception. Her perceptions lay locked in her dead consciousness. Nevertheless, he felt it suddenly tremendously important that Grace hear his side of it.

Grace had remained silent until he had emptied himself. Then she sucked in a deep breath and shook her head.

"I don't know what to say," she said.

"I suppose I've taken you by surprise."

"You're right about that, Sam. It's a little scary."

"Scary? I hadn't realized I was frightening you."

"Not frightening exactly. It's the idea that what you just told me about your relationship with Anne is so different than I had imagined. I'd never have guessed."

"Nor would anyone else," he agreed. "She was a fabulous wife in every other respect."

"Except where it counted most."

"She just wasn't aware of how important it was to me."

"Why didn't you explain it to her?"

"I decided that it would only have made it worse, heightened the trauma. Maybe I didn't want to see it as an obligation on her part, or, as you suggested, a kind of duty. Did you enjoy your so-called duty, Grace?"

He watched her grow thoughtful for a long moment.

"I didn't think about it. I just did it. I figured it was part of the game. Was it fun? Sometimes."

Sam nodded.

"Well, it wasn't part of the game as far as Anne was concerned. That's why the other way, me catting around, was a lot easier. I gambled that I could get away with it."

"And you did."

"I wish I could understand why she was like that. She apparently didn't seem to want to know or care. Maybe the sparks went out of it or the chemistry spoiled or the mysterious reactors that turn on sexual energy went blank. I don't know the answer. I wish I did. All I'm saying is that it changed the entire pattern of my life. I married to be true, honest and faithful. Till death do us part. That may sound like a naive concept, but I believed it at the time and I swore allegiance to it. No need for that now."

"I'd say you kept your word, Sam," Grace said. "Sounds like one big guilt trip to me."

"You think so?"

"I mean this need to tell your story now. It's so Catholic." She chuckled. "And this." She kissed the head of his penis. "It salutes your confession." She giggled for a moment, then continued her ministrations. Stopping, she looked up at him. "Poor Anne. Look at this wonder. Look what she missed."

"And what I missed," he said, feeling the full pleasure of it.

She started again, then stopped and inspected him.

"It's like a pillar of ivory. And a perfect fit."

He smiled at the reference.

"So I've noticed."

Gently, he moved her upward and kissed her deeply. He was silent for a long moment.

"What was your marriage like?"

"You mean sexually?"

"Yes."

She grew thoughtful.

"Not like yours," she said. "He was not deprived. I was available. I let him use me until it sort of petered out."

She giggled.

"And you were faithful?"

"Damned right," she said. He sensed her pride in that. "I was hit on by strange men more than once, but I felt uncomfortable about . . . affairs. Oh, I thought about it. I might have even imagined it. But I didn't do it."

"Because you were afraid to be discovered?"

"Yes, that, too. But the truth is . . . I didn't want to feel . . . well, disloyal."

"As I was?"

"I didn't mean to compare. I'm just telling you how I felt about it. I'm a woman, which makes me different from you."

"Do you think men and women are that different? I mean in the way they perceive things, the way they think and feel?"

"Totally. I can only judge by me. To tell you the truth, I don't think I understand men, men in general." She chuckled and brushed her hand against his cheek. "I've never been very successful in knowing men. My experience hasn't exactly been wide-ranging."

"Do you think you can understand me?"

"I'll try. But you do represent a hefty challenge."

"Why hefty?"

She seemed to hesitate. Then she reached out and gently grasped his erection.

"By your own admission, you put a lot of stock in this guy's happiness."

He laughed. "You've got a point."

"No, you have."

Now they both laughed. Her sense of humor had emerged and he loved it, loved this play between them.

"It's a measure of my manliness."

"I'd say . . ." She used her fingers as a yardstick. "A foot long."

"Thanks for the compliment."

"I'm only estimating what it seems like to me."

"Then let's leave it at that."

"Why leave it at all?"

She bent down and kissed it. Again, he eased her up and kissed her on the lips. Then she nestled her head in the crook of his arm.

"Do you think I'm exaggerating its importance?"

"I don't know. I'm learning. I've never met a man like you. As I told you, my experience of men is limited."

"Were you a virgin when you married?"

"No. We did it before we were married. It was the first time for me."

"Was it . . . was it satisfactory?"

"It was okay, I guess. I can't say it wasn't enjoyable. I suppose I loved him. And I felt good about letting him be the first."

"Did you have any relationships after you separated?"

"I see you're getting personal, Sam."

"Sexy talk turns me on."

She reached down and caressed him there.

"See," he said.

"It never seems to rest."

"Not with you, it doesn't. If it did, I'd stoke myself with Viagra."

"You're not a candidate."

"Not yet."

She was silent for a long time. He hoped she wasn't thinking about their age difference.

"So tell me about these others, after you separated."

She sighed and patted his stomach.

"There was Alfred. He was four years younger than me. Very pretty. Very stupid. Very boring. It lasted a week. He left me. End of story."

She told him about her brief experience with her dentist.

"He had a strange definition of fillings," she said, giggling, obviously enjoying the byplay. He, too, seemed to enjoy the humor.

"That's it?"

"I told you. My experience is limited."

"You could have fooled me."

"With you, I guess I'm doing what comes naturally. I can't believe this is me. I'm finding I can't get enough of you."

He moved parallel to her and she inserted his penis.

"Yes," Sam said, "A perfect fit. Made to order."

He saw her in the half-light, beside him, her head back, her hair flowing beside her, her eyes glistening. She was smiling, a happy, contented smile.

"All I'll require," he whispered "is doing this daily; that means, according to my calculations, five thousand times a year."

"How did you come up with that figure?"

"I'm sixty-four. I'm looking for fifteen active years, give or take . . . if I'm lucky."

"If today is any indication, you're moving ahead of the curve," she said.

"I'm making allowance for bad days," he said. "If all goes well, it will average out."

They were silent for awhile. He felt her muscles pulsating around his erection.

"It's never been like this, Grace," he whispered. "Never."

"Never?" she asked. "Not even with those others?"

"Never. Not with them. Or anyone. And you?" he asked. "Has it ever . . ."

"Been this good?"

"That is the question. Yes."

"Would you believe me?"

"Absolutely," he said. "Always."

"Never, never, never," she said, moving her pelvis in a circular motion, as if to emphasize the point. "Am I going too fast?"

"Yes," he said. She stopped her movements.

"Is it me, Sam? I mean, are you imagining I'm Anne, that you're doing this to Anne?"

"No. I'm not imagining doing this with Anne. I'm doing this with Grace."

"What are you doing to Grace, Sam?" she asked, her breath coming faster. He knew she was climbing her way to a charged orgasm. She was definitely not Anne.

"Making love to Grace," Sam whispered. She started to move her pelvis again.

"Say it dirty, Sam."

"Fucking you, Grace."

"Fuck me, Sam." Her words seemed to signal that he join her movements, which he did.

"It's going to happen, Sam," she purred.

"Then let it happen."

"Is it happening for you, too?"

"Yes. For me, too."

He felt her letting go, moaning with pleasure. Then he felt his own come, the joyful spasms. She seemed to rear up, pummeled by some inner waves. After awhile they both started to cool, remaining locked together. She seemed to doze.

He closed his eyes, but he did not sleep. He was wondering how and why this had happened. Where was this energy coming from? How did it begin? Was it really the clothes, her wearing Anne's clothes that had triggered this response in both of them? How wonderful and exciting it was when she walked across the room modeling them for him.

And then, when she had taken off the ermine coat . . . My God. What an explosion of sexual energy. It was as if she knew exactly what he needed, the rush, the explosive effect, the pleasure. But the thing that made it special was what she herself was obviously feeling, the honesty of her own pleasure, their mutuality. All the money in the world couldn't buy that feedback. And no actress could invent her reactions, the way she came, shivery, abandoned, appreciative, like some great earth mother opening joyously to receive him.

He began to feel drowsy and slept. When he opened his eyes again the sun had fallen in the sky. It had become dusk, an orange dusk. She was sleeping quietly beside him. He leaned over and kissed her deeply again on the lips.

She awakened, smiled and returned his kiss.

"Do you feel good, Sam?"

"Yes, darling, very good."

"Who am I, Sam?" she asked.

"Grace," he replied.

He reached for her hand. Their fingers locked. It was a day never to be forgotten and he hoped that he would not let a single detail of it fade from his memory.

CHAPTER EIGHTEEN

It was beyond anything she could have imagined. Sam Goodwin had become the dominant force in her life, an all-encompassing, overwhelming presence. She moved through time and space giddy with erotic energy, carried along in a whirlpool of excitement that defied either definition or analysis. She dared not believe that her goal was in sight, but events were taking on a life of their own and heading in the right direction.

Her life with Sam, after an upsetting incident with Carmen, grew into a comfortable daily pattern of easy companionship spiced with a continuing menu of sexual excitement.

Carmen had, a few days after their first memorable experience together, discovered them in bed in, as the lawyers say, *flagrante delecto*. They were too involved in themselves to notice her observing them until she had fully absorbed the situation and had left the room and slammed the door behind her.

Disturbed by her action, Sam had put on his robe and hurried downstairs to talk with her. Grace put on one of Anne's silk robes and listened in the upstairs corridor. She heard every word of the unpleasant encounter.

"This is none of your business, Carmen," Sam told her.

"She a devil, this woman. She make you crazy."

"I don't appreciate that comment, Carmen. This has nothing at all to do with you."

"You men stupid and blind. She after your money, mister."

"You're pushing it, lady."

"I no care. I loved Madame. She still warm in her grave, and look what you do. Have you no shame, no feeling in your heart for Madame?"

"This has nothing to do with Madame."

"I feel her anger in myself. Mister, I think sometimes this house will burn in hell because of what you do to her."

"I've done nothing to her. You know I loved her."

"You men, you think only with your *cojones*. You love only your *cojones*. She love only your money."

"How can I ignore what you've just said, Carmen? How long have you worked here . . . fifteen years? Why are you doing this?"

"I not do nothing. I see with my eyes. This whore in your bed bring you nothing but pain."

Grace felt the rage rise in her gut. Disgusted and insulted, she was tempted to go down and join the confrontation, say her piece. Above all she resented Carmen putting this idea into his head.

"I'm sorry for your attitude, Carmen," Sam said. She caught the sadness and resignation in his voice. "But you leave me no choice. You have two hours to leave here. I'll write a check for six months' pay. I'm really sorry about this, but you've overstepped the line."

"I no need two hours," Carmen cried. Sometime later she heard the front door slam.

When Sam came back to the bedroom his face was ashen. He looked at Grace and shook his head.

"I'm sure you heard that, Grace."

Grace nodded.

"Yes, I did. I was furious. I'm better now."

"I hope you don't take it to heart," Sam muttered.

"She was very devoted to Anne," Grace said, watching his face, wondering if any permanent damage had been done. "From her vantage I guess that's the way she sees me, a whore with an eye on your money."

He seemed to reflect on her words for a moment but did not pursue it.

"I'm sorry you had to hear that."

He moved toward her and they embraced. After awhile they disengaged and moved out to the patio, where they stood by the railing and watched the sun spangle on the water while both of them contemplated the situation.

The logic of Carmen's words were underlined in Grace's mind. Perhaps at heart she was the whore of Carmen's representation. She could not deny, not to herself, that she had come for exactly that purpose, to benefit from Sam's money. There was no escaping the truth of Carmen's assertion. The fact that she had thrown herself wholeheartedly into the effort did not negate the truth of it. From the very beginning Carmen suspected her motives.

"She was upset," Grace said. "I can understand that."

"She had to go," Sam murmured.

"Perhaps she felt it was too soon after . . . she had a point."

"It's my life. Our lives. Time doesn't stand still, especially for a man of my age. Besides, you know how I felt about Anne. I did not betray her. You mustn't let it worry you. It's not the first time in my life that I've fired people."

"I've never been at that end of the stick," Grace sighed. Her candor surprised her. It was not part of her contrived persona.

"Well, I have," he said. "And I did what I had to do." He averted his eyes. "She crossed the line, insulted you, made you out to be something you're not."

"Can you be so certain of that, Sam?" Grace said, wondering why she had said such a thing. She had deliberately endangered her project. Was this to be another thing in her life that she screwed up? But his reaction relieved her.

"I pride myself on my judgment about people."

He turned to her, and she felt the piercing intensity of his gaze. The bright light made the color of his eyes seem a deeper blue.

"Besides, we didn't need her negativity around us," Sam said. He was silent for a long moment. "Do you think I was too harsh?"

She hadn't expected the question, which made her confront her hypocrisy. Of course Carmen had to go. She would have gummed things up for sure. *Be real, Grace,* she admonished herself. *Keep your eye on the ball. Remember Mrs. Burns's caveat. Ring around your finger.*

Nevertheless it was troubling, a clarion call of things to come. But then, this was all new territory to her. She must face the cold facts. If, by some miracle, this relationship continued, she would be known forever as the woman who seduced Sam Goodwin before his wife's body was cold. She had her own justification. She, too, was in a race against time. Financial ruin loomed just over the horizon. She had no income and a daughter who had to be extracted from an untenable situation. She had narrowed her escape route down to one path, the one that led to Sam Goodwin.

"Wipe this little incident out of your mind," Sam said.

"You, too," Grace replied, worried suddenly about a new terror, debilitating guilt. At this point, she knew, guilt was the enemy; guilt could trivialize what was happening between them.

"If it's all right with you, Grace, we don't even have to expose ourselves to the viciousness of others. With Carmen gone I'll hire a complete stranger. What happens here is nobody's business but our own."

"We can't hide forever, Sam," Grace protested mildly, but mostly for form's sake. Sam was right. There was no point in complicating matters by exposure. The more time that passed, the less people would take notice.

"As far as anyone knows, you come here to dispose of Anne's wardrobe."

"Among other things," Grace said, winking deliberately, putting a playful spin on the issue.

"The important thing, Grace, is that, whatever others might say or think, we know the truth of it, the truth of ourselves."

She nodded agreement, eschewing words. In his mind, truth was an absolute, a condition of their relationship. It frightened her to contemplate. That was something else that had to be pushed from her mind.

On balance, she decided, returning to cold calculation, the idea of staying out of sight favored her ultimate goal. It would isolate them, keep him away from the competition and reserve him for herself.

She smiled and caressed his cheek. She detected in herself a sense of growing possessiveness, instantly recognizing the dangers and pitfalls of such an emotion.

"Anne would understand," he whispered, more to himself than to her. He looked out of the window, as if he were searching for Anne's reassurance somewhere out in the horizon, beyond the sea. It allowed her time to consider her own uncertainty. Was this "arrangement" for him anything more than a passing erotic episode, a bridge of pleasure across the waters of mourning and loss, grief-chasing medicine, a temporary intermission to give him time to pick up the threads of a new life?

After a few moments he shook himself out of his sudden reverie and kissed her deeply on the lips. Despite her uncertainty, she returned his ardor and they made love. She felt no hint of grief or guilt in his performance.

CHAPTER NINETEEN

When she returned the next day she found a new housekeeper already installed.

For the past month she had lived in a kind of cocoon of pure pleasure, residing in another dimension of reality, as if her spirit had entered a new body and was living a separate life from the one she had always known. She was, in fact, reinventing herself, deliberately, with glorious abandon.

The lies that spewed out of her imagination were like a fecund plant, growing like the great beanstalk in the fairy tale, tendrils popping before her eyes. She was deliberately creating a new person, complete with a new identity and history, solely for Sam's consumption and approval and, above all, for her own selfish benefit. She was convinced that the real facts of her life, the boring truth and unexciting emptiness of it, the recounting of her failures, would cause her immediate expulsion from serious consideration for a lifetime commitment.

As the details of her false history escalated, she forced herself in self-protection to burn the facts into her memory. Sam was too relentlessly curious about her for her to get away with evasions and incomplete facts. And, of course, she needed to keep the story logical, factual and accurate.

"Why so many questions?" she would ask periodically, when she felt her imagination tire. They had this great luxury of time between them, lying in bed, their bodies cooling from the profound energy of their lovemaking, alert to each other. They were the only human beings in the center of their circumscribed universe.

"I need to learn you," he would respond.

Learn me? Considering the false facts she was bombarding him with, she could not imagine his ever *learning* her.

"But you know me, Sam," she would reply.

As for the unspoken truth, the nonfactual reality, there was no way her body could lie to him. She was not faking it. She hoped that was obvious to him. And truthful. Her explosive responses were genuine and their mutuality beyond argument. Certainly, after this first month of pure rapture, there were no sexual secrets between them. There was not a mark on his body that she did not know. Nor could there be one on hers that he had not confronted in his own exploration.

She knew instinctively that the sexual aspect of their lives could never be the deciding factor for him, as it hadn't been the deciding factor in his relationship with Anne. She clung tenaciously and impatiently to the idea that originally had motivated her, to be legitimized in marriage. It had from the beginning been her ultimate goal. She vowed never to lose sight of it, despite all other temptations that might waylay her.

Ring around your finger, dummy. The words reverberated in her mind. She was not, she believed in her heart, constituted to be a kept woman, however financially secure it made her life.

Despite the glorious time she was spending with Sam, she could not evade the facts of her finances. Unfortunately, the rosy possibility that Mrs. Burns had painted made no allowances for time or money.

Her money was running out, and among her many anxieties on that score was that Jackie might buckle under the pressure of her newly acquired expenses, meaning that she might drop out of school or otherwise blunt her chances for a better future. If Grace's gamble didn't work out—and it was a long shot—Jackie's future would be doomed. Not to mention her own. She had invested all of her hopes in this enterprise.

Yet she dreaded the possibility that he might offer her money. However proffered, she knew she would, as a matter of both dignity and tactics, have to refuse. The slightest show of desperation, she calculated, would be fatal.

Above all she needed Sam's respect, and to avoid being tarred with the brush of Carmen's definition of her character and motives. Besides, she had portrayed herself as financially secure. Would she accept a gift? No; that, too, would have to be rejected. In fact, she had decided irrevocably that anything that hinted of an exchange of value for sexual favors had to be rejected. The stakes were too high for compromise.

She liked to think that she was acting in a way true to her Catholic roots, with its rigid morality. But, on reflection, that hardly held water. She felt no guilt on the erotic front, not in the slightest, no sense of sin or soiling. She loved that part of it, hungered for it without any hint of second thoughts or conscience.

What bothered her most was the lying, the proliferation of false testimony. She was not by nature and upbringing a liar.

On the other hand, she found that she could disregard the anguish over her lying by defining it as simply a means to an end. This, too, was a paradox, since the end could be dangerously compromised by revelation. The fact was that she had gone too far to retreat, and to worry about being exposed would only inhibit her budding relationship with Sam.

Day after day the lies continued, the soft, intimate cadence of her whispering voice, spinning its frail web of deception with relentless and, to her, surprising creativity and eloquence. Even when she told the truth about her history, it began to seem like a lie.

"What were your parents like, Grace?"

"Loving, involved and interested in my life."

"What did they do?"

She had forgotten. Anxiously, she searched her mind for what she had told him earlier.

"Oh, yes," Sam said, "You told me. Your dad was an engineer and your mother taught piano."

"You have a good memory, Sam," she said, relieved. She needed to be more alert, she told herself.

"You must be musical, then."

"Oh, yes."

"The classics, I suppose. Brahms, Chopin, Beethoven."

"All of the above."

"How old were you when your mother died?"

"Mom was in her late seventies."

"Which made you a kind of late baby."

His drive for information was maddening.

"Yes."

"What they used to call a change-of-life baby."

"They wanted children badly."

"So you're an only child."

"Yes, I am."

"I'm one myself. Unfortunately, I became the object of my parents' possession. It was stifling. It was important to get away."

She had hoped that such an intimate insight might set him off on his own path and sidetrack his curiosity about her. It didn't. Nevertheless, she was alert to any opening that might get him talking about himself and short-circuit her having to continue her inventions.

"Did you enjoy working in Washington?"

In the brief silence that followed she had to jog her memory. Yes, she had said that. Hadn't they discussed that earlier?

"Yes. I loved it. I worked for a senator."

"Did you? Which one?"

For a moment she was stumped. She could barely remember a name from that long ago. How old would she have been? Twenty-two, twenty-three. Then a name popped into her mind, another gift of fate.

"Kennedy. I worked for Kennedy. I was pretty low on the totem pole."

"He's still there. What staying power!" He paused, became reflective. "Anne was a great fan of the Kennedys. They were a bit too liberal for me. I'm more of a centrist."

"So am I," Grace said, hoping that he would veer off the subject. She was way out of her depth.

"We have gone a bit too far to the right, but we do have a way of adjusting. Don't you think so?"

"Yes, I do. That's what makes our country so great."

"I agree," he said. "But we do have to stay ahead of the game in every area. Do you realize that in my lifetime the population of America has doubled?"

"It's very troubling, Sam."

"In your children's lifetime it will double again. Can you imagine how America will fare with a population of half a billion? And a billion in your grandchildren's lifetime."

"It is staggering."

"Anne and I had some lively political discussions. She was very opinionated." He chuckled. "I liked that."

In that area, she knew she would suffer by comparison. The fact was that she didn't know enough to have firm opinions. She wished he would change the subject.

"Is Washington where you met your ex?"

It had been his own conclusion and she did not resist, hoping it would channel his thoughts away from any political discussions. Quickly, she reviewed the time frame.

"Yes," she said.

"What was he doing?"

"He was with a law firm, just starting out."

"How did you meet?"

"A blind date."

It seemed innocuous and vague enough, and gave her an opening to ask him a similar question.

"And you, Sam? Where did you meet Anne?"

"Anne and I met at a dance in Wellesley. I had this friend Carl who was on the prowl for wealthy young ladies. He dragged me up there one weekend and fixed me up with his girlfriend's roommate, who was Anne."

Cutting too close to the bone, his revelation about seeking a rich girl aroused her curiosity and prompted her to want to further her exploration.

"Were you looking for a rich girl?"

"Among other things. I certainly didn't rule it out. Wellesley was pretty toney for me, a kid from Brooklyn College without a dime."

"Was Anne rich?"

"I guess by the standards of the time. Her father was a stockbroker. They lived in Manhattan in a huge apartment on the East Side. Family came to Palm Beach for the winter." He grew wistful. "They were real white bread WASPs. I was the Jewboy from Brooklyn."

"Anne wasn't Jewish?"

"She converted, went through the whole *megillah, mikvah* and all. She became more Jewish than me. Her family didn't speak to us for ten years. By then I had made big bucks. Amazing how much difference money makes. Suddenly, I was acceptable. Just barely, but acceptable. I have to say, Anne was great about all that. She thought her family were bigoted assholes, which they were."

Grace wondered if she would be subjected to conversion if she married Sam, not that it mattered. Ring around the finger. Above all else.

"What's a mick . . . mick something?"

"*Mikvah*. Rabbis put the lady in a pool, supposed to wash away their gentileness. Something like that. My Orthodox grandparents were still alive then. Anne insisted on doing it out of respect for them. Frankly, I didn't much care either way. But, I must say, Anne did like the idea of being Jewish, daughter of an ancient people, an underdog and a minority. My son was *bar mitzvahed* and my daughter was *bat mitzvahed*. Not that it made much difference in their lives."

Grace had noted that he hadn't talked much about his children, and what he had said indicated disappointment about how they had turned out. Of course she wanted to know more about them, but he did not seem to want to continue on that path.

"Considering the gap between you, it's amazing how well things turned out," Grace prodded. She wasn't referring to the sexual gap and Sam understood. Since the gap between her and Sam was at least as wide, probably wider, she needed to know how it had been bridged.

"We came from different worlds. Anne was the product of American ancestor-worshippers, of people who came over on one of the first waves, way back in the seventeen hundreds. Her mother was DAR and her father was Society of Cincinnatus, a descendent of a Revolutionary War officer. They considered themselves the American aristocracy, and they had imbued Anne with all the attributes of that class. It used to be called breeding. Anne knew all the little rituals of the class, the way they spoke and thought and acted, the way they entertained, their confident coolness and sense of superiority. Oh, they were bigots. Catholics were way down on the social scale and Jews were below that. And what was I, a hustling Jew from Brooklyn who fit all the stereotypes. I was a natural at business. Didn't matter what kind. I could squeeze a buck from a stone. But what I didn't have was Anne's sense of taste and class with a capital *K*. What good was money if you didn't have that? Anne taught me how to be perceived as someone with class. Hell, just look at the possessions in this house, the antiques, the paintings, the look of old money. It's a genuine look, not phony, because Anne was genuine, the real thing. She taught me how to act, how to look, how to live."

It seemed so strange and incongruous for Grace to be lying there naked, intimately entwined with this man, while listening to this relentless drumbeat of praise for the lost wife, perfect Anne. Anne the classic mate. Anne the wonderful. She snickered to herself, taking refuge in the one place where she, Grace, dominated. Anne the unfuckable!

Except for that single aspect, it was impossible for Grace to think of herself in the running to replace such an object of awesome praise. Certainly, she, the daughter of a barber, badly educated, at the bottom of the economic ladder, with a loser's past and a child who was slipping into the netherworld of white trash, could not possibly aspire to be the mate of this man who had experienced the instruction of an American aristocrat. She wanted to scream out her true reaction to his litany of admiration, but, of course, she held back, knowing that she still had one golden pointed arrow in her quiver that could not be attributed to Anne.

She kissed him on the lips, then disengaged and kissed her way downward from his chest to penis, which rose to the occasion. Her lips teased him as they pecked along the shaft and below, pausing to whisper, "Did she ever do this?"

"Never."

"Or this?"

"Never."

She felt him tense with pleasure as she ministered to him, her hands busy elsewhere, searching for his most vulnerable points of pleasure, feeling the sense of sympathetic joy.

"Did she ever say how wonderful and beautiful and manly and strong and hard you are?"

"Never," he gasped.

On another level, it was impossible to believe that she was doing this, competing in this way with the perfect Anne, the dead Anne, who had not been even remotely perfect in this one regard. Grace herself was not a woman of sexual experience, and everything that she was doing came from some weird instinct buried deep in the female psyche.

"Is this good?" she asked, knowing the answer but wanting to hear it spoken.

"God, yes."

"The best, the very best?"

"Absolutely."

She stopped for a moment and looked up at him.

"I want to taste you, Sam. Is that okay?"

He hesitated, then nodded. She had never done this and wanted him to know, wanted it to be remembered as something that had never happened between him and the perfect Anne, the neutered Anne.

She bent over him again and felt him tense, then explode in her mouth.

Later, when they had cooled and she lay in the crook of his arm, she felt oddly victorious and was certain that she had made her point. It had also brought his focus back to her, and the questions began again.

"When you were married, Grace . . . did you have secrets from your ex?"

In the context of the moment the question was worrisome, as if she had overplayed her hand in exhibiting what might have seemed to him too much sexual expertise.

"Not like yours, Sam." Another absolute truth.

"Odd, isn't it, that I should feel guilt about it only after she's gone?"

"Why torture yourself, Sam? It's over."

"The memory isn't over."

"Then maybe you should have told her. Confessed."

"I was a coward. When she was alive I was afraid to risk telling her, and when she was dying I didn't want to add to her pain."

It occurred to Grace that maybe her little exhibition of sexual prowess had been counterproductive after all. Somehow it had recalled his deception.

"Do you believe your husband was faithful?" he asked suddenly, after a long pause.

"How can one be sure? Like Anne, though, he didn't show much interest in that area." A half-lie, she decided. Jason's indifference had come later.

"I admire your self-discipline, Grace."

"It wasn't discipline, Sam. I didn't care."

"Not care?"

"Frankly, I was as bored as Jason when it came to that." She turned upward to look at him, then kissed his cheek. "Not until you came along, Sam."

She immediately regretted the comment, although that was another truth. She could tell by his facial expression that he might have doubted the assertion and she let it pass. Naive older men, she supposed, could be vulnerable to wishful thinking and might accept such an explanation, deluding themselves. Not Sam, she decided. Millicent Farmer would have kept up a drumbeat of praise for her unfortunate dupe.

"I hope you believe me, Sam," she said, watching his face.

"Why shouldn't I?"

"It sounds so . . . phony," she sighed, mimicking herself. "'Not until you came along, Sam.'"

"Some things you can't lie about."

"Women fake it all the time," Grace muttered. "You men are such ninnies."

"I told you, I'm a good judge of people. And I don't think you're a very good actress."

"Well, you're wrong," she said, displaying a childish pout. "I *am* faking it."

"Well, I'm not." He chuckled.

"That's pretty obvious."

Her hand felt his penis harden again.

"You can't fake that. No way."

Suddenly he reached out, brought her face to his and kissed her hard on the lips, their tongues intertwining. When they had disengaged he said, "There's more to this than meets the eye."

For a moment she was confused. Had he discovered the truth?

"Yes, there is," she agreed. She had, after all, the advantage of knowing the truth about herself. For a while they slid into silence.

"What was your husband's name, Grace?"

Oh, God, she thought, digging into her memory. Had she lied about his name? She couldn't remember.

"Martin," she replied, unable to bring herself to acknowledge Jason as a real person, further distancing herself from the truth of her past.

"And you never had a clue? You know, about his being gay."

"Not a clue."

Again she was entering territory that was unfamiliar.

"If you're not comfortable talking about it, we could drop it."

How could she be comfortable? she thought. Creating another person out of whole cloth was an uncomfortable process. Yet she feared dismissing it out of hand.

"Were you devastated?" he asked.

"How would you react?"

"Not well, I think."

She wondered if she had gone too far out on a limb. But on reflec-

tion she decided that it did have a certain logic to it. If she had said
that her husband had left her for another woman, which was equally
untrue, it might have diminished her in his eyes, marking her as a
woman who could not hold her man, undesirable and boring.

Above all, she had to protect this image of herself as desirable, intelligent, educated and cultured. She had never considered herself
to have any of these attributes, although she was beginning to suspect that she had not done herself justice about her intelligence.
How, then, could she have developed such cunning?

His reactions to her fictive creations, she was discovering, were beginning to give her an outline of how he wanted her to be, as if she
were connecting numbers in a child's drawing and watching a recog-
nizable shape emerge. It was, she realized, up to her to place the
numbers in the proper position. She was beginning to realize that his
questions were equally informative about him as her answers were
about herself.

These conversations, recalled in bits and pieces, stuck in her memory as she contemplated what was happening between them. As
much as she tried, she could not keep herself from assessing her
progress. Had she engaged his interest beyond the sexual component of their relationship? Was he beginning to consider her as a
marriage prospect? Or was she merely a sex object, a roaring good
fuck who he would toss aside as soon as he grew tired of her? Did he
suspect her real motives, her subterfuge? Was he buying her lies?

She tried, of course, to strip such an assessment of all emotion, discounting her own feelings toward him, fearing that her own needs
and desires might inhibit her progress toward her ultimate goal. In
the process she was discovering strange things, about herself, depths
to her inner psyche she had never noticed: her explosive sexuality,
her calculation, her cunning, her imagination and resourcefulness,
her singleness of purpose.

It was particularly strange, since she had never considered herself
anything but mediocre, somewhere in the lower middle of the status
ladder, ordinary and uninteresting. Looking back to her occupation
as a cosmetician, she felt a sense of humiliation and disgust. She had
been little more than a face painter and ego massager, a servant to
vulnerability and vanity.

Of course, she had always seen her marriage as a dreary folly, a relationship with a weak and limited man. Now Jason seemed even beyond that—hollow, stupid, empty. She resented more than ever the

wasted years and enjoyed the idea that in her re-creation of herself she had even eliminated his name from that history.

In fact, everything that had occurred up to the moment she had met Sam Goodwin had been dismal, bleak and unpromising, her childhood a nightmare of religious repression, conformity and ignorance, her teen years aborted by her ridiculous relationship with Jason and the years after, a struggle for crumbs that had corrupted her daughter and diminished further her own self-esteem.

What was happening to her now was awesome, a kind of miracle, a self-created reincarnation. Yes, despite the sheer joy of it, the sense of liberation from the humdrum reality of her old self, she could not shake the dread that it portended, and the occasional projection of herself sitting among the ruins of her fantasy seemed more frightening than death itself.

The new housekeeper, a Puerto Rican woman named Felicia, seemed to float silently through the house, paying little attention to them, except at mealtime, when she became somewhat more obtrusive as she served.

They walked the beach, swam in the ocean, made love and stayed within the confines of Sam's house. There were telephone calls discreetly taken by Sam in his den. She assumed he was conducting business and returning calls from friends, and she used these interludes to cull through Anne's closet and set aside those clothes she would remove. So far, she had managed to clear out less than a quarter of the woman's wardrobe, fearing that the end of that project might signal the end of this idyll.

She had worked out a regular routine, researching the various charities that took such clothing donations and dropping them off in person. Often, the volunteers on duty would comment on their quality, but she avoided all conversation. She no longer gave out her name and telephone number, fearing that an inadvertent call might alert Jackie to what she was doing.

As he had indicated earlier, he avoided all socializing, begging off any appointments for lunch or tennis at the club and discouraging all visitors. She wondered how long he would be able to use the excuse of his grieving to keep himself, and her, isolated. But she would not give herself permission to speculate beyond the present on that score.

On most days she would come back to Sam's house after dropping off the clothes and they would enjoy a candlelit dinner. Then she would return to her own apartment, usually before Jackie got home from her night job at the movie theater. Yet, despite the routine, she considered those moments with Sam an exciting adventure and couldn't wait until she got to his home in the morning for their walk along the beach.

Back at her own apartment, Grace floated through the old reality barely able to sustain a credible attitude, hoping that Jackie wouldn't question her whereabouts too closely. It was one thing to lie to Sam, but another to lie to her daughter.

Instead of being a detriment to their relationship, she considered the acquisition of the little yellow Honda as a blessing in disguise, another nudge of destiny. It gave both Jackie and herself the freedom and latitude to pursue their own agendas. There were, of course, nagging thoughts about her daughter's relationship with Darryl and the legitimacy of the car transaction, but she dismissed them, hoping they would not get in the way of what was happening between her and Sam. For the moment, that would have to be her top priority.

Aside from school, Jackie worked the breakfast shift at McDonald's, which required her to be at her job very early in the morning. This burst of ambition—or was it a frenzy of illogical independence?—was troublesome to Grace, who was concerned that her daughter's furious pace would prevent her from keeping up with her schoolwork.

The fact of her daughter's new physical independence and her own use of time, spending practically all of it with Sam, inhibited their communication. As she grew more and more intimate with Sam, she recognized that she was growing less and less intimate with her daughter. Even their brief conversations when Jackie came home from her night job seemed coldly evasive, deliberately so on her part as well.

But the central issue between them remained the same: money and its scarcity. With the remainder of her severance money nearly gone and her unemployment check barely covering expenses, Grace was heading into a financial morass.

She had calculated that Jackie, considering both jobs at minimum wage, and what Grace could spare from her unemployment check, would never come close to the hundred-and-twenty-five-dollar payments for the car. Nevertheless, she was determined not to intervene. Jackie had to discover the true value of money and financial responsibility for herself. As for Darryl, Grace hoped that Jackie would discover the folly of that relationship.

"Is everything going okay, Jackie?" Grace asked one night about six weeks after she and Sam had become intimate. Jackie, looking haggard and pale, had just returned from her night job.

"I'm doing fine," Jackie said with a strong hint of bravado.

"You look tired, Jackie," Grace said, suddenly realizing that she had neglected to appraise her daughter with her usual scrutiny since becoming involved with Sam.

"You don't," Jackie snapped. It was an observation that surprised her. She had assumed that her subterfuge was credible, and Jackie had given no hint of questioning it. Until now.

Grace knew she looked good. She was rested and tanned from her daily walks in the sun and her swimming exercise. Her relationship with Sam was revitalizing, and the daily lovemaking seemed to create a profound inner glow of contentment that apparently was more obvious than she might have assumed. She felt a sudden tension as she prepared to deflect Jackie's observation.

"When you're scrounging for a job you have to keep yourself looking as if you don't need it."

"I can't understand why it's so difficult. It's not like you're trying to be president of a company."

"I just don't want to take anything."

"Beggars can't be choosers, Mom."

"Let's not get into one of those, Jackie. I'm doing the best I can."

"Are you playing that song again?"

"You're tired, Jackie. Maybe we should discuss this some other time."

"Hell, you're hardly around," Jackie snapped.

"What's that supposed to mean?"

"It means, dear Mother . . ." Grace could see her daughter's hesitation. "A couple of times in the last few weeks I've stopped by after school to catch a nap before getting to my night job. You weren't home."

The revelation startled her.

"Could be those were the times I went to the movies."

"Mom, I've been calling from the job. You're not home at night."

"I might have been in the shower."

"Mom, I'm not stupid. Where do you go?"

She felt a sudden knot in her stomach. Was this the time to make a clean breast of it? She pondered the question briefly, then rejected the idea, hating herself for mistrusting her own daughter.

"Are you still involved with the clothing? You know, the charity thing?"

That again? Grace wondered. Was that still on her mind?

"It's over," she replied, gagging on the lie.

"You mean the source has run out?"

"It's over. That's what I mean."

She held her temper, watching her daughter's face, sensing her suspicion.

"You look as if you don't believe me," Grace said, regretting the comment instantly.

"Did I say I didn't?"

"Please, Jackie, no games. We've been through that. Let's drop the subject."

"Why are you so touchy about it, Mom?"

"I'm not touchy. It's just that . . . whenever we get on the subject, it causes problems."

Jackie turned away and began to get undressed for bed. Grace wished she didn't have to be so closemouthed and oblique. But she couldn't risk the truth. Not yet. *Someday,* she assured herself. *It's for us, Jackie. You and me. Be patient,* she told herself. *I'll make it up to you.*

"I know it's not easy, Mom," Jackie said. "Believe me, I don't want problems between us."

"I know, Jackie," she replied, calling upon her inventiveness. "It's not as easy as you think. Good jobs don't grow on trees. Besides, I'm a little burnt out on being a cosmetician. And the reason I'm away so much is that I don't like spending time alone in this place."

"Mom, the unemployment checks won't last forever."

"You think I don't know that?"

"It's scary."

"I know, Jackie."

"But where do you go, Mom?"

"That again?"

"You'd expect the same honesty from me," Jackie said.

"I know I've been evasive, but it's only to spare you. Sometimes I go to the movies. Sometimes to a shopping mall; not to buy, just for kicks. Sometimes, I just drive around."

"Gee, Mom, I hadn't realized things were that bad." Jackie managed a smile. "I was hoping that you found some guy."

Grace shrugged, unwilling to articulate the lie. She thought suddenly of the life she had superimposed on her daughter, the smart young woman who had chosen to pursue a medical career, who would have little trouble getting into Princeton, her brilliant, attractive, wonderful daughter. Her heart sank as she considered the prospect of Jackie being confronted by Sam.

"What's going to happen to us, Mom?" Jackie shook her head. "I feel like I'm on a treadmill, going nowhere. I hate my jobs, and Mom . . ." Grace worried through a long pause. "I'm doing lousy in school. I'm thinking maybe I should drop out for awhile."

Grace felt a thump in her head.

"No way, Jackie. I won't have that. No way."

"Don't go ballistic, Mom. Just for the time being."

"There is no time being, Jackie. If you hate the jobs you have, think of what's ahead of you. More of the same. Without skills, you're a dead duck."

"I'll be a dead duck no matter what, Mom."

Grace studied her daughter. In her present state, tired, pale and obviously depressed, she looked pitiful.

"You're just exhausted, Jackie. You took on too much of a burden."

Grace moved across the room and embraced her daughter, who did not resist.

"I'm so tired, Mom."

"I know, darling."

"It all seems so . . . so discouraging. I haven't got time to breathe."

"It will all work out, Jackie," Grace said, upset at seeing her daughter so tired. "I know it will. I'm angling for something now that could be wonderful for both of us. Just have patience."

"Mom, please, don't raise false hopes. I couldn't bear it."

"Maybe . . . well, maybe if you quit the night job . . ."

She felt her daughter stiffen against her.

"But I won't be able to make the payments. That's the one thing Darryl insists on."

"Let's not start on Darryl," Grace said. She dreaded talk about Darryl most of all.

"I know you hate him, but the fact is, Mom, he's the only bright spot in my life."

"Then everything else must be awfully bleak."

"It is, Mom. Sorry about that."

"He's making a slave out of you," Grace said, holding back her anger. "Can't you see that?"

"What I see is that if I don't pay the hundred and twenty-five, Darryl will take the car back. And I'll lose the down payment. That's the deal."

"Then let him take it," Grace snapped.

"You'd love that, wouldn't you?" Jackie muttered.

"Yes, I would."

It brought back the terror of the car transaction and the distasteful memory of the monstrous Darryl. Had she talked to him yet about the matter of the documentation? Considering Jackie's present condition, Grace decided it was better for now to keep quiet on that subject.

"Okay," she said. "I'll drop it. I just hope the day of reckoning won't be too painful."

"For you or for me?" Jackie sneered.

"For both of us." Grace sighed, thinking of Sam, wishing for resolution. And deliverance.

CHAPTER TWENTY

Sam decided that it was pointless to analyze, scrutinize or speculate about his relationship with Grace. It was easier to simply accept, enjoy and go with the flow. He felt neither guilt, pressure nor remorse. For her part, Grace seemed to be of the same mind. There was no game plan, no subtle hints of the future, nothing but the present.

Not that the past, especially his life with Anne, could be erased like chalk on a blackboard. It had been cleansing to lift the burden of memory, to clear away the cobwebs of guilt and betrayal that had inhibited his life with Anne. With Grace he could revel in the freedom of honest communication, undo the restraints of withholding elements of his true nature, give free reign to his sexuality, enjoy the openness and inner tranquility that complete candor provided.

As much as he was observing her, learning about her, prodding her for more and more of her history, he supposed that she was observing him with equal eagerness. Both of them seemed to prefer this state, where not only did the present count, but the past, the intimacy and honesty of it, was a prelude, a foreshadowing of the present and, perhaps, the future. It was deliciously comfortable, free from repression or cant.

No overtures had been made by either of them for a more permanent arrangement. By silent agreement, he supposed, such a
prospect had been taken off the table. She had, in her special way, set
the conditions of their relationship, which seemed to mean keeping
the status quo. She seemed to have no desire to pursue anything material. She expressed no interest in possessing any of Anne's clothes.
There was no hint of wanting gifts of any sort, especially gifts of
money. He would have gladly obliged, although, in truth, it would
have put him on his guard. Above all, he hated being on guard. He
had been on guard a lifetime with Anne.

Many women of Grace's generation, more than one removed from
his own, with an inherent sense of independence, might be humiliated to accept any arrangement that smacked of dependency on a
man's favor. She didn't have to say it. He could sense it. Besides, as
she indicated, she was apparently financially comfortable in her own
right.

Although he would very much have wished to shower her with
gifts, he assumed that her refusal, spoken and unspoken, was her way
of saying that she preferred her complete freedom from any obligation and commitment. Or, he feared, this was her way of saying that
this arrangement was transitory, that she considered the age gap between them unbridgeable.

Or, more optimistically, perhaps she wanted no hint of materialism
to corrupt their relationship. Not that she had said or even hinted
that she held these views. Yet he was sure of it. This, he supposed, was
the real meaning of intimacy, knowing for sure what was meant between them.

He yearned for her to spend more time with him, especially
nights. Night accentuated the terrors and turbulence of loneliness
and brought the darker side of imagination into play. It was a time
when one came to grips with the transient nature of mortality, the reality of diminishing time, the looming threat of the relentless hand
of death.

Grace had shown him the power of life. Her flesh had infused him
with the energy of youth. When she was gone his powers seemed to
wane, the lights dimmed. At night he yearned to touch her and hear
her living sounds beside him. There was too much space here alone.
He needed her to fill it with him.

Yes, he wanted her with him, days, nights, as long as he could project his future. But to suggest that would imply a giant step forward

in their relationship. Most of all, he feared that she would reject any idea of permanency.

He had agreed to the isolation for both their sakes. This was too delicate a time for them to endure the pressures of observation, of lending themselves to other people's opinions. He had no wish either to expose Grace to inevitable harsh judgments or have Anne's memory suffer by indirect defaming.

Old friends would call from time to time to suggest various proven recipes to deal with his grief. Many invited him out, although no one had yet suggested that he seek solace in female companionship, although he knew that it was on their minds. He did not go to the club. From force of habit, despite his diminished interest, he continued to consult with his various financial advisers.

Mostly, he looked forward to his moments with Grace, which were the only times he felt fully alive. He acknowledged that it was mysterious that such an overwhelming wave of passion had engulfed him at the moment of his greatest grief. Was he being somehow unfaithful to Anne's memory, as he had been unfaithful to her in life? It troubled him. He could see how others might interpret his actions as callousness, indifference and disrespect for his late wife.

Bruce continued to call him, always under the guise of filial love and caring, offering various caveats and instructions to him for protection against predators of the female gender. He zealously exerted pressure on him to better arrange his estate for future preservation, which meant, also, the avoidance of estate taxation and, consequently, more inheritance for Bruce and his sister. What he had done previously was to draw up conditions that would protect Anne from the conflicting desires of his children and the possibility of her being besieged by predators. Lonely widows were easy pickings. Her death had skewered that arrangement.

Carol, too, called, but her needs were mostly immediate. He usually obliged to some extent, knowing that the money would be thrown into a rat hole, if only to shield himself from her constant whining.

He often speculated that Bruce and Carol truly believed that his refusal to make these arrangements was a way for him to maintain control over them. But he had concluded instead that what he really wanted was exactly the opposite, to maintain his independence from them, to divorce himself from their prospects. In the end, he felt certain he would take steps, from force of habit, to keep his estate from the clutches of the tax collector.

As for potential predators, which by his son's definition, meant scheming women fortune hunters who preyed on wealthy aging widowers, any precaution seemed laughable. He considered himself too aware, too street smart, too cunning and shrewd, too far from senility, too practical and cautious to allow female predators to come near him, no less feast on his carcass. It was an amusing irony to him that Grace was exactly the opposite of such a definition.

What he insisted on was that any arrangement he would devise for his estate's disposal must be his own decision, not his children's. Pressure from them made him particularly resentful and defensive and, above all, unwilling to accede to their wishes.

He knew, of course, that it was only a matter of time before his son would find a way to discover the truth about him and Grace.

"I know what's going on with that woman, Dad," Bruce told him finally. By then Sam had been intimately involved with Grace for about a month.

"I was wondering when you would get around to that."

"It was quite by accident, Dad. A woman called asking for a reference on Carmen. Frankly, I couldn't believe you got rid of her. I called her and she told me . . . well, that you were involved with the woman who had come to dispose of Mom's clothes."

"I offered them to you and your wife. And to Carol. Apparently you didn't want them."

"Just because we left them in the house didn't mean we didn't want them," Bruce said with a pained air.

"It's the first I've heard about it."

"Anyway, that's not the issue, Dad. It's really your call about the clothes."

"So you don't want any of them?"

"I guess not, but that's still not the issue."

"What is, then?"

"I'd say it was a matter of respect for Mom."

"What is?"

"I called a number of your friends. They said you hadn't been to the club and remained holed up at home. Am I right to conclude that you're carrying on with that woman?"

"Carrying on? You can conclude anything you want, Bruce."

"Dad, if I'm right, you could be heading for lots of trouble."

"It's none of your business, Bruce."

"Yes, it is, Dad. Mom isn't around to protect you anymore. I've got to do it for you."

"That is the most presumptuous, asinine thing I've ever heard."

"Don't get mad, Dad. All I want is for you to face the facts. Mom hasn't been gone, what six, seven weeks, and here you are . . . with another woman. Really, Dad. Okay, don't get upset. I suppose there are certain physical needs, even for men of your age. That, maybe I can understand. But beyond that, Dad, don't get carried away by the physical aspect. Oh, I know the rationalization about people who had a good marriage and are so traumatized by the loss of a spouse that they need another replacement mate immediately. I've consulted some well-known psychologists on that score. Believe me, I understand."

"You understand shit, Bruce," Sam said.

His conversations with Bruce were getting increasingly acerbic, but still he couldn't bring himself to cut the paternal cord. It was Anne who was always the voice of reason when it came to conflicts with his children. He could still feel her influence. Bruce might have sensed this as he continued his avalanche of advice.

"Dad, according to these psychologists, grief makes people irrational. You're not yourself. Can't you see that? It takes time to get through this. I hate being the bad guy about this, but I feel I owe you this cautioning note. You're my father and I love you. I do, you know. And Carol loves you. So our advice is, believe me, separate from the other, the matter of the estate. I know you're touchy about that as well, but you didn't work hard all your life for a big slice of your estate to go to some fortune hunter. It's bad enough that Uncle Sam will take a big bite out of it. Now, I'm not saying that this woman is out for no good. She may be genuinely interested in you as a person. But the fact is, you're a very rich man, a mark for any designing woman. Be real, Dad. Protect yourself. I'm not saying you shouldn't see other women. Believe me, I'm a man like you, Dad. I know about certain needs. If that is what you want, then pay for it. Make it impersonal. What I'm talking about is emotional involvement, getting yourself so wrapped up in a woman that you can't see the forest for the trees."

"It's none of your damned business."

"I'm your son, Dad."

"Then be my son and stop worrying about the fucking money."

"You're wrong, Dad. That thought isn't worthy of you."

"Don't lecture me on the worthiness of my thoughts."

"You're being irrational. That's exactly the point."

"Bruce, your father is not an imbecile. I'm not exactly stupid when it comes to human relationships."

There was no point in arguing. His position, Sam supposed, made perfect sense from Bruce's perspective. But Sam was still alive, rational and, despite popular myth, physically vital. Bruce might even be sincere about his professed love for his father, although Sam doubted that it carried the emotional weight his son had cited.

Sam supposed that Bruce was no worse nor better than other children with a wealthy father and a healthy appetite for possessions and further fortune. This, Sam knew, was the dark side of having money, too much money.

In that context, Bruce and Carol's real agenda had only to do with his death and thereafter. He had a nagging suspicion that their dutiful little homilies about love were the expected lip service of grown children. It wasn't a comfortable presumption, but he could not get it out of his mind that his own love for his children had more to do with nostalgia for their childhood and his own youth, for another long-lost, more hopeful time, than present reality.

It occurred to him that these thoughts were a generational journey that proceeded through a time-worn passage. He was not the first aging parent to think them and he wouldn't be the last. Apparently this was the final stage of parenthood to be endured and clearly the worst, most frightening part of the process.

"Just in case, Dad, I've drafted a prenuptial agreement. Don't get mad, Dad. I know you'll think that's also presumptuous of me. Frankly, I don't expect it to be anything to be seriously considered at this point. No way is it a reflection of your present state of mind. But it does give you a sense of how you should be looking at your future estate-wise. I'll fax it to you. . . ."

"Isn't that a little like putting the cart before the horse? The idea hasn't even entered my mind."

Of course Bruce was being presumptuous. But wasn't he being a bit ingenuous as well? Sam wondered.

"All it does is give you guidelines . . . just in case. Something to think about."

"I don't want to think about it."

"You've got to, Dad."

"You're patronizing me, Bruce. The fact is that with all your education and lawyerly bullshit, you're still a little pisher."

"You're always misunderstanding, Dad. Someone has to speak up for Mom's point of view. She was an integral part of your success, Dad. She wouldn't want what you and she have built to inure to the benefit of a stranger."

Inure to the benefit, Sam sighed. Lawyer talk. It was starting to depress him.

"In the first place, Bruce," Sam said, though he had no wish to continue the conversation, "what I do is my business. Not yours. You know I cared for your mother, loved her very much. She's gone now, and I have to get on with my life. Yes, I am seeing another woman. Believe me, she has no designs on my money. She's financially independent, her own person. She would be insulted by this conversation. Carmen was summarily fired for almost exactly the same reasons. She did not mind her own business. At this stage, we haven't discussed anything that remotely suggests those things on your mind. At some point, perhaps, it will be dealt with. But it's far too premature. I'd appreciate it if you'd stow it for the time being. I have no intentions of doing anything hasty or stupid. I never have. I never will. Frankly, I don't want to hear any more about it."

"So you are involved," Bruce mused.

"I don't need this conversation, Bruce," Sam said in frustration. "And I'd like to hang up now."

"I know you hate hearing anything negative, Dad. But someone has got to voice concerns."

"Concerns noted, son."

"And please read what I've written, Dad."

He hung up, livid with frustration and rage. It always came down to this: money, money, money. He wondered if his children saw him as a human being. Perhaps they never had. He was the father, the provider parent, the authority figure, the teacher, the disciplinarian, and the enforcer . . . but never, from their circumscribed view, to be seen as human, with needs beyond their welfare and protection.

Trying to sleep was impossible. His mind churned with angry possibilities. Perhaps he should redo his will completely, give everything he had to charity. Everything! Leave them nothing. Let them vent their anger over his dry bones. He felt constricted, confined, straitjacketed by convention and responsibility.

He got up, roamed the house, then went out on the balcony. It was a moonless night. He couldn't see the ocean, although he heard its relentless pounding on the shore. It reminded him of Bruce, equally relentless, his harangue never-ending.

Grace a designing woman? The concept was laughable. He prided himself on his knowledge of people. Grace was too proud a woman to demean herself by accepting any gift from him, whatever its value.

She was obviously trying to maintain her integrity, accepting him for himself alone, showing little interest in what he had. There wasn't a covetous spirit in her mind or body. He was sure of it, dead certain, in fact. Besides, she did not lack for material resources. She was interested in him solely as a human being, a man, a companion, a friend, a lover.

Fearing rejection, he fought off any contemplation of a future with Grace Sorentino. He had deliberately deflected such speculation and he wasn't going to allow his hopes to rule his conduct. Not in his present state. But he could not stop thinking about Grace, going over the events and episodes of each day with her, the sheer joy of it. He missed being with her, missed her embrace, the touch of her, missed her soft, soothing voice.

It was after midnight. She had been away three hours and it felt like an eternity. How was he possibly going to get through the night without her? For days, he had fought the truth of it, hoping that his mind, his rational intelligence, would triumph over his emotions. He had deliberately avoided any suggestion that she spend her nights with him. She was already spending her days with him, but it was at night that he was most vulnerable.

He missed her, ached for her. And yet he dared not confront her with such feelings. Would an offer of a more permanent arrangement insult her? Chase her away? Above all, he could not risk abandonment. Anne had already done that.

Had he felt this way about Anne? He tried to remember how it was at the beginning. It was too murky, too confused by what went after. With Anne, although he could not find perfect recall, his feelings seemed as if they were more cerebral, and, therefore, more calculating. Anne represented an entry into what he then had considered a higher world, the American aristocracy.

Had he considered such ambitions when he had courted Anne? Courted? It was such a proper word. But that was exactly what he did with Anne, who was a virgin when she came to the marriage bed. Not once before their marriage had he touched her naked flesh, meaning her breasts and her vagina. Even then, he had sensed the missing link, the total absence of passion.

With the exception of that one time he had called Grace, he had never done it again. For some reason it had become a silent pact between them. He would not call her. She would not call him. It had no logic, only precedent, as if they were allowing total absence from each other to heighten the joy of the morning reunions. That might have been the rationale. Or perhaps it was something else, a compartmentalizing of their lives, a device to avoid commitment beyond their days together.

At that moment he refused to conform to this silent pact. He needed her, needed her voice, as if it were the only remedy for his agitation. He reached for the telephone.

"It's me," he whispered.

"Sam?"

Her voice was barely audible. She was whispering.

"Himself."

"Is anything wrong?"

"Nothing wrong. I . . . I couldn't sleep. I . . . I miss you."

"I'll be there in a few hours, Sam."

"I know. I . . ."

"What is it, Sam?"

"I wish you were here, Grace."

"And I wish I was with you."

"Really?"

"Really."

"It's not enough. Just days together."

"I know."

Her voice was barely audible. Suddenly he heard an intrusive sound.

"Are you still there?"

"Yes. But I can't talk now."

Can't talk? Why? He left the questions unsaid.

"Tomorrow, then."

"Tomorrow."

Hanging up, he felt troubled by her abruptness. What had happened? Had someone picked up an extension? Suddenly he felt an uncommon sensation, a psychic stab, a kind of agony. Defining it instantly, he knew it was jealousy. Another man? Was it possible? He turned the possibility over in his mind, then dismissed it, annoyed that it had even entered his consciousness. Another man, perhaps a husband, not an ex, was in the picture. That would mean she was lying about her situation. Never, he decided. She would explain it all tomorrow.

But it did illustrate the extent of his feelings, this instinct to exclusively possess her. He knew what it meant, although he was not certain that he had ever experienced it with the same powerful sense of totality. Not with Anne. Not with anyone.

He was . . . there was no other way to describe it . . . in love.

CHAPTER TWENTY-ONE

"So that's it," Jackie said. She had come into her mother's bedroom and sat down on the edge of the bed.

"That's what?"

"Mom has got a guy."

On one level Grace felt a weight removed, a burden lifted. On another she felt terrified.

"I don't appreciate your listening in on my personal conversations," Grace rebuked.

"I didn't listen in on purpose, Mom. A call comes in the middle of the night, it's only natural. Anyway, that's beside the point. Who is this man?"

"A very nice man."

"You could have told me. I tell you everything."

"It didn't seem appropriate. Besides, you don't tell me everything."

"Is it serious?"

"I can't say."

"Are you balling him?"

"Jesus, Jackie."

"Bet you are. I'd like to meet him."

"In due time."

"So this is where you go when you're supposed to be looking for a job."

"I'm still looking for a job, Jackie."

"What kind of a guy is he, Mom?"

"Very nice and kind. A good person."

"Does he know you have a daughter my age?"

"What is that supposed to mean?"

"It means you might be lying about your age, or maybe he doesn't know you're carrying the baggage of a teenage daughter. It's obvious from the way you cut short the conversation that you were hiding the fact that I existed."

Despite her skewed interpretation, Jackie was closer to the truth than she knew.

"It isn't that," Grace admitted. "He knows I have a daughter."

Jackie cocked her head in skepticism.

"Is he older or younger than you?"

"Older," Jackie admitted. "But then, anyone over forty must seem ancient to you."

She contemplated her answer through a long pause. "Is that where you got the clothes?"

"I told you," Grace said, annoyed now. "I won't discuss that."

"That's it, isn't it? A dead person's clothes. His wife's, right?"

"I told you . . ." Grace began, then aborted her reply. She wished Sam hadn't called.

"Dead wife," Jackie said. "I'm not an idiot, Mom. There's dough there. I can smell it."

"That's all you think about."

"What else is there to think about? We're bleeding down here. If you're balling a guy with money, the least you can do is hit him up for a few bucks. Mom, you're not in a position to just give it away."

"My God, Jackie . . ." Grace sputtered, her anger accelerating.

"Why are you so touchy about it, Mom?" She clicked her tongue. "Not love, Mom. Not that. You're too old for that. You've got to be more practical. What we need here is security, Mom. That's where it's at for us."

"This conversation is over," Grace sputtered.

"See how touchy it makes you. See?"

"I . . ." She was momentarily at a loss for words. "I . . . I just don't want anything to spoil things."

"You think I'll spoil things?" Jackie said belligerently. "Is that it?

The bigmouthed daughter. Hey, Mom, I'm not stupid. If you're bull-shitting the guy, I'll play along. I won't fuck it up."

"Can't you just please leave it alone for now? Can't I have some privacy about this? Believe me, Jackie, if anything happens . . . you'll be the first to know. And you don't have to be so crude about it."

"Crude? This guy must be veddy fancy. Well, thank you very much. Just wonderful. You want me to tell you everything, but you won't tell me anything. That's fair, isn't it? Shit!"

Jackie stormed out of the room. Grace wished she could confide in her daughter and hated the idea that she couldn't really trust her. She wished that Sam hadn't called; but then, how could she have forewarned him? It was a dilemma that she knew she would have to confront sooner or later. She hoped it was later, much later. One probing conversation between Sam and Jackie would be enough to topple all the dominoes.

Jackie was gone when Grace got out of bed. Her job with McDonald's started at seven in the morning. Grace hadn't slept much. Her mind churned with ideas, mostly dire imaginings. It seemed an overwhelming irony that the only person who could advise her on how to proceed was Sam himself, wise, practical, thoughtful Sam.

By then, she realized, she had dug herself a hole so deep there was no possible way to extricate herself without harm. Worse, she had no illusions about her own emotional involvement with Sam, although she refused to characterize it.

At this point, what she feared most was that she would succumb to an arrangement that would derive more from the heart than the head.

Yes, she missed him when she was away from him. Yes, she longed for him in both physical and psychic ways. Yes, she could think of no more wonderful way to spend her days than with him. Millicent Farmer would ridicule her for being such a weak ninny. She remembered her words: "This has nothing to do with feelings. This is business."

Yet so far nothing had happened on this business side. He had not brought up the matter of the future, their future. Nor did she have any idea whether he was mulling the idea, considering a future with her.

She had deliberately not broached the subject, fearful that he would reject the basic premise of her involvement. Marriage. Ring around the finger. It was a mantra endlessly churning in her mind.

The reality, of course, was that the matter could not be postponed for long. Her unemployment check wasn't enough. She was behind in everything, her rent, her car payments, the utility bills, everything. And there was Jackie.

Yet, despite Jackie's reaction to this call, Grace could not deny the pleasure of his declaration. It confirmed what she wanted to believe, that she had made a profound impact on his life, although she dared not give it the name it demanded, fearing that it would describe his impact on her as well.

Any acknowledgment of her own feelings for him would be contrary to Millicent Farmer's caveat not to get emotionally involved. Emotion compromised judgment. Unfortunately, it was a lesson better understood in a vacuum. She had violated the caveat. The alarm bells were deafening.

Just as she stepped out of the shower the phone rang. She rushed to answer it, feeling certain that it was Sam.

"Is this Mrs. G. Sorentino?"

It was a woman's voice, vaguely familiar.

"Yes."

"I'm sorry to call so early, but I wanted to be sure to catch you before you start your day. My name is Margaret Carlson from the Salvation Army."

Grace groped for some shred of memory.

"You dropped off some wonderful clothing for the needy about a month or so ago. I was the person you dealt with. Do you remember?"

"Oh, yes," Grace replied. "I do remember."

"One of the recipients of our program came by yesterday with some material that was found in one of the pockets of the jeans. Believe it or not, we keep excellent records of our gifts. And our recipients are very grateful."

"What sort of material?"

"Letters. Personal letters. I thought you might want them back."

"Really," Grace began, "it's all right. Just throw them away."

"I thought perhaps they might have sentimental value."

"It's all right . . ." Grace began, but the woman persisted.

"I . . . I . . . well, I must confess, I started to read them . . . I don't usually do such things, but you understand I had to identify . . ." Obviously embarrassed, the woman cleared her throat. "I just thought you might want them as a keepsake. I thought they might have sentimental value."

"Whom are they addressed to?" Grace asked, her curiosity aroused.

"A box number in Palm Beach. No name."

"And the salutation?"

"Really, Mrs. Sorentino, this is none of my business. I just thought I'd call as a courtesy . . ." Grace caught a trace of indignation. ". . . but if there's no interest . . ."

"No," Grace said quickly, oddly intrigued, invoking the idea of destiny again. "I'll pick them up."

"You know where we are . . . where you dropped the clothes off. We're open until seven."

Grace looked at her watch. There was more than enough time to pick them up and be at Sam's on schedule.

"I'll be there shortly . . . Mrs. . . . was it Carlton?"

"Carlson," the woman said. There was a moment of hesitation. "And Mrs. Sorentino . . ."

"Yes?"

"Darling. The salutation was just that . . . darling."

"Darling?"

"Oh, I didn't read beyond that. None of my business. But when someone writes darling . . . kinda personal like that . . . you know how it is."

"Certainly . . . yes . . . very kind of you. I'll be there."

Grace puzzled over the call and especially her decision to pick up the letters. Darling! She didn't know what to make of it, except perhaps that they were letters to Anne from Sam. Then why would she want to see them? On the other hand why was her curiosity so compelling?

But then, everything to do with Anne's clothing had been compelling. They were the axis on which everything between Grace and Sam had revolved. Anne's clothes were the catalyst for the introduction, the heart of the ploy, the central erotic prop of the seduction, the fuel for their sexual conflagration. It was eerie, as if the dead wife, Anne the frigid, was ordering these events from her icy headquarters beyond the grave.

CHAPTER TWENTY-TWO

When she got to the Salvation Army drop-off center in West Palm Beach, the woman handed her a small packet of letters.

"I knew you'd want this," she said with a knowing nod.

"Thank you."

"And I'm so happy that you're feeling better."

"What?"

"I think you look just great."

Puzzled by the woman's statement, Grace went outside and got in her car. She sat for a long time contemplating the envelopes, all neatly slit open, obviously by letter opener. There were three of them, all addressed to a Palm Beach post office box, as the woman had stated. There was no return address on the envelopes, which were all written on blue stationery and addressed in a hand that seemed, even to her unpracticed eye, to be masculine.

She noted the place and date on the postmarks. Miami. Last year. Each posted in a one-month time frame. She arranged them by chronology, the earliest first.

Before opening the first envelope, Grace speculated that these might be letters from Sam and that reading them would be tantamount to an unwarranted and immoral intrusion. Besides, she didn't want to suffer the irritation of reading Sam's sweet words of love to his late wife. But even then, before reading the letters, she noted that the handwriting on the envelope just didn't *seem* like Sam's.

But then, she reasoned with a detective's zeal, why the post office box, unless it was meant to be a little game between them? Sam, after all, did have an imaginative streak and was capable of inventing games. And if not Sam, who? And why the salutation *darling?* She wondered if her curiosity was turning salacious. Destiny again, she told herself, imagining that fate was throwing luminescent dust in her face, lighting the way to some crucial discovery.

With shaking fingers, she drew out the first letter and began to read, her heart pounding with trepidation at what was clearly an unhealthy violation of Anne's privacy. It wasn't a long letter, a mere note covering only one side of the page. But as she read, she became more and more perplexed and eager to know more.

"Darling," the letter began. It was, as the woman had said, the only salutation.

> *After all these years, Anne, my dearest love, how can you just remove me from your life? I thought our love was too strong, too consuming, too everlasting. I wish I could find the words to express it. The fire of your passion and its memory even now has sustained me all these years. Our intimate time together is the only thing that makes my life palatable. How can I survive without you? Please, Anne, my darling, my all, reconsider.*
>
> *Love everlasting*

The letter was signed with the "happy face" graphic, but the smile was turned down.

Admittedly, she was stunned but did not let herself jump to any firm or rash conclusions. Just follow the silver dust, she commanded herself. The devil is in the details.

Despite her shaking fingers, she carefully refolded the letter and, blowing the envelope to widen its opening, she slipped it neatly back in place. Handling it carefully, perhaps as evidence for some future revelation, she set it aside and opened the next one.

Before reading it, she contemplated the words of the first letter she had read. "The fire of your passion." Frigid, was she? Really! Don't jump to conclusions, she warned herself. So far this was merely circumstantial, a transient idea remembered from an occasional foray into Court TV. Things are never as they appear.

With fastidious care, she removed the second letter, which covered the full four pages of the stationery. An errant thought crossed her mind and made her giggle. This was a miniseries.

> *Darling,*
>
> *My mind can barely accept this. Terminal. You wrote terminal. I'm stunned. Have you considered all the alternatives? I suppose I should feel flattered that you wanted to stop seeing me, not because you no longer loved me but because you thought I might be turned off by your declining health. Never. Ever. I told you. I will love you forever and ever and ever. Do you realize, Anne, that it has been more than twenty-five years? A quarter of a century. It was wrong, Anne, wrong to deprive us of each other, wrong to steal only moments, instead of being with each other always. For what? Life with our spouses was never "real life." Never a passionate life, body and soul. Who have we hurt? No one but ourselves. I can't stand the idea of it, the stupidity of it, the waste of it. Anne, please, let's acknowledge it publicly before we part forever. We owe that to ourselves.*
>
> *Love everlasting*

That, too, was signed with a happy face, the smile turned downward.

Still reserving your judgment? Grace asked herself smugly. The letter writer was, obviously, Anne's longtime secret lover. So this is where she spent all her passion. *Anne, you cagey bitch,* she thought, *you weren't frigid at all. You were just being faithful to your lover. How noble! How romantic! How could you be so two-faced?*

The knowledge brought an odd sense of elation. The icon was off its pedestal. In a flash her elation turned to anger. At first toward Sam. *You blind, deluded dupe,* she railed at him silently, banished from his wife's embrace, sentenced to a lifetime of guilt by a faithless woman. Worse, his not knowing, not having a clue, worshipping at the shrine of her memory. *Where was your vaunted insight, Sam?*

Then, suddenly, her anger found it's real mark: Anne! Anne the virgin queen, Anne sitting on the golden throne of memory. What was she, after all? A liar, a cheat, a whoring cunt, forcing Sam to find sexual solace with prostitutes and inducing a monumental guilt trip on a lovely, wonderful, devoted, blameless man. "Ball-busting bitch," she hissed aloud. It was all Anne's ruthless ploy to maintain her status while she fucked her brains out with a secret stud. Sam was the cuckold, the injured party. She felt his humiliation, his forced entry into a secret world of lies and dissimulation that, she was certain, were foreign to his nature.

Surely Anne had known that he was finding gratification elsewhere. It hadn't fazed her. She was getting her fill. Dear, sweet, phony, coldhearted Anne. It was hateful of her. Poor, dear, trusting Sam, an innocent victim of this unfaithful woman, this fraud.

Venting her anger for a few moments more, Grace finally calmed somewhat and opened the last letter.

As always it began with "Darling."

> *Your last word, your farewell. How can I endure such a thought? I could have visited you at the hospital or now, at home. You could have given me at least that farewell in person, a parting embrace. I couldn't care less what Sam might think. What would it matter now? Nevertheless, my love, I will defer to your wishes. Farewell, my dear, sweet darling, my true love, my life. Farewell, my princess. I will terminate the PO box. Life will never be the same without you. Never! Never! There will never be another woman in my embrace. Never! In a real sense, my life, too, is over. Good-bye, my dearest love.*

Inexplicably the letter was not signed. It was, of course, both heartfelt and pathetic, but Grace's anger and disgust strongly repressed any sympathy for the writer or Anne.

She sat in the car for a long time, mulling over this strange surfeit of unwanted information. She was convinced that Sam had no knowledge of her perfidy. She had gotten away with it for a quarter of a century.

She put the letters in her purse, started the car and headed toward the bridge. In her possession she had the hard evidence of Anne's unfaithfulness. The woman had deliberately maintained her pose of frigidity, had deprived Sam of his rights as a husband, had forced him into a life of infidelity, exposed him to danger, goaded him into secrecy and guilt, stunted their marriage. It was infuriating.

Her anger simmered at white heat. At that moment she felt no elation in the discovery, no sense of vindication, no joy in it, only despair. Her heart went out to Sam.

Worse, Anne had apparently saved the letters deliberately, as if it was necessary for her to preserve the evidence of her unfaithfulness, perhaps hoping that one day they would be found, as they were. It couldn't have been an oversight. No way. Perhaps there were other letters as well. Why, then, would she have set up a clandestine PO box? She would have to search through the clothes to be sure.

In her meanness, Grace speculated, Anne, Anne the wonderful, had reached beyond the grave to hurt her husband. Imagine! Twenty-five years of faithlessness. It was, she supposed, something of a record. She had taken her pleasure elsewhere. She had been faithful to her lover only, while depriving her husband of her wifely favors, forcing him to consort with strangers. Grace turned it over and over in her mind, like a perpetual drumbeat. How could she have been so callous and unfeeling toward Sam?

Whatever Anne's rationalization for her action, Grace continued to be furious over her subterfuge. How clever she had been to keep the secret! Think of the creativity required, while, all the time, enjoying the largesse of her husband's millions.

Then it occurred to her that perhaps Sam had known all along, had made his peace, had taken refuge in denial, had, as any good businessman might have done, considered the bottom line. Anne, after all, represented his entrance into the heady world of upper-class social acceptance, where money could grease the skids and antecedents might be, however reluctantly, overlooked. No, she decided finally, Sam had simply been gullible. Her own relationship with him was proof positive.

She crossed the Royal Palm Bridge and rode north on Ocean Drive toward Sam's house. As her anger dissipated, she discovered that the evidence of Anne's infidelity had provided her with an extraordinary weapon. It had the power to destroy the myth of Anne's perfection and to expose her as a fraud.

Her satisfaction over such an idea was short-lived. How would Sam react to such a revelation? Would the destruction of Anne's image further her own cause? Or would it hurt? Grace, too, was culpable. She, too, had lied, dissimulated, falsified. Would her exposure of Anne's guilt make Sam resentful of Grace? Often, the bearer of bad news became associated with the news itself. Sam was deeply involved with the worship of his wife. His mind might not accept the truth of it, making Grace the villain. It was a dilemma.

She acknowledged that the temptation to expose Anne was tantalizing. She had it in her power to place doubt in Sam's mind and possibly destroy his image of dear old Anne, classy Anne, perfect Anne. Unfortunately, she also risked being caught in the crossfire.

She parked the car and saw Sam's smiling face in the open door, ready to receive her into his arms. Marilyn, bonded with her now, came out to greet her. No, she decided. This was not the time to reveal Anne's secret. Nothing must disturb the calibration of their current mood. Perhaps someday. But definitely not now.

She fell into his arms and folded herself into his embrace.

"I need you," he said.

"No less than I need you," she assured him.

They did not take their morning walk. Instead, arms around each other's waists, they walked up to the bedroom and made love. It was a mutual initiation, spontaneous, frenzied and immediate, the culmination coming swiftly, in tandem, as if they had been deprived for years.

"After I called I spent a night of agony," he said when they had cooled and lay comfortably in each other's embrace.

"Why?"

"Don't laugh, but I was jealous. I fantasized that you didn't want to talk because there was a man in your bed."

"Are you serious?" she asked, unable to suppress a giggle.

"I was at the time."

"There is room in my bed, Sam, but only room in my life for one man."

"You were abrupt. It made me insecure."

She decided on the absolute truth, wondering if it was possible to find her way back to square one, original truth.

"My daughter had picked up the phone. I haven't told her about you, Sam. Not yet."

"I guess I blew it, then," he sighed.

"You certainly piqued her curiosity."

"And did you tell her?"

"I sort of danced around it."

"How so?"

At that point she knew that absolute truth was impossible.

"I told her I had a very close friend."

"That's all?"

"What would you want me to tell her, Sam?"

It was, she knew, an opening to a discussion of their future. She waited with trepidation for his response.

"It's your call, Grace," he replied evasively. "I'd like to meet her. She sounds quite wonderful."

The idea filled her with dread. Even if she coached Jackie in the details of the big lie, she knew that Sam would discover the subterfuge with a few well-aimed questions. Such a meeting would be a disaster.

"Why not invite her over, Grace?" he asked, in a sudden change of focus, which took her by surprise.

"She's extraordinarily busy with her schoolwork."

"On a weekend, then," Sam persisted.

"Yes," Grace replied. "Might be a great idea."

She paused for a moment, then winked and smiled, knowing it was pure sham.

"First, I think I should explain to her what's going on here."

Considering what she had discovered that morning, was she any worse than Anne?

"And what exactly is going on here, Grace?" Sam asked playfully, raising himself on his elbow and studying her face.

"An involvement," Grace said cautiously, putting her hand up to his face, patting his cheek.

"With a very mature man," Sam said.

"That again?"

"It's on my mind, Grace."

"Well, then, take it off your mind. Maturity is good, Sam. There's a lot to say for experience. Besides, I'm not exactly a spring chicken."

"You are to me."

He kissed her on the forehead, then insinuated his arm under her neck until her head rested on the crook of it.

"We're lovers, aren't we?" Sam asked.

"I'll buy that," Grace acknowledged. She reached for his hand, grasped it and kissed his fingers. She felt secure and comfortable in his arms, although her mind churned with nascent possibilities.

Again she contemplated revealing what she knew about Anne. Perhaps in some way such a revelation would have some benefit to her. The evidence remained in the pocketbook that sat on a chaise in the bedroom not ten feet from where they lay. She even considered a new ploy, an accidental discovery. Maybe she would simply tell Sam that she had found the letters on Anne's closet floor, which wouldn't be that far from the truth. She would, of course, have to deny reading them. Another lie. No, she decided, not now, not yet, maybe never.

"I love you, Grace," Sam whispered.

"Love?" His assertion, coming when least expected, stunned her. It occurred to her now that they must have deliberately avoided the word, as if it were a dangerous shoal. Even in the throes of sexual ecstasy neither of them had uttered it out loud since, she was certain, the saying of it would somehow diminish its sincerity. Now he had said it. It was an admission that she wanted with all her heart but had dared not hope for. Nor did she expect what followed.

"Beyond a shadow of a doubt, Grace. I long for you, yearn for you, hunger for you." He paused, kissed her on the cheek and placed one hand on her heart and one on his. It was a gesture she had never experienced before, a kind of oath, she assumed, made to dispel any doubts in her mind. "I swear it. I love you, Grace." He sucked in a deep breath and appeared to have entered a state of deep and demonstrative emotion. "I know I'm playing in a young man's arena. I don't even know how it happened or why. But I'm sure of it. I do love you, my darling. I do."

He embraced her lengthwise, flesh to flesh, and looked into her eyes, searching, it seemed, for affirmation. His breath tasted sweet and his lips were warm against hers, just touching lightly.

She felt a wave of giddy elation roll over her. Yet she could not find a touchstone for her own reaction. She was too confused, too overwhelmed and, despite hearing his words and wanting desperately to believe them, she sensed in herself a growing feeling of doubt; not doubt in his assertion, but doubt of her own worthiness.

Suddenly, a brief phrase entered her thoughts. *Beware of what you wish for; it may come true and be more than you bargained for.*

Above all, she wanted to accept his revelation as an indisputable fact. *He loves me.* The phrase rolled over and over in her mind. Had it come naturally, or was this the result of her blundering but apparently effective manipulation? *Accept it,* she goaded herself. *Run with it. Tell him what you feel.*

She knew he was waiting for her declaration, knew that he was too clever a man to declare himself without having concluded what her own response was likely to be. Certainly she had demonstrated the supposition by her action, by her sexual response, by her body language, by the hundred little special ticks of affection, deep affection that could be interpreted as "love."

"I seem to have the same symptoms," she said, emphasizing it with the physical pressure of her embrace. She felt him waiting in silence for the ritual words to emerge. "I love you, Sam," she whispered finally. "I love you with all my heart, soul and body." They struck her as clichés, but they were the only time-honored way to articulate her feelings.

She kissed him long and hard on the lips, reaching down to caress his genitals. His penis had hardened again.

"I salute you, my sweet love," he whispered.

"So I observe," Grace said, tracing his smile with the fingers of her free hand.

"Is such an emotional condition possible for a man over sixty? Well over."

"Apparently more than you think," Grace replied, caressing him. "As possible for a woman nearing forty."

She giggled and kissed him again, then moved under him and inserted him.

"We belong like this," she said.

"Absolutely," he agreed. Eye to eye, they watched each other.

"Say it again, Sam," she said, giggling with playfulness about that old movie line.

"I love you, Grace."

"Say it again, Sam."

"I love you, Grace."

For the first time since they had been intimate she sensed that they were sharing another dimension, beyond the pure pleasure of sexual stimulation and culmination. She felt a bonding process at work, an understanding that what was happening between them was important and enduring. She could not remember ever feeling happier or more joyful.

"Good God, Sam, I am so happy, so fucking happy," she cried.

"Say it again, baby."

"I am so fucking happy."

Tears welled in her eyes. Yet somewhere in the back of her mind, a nagging thought had begun to emerge. Would this have happened without the lies? She had no doubt about the shared truth between them, the fundamental essence of their genuine feeling for each other. Would it have happened naturally, without deliberate embellishment? Had the crooked means justified this honest end?

They began moving in tandem, her pelvis circling as her sex tightened around his until they reached a simultaneous orgasm. No instructions were needed now. No words. Their bodies melted into each other, in perfect rhythm.

In the languor that followed she waited through the silence for what she believed would be the next phase of his revelation, the plan for their future. They had discussed loving and need. That bridge had been crossed. What she wanted now was some practical assurance of permanency. Wasn't that supposed to happen next? Or was she being naïve?

It did not come, not through the later walk along the beach, not during lunch or their afternoon lovemaking, not through their romantic candlelit dinner. Perhaps, she reasoned, their joint declaration of love had an odd silencing effect on him, on both of them, as if any further discussion beyond their feelings about each other was moot. Still she waited for his declaration. Surely it was running through his mind. Surely.

The day slipped by in a euphoric haze. But as they stood sipping champagne on the back patio, watching the moon and stars throw spangles on the water, she began to feel a tremor of anxiety. Questions began to nag at her.

Wasn't it in the natural rhythm of the mating process that commitment followed the affirmation of mutual love? And didn't this joint profession of love, in the case of two unattached lovers, define as its ultimate goal some traditional binding state, some promise of meaningful attachment? If that was the case, she told herself, then he was now supposed to declare himself.

Why was he holding back? she wondered. Was such an idea really under consideration by him? How high was it on his list of priorities? No, she had vowed to herself repeatedly, she would never consent to being a mere mistress, whether she lived on or off the premises. Discounting what she had been doing for the past month, she understood that consenting to such a role would sooner or later undervalue her. Ring around the finger; the words echoed in her mind.

She wanted to be a wife, Mrs. Samuel Goodwin, with all the perks consistent with the role, the same perks that he had afforded to the deceased wife, the faithless Anne. Knowing what she knew, she was ashamed, ashamed for Sam, to see the props of his undeserving Anne worship strewn around the house. Row on row of photographs of her in silver frames scattered in every room, her image elaborately portrayed in three oil paintings, the endless racks and drawers of clothes, these assets of her memory, tangible and intangible.

Destiny again had intervened to point the way. The Anne he had lived with was a fiction, her life with him a story written in disappearing ink. Grace must think of herself now as a protagonist, an armed warrior in the battle against Anne's memory. It was a tissue of lies, pure bullshit.

She was well aware of her changed mission, which was to wipe out all visible elements, remnants really, of the old Anne. The idea of eliminating Anne's clothes from the house now had a much higher priority than when it had first been suggested. Before it was a device for meeting Sam by allegedly sparing him the pain of removal. Now it was a first step in a campaign to rid the house of Anne's memory.

Her growing belligerence surprised her. Was she simply taking out her frustration on the dead Anne, the memory of the dead Anne, because of Sam's unwillingness to speak about further commitment?

She felt no serenity in the situation, despite her acknowledgment of loving him, which, to her total surprise, felt like the real thing. Now the dilemma for her was whether she had to take the bull by the horns and broach the subject of marriage. But how? Despite her earlier cleverness in insinuating herself into his life, she was frightened. Did he really love *her*, or the image of herself she had concocted out of thin air, out of desperation?

Certainly there was no logical explanation for her being in love with him. Was it possible to induce such a feeling based on tangible considerations—his wealth, his character, his sexual performance? If so, it was certainly not in her frame of reference. Wasn't love, the romantic variety she was now experiencing, one of life's eternal mysteries? These were heady thoughts for a poor, not well-educated lady perched on one of the lower rungs of the ladder, looking upward, just another wannabe looking for a way to climb out of the crapper.

As she looked out to sea, she contemplated the disaster that was waiting to happen. She had, she realized, done the unthinkable, according to the Millicent Farmer gospel. She had gotten emotionally involved, the ultimate no-no.

It wasn't supposed to happen this way. The lies, as originally conceived, were only to be little white lies, inducements really, tiny falsehoods meant to boost herself in his esteem, a harmless sales device, not anything that might endanger the ultimate objective.

Maybe, despite her deliberate effort, she hadn't really expected this to happen, not in her heart of hearts. He was, after all, far above her in background, status and intelligence. He was successful, older, presumably wiser, of another religion and background. Against that, what did she have to offer?

It struck her that maybe, despite his declared feelings, he wasn't buying. So far he had made no further commitment. And if he had? She would be faced with yet another dilemma. How could she possibly explain away the lies? Perhaps she could downgrade them to silly little fictions of no merit or importance, even laugh them away as ridiculous notions, the figment of an overheated imagination.

Would such explanations fly? she wondered. And the business about the disposal of Anne's clothes, the revelation that it was only a ploy to get to know him. Then further back in the chain of events, the deliberate haunting of funerals to find Mr. Big Bucks.

Didn't love conquer all? Supersede judgment? She pondered her own reaction if the tables were reversed and he was the one concocting lies, piling lie upon lie about the state of his finances . . . that he owned nothing, was in debt over his head, that he was on the verge, or already in bankruptcy, that he was not sixty-four but seventy-four, that he had been diagnosed with terminal cancer, that he had used these lies for the express purpose of getting him through his grief, consoling himself through sex.

How would she react to those revelations? Not well. It was something she was almost too frightened to contemplate. She was certain his reaction would be explosive. He would surely ban her from his sight, like some stalker who is prevented from coming within a hundred yards of him by court order.

But then it struck her that, perhaps, if she was clever enough and if she coached Jackie carefully or, better yet, bribed her with Sam's largesse, she might take this tangle of lies with her to the grave, just as Anne had done. How clever the bitch must have been. Grace envied her lying skills. For twenty-five years she had a secret lover to whom, wonder of wonders, she was apparently faithful, leaving poor Sam to fend for himself in the sex department. It continued to infuriate her. Perhaps it was time for him to learn the truth about that two-timing wife of his who had brainwashed him into believing she was little madame wonderful.

Not yet, she decided. She needed time to consider her next move. She could blow the whole thing between them out of the water. People in such situations were known to shoot the messenger. Hold off, she begged herself. But for how long? Time was running out. She was going broke. Her personal position in practical terms was getting hairy.

She fully realized now how out of step she was with her generation. Yes, she told herself, she had been overlooked, uninformed, left at the post. Absolute candor would have been the way real women, aware women, stronger women, today's women, would have handled this situation. And let the chips fall where they may.

She envied them their courage and fearlessness, their arrogance and independence. She was no better than her mother, and all the women who came before her, frightened and dependent. Jackie would tell him to fuck off. Shit or get off the pot. Where would that have got her? She dismissed such a course, not only because of her lack of courage but because she was fearful that Sam would be confused by this new attitude on her part.

Let it simmer, she told herself, disappointed but optimistic. They went through the ritual of parting for the night with their usual fervor.

"Tomorrow," he said, holding her in a tight embrace.

"Tomorrow," she agreed.

"Same time, same station." He paused, kissed her eyes. "I love you, Grace."

"And I love you, Sam."

So, she thought, *what the hell are you going to do about it?*

He walked her to her car and she got in, waved and drove away. She was both relieved and regretful at the same time. But as she drove across the bridge, facing the prospect of Palm Court, her regret held sway over her relief. He hadn't offered any option at all. Apparently this arrangement was to stay exactly where it was for the foreseeable future.

In the face of such inaction, how could she remain silent? She contemplated calling him on the telephone, having it out, maybe telling him the truth about Anne. Hell, she had the evidence right here beside her. She patted her pocketbook. Right here.

Where do we go from here, Sam? You can't just leave me in limbo. Not now.

CHAPTER TWENTY-THREE

As she neared her apartment, Grace grew increasingly depressed. Was this her fate, to live in this dump forever? Had she constructed too noble an image of herself? Too independent? Too self-contained? Was she wrong in not telling him about Anne, Anne the faithless, Anne the cheat and liar?

By the time she reached Palm Court she was too mentally exhausted to reason logically. Opening the mailbox, she took out the contents, knowing without even looking that they were either overdue bills or junk mail.

She dreaded any confrontation with Jackie. Jackie the needy. Jackie the wanter. She let herself into the apartment, noting that she had kept to her schedule of arriving home before her daughter.

As she slumped in the chair of the darkened living room, she felt a sense of cold remoteness. She wished she were someone else, in some other place. What she craved now was blankness, invisibility. Then she heard a click. The door opened and Jackie came in. Because of the darkness she didn't see Grace and moved quickly to the little kitchen and flicked on the light.

Throwing her books on the Formica breakfast counter, Jackie grabbed the phone from its wall cradle and dialed. Grace was about to make her presence known but, for some unknown reason, she hesitated, listening instead to her daughter's voice.

"Mr. Barlow, this is Jackie," Jackie said, uncharacteristically breathless. "You have to make it fifty. Twenty-five is just not enough. And you promised that this would not have anything to do with my job at the theater. Right? It's just a business deal between you and me. Forty? But I needed fifty. How about forty-five?"

Grace's first instinct was pride; her daughter was asserting herself, standing by her guns. *Good girl, Jackie,* she thought, listening further.

"Okay. An hour then. As much as you want. Yes. Everything. That, too. I'll come in an hour before the theater opens on Saturday morning. No. You don't have to worry about my mother finding out. And you can trust me, Mr. Barlow. Yes. I know you are, and I know you'll keep your word about the condoms. No, we don't want any repercussions. Not from your wife or my mother. Just for the fun of it. Believe me, I won't make trouble. But only on Saturday. Anything you want. I'm not exactly a dumb little virgin. Yes, Mr. Barlow. Not a word. I promise." She hung up.

Grace felt the sensation of a fist squeezing her gut. Her heart suddenly pounded like a sledgehammer in her chest. At first she thought she had mistaken the context. No. It wasn't open to misinterpretation. Jackie was making a deal to prostitute herself. After a brief pause, during which she tried unsuccessfully to get herself under control, Grace erupted.

"Have you completely lost your mind, Jackie?" Grace shouted, standing up.

"Mom. How could you . . . listening to my private conversation?"

In the harsh light of the kitchen, Jackie's face turned a flat ashen, as if all the blood had drained out of it.

"Don't you understand what you're doing?"

"I didn't mean for you to hear it. . . ." She turned her face away and her shoulders indicated that she had begun to sob.

"You're a sixteen-year-old child, for God's sake, Jackie. Has this man been pressuring you, harassing you? We could call the cops or something."

Jackie shook her head in the negative and averted her eyes.

"Look at me," Grace commanded.

She felt her heart breaking. She was devastated, as if Jackie had just been discovered to have a terminal illness. As always she blamed herself for Jackie's transgressions. Hadn't she taught her right from wrong? Apparently the lessons hadn't stuck. It was just one more parental failure chalked up on the scoreboard.

In a burst of frustration and anger, Grace stepped across the room and, grabbing Jackie's shoulders, spun her around. Tears were streaming down Jackie's face.

"Did he harass you into this?" she shouted. "Answer me."

Jackie bit her lip and again shook her head in the negative.

"No, he didn't," she croaked.

"Then why . . ." Grace demanded.

"Money," Jackie said, swallowing hard, finding control. "I approached him. I needed extra money. It was my suggestion. The only thing we haggled over was price."

"Doesn't he understand the risk he'd be taking?" Grace snapped.

"It's my fault, Mom. Not his." She raised her voice. "He isn't a bad man. He's married with two very nice children. He's fifty-one years old. And I could use the money, Mom. It wasn't meant to harm anybody."

"No harm. No harm," Grace cried. "Never mind the psychic harm to yourself. Where is your pride? Where is your self-respect? This is prostitution, Jackie. And your dear Mr. Barlow—we'll nail that son-of-a-bitch to the cross. He agreed to this. How could he be so awful? Risking statutory rape, sexual harassment, contributing to the corruption of a minor. Hell, we'll get this bastard." She felt herself hyperventilating and needed a few moments to get herself under control.

"Please, don't do anything like that. It wasn't meant to be a big deal, Mom. It was my fault."

"He's the one with the money."

"I sort of threw it in his face."

"And he caught it."

"Darryl said . . ." Jackie began, then realized that she had made a terrible mistake.

"So it was his idea," Grace fumed.

"Sort of . . ." Jackie started to cry again. "Please, Mom. Leave it alone. Please."

"You've got yourself a pimp."

"It isn't like that," Jackie muttered. "A one-time thing."

"It's the beginning," Grace said. "He's making you a hooker."

"It was just Mr. Barlow, Mom," Jackie whined. "One guy."

"I can't understand what's happening to you. It's . . . it's pure prostitution, that's what it is. You're selling yourself, throwing away your self-respect. Don't you understand the difference between right and wrong? I'm not going to let this pass, Jackie. Darryl . . . that filthy bastard."

"How else was I supposed to get the money, Mom?"

Jackie wiped her eyes with a tissue. Saturated, she balled it and threw it into the sink and took another from a box on the Formica table. Then she cleared her throat.

"This was a business transaction, Mom. I couldn't meet my car payment. Darryl had no choice. And I need my car."

The car, the car, Grace screamed within herself. The image of Darryl jumped back into her mind. The shaven-headed Darryl with his black leather jacket, swaggering in his high-heeled black cowboy boots, his proud, pooching bundle of genitalia in his tight jeans, the real dagger with the swastika and the tattooed dagger on his arm, encircled by the snake and the words, DEATH BEFORE DISHONOR.

She studied her daughter, a child caught in a whirlpool of contradictions, unable to understand the consequences of her actions, victimized by the demons of adolescence and the ineptitude of her parents, especially herself. In Jackie's mind, Darryl was the avenging angel come to rescue her from the black pit of despair. Again she blamed herself for not working harder to keep Jackie from his evil intent. A wave of painful guilt washed over her.

"I'm not going to let him get away with this," Grace said. "I should have stepped in earlier, been more aggressive."

"You'll be making more trouble than you need, Mom. You don't know him."

"I'm not afraid of him. Not afraid of his stupid knife and his macho posing."

"All Darryl wants is his money. He doesn't want to hurt me. I owe it to him. A deal's a deal." Jackie looked at her mother, biting her lip, her now dry eyes flashing with anger. "Hell, you can't give it to me."

"Jesus, what have I raised here?"

"Well, I can't depend on you. You're a goddamned loser, Mom. That's what you are. Nothing is lower than a loser."

"And what are you—" Grace began, feeling a sob begin deep inside of her. She had the urge to explode with horrible, hurtful words, words of rebuke, words of anger and frustration. She managed to tamp down her rage, bottle it inside of her, searching her mind for some direction that would not make the matter worse than it was, if that was possible.

"Darling, please. Let's not focus the anger on ourselves. We're in this together, you and me. All I'm trying to do is keep you from hurting yourself. What you're doing with Mr. Barlow is, to be kind, just plain wrong. Can't you see that? Above all, you've got to respect yourself. You're a beautiful young woman now. Don't make yourself . . . a . . ." She groped for the right word. "A commodity. You're a person . . . the future will be what you make it." She sucked in a deep breath. "I love you, darling, with all my heart. A mother wants the best for her daughter. I know, I know. So far I have been a loser. I admit it. But there is hope. Believe me. Trust me. I'm trying to turn things around. I need time. . . ."

She felt tears coming and turned away, clearing her throat, then wiping them away with a tissue. Suddenly she felt a hand on her back.

"I'm sorry, Mom. I didn't mean—"

Grace turned and embraced her daughter, feeling her body wracked with sobs.

"It's about time we had a good cry," she managed to say, hoping that the gesture would bridge the growing gap between them.

Jackie quieted, then disengaged.

"If I don't get Darryl the money, he's going to take the car back. I just didn't know what to do. I had no choice."

"Now, let's put our heads together on this," Grace said, feeling she had regained some of her parental authority. "I stick with my premise. I'll bet that car was stolen, or, at the least, its ownership is suspect. There are worse things as well. . . ." Her voice trailed off as she hesitated.

"Like what?" Jackie asked, frowning. Grace sensed some of her belligerence returning.

"Let's face it. Now don't get upset, but it must be said. Inducing a minor to prostitution, statutory rape. Maybe stolen cars. Jackie, you can't ignore the obvious. The man is vulnerable."

Jackie shook her head and bit her lip.

"You can't, Mom."

"Why not? He can't just terrorize you like this."

"He's not terrorizing me, Mom," Jackie muttered.

"You can't still be defending him?"

"I don't want him to hurt anybody."

"Hurt anybody? He's already hurt you, Jackie."

"Not really," Jackie whispered, averting her eyes. Grace shook her head in despair, feeling the rage begin again.

"Jackie, Jackie, my poor baby. Can't you see it? This whole thing stinks to high heaven. This terrible person has you in his clutches. He's not just terrorizing you. He's deliberately and ruthlessly taking advantage of you, trashing your life. Wake up, baby. We've got to stop him."

Grace looked at her daughter, a sad, frightened little girl. Watching her, she felt as if she were confronting her own failure and her anger dissipated.

"You mustn't do this, Jackie," she pleaded, her voice calming. "This would only be the beginning of a downward slide. He's using you for his own evil purposes. How can I make you understand?"

"Look, Mom, none of this is helping. It's still a matter of the money."

"It's more than just money . . ." Grace began.

Jackie suddenly erupted.

"More than just money. More than just money. Are you crazy? It's all about money. Mom, money is the most important thing in the world. We have nothing. Nothing! What kind of a life is this? Look at this shit house. Look in my closet. Rags. Cheap crap. Other kids have cars, clothes. I feel like a beggar. I don't want to feel like a beggar, Mom. I like nice things. And . . . and . . ." She seemed on the verge of hysteria. "If I have to depend on you . . . we'll never get out of here and I won't ever have anything."

"Well, don't pin your hopes on Darryl and his stupid bike. Follow him, he'll lead you straight to the gutter."

"At least I have a car," Jackie shouted. Her adolescent arrogance had returned. "That's more than I ever got from you."

"You think that's your car, Jackie? Don't delude yourself." Grace walked to the phone and picked it up.

"What are you doing?"

"Calling the police."

"I wouldn't do that, Mom," Jackie cried, panicked, as she moved toward Grace and grappled for the phone. "Please. He can get real nasty, Mom. Please. I'm begging you. He's dangerous. He'll hurt you, maybe worse."

Jackie seemed on the verge of hysteria and Grace let go of the phone. She searched her daughter's face, seeing abject fear in her expression.

"Has he threatened you, Jackie?"

"He can make trouble Mom . . . big trouble . . . for both of us." Jackie hesitated. It seemed a reluctant admission.

"For both of us?"

Jackie's thin facade of arrogance was crumbling again. Her eyes filled with tears, which began to roll down her cheeks.

"I just don't want any trouble, Mom. He could hurt you."

"You're worried about me?" Grace said, the full weight of her guilt descending on her like a rock on her chest. Her parenting had been an abysmal failure. She would never forget it. It was all her fault, hers alone. She couldn't even cast blame on Jason.

"Yes, Mom. I'm worried about you."

"I hadn't realized . . ." Grace began, sucking in a deep breath. "Look, I'll find a way out of this mess, Jackie. And I won't make trouble. And Jackie . . ." She wanted to tell her about Sam and the possibilities her relationship with him boded for a better future. Not yet, she decided. "And I promise you things will be getting better."

"You always promise, Mom, but nothing happens." Jackie wiped away the tears with the back of her hand.

"It is happening, Jackie. It is . . . you'll see."

Jackie's perceived need for money and her obviously self-destructive relationship with Darryl had driven her to take desperate action. Her discontent was far deeper than Grace had realized. Perhaps a faulty gene had come down from her and Jason's blood that had blurred the line between the good and the bad.

Jackie was right about one thing: Their lack of money was a terrible disaster. It was humiliating. It ate away at their self-esteem and dignity. It made them feel crippled, unfit, desperate. It corroded self-respect. Even Grace's visits to the unemployment office, where she stood in line with the other unfortunates, was a demoralizing act.

Thinking this, Grace faced the full scope of her frustration. She felt shackled, imprisoned, unable to make a choice on her own. Her only avenue of hope was Sam. Why didn't he act, declare his everlasting fealty, get down on bended knee and beg her to marry him?

She recalled Mrs. Burns's words, echoing and reechoing. Ring around the finger. Perhaps she should speak up, demand his consideration, force him to declare himself. Would he back off, grow fearful, have second thoughts? Of one thing she was dead certain: Sam was not a man for ultimatums.

"All right, Mom," Jackie said between sniffles, obviously emotionally spent. "Don't worry about Mr. Barlow. I won't do this ever again. I didn't want you to know. I didn't want to hurt you."

"You would be hurting yourself."

"It's over, Mom. I'm sorry. I promise. Never again."

"What about dear little Darryl?"

"I don't know, Mom." Jackie shrugged. "I just don't want him to hurt you."

"He won't," Grace said, taking a brave stand.

"He wants his money, Mom. That's the deal."

"Then we'll give it to him," Grace said, her mind groping for some plan to raise immediate cash. This was, indeed, a crisis, and it had certainly rearranged her priorities.

"But how, Mom? You said you haven't got any."

"Can I extract a promise from you, Jackie?"

"Of course you can, Mom."

"Please don't question me about anything. Not now. I'll tell you what you have to know in due time. All I can say is that something good is happening between me and the man you questioned me about yesterday, something good for both of us. Financially rewarding, too."

"Really, Mom?"

"Really."

"Can you tell me anything about him, Mom? I'll bet he's rich."

"You promised," Grace said, lifting her hand like a traffic cop.

"Okay. But you won't keep it from me too long?"

"Trust me."

She reached for her pocketbook and took out her checkbook. Her balance was just under two hundred dollars.

"How far behind are you?"

"Two hundred and fifty dollars."

She thought about postdating it, then rejected the idea. Somehow she'd cover it. She wrote it out, then handed it to Jackie.

"This should give you some breathing room."

"Thanks, Mom."

"On second thought, mail it to him. I don't want you to see him again. That's the deal."

Jackie studied the check.

"I promise, Mom."

It crossed Grace's mind that what she had been engineering was not much different from what Jackie had been setting up. Like mother, like daughter, she admonished herself. She was no less a hustler doing what she had been doing. Who was she to judge Jackie's act of desperation?

Grace wondered if Jackie saw any of this in moral terms, the right and wrong of it, the black and white of it. Or was it simply Grace's discovery of that action that had made the idea unpalatable? At this juncture she didn't take the fork in the road that led to denial. The sad fact of Jackie's assent to the idea of prostituting herself was, to her mind, an act of depravity, not merely stupidity.

What had Grace done to have allowed such moral neutrality to be planted in her daughter's mind? This was, she decided, the essence of her parental failure, and it was up to her, if it wasn't too late, to take whatever corrective action was possible.

"You call this Mr. Barlow tomorrow and quit your job instantly. I don't want you to ever go back there again. And if he makes a stink, tell him how vulnerable he is."

"He won't . . . but it was a good job, Mom."

"No more jobs, Jackie. You have one job, getting good marks, getting into college. That's your job. Do we understand each other?"

"But what will we do for money?"

"Leave that to me, okay?"

Jackie nodded.

"Yeah, sure, Mom."

"Trust me, darling."

"Sure, Mom."

"You don't believe me, do you?"

"I want to, Mom. I really do."

Grace held out her arms and Jackie, with some reluctance, moved into them.

"Never go that far again, Jackie. Never. Never. Never."

"I won't, Mom."

"And no more Darryl. I swear to you, you see him again and I'm going to the police. Do you understand me?"

"Yes, Mom."

They held their embrace for a long time. Then Grace disengaged and went into her bedroom. She fell on her bed and studied the ceiling, groping in her mind for some answer that would rescue them and still keep open her options with Sam.

It was obvious that her timetable wasn't Sam's. What she needed was money, immediately. Sam could wait. Despite her so-called wiles, she had not created in him any sense of urgency.

Weighing her options, she speculated that perhaps it was time to make a clean breast of it, tell Sam the truth. Truth was his watchword, wasn't it? Why not confront him with its starkness, the truth untarnished? Take the risk. Throw herself on his mercy. The image suggested by that idea, her kneeling before him like a supplicant, begging for understanding, while she confessed her sins, was too distasteful to contemplate.

He would certainly be stunned by the blatant cynicism of her action. Be brave, she urged herself. Let the chips fall where they may. Tell it as it is. None of those clichés were helpful. They hadn't been helpful to Anne either, Anne the wonderful, Anne the traitor, who got away with cheating for twenty-five years.

She stopped pacing and threw herself on the bed again, hoping that exhaustion would send her into oblivion. It did.

When she awoke she was surprised by what could only be described as a major miracle. It was as if a computer had been silently operating in her subconscious as she slept. It had weighed all available options and spit out the one that best suited her condition. Convert Anne's clothes into immediate cash!

Of course, it had been there all the time, and she had once rejected the possibility on other grounds. But that had been a different time, eons ago, when her priorities were different. Ironically, it was Jackie's entrepreneurship that had pointed the way. Once she had worried about exposure, but the earlier experience had not met with repercussions, and there was no reason to believe that they would occur now.

As for the ethics of the action, which once had concerned her, Grace rejected such a notion. In the game she was playing, ethics were a foolish abstraction. Selling Anne's clothes was nothing more than another lie in a more tangible incarnation. What did one more lie matter? She was still able to maintain the purity of her promise to herself . . . well, almost . . . not to take money or kind directly from Sam.

This condition, too, she knew, was less ethical than tactical. Above all, he must never believe that her motivation was in any way related to his money.

Jackie's act of desperation had changed everything. The mother instinct was operating now, with all the fierceness and protective zeal of a lioness with her cub. And she had been touched by Jackie's concern for her, which seemed quite real. The fact was that Grace *was* afraid. There was no telling what an evil man like Darryl might do.

She heard Jackie busy in the living room, putting up the studio couch, which was always her last task before leaving the house in the morning. She was, as she had been for the past few weeks, off to her morning job at McDonald's.

"I want you to quit McDonald's today, too, Jackie," Grace said as she moved into the living room.

"Are you sure, Mom?"

"Very sure."

Jackie studied her mother's face.

"You're going to get the best, Jackie. The best of everything," Grace pressed. "Cross my heart."

She wanted to say "Trust me" again, but she held off. It was getting to be too much of a cliché to be believable.

"You still won't tell me what's going on, Mom?"

"When it happens you'll be the first to know."

If and when, she had wanted to say, knowing the *if* would plant a seed of doubt. This wasn't a morning for doubt.

Jackie smiled and shrugged. It was obvious that the implied promise of financial gain had considerably buttressed Jackie's optimism. The power of money, Grace thought, hating the reality of it.

When Jackie left the house Grace sprang into action. She looked up all the secondhand clothing consignment shops in the phone book and began her calls. Charity begins at home, she decided.

CHAPTER TWENTY-FOUR

She arrived at Sam's house with a U-Haul connected to her car. He came out to greet her. They kissed deeply, their embrace fervent.

"God, I couldn't wait until you got here," Sam said.

"And I can't wait to be here."

After a few moments he noticed the U-Haul.

"I'm feeling very industrious today," Grace said. "I've been neglecting my work."

He chuckled with amusement and shook his head, as if it had become a matter of growing indifference to him. She would be killing two birds with one stone: The money, of course, and what could be the biggest bonus of all, getting rid of more reminders of his unfaithful, deceased wife.

"We have to be true to Anne's wishes," Grace said, repressing any hint of sarcasm. "It was beginning to bother me."

"Of course, darling," Sam said, taking her hand and leading her into the house. They didn't allow the heat of passion to interfere with their beach walk and swim, as it had yesterday, and soon they were ambling along the shore, arms around each other's waists.

Today, Grace knew, would mark the first drastic change in their usual routine. Her mind was filled with the logistics of what she had planned. She calculated that with speed and efficiency it would take her at least a week to empty Anne's closet. That was her goal.

She had talked with a number of the store owners, told them the types of clothes that were to be consigned, mentioned the various famous designers involved and, in an uncommon burst of business acumen, insisted on a cash advance.

"Do you mind if Felicia helps me?" Grace asked, still working on the practicalities of the chore.

"Of course not," he replied.

As usual Marilyn chased the sandpipers and ran along the foamy edge of the surf. At intervals they stopped to kiss and embrace on the deserted beach. She loved being close to him, loved the spontaneity of their actions. She was also relieved that she had discovered a method that would take the pressure off, give him time to resolve things in his mind and, hopefully, meet her ultimate objective.

After their walk they had their swim and came back to the house and made love.

"I really like the idea of your wishing to fulfill this commitment to Anne," Sam told her when they were winding down. Normally she loved this time, the talk, the conversational exchange. Sam, she had discovered, was a very verbal man, introspective, with wide-ranging interests.

She loved hearing about his early life, his affection for his parents and his struggles to succeed. He would tell her about the world in which he grew up, so different from her own. He seemed compelled to tell her his story, not only the narrative of his marriage, which she endured stoically, but his life before meeting Anne, which was much more exciting and far less stressful on her. Unlike her own story, Grace knew it was an honest portrayal, embellished more with sentiment than inaccuracy.

He had begun, too, to discuss national and world events, his perspectives on these matters and his opinion about politics, government, foreign affairs and economics.

Even though it pointed up her lack of knowledge on these subjects, she listened carefully, treating his conversation as if it were an educational experience. She marveled at Sam's knowledge and considered herself extraordinarily fortunate to have won the affection and love of such an intelligent man.

It surprised her, too, that she had absorbed enough to make reasonably acceptable comments at appropriate moments, comments that probably indicated to him that she knew more than she did. She was certain that such discussions were a way of life in his marriage with Anne, and she tried to mask her lack of knowledge, which troubled her. It was, after all, another form of lying. Sometimes he would lead her into discussions that referred to events in her own fictitious history.

"The fact is," he told her, "the country is in a compensation phase, swinging now somewhat to the right of center, but not quite like it was in your Washington days."

"Not quite," she replied, frightened by the reference.

"It had to come. It's like a pendulum."

"Absolutely."

"I used to argue with Anne on this point. I never won, of course. She was adamant. Very articulate, too. She believed in her heart that anyone right of center was a hypocrite. She was really down on anything that smacked of hypocrisy."

"Was she?" Grace said, thinking of the letters in her possession.

"Vacillating politicians would drive her up the wall. Anne had this thing about telling it like it is. She could be pretty damned passionate in an argument."

Elsewhere, too, Grace thought, triggered by his mention of passion, remembering Anne's lover's phrase, the "fire of passion."

Now when he referred to Anne she could barely contain her anger and disgust. Why did he continue to extol his late wife's virtues? *She was a fucking whore, Sam*, she wanted to say, to shout it out, blast it into his mind.

"When she believed in something she refused to accept anyone else's point of view. She considered it a kind of surrender, a compromise of her integrity."

When Sam stressed this quality of integrity in his dead wife he would grow reflective, suggesting that he was again beating himself up because of is own infidelity. Grace tamped down her anger, forcing her silence. The Anne myth was obviously too firmly established in Sam's mind to accept any challenge from her.

Thankfully, he seemed less and less interested in interrogating her about her past, as if, she hoped, he might have finally put his mind to rest as to her suitability as a replacement for Anne.

Before she learned of Anne's betrayal, she had been able to tolerate his endless paeans of praise for Anne's taste, integrity, poise and intellect. Always after these outbursts she would counter in the only way she knew Anne was beatable . . . in the sack.

At those times, when she was consciously competing with the

"frigid" Anne, she would marvel at the intensity of her sexuality. She would become the aggressor, the director, putting him through a series of physical gyrations that would make a hooker blush.

Often, during these episodes, she would wonder if she had carried things too far. But his expressions of gratification, sometimes loud and vocal, as uninhibited and resonant as her own, put her mind at ease. In this area their compatibility could not be challenged.

Because he respected the idea of fulfilling her so-called commitment to Anne, he didn't object to her spending most of the afternoon carrying out armfuls of Anne's clothes. She sent him off to his den to do his business while she and Felicia took the clothes off the racks, sorted them and laid them carefully in the U-Haul.

"You give all these to charity?" Felicia asked her as they worked. Although Felicia was a woman of few words and normally kept her personal thoughts to herself, Grace knew a broad hint when she heard one. She did not take the bait.

"Yes, Felicia. This was the late Mrs. Goodwin's wish."

"Fur coats for people on the Welfare?"

"The charity people know how best to help the poor. They'll probably sell them and recycle the money for various good purposes."

Grace could sense that the entire operation puzzled Felicia. She was probably even more puzzled by the goings-on between her and Sam. Thankfully, she posed no threat or interference. Grace timed it so that she was able to make stops at the two secondhand clothing stores she had chosen and still return in enough time for them to have their usual candlelight dinner.

The proprietors of both stores were amazed at the treasure trove she had provided, and Grace walked away with advances of a thousand dollars from each store. Grace's deal with them called for an additional commission coming, less the advance, if the clothing was sold.

She deposited the cash into her checking account. Both proprietors agreed that it would not be difficult to find customers for such high-quality clothing.

Neither of them questioned her as to where the clothing had come from. Since all transactions were in cash, they didn't require any confirmation of her real name. She told the proprietors that she would call or visit periodically to check on the progress of the sales. To further cover herself, she had gone through any pockets that might hold clues to the origin of the clothing or additional details of Anne's secret life. She found nothing.

Grace admitted to herself that she didn't feel very good about these transactions, nor did she believe that she was getting more than a fraction of their value. Survival required compromise, she assured herself. But the money was comforting and, surprisingly, ameliorated the effects of the betrayal of her earlier principles. After all, no one was harmed by these activities, and the benefits to herself and Jackie would be significant.

She was pleased to discover that Sam was no longer curious about the various charities to which the clothes were consigned.

"Would you like to know where they went, Sam?" she would ask.

"Darling, I'm sure they were put to good use."

"Yes, Sam. They were."

CHAPTER TWENTY-FIVE

As she had figured, the disposal of the clothes took nearly a week. Emptied, the interior of the closet had an eerie feeling. It was cavernous without the clothes. She had removed everything, all of Anne's possessions, even her costume jewelry and her makeup. The latter she disposed off as garbage; the former was consigned to the secondhand stores, with advances totaling another thousand dollars.

Except for the photographs displayed in the bedroom, which she feared removing, there was no longer any sign that Anne had lived in that space. Not so with the rest of the house. The photographs and the paintings were still in place and, of course, the totality of the design and decor bore Anne's stamp.

Still Sam didn't mention any further suggestions about their future together. She would give him time, she promised herself.

When she returned to her apartment in West Palm Beach at the usual late hour, Jackie was home. She had assured her that she wouldn't see Darryl and she had quit both jobs. Also she seemed to be devoting herself to her schoolwork. With cash coming in, Grace was able to increase her allowance, although the car, which was still in Jackie's possession, remained an issue.

"Things seem to be going very well with you and your mystery man," Jackie said with a wink. Grace wasn't happy with the implication of the wink.

"Yes," Grace said, deliberately noncommittal.

"What is that supposed to mean?"

"Can't we just drop it, Jackie? You did promise, remember."

"That doesn't mean I'm not curious, Mom. I figure you're spending most of your time with him. You said you're not working. So it must be very serious between you two. And it is paying off."

She was right about that, Grace thought, noting the irony. The week-long foray into the secondhand shops had produced ready cash. And it hadn't made the slightest impact on her relationship with Sam. If anything, it seemed to grow more and more intense, and she began to foresee the inevitability of some decisive action on his part.

She had, of course, rationalized her actions in selling Anne's clothes on the basis of desperation and necessity. She felt slightly more relaxed about her relationship with Sam. He told her he loved her often, but she didn't press him for any further commitment, frightened about pushing him too hard. She continued to withhold what she knew about Anne. That, she told herself, was her ace card. By contrast Jackie's pressure on her for more knowledge about her mysterious boyfriend was increasing.

"I am your daughter, you know. What I don't understand is why you haven't brought him around. The least you could do is introduce him to me. Or are you afraid he'll run when he finds out you have a daughter my age?"

"He knows that. We'll bring you guys together in good time."

"I don't understand the big deal. Are you ashamed of me?"

"These days I'm quite proud of you."

"Then why am I such a big secret?"

"I told you. He knows about you."

Not really, she told herself, upset that she was lying to her daughter. After all, what he knew didn't in any way describe Jackie's background.

"Has he got kids?"

"Yes. But they're not kids."

"So he's older," Jackie said, smirking.

"Yes, he is. But that's all I'm going to say."

"Have you met his kids?"

"No," she lied, not wishing to tell her the details of attending Anne's funeral.

"And he's not curious to meet me?"

"You agreed not to ask a lot of questions, remember?"

"It just seems strange is all."

"All right," Grace agreed, relenting somewhat. "Here's all you have to know. I'm going with a very nice man. Neither of us has explored any options for the future. That means we don't want to get involved with each other's families. Not yet."

Grace paused. Once again she was shading the truth. Sam had indicated that he would like to meet Jackie.

"Does that satisfy you?"

"No."

"Well, that's the only information you're going to get out of me at this point."

Jackie shrugged grudgingly.

Of course there were still other issues between her and Jackie that had to be faced, especially the matter of the car. They had avoided any discussion of the subject for the last week, although it still hung in the air between them. But with money in hand, Grace felt it was best to put that problem behind them.

"Now for the car," Grace said, taking a deep breath. "Here is what we're going to do. We're going to give Darryl, wonderful Darryl, a check for the full amount of what's owing in exchange for the proper documentation on the car. Is that fair?"

Grace watched Jackie's face drain of all color. Her eyes opened wide.

"The whole amount?"

Grace nodded.

"You'd pay the whole amount? Twelve hundred dollars? Do you have that much?"

"I do. We're going to pay it all off so you'll be released from the obligation. Fair and square. That's your deal. Am I correct?"

"Yes, Mom. That's my deal, but . . ." Jackie said. She seemed oddly confused.

"No buts . . . that's the least I can do for my daughter."

"You don't have to, Mom."

"Oh yes I do. I have the money."

"Where—" Jackie began.

"Please, Jackie. No questions."

"Him? Right?" Jackie asked.

"Do you want me to do this or not?"

"I guess . . ."

To Grace's surprise Jackie didn't seem as pleased as she'd expected.

"I thought you'd be delighted that we'll be taking the pressure off
you. Isn't that what you want?"

"Yes, Mom . . . I . . ."

Her hesitation was surprising, but Grace shrugged it off.

"I thought you'd jump at the chance."

"Sure, Mom," Jackie said, but the color had not yet come back to
her face.

"Then you'll own the car outright. Am I correct?"

Jackie nodded, still in an obvious state of confusion. Grace studied
her, puzzled.

"I guess so," Jackie replied.

As she spoke, her mind was ticking off possibilities to which she
had devoted lots of thought. She would give Darryl the benefit of the
doubt about the documentation. She was determined to tread carefully and, bowing to Jackie's fears, not to lose her cool and tempt his
anger.

But she had gone way out on a limb to get the money, done what
had earlier been the unthinkable. Of course, she was resentful that
she had been reduced to such an action. But what choice had she?

Ironically, she wished that Sam could handle this for them. Sam
was a shrewd businessman who would know what to do. Sam wouldn't
be afraid of Darryl, whom he would be sure to characterize as a third-
rate punk manipulating a confused teenager. Sam would send the
bastard packing.

"Here's what we're going to do," Grace said. "We'll meet Darryl in
some public place, say a restaurant, where we can discuss this in a
businesslike way."

Inexplicably, Jackie's eyes seemed to glaze over.

"What is it, darling?"

"It's just . . . well, I'm sort of afraid."

As Jackie spoke, her lips trembled.

"Afraid of what?"

"I shouldn't be. I know I shouldn't, but I am."

"There's nothing to be afraid of, darling. We're paying off a debt.
Believe me, I don't want any trouble."

"Suppose, well . . . suppose . . ."

"That he can't give us any documentation, any papers? Is that what
you're worried about?"

"Probably. Yes. I am worried about that."

"I'm not going to do anything stupid, Jackie. I just want to be sure he doesn't bother you . . . us . . . ever again. It has to be done, Jackie. The sooner the better."

"I guess . . ."

"Good," Grace said gently. "Call him now and arrange for us to meet. Get it over with. Okay?"

"Now? It's . . . it's late."

"He's a big boy. I'm sure he's up."

She watched as Jackie picked up the phone.

CHAPTER TWENTY-SIX

They met in an all-night coffee shop in downtown West Palm Beach, a throwback from another era, complete with booths made of naugahyde and Formica-topped tables. They were approached by a sour-looking middle-aged waitress. Grace and Jackie were the first to arrive. They slid into the booth, sitting side by side, watching the entrance.

They heard the loud sputter of his motorcycle, which came into view through the glass doors. He parked it directly in front of the place and swaggered in, swinging his helmet by its chin strap. He wore the same biker's uniform she had seen him in before: black leather jacket, spangling with metal-stamped swastikas, black leather boots, tight jeans that showed off the bulge of his crotch.

"Hey, mama and daughter, two peas in a pod," he said, smiling crookedly in a way that clearly suggested ridicule.

Grace had an opportunity to observe him more carefully than before. His head was freshly shaven, shiny, his brown eyes feral and wary behind his high cheekbones. Only his short cleft chin belied his stance of arrogance. He slid into the booth opposite them and laid his helmet on the seat beside him.

"Hi, Darryl," Jackie said awkwardly.

"Lookin' great, Jackie." He turned to Grace. "You, too, Mama." He slapped the tabletop. "Offer for a twofer still stands."

The sour-looking waitress, with a noticeably disapproving glance at Darryl, took their order for three black coffees. "Mean lookin' bitch," Darryl whispered. He turned to Grace and Jackie.

"So what's the pitch? Jackie says it's about the car."

"We're here to pay it off," Grace said, forcing herself to be pleasant. "The full amount owing." She opened her pocketbook and drew out her checkbook and a ballpoint. "What is the exact amount owed?"

"Twelve big ones."

Grace snickered inwardly at his reference to hundreds as big ones. Sam, she knew, would have laughed out loud.

"Who do I make the check out to?" Grace asked.

She noted that Darryl and Jackie exchanged glances.

"This time, I'd rather it was cash," Darryl muttered. Grace caught a change in his attitude. He seemed to have grown more serious.

"Believe me," Grace said, "the check is good."

"I ain't saying it's not. But cash is better."

"Come on, Darryl. Don't be ridiculous. Who do I make it out to?"

Again, Darryl and Jackie exchanged glances.

Grace held her pen poised to write; then she looked up. "I assume you brought the documentation, the title and registration."

"I'm not stupid, Mama," Darryl grunted. "You can stop that check first thing in the morning."

"I guess you didn't bring it then," Grace said, pausing, watching his face. "How do I know you have it?"

Darryl shook his head, forced a laugh and looked at Jackie.

"I don't think Mama trusts me, baby."

"It's not a matter of trust," Grace said. "It's a matter of business."

She wondered if she should catalog her misgivings about the transaction and, in general, the relationship with her daughter, who, at that moment, looked frozen with fear. Instead she held her peace, determined to tough it out and end it once and for all.

"Looks to me like your mama here has developed a very shitty attitude about me."

"Look, Darryl," Grace said, pausing as the waitress brought their coffees, "my daughter is a minor for whom I'm responsible. She made a deal with you and all I'm doing here is fulfilling her obligations. This is a simple transaction. I have the money, but what good is the car if it isn't properly registered and titled? There are license plates on it, and I'm certain they can be checked out for their legality. I haven't done so. I'm giving you the benefit of the doubt. I'm sure your bike is properly documented and you know the danger of being caught in an illegal transaction. The fact is that we both know, under the circumstances, that Jackie has been driving it illegally. . . ."

Darryl held up his hand like a cop directing traffic.

"Are you accusin' me of somethin', Mama?"

As if to back up his statement, he suddenly reached behind him and pulled out his knife. Jackie tensed beside her. He started to clean his nails with the point of the blade.

"Put that damned thing away, Darryl," Grace said.

"Just cleanin' my nails, Mama. No law against that."

Grace could see the mechanics of his usual pose of menace and, surprisingly, she felt no fear for herself or any sense of intimidation.

"Darryl, please," Jackie said. "Put it away."

"Little pussy scared?"

"Come on, Darryl," Grace said calmly. "There's no need to get dramatic. Just put it away."

He sneered, shook his head and slipped the knife back in its pouch.

"I have the money," Grace said. "Just provide us with the legal documentation." She spoke slowly and softly, barely above a whisper.

"You got a fuckin' lousy attitude, Mama." His hand shot out with an accusing finger pointed directly at her right breast. Grace looked down at Darryl's finger. It seemed a cue for him to press it forward.

"Get your filthy paw off me, you pig," Grace said. She felt her anger break through. "I should go right to the police and expose you. They'd throw the book at you. Statutory rape, probably car theft, inducing a minor into prostitution. Hell, they'd have enough to put you away for a very long time."

"M-o-m," Jackie whined.

She watched Darryl's face grow dark and ominous. Then his lips broke into a crooked smile. But he had withdrawn his finger from her breast.

"You won't do that, will you, Mama?" Darryl said.

"Wouldn't I?"

Darryl looked at Jackie, his eyes narrowing.

"It's not only for cleanin' my nails, Mama."

"Don't, Darryl. . . ." Jackie began.

"I don't think the kike would be too happy with that, Mama . . ."

He paused, continuing to smile, watching her face. He could not fail to notice her stunned expression. Her heart had seemed to break its rhythm, thumping heavily in her chest. She couldn't believe what she had heard.

"You promised, Darryl," Jackie whined.

Grace closed her eyes tightly, hoping that when she opened them all this would go away.

"And I don't think he'd appreciate what you did with those clothes . . ."

Grace, feeling a strange flutter in her heartbeat, turned to her daughter, who cowered in the corner of the booth.

"You knew this?"

Jackie bit her lip and turned her face to the wall. Then she turned back to face Darryl, whose eyes seemed to burn into her face.

"I saw you, Mama. You and that old Jew boy walkin' the beach hand in hand, kissin' and cooin'. Bet you're fuckin' the old guy's balls off, takin' in that cut salami of his." He cackled and shook his head. "I been followin' you, Mama. Tellin' your little girl here that you were puttin' them clothes into charity. Bullshit. You gotta nice scam goin' with that fuckin' kike."

"How dare you . . . how dare you. . . ." Grace began, trying to get herself under control. She turned to her daughter. "And you . . ."

"I didn't mean any harm, Mom. I just . . ."

"Ain't her fault. Likes money, this little pussy of yours. Figured you got somethin' good workin'. Got yourself a Jew fat cat."

"I won't sit here and listen to this," Grace said, feeling hysteria growing inside her. But she couldn't find the energy to stand.

"What did I tell ya, Jackie?" Darryl said. "She's scared shitless." He turned to Grace. "You keep pushin' that stuff about the cops. I go to Sammy Goodwin . . ."

The name on his tongue was appalling. She felt her flesh turn to ice.

"See, Jackie? She ain't so cocky no more. Got this good thing goin'. Rich old Jew boy. All them clothes you carted out of there this week—bet there's more where that came from, right, Mama?"

Grace tried to work through her anger. She felt utterly desolate and alone. She turned toward Jackie.

"How could you?" she whispered, unable to find her voice.

"I just wanted to know what was going on, Mom," Jackie said. "I had a right to know. I'm your daughter."

"Are you?" Grace asked, taking a deep breath, then turning to Darryl, but unable to find words.

"Hey, Mama," Darryl said, "don't get me wrong. I don't wanna rain on your parade. No way. Pork your Jew boy day and night. No big deal. It's just that . . . well, me and Jackie figured you got yourself a scam goin', here. You know . . . the deal with the clothes, and I'll bet the Yid's been given you a few extra bucks for the use of your ass. And me and Jackie figure you want to share your good fortune with your daughter and her friend."

"Mom, I never . . ."

Jackie had suddenly erupted, attempting to stand, but inhibited by the stationary table.

"Now take it easy, little pussy," Darryl said. "You been bitchin' and moanin' about your mama puttin' out no bread in your direction. Here's your chance. Hell, she's not goin' to blow this deal. Right, Mama? We understand each other, right? She ain't gonna make no trouble for me and you and we ain't goin' to make no trouble for her, right, Mama? From now on she's gonna share . . ."

"I won't sit here and listen to that," Grace said, sliding out of the booth. It was like a bad dream. She felt unclean, humiliated, betrayed. She could think of no logical response beyond her own disgust and disappointment. Her mind was a jumble of contradictions. She needed Sam now. Sam would know how to react. Sam would know how to deal with this monster.

"You just don't know . . ." Grace began, her voice wispy and unsure.

"I don't know what, Mama?" Darryl sneered.

"You just don't know . . . just don't know . . . what desperation can do . . ."

Grace's legs felt rubbery as she moved out of the coffee shop. In the street she felt disoriented. Then she heard Jackie's voice behind her.

"I didn't mean it, Mom. I didn't know he would go this far."

Grace turned toward her daughter. Although Jackie looked genuinely contrite, Grace felt little compassion.

"You knew all along."

Jackie looked down at the sidewalk, locking and unlocking her fingers.

"You lied," Grace said. "Your promises meant nothing. How could you?"

"I'm so sorry, Mom. Really I am. I was mad."

"Mad?"

"That you weren't telling me everything . . ."

"Money, too. You thought I was holding back."

"I was working two jobs, Mom. I was tired. It was his idea to follow you, not mine. Not really. I'm sick of this, Mom, sick of everything. I just told him to get lost. Let him keep his stupid car. Mom, please, no more trouble over this. I was mixed up. I was wrong."

"Your Darryl is an evil man," Grace said, only half believing her daughter's contrition, unforgiving about Darryl, dear Darryl. His hateful remarks about Jews echoed in her mind. She felt as if they were directed at her as well. *God, Sam,* she cried inside herself, *help me.*

Then, suddenly, Darryl was standing beside them, helmet swinging from his hand.

"You ain't off the hook, Mama," Darryl sneered with a movie tough-guy flourish to enhance his menacing pose. He turned toward Jackie. "You neither, little pussy. Don't think you can just throw back the car without payin' nothin'."

"Enough," Grace shouted, finding her voice again, beyond fear, feeling the white-hot purity of her rage. "Don't you pull that intimidating crap on us . . . not ever again. Just get the hell out of our lives." She moved fearlessly toward him and pounded her finger into his chest. "And see to it that you get that car out of our face by morning. You hear that, stud? By morning."

"Or what?" Darryl croaked.

"You're not out of the woods, pal," Grace said, her voice lowered, determined to be equally menacing, as angry as she had ever been in her life. It was as if all the frustrations she had ever suffered, her many losing battles and disappointments, her bad marriage, the struggles with Jackie, her humiliations, her fearsome economic circumstances, all her dead and dying dreams, erupted inside her with volcanic force. "You sick Nazi bastard. I'll see you in hell if you ever come near us again."

"Don't fuck with me, lady," Darryl said, momentarily stunned by her outburst, then quickly recovering his arrogance. "You don't know what trouble is." He turned to Jackie. "Tell her. She fucks with me, you're both dead meat."

Grace, sensing a rising inner hysteria, turned away and, grabbing Jackie by the arm, headed toward her car. Darryl came up behind them and spun Grace around to face him.

"You diddle me, bitch," he shouted, "I'll fix you and your kike buddy." He shot an angry glance at Jackie. "You tell her not to make trouble for me, you hear me, Jackie? And make sure I get the dough. . . . You got my meanin'?"

Grace felt a pounding in her head, fighting her rage. She turned away from his ugly, twisted features and evil stare and, dragging Jackie, ran to the car.

"I'm warning you, both of you," Darryl shouted behind them. "Don't fuck with me."

They got into the car, and Grace quickly locked the doors, turned the ignition and gunned the motor. The car shot forward.

"I feel so terrible about this, Mom," Jackie whined beside her.

"Less said the better," Grace said, her anger still simmering. They drove for a while in silence.

"If he doesn't get that money, Mom," Jackie whined, "he means it. He'll make trouble for you and your boyfriend."

"He'd better not," Grace said. Would he? She wondered how Sam would react if Darryl confronted him. She shuddered to think about it and tried to chase the idea from her thoughts.

As she drove, she saw him suddenly in her side mirror, coming up fast in his motorcycle, the shiny metal of the bike reflecting the street lamps. With his black helmet clapped on his head and the visor closed, he looked like Darth Vader descending on them to attack. The road was almost deserted at that hour and he drove the bike past them, then cut in front, then circled around them and repeated the maneuver.

It was nerve-wracking and dangerous. Grace's heart pounded with fear.

"He's trying to make us crash, Mom," Jackie whimpered.

She held the wheel steady, determined to keep herself together. Then, finally, he lifted one hand, gave them the finger and headed off down the road.

"He's crazy," Grace mumbled.

"Don't mess with him, Mom. Please. He'll do something awful. You don't know what he's like."

"And I don't want to know."

"Please, Mom. I'm not kidding. I'm so, so sorry."

"Are you really, Jackie? He messes with us, I'm not going to roll over. I mean it."

She parked the car next to the yellow Honda.

"It better be gone by morning," she said, banging her car door shut, as if the added sound was needed to buttress her courage. "Leave the keys on the seat. I hope he got the message."

Jackie fished in her pocketbook, found the keys, opened the car door and put them on the driver's seat.

"He'll be after the money, Mom," Jackie said. "He won't give up. "
Grace turned and faced Jackie.

"You make it sound like you're his partner," Grace said.

"Well, I'm not," Jackie pouted.

"Remains to be seen."

"You sound like you don't trust me, Mom."

"Do I? How perceptive of you."

She opened the door of the apartment and headed directly into her bedroom, undressing quickly, throwing herself naked on the bed. By then anger had turned to fear as she imagined what could happen if he carried out his threats.

Confronting Sam would be a disaster for Grace. Everything between them would end. He would quickly learn the truth about her and the grim circumstances of her life. All her lies, all her sad, cynical manipulation of his grief would be revealed. She would be unmasked as a phony, a cheat, a gold-digging whore. It would be over. Kaput. The death of hope.

As for Jackie, Grace was bewildered by her actions. How blandly she had acted her part, pressing her for information that she already knew. It was depressing to contemplate. Her own daughter.

The pressure of all this horror overwhelmed her. She confirmed to herself, yet again, that she was not built for subterfuge. It was out of character for her. She detested the idea that she had created this fictional persona to enhance her position with Sam. But then, hadn't Anne, sweet, faithful, accomplished, wonderful Anne, blandly lived a lie for more than two decades? Two wrongs didn't make a right, she told herself.

She was growing tired of this debate within her mind. Soon her fear began to dissipate. She knew in her heart and soul that she loved Sam Goodwin, loved him as she had never loved anyone in her life, loved him unconditionally and was fully prepared to give him a lifetime of devotion. Did he feel the same way? *Show me, Sam,* she cried in her heart. *Show me the power of your love.* The idea calmed her and she crept under the covers.

How far afield she had come from her original intent! Life was dynamic and unpredictable. She had been caught in a web of her own creation. She speculated about what might have happened if she had told him the truth from the beginning. *Oh, Sam,* she cried, *if only you could look into my heart.*

What had happened to Mrs. Burns's various caveats? And Millicent

Farmer's dictum? Ring around the finger? A fool's notion. None of that seemed relevant anymore. Emotion had won over reason. Was that victory or defeat?

It was time, she decided. Time for a full confession, time for truth, for total honesty. There was no way to predict his reaction. Certainly he would be shocked and confused and consider her deliberate lies a betrayal of trust. How would she react if their roles were reversed? Would there ever be room for trust again?

Then she remembered the evidence of Anne's infidelity, the letters she still carried around in her pocketbook, ammunition at the ready. Ready for what? Perhaps, as a last resort, she would show him how simple it was to misplace trust, to be fooled, to be manipulated into believing deliberate lies.

Anne had done it, and he continued to worship her memory, continued to keep her spirit enshrined in his heart, Anne the betrayer. How would he react to that knowledge?

The idea of such exposure filled her with dread and yet, here she was, contemplating telling him the truth about herself. And didn't the truth about herself, she rationalized, the absolute truth about her past, have to include what she knew about Anne's infidelity?

There was only one reality for her—to tell him, at a minimum, about her own lies. That was her resolution. If his reaction was to reject her, then she would tell him about Anne, show him the evidence. Would one betrayal cancel out the other? She wished she could tell Sam about her options, let him choose. She was appalled at the stupidity of the idea.

What was she, after all, just a dumb, half-educated girl from the lower middle classes of Baltimore.

She felt herself growing drowsy, and soon her thoughts drifted to happier associations. Like being with Sam, making love, walking the beach, enjoying the wonderful, isolated world they had created for themselves. Concentrating on these moments, Grace found that she could keep all negative thoughts and possible perils at bay. In such a tranquil state of mind, she disappeared into the void of dreamless slumber.

She awoke to a sense of foreboding and, remembering the events of the night before, she dashed into the living room. The studio couch was closed, the bedclothes folded. She looked out the apartment window. The yellow Honda was gone. Checking the time, she assumed that Jackie had taken the bus to school.

Perhaps she had won her point with Darryl, despite all his threats and bluster. Looking on the bright side, she considered that the incident might have brought Jackie to her senses.

She showered and dressed and went off to meet Sam. At least she had something wonderful to look forward to, she told herself, refusing to allow ominous possibilities to spoil her prospects for the day.

In the car, driving toward Sam's place, she remembered her resolve of the night before. She must tell him the truth. There was no other way. Was it necessary to tell him about Anne? That was a separate question. No debates this morning, she decided. She knew what she had to do. Let the chips fall where they may.

CHAPTER TWENTY-SEVEN

Sam stood on the balcony off his bedroom and watched the full moon rising above the ocean's horizon. Because of the light he could see the turf churning at the edge of the beach and, in the distance, a cruise ship moving its cargo of revelers southward toward the Caribbean.

He wished Grace was beside him. Even the salt tang that twitched his nostrils couldn't completely eliminate the aroma of her flesh. His taste buds, too, recalled the memory of the taste of her, particularly their last good-bye kiss.

He still remembered Anne, of course, but in a more cerebral way. His grief had receded and he no longer felt the same anguished feeling of loss. The missing Anne, he assured himself, had become or was fast becoming more of a historical fact than an emotional condition. Everything about her was fading into a kind of mythology. Even the old, gnawing guilt about his infidelity was losing its power.

Nor did he sense in himself any inhibiting constriction of conscience about thinking of Anne in this way. Her presence in his living reality was over. She had been replaced in her role by a new player with a totally new take on how the part was to be played.

Acknowledging the fact of this replacement had been his most difficult decision. Anne was over in his life. Grace was a new beginning. At that moment, standing on the balcony, watching the infinity of the sea, he rebuked himself for not facing the truth of the situation, for avoiding the inevitable truth. What he feared now, most of all, was losing her.

He had wrestled with the idea that saying good-bye to Grace every night was, in fact, an unnatural state. Although two months had passed since Anne's death, he was now willing to believe that he had mourned her sufficiently, that he had by his grief acknowledged their long marriage, and despite his long catalog of infidelity he had done his duty by her.

He was well aware that he had deliberately avoided the subject of a permanent arrangement with Grace, even marriage, especially marriage. She had not pressed him. Indeed, at times it seemed that she, too, was deliberately avoiding the subject. He wondered why. Perhaps she wasn't sure their relationship had the stamp of permanence, or she had decided that the difference in their ages was a drawback.

At first he had thought so himself, but after spending time together, talking, making love, interacting, he was convinced that their relationship was workable, pregnant with potential. Certainly from a physical point of view they were enormously compatible. It was marvelous, a miracle. He was, above all, a realist. The aging process was relentless. Down the line, perhaps five, maybe ten years from now, if he were lucky, his powers would certainly diminish, although new drugs held the promise of extending potency. Yet, even with that, one couldn't ignore the body's inevitable natural breakdown.

But he knew, also, from his years with Anne, that the physical aspect, specifically sex, was not the whole story of a relationship. For him and Anne, money had been the leavening ingredient. It had made the bread of life rise, made it tastier, more palatable, despite the absence of a sexual component.

There was, of course, great truth in the idea that man did not live by bread alone, yet few could deny the inherent joys of creature comforts, of being totally free from the tension of material need. Money enhanced life. Lack of money diminished it.

By the same standard, sex, aside from the issues of propagation and survival of the species, enhanced life as well. Its practice gave undeniable pleasure, both physical and psychic. At puberty he had recognized it as a powerful and profound personal need. With Grace, from his point of view, he had closed the full circle of that need. As long as it lasted their sex life enhanced and embellished the joy of their relationship.

Certainly she had exhibited a sexual drive at least equal to his, but he wasn't certain that its equality represented the same importance to her as it did to him. Repetition might diminish its impact. She might grow tired of him. They were, after all, only in the first flush of desire. At some point, surely, the novelty would wear off and evolve into humdrum routine. He feared that over time, as he aged, she might lose interest in him. Perhaps that was why he had decided to wait before he suggested a more permanent arrangement. The fact was that, fearing her rejection, he was too afraid to ask.

Perhaps it was Bruce's telephone call from the airport, coming at the precise moment when he was approaching a resolution about his future with Grace, that had pushed these thoughts into the forefront of his mind.

Bruce had not previously announced that he was coming. In fact, Sam had just spoken to him two days earlier. There had not been the slightest hint that he was coming to visit.

Their conversation, as always, revolved around the same subject, the fear of his vulnerability, his involvement with Grace and the implied disrespect of Anne, as well as the perennial subject, the preservation of Sam's estate. The dialogue with Bruce was getting increasingly contentious.

Was this, then, his last ditch effort? Probably, Sam groaned inwardly. And the coincidence of his calling at a time when Grace wasn't in the house was equally ominous. In fact, the impromptu visit had an emergency air, which was enormously troubling.

"Dad . . ." Bruce had come up behind him. Sam, lost in thought, hadn't heard the taxi over the sound of the pounding surf, and Bruce had his own key to the house, which reminded Sam suddenly of his son's sense of possession over his father's property. At that moment he vowed to change the locks. Sam turned and faced his son, who moved closer to embrace him and kiss him on the cheek.

"I know you must be tremendously surprised, Dad," Bruce said, his features murky even in the moonlight. "I just felt that this had to be done face-to-face."

"Well, here we are, face-to-face," Sam said, not knowing what else to say. It occurred to him that he wasn't exactly overjoyed at seeing his son.

"Can we go inside, chat in the den?" Bruce asked.

Sam shrugged his consent and followed his son down the stairs to his den. Here, they had always had their more serious discussions, another ominous note.

"Are you hungry?" Sam asked.

"Ate on the plane, Dad, but I could use a drink."

Bruce moved to the bar and, lifting the twenty-year-old malt whiskey bottle, silently asked his father to join him. Sam nodded. He was certain he would need a stiff drink to face what was coming.

Bruce poured out two generous drinks and handed his father a glass, then took a seat in one of the two facing wing-backed leather chairs. Another ominous note, Sam thought, taking the opposite chair.

"Very lawyerly," Sam snickered, looking at his son, who had not even removed his jacket. He took a deep swallow of his drink. "It must be pretty important to bring you cross-country."

"It is," Bruce said, halfheartedly sipping his drink, then putting the glass down on the table beside him. He cleared his throat. Sam noted the complete absence of the amenities, the usual small talk expected between father and son; but then, he decided, they had disposed of such questions in their earlier conversations on the phone. Sam recognized that he was not being forthcoming either, having not asked after his son's wife. A deliberate avoidance, he acknowledged to himself, thinking suddenly that he had never really agreed with Anne's assessment. Sam had never liked her.

"I don't know how to put this, Dad," Bruce said.

"How about straight." Sam said. He studied his son, his features more like Anne's than his own, the high forehead, straight nose, square cleft chin, a strong face with Anne's blue-gray eyes staring out at him.

"This is your most vulnerable time, Dad," Bruce began. He was obviously nervous, trying to follow a scenario that he must have worked out for himself in advance. "Considering the circumstances, it's perfectly natural. I'm not faulting you at all. You must understand that. This is coming out of genuine love and concern for your future."

"And yours," Sam interrupted.

"Dad, please, don't be unkind. I don't want this to be hurtful. I just want you to face the reality of the situation."

"What situation, for Christ's sake, Bruce? Enough prologue. Let's get down to the cream cheese. What the hell are you talking about?"

Bruce lifted his glass for another dainty sip of scotch. His hand shook as he lifted, drank and put down the glass. He cleared his throat again.

"Grace Sorentino," he said hoarsely.

Sam had, of course, expected it. Despite their attempts at secrecy, he had always known that his son's resourcefulness would eventually ferret out her identity.

"Okay," Sam said. "So you know her name. Good for you. Yes, Grace Sorentino. She's a dear friend. And, I might add, she has been extremely helpful and understanding . . ."

"I'm sure of that, Dad."

Sam detected a note of sarcasm.

"What's going on here, Bruce?"

"Do you know much about her?" Bruce asked.

Somewhere in the distance, deep inside himself, Sam could sense an odd disturbance begin, like distant thunder. He was instantly wary.

"I know all I want to know," Sam said, feeling his throat constrict.

"And you're not even remotely . . . well . . . concerned?"

"What are you talking about Bruce? She's a lovely person."

"And apparently you're quite involved with her."

"Am I on the witness stand, Bruce?"

"Don't get defensive, Dad. Please. I told you, I'm trying to be protective, not harmful."

"Well then, get to the point."

"Are you comfortable with what you know about her?"

"Where are you heading, Bruce?"

Suddenly all sorts of warning flags went up in Sam's mind.

"We had to know, Dad," Bruce said. "It's you we're thinking about. Oh, I know you don't believe that. And I'm not here to tell you what to do. All I want is for you to know . . ."

"Know what, dammit, know what?"

"About this person."

"Person? You know her name and she's still referred to as a person, more like an object than a real person. Oh, I can see where you're leading me, Bruce. You realize that this is none of your damned business?"

Bruce uncrossed his legs and took out an envelope from his inside coat pocket. Sam, his agitation growing, watched as he slipped out a paper from the envelope and opened it.

"It is our business, Dad. Just don't get emotional. Look at it from our point of view. We had to hire someone, a very reputable, discreet person. You wouldn't tell us anything. How could we protect you?"

"Protect me from what?"

Sam reached for his drink and swallowed it in one gulp. He noted that his fingers shook.

"Grace Sorentino," Bruce said, reading from the paper he held in his hand. "Age thirty-eight."

"Well, there's a revelation. You think I don't know that?"

Bruce did not look up from the paper.

"She has a daughter age sixteen, nearly seventeen. Jackie."

"Your boy really earned his fee," Sam sneered. "Do I have to listen to this crap?"

"She lives at Palm Court in West Palm Beach."

"So?"

"Dad," Bruce said, shaking his head, "she was recently fired from Saks Fifth Avenue, where she worked at the cosmetics counter for three years." Bruce sighed. "Apparently fired for insulting one of their best customers." Bruce looked up. "She sold cosmetics."

Surely a sin of omission, Sam reasoned, refusing to allow himself to be shocked or show surprise. Was there anything sinister in her refusal to tell him about that? She might have wanted to keep busy, keep her hand in. Perhaps it was a kind of hobby. He cleared his throat, which had suddenly become constricted. He knew, of course, that Bruce had thrown down the gauntlet and tried to steel himself against the bad news yet to come.

"A few weeks ago she blew another job at a beauty salon, Mary Jones. Same story. Insulted a customer," Bruce continued. "She is currently on unemployment insurance."

"So?"

It was the only word he could get out without revealing his real feelings.

"This place where she lives, Palm Court . . ." Bruce continued, his tone even and lawyerly, holding any obvious negative expressions in check. "Not very up-to-date. I don't want to be a snob about it, Dad, but it's not exactly first class. I have photographs. It's pretty grungy. Would you like to see them?"

"No, I don't think that will be necessary. Fact is, I've never been there," Sam said, his heart sinking, forcing a posture of nonchalance, knowing it was transparently phony. He got up, crossed to the bar, poured himself another drink and carried it back to his chair. He didn't offer one to his son.

"Born in Baltimore," Bruce continued, concentrating on the paper in front of him. "Grace Frances Sorentino is her full name. Attended Baltimore Junior College, dropped out after a year. Both parents born in Sicily. Mother dead. Father a barber. Lives above the store in the apartment where she grew up." He read it perfunctorily, not looking up. "I'm sure you know all this."

"Of course," Sam whispered. His heart was breaking. He wanted to cry.

"Married Jason Lombardi. Apparently he dropped out of high school. She was nineteen. Mr. Lombardi seems to have been a hustler of sorts. He left quite a paper trail of bad debts, various judgments against him. A pretty bad apple." Bruce shook his head. "They were divorced six years ago. He's behind in his support payments. Rather messy."

"So she's had a lot of bad luck," Sam said bravely, wondering if he was effectively masking his denial. He wanted to question the report, wanted to tell his son that it was nothing but a pack of lies. There was some mix-up here. It wasn't his Grace Sorentino. Not his Grace.

"I'd like to assume you know all this, Dad," Bruce said.

Sam couldn't find the will to reply. Instead, he reached for his drink, spilling part of it because of his shaking hands. He put the drink down without bringing it to his lips.

"Her daughter," Bruce went on, "Jackie, goes to West Palm Beach High School. Not a very impressive student. Apparently she has a boyfriend, a skinhead with a record. Minor stuff. Petty thievery, things like that. She seems to be quite active sexually." Bruce looked up suddenly. "I'd take that as hearsay. He's very thorough, but I think in this case he might have gone too far. What I think he's trying to say is that the kid is a bit on the wild side."

"I thought . . ." Sam began, then realized that he was mounting a futile defense. He stopped himself. Above all, he didn't want his son to see his naïveté, his vulnerability.

"And here's something that really confuses me, Dad," Bruce said, frowning and studying his father's face. "She apparently gave some of Mother's clothes to various charities . . . but then . . ."

Sam turned away, fearful of what was coming next. He felt his stomach sour and nausea begin.

". . . she brought the bulk of them within the past week to a couple of secondhand consignment shops. Apparently got some advances against future sales."

His disappointment was palpable now. He felt awful as he assessed the extent of his gullibility. How could she? His memory groped through the endless catalog of her lies, each one offering a painful stab into his soul. He had no reason to believe that Bruce was manufacturing the information.

He recalled her alluding to her successful father, the lawyer husband, Johns Hopkins, her work for the senator in Washington, the brilliant daughter who needed no help getting into Princeton, who wanted to be a doctor, the luxury condo in West Palm, her financial independence, the endless cacophony of lies, lies, lies. He felt brutalized, used, unclean.

Was this the same woman he had contemplated marrying? Was this the woman who compared with Anne, the sainted Anne? She was a total fraud, a whore, a monstrous, lying bitch. He remembered how she had come to him after the funeral, proposing to spare him the pain of disposing of Anne's clothes. How naive he had been not to have seen through her ploy. He felt his disgust amplifying as he remembered her sexual acrobatics, the declaration of her love and, above all else, the filthy lies. God, what a fool he had been, what a monumental fool.

He got up from his chair and, without looking at Bruce, walked to the bathroom. He felt nauseous and dizzy. Stooping over the toilet, he lost the drink he had just imbibed. He looked at himself in the mirror. His complexion was blotchy, his eyes bloodshot with anger, sweat rolling down his cheeks.

"Asshole," he cried to his image in the mirror. "Asshole."

Suddenly tears rolled out of his eyes, his nose reddened. How could this have happened to him? He, who had amassed a fortune. He, who had always been in control of his life. He, who prided himself on his judgment of other people. Suddenly he felt the full burden of his years. Old!

Bruce was right. He had been vulnerable, an idiot. Worse, a slave to his hardon, a naive, vanity-obsessed moron. How easily he had been duped. God, how sincere she had seemed, how glib. Lying bitch, he cried to his image in the mirror. How dare Anne leave him in this state, alone, a target for a clever, fortune-hunting whore. He was a mark, a patsy, a sucker.

Bending over the sink, he washed his face and tried to clear his eyes of any signs of tears.

"Are you all right, Dad?" Bruce said from behind the bathroom door.

"Of course," he grunted. "Can't a man go to the bathroom without being bothered?"

"Sorry, Dad."

He took a last glance in the mirror, feeling some semblance of control return. All right, he had been taken. But, hell, there was no damage done. Yet he had come this close. He lifted his fingers to the mirror to illustrate the margin by which he was rescued. This much, he sighed.

In an attempt to rationalize his position, he characterized the episode as just what the doctor ordered to rescue him from his grief, the ministrations of a fuck-happy whore. And he certainly had fucked his brains out. That was one way to chase grief. Fuck your brains out. Maybe he could rent Grace out to other old widowers. Need a blow job to chase the blues? Got the goods, the real thing. He laughed at his image in the mirror. It came out as a cackle, but he felt secure enough to join Bruce again.

"Stomach's been acting up," he told his son. He took his seat in the leather chair again.

"Now, where were we?" Bruce continued. Sam was certain he was reveling in his newfound power. "This is obviously a woman who lived in the margins. I don't know how she got in your good graces, but she sure as hell did. I'm not saying that she might offer perfectly decent companionship, but beware of anything more. I'd say that if anything she told you didn't jibe with my investigator's facts, this seems like a classic case of deliberate and cynical fortune hunting."

Sam forced a chuckle.

"Do you think I'm that naïve, Bruce? Did you get it into your head that I was looking for a long-term relationship? The woman was pleasant and no threat at all. Did you think I was going to give away the store? Did you think your old man was an idiot?"

"She's been here every day and night for weeks, Dad. You can't deny that."

"That private dick of yours sure was thorough."

"You want his opinion?"

"If I didn't, I'd get it anyhow."

"He thinks it was a setup. They were all in on it. He saw the kid's boyfriend on his bike watching the house. He thinks she found a way to pick up a few easy bucks on Mom's clothes. I'm not saying you didn't give her permission, but I'm sure you never expected her to sell them. Anyway, he thinks she was trying to get into your good graces, separate you from your bucks, Dad. I'm sorry to say it that way. But that's what he thought."

"And you think I didn't know what was happening?"

"I didn't know what to think."

"I'll bet you thought your old dad had lost it, maybe was going to put a ring on her finger, right?"

"It crossed my mind," Bruce said, smiling, as if he was certain his father was letting him in on some joke. "I've had some research done on the subject. A grieving man after a long and happy marriage can get carried away. And it doesn't really matter how old he is."

"Well, I wasn't carried away." His courage was ebbing again, his heart sinking. *Grace,* he cried within himself. *What did you do to me?* "You wasted your money on that report. I know everything that was in it. She was useful to me in certain ways. She made me laugh, had a good gift of gab, and maybe in other ways as well. But, Bruce, there was never any danger of her taking your mother's place. No way. Your mother was everything to me. Everything."

Bruce watched his father's face, then put the paper back into his jacket pocket.

"I'm relieved, Dad. I hope you now see why I was so concerned."

"As a matter of fact, I was getting ready to . . . you know . . . show her the door. What more is there for her to do around here? As for the clothes, believe me, I couldn't care less if she made a few bucks on them for her trouble. You saw your mother's closet. It would have been too painful for me to go near it. She did her job well as far as I'm concerned. Now that's over. Take a look yourself if you want to. The closet is bare."

"You had me really scared, Dad," Bruce said. It was hard to tell whether he had bought his story. But then, Sam had lost all confidence in his ability to read people. It galled him how easily he was taken in, believing that he loved her, actually loved her. It was ludicrous. Loving this woman who had betrayed him.

Sam got up and poured himself another drink, then brought the bottle to where Bruce was sitting and poured him a slug.

"Cheers, son," Sam said as they clinked glasses.

After they had drunk Sam said, "You could have saved yourself the trip. Told me what you had to say on the phone."

"I'm glad I came, Dad. It gives me a chance to discuss again what I think we should be doing about the estate."

"Oh, I've been thinking about that, Bruce. I think you have made

some good points. I'm almost there. Just give me a little more time
and we can refashion things to your specifications."

"That's great news, Dad." Bruce said, holding up his glass and
shaking his head with obvious pleasure.

This was all a charade, Sam was thinking as he looked at his son.
The fact remained that his son had spied on him. Whatever the out-
come, that was a terrible thing for a son to do. It was true that he had
the urge, figuratively at least, to shoot the messenger. He had never
been happier than his times with Grace, and he hated his son for
bringing him the news of her treachery.

"Well," Sam said, slapping his thighs and standing up, "I'm bushed.
You can sleep in your old room. When are you heading home?"

"First thing in the morning. I ordered a taxi for seven. This was just
a quick trip, Dad, a spur-of-the-moment kind of thing. As soon as I
got this report, I knew I had to come."

"Sure, son. In your place I'd do the same."

He looked at Bruce, studied him for a moment, realizing suddenly
that he held no love in his heart for him. Whatever obligatory love he
had once felt for him, and for Carol, too, was little more than nostalgia for his own youth. Having progeny, he supposed, cheated death,
kept the genes alive, assured immortality. So what? he told himself.
His son had set out to destroy his father's hope and potential happiness, and he had. Sam didn't feel as if he had been rescued from a
fate worse than death.

On the contrary, he had been dealt a deathblow. He had no wish
to see his son again, ever.

After Bruce had left him, Sam walked out to the beach, then to the
water's edge. The surf rolled and pounded and slapped against the
wet sand. He took off his shoes and rolled up his pants. Above him
stretched an infinite canopy of stars, ahead the vast expanse of endless ocean.

He felt the terrible ache of abandonment, of total aloneness, as if
he were the last person left on earth. Surely the Grace whom he
adored, loved, longed for, was not the Grace of Bruce's report. The
Grace he had loved had been strictly in his imagination. Hers was a
giant hoax.

He started to move deeper into the surf, to his calves, to his knees,
still feeling the earth under his feet; then, suddenly, a wave lifted him
and he felt weightless and strangely unburdened, detached from life,
as if he were entering a void.

He was aware enough to sense the temptation to end his life. Death did not frighten him, nor did he feel any need to sum up his life, which had, by his standard of truth, been disappointing—an incomplete marriage, unloving, greedy children, the dubious glory of wealth, hardly an asset in his present state. If there was a single positive note to all this it was that he would leave his progeny in financial knots, all loopholes closed, forcing them to be the full partners of a covetous Uncle Sam. Oh, there would be more than enough left to sustain the most lavish consuming habits of his children, but the pain of unsatisfied greed would be unbearable.

Perhaps it was the idea of that that lifted his spirits and restored him to the living again. It was indicative of the way he saw himself now. He was not a nice man. He was a fraud. An empty suit. He deserved the hand that fate had dealt him. Above all, he hated himself.

He let himself float in on the incoming tide and lay, beached like a whale, along the water's edge. He imagined himself laying there, another of life's victims, an old man betrayed by the illusion that there was still much ahead to enjoy. This thing with Grace was to be his last hurrah. In the distance he had heard the applause of the gods. He had, for one brief, shining moment, actually believed that he had defeated age, found that illusive grail, a late and glorious love. It had turned out to be yet another of life's mirages. At the water's edge he knelt and, in a wave of anger and self-pity, pounded his fists into the wet sand.

CHAPTER TWENTY-EIGHT

Immediately upon entering Sam's house, Grace was assailed by an odd feeling that somehow the environment had changed. Perhaps it was the fog, she thought. It was thick over everything, like a gossamer veil. She heard the pounding of the surf, but the ocean wasn't visible.

Sam, who usually met her at the front door, was not there. Felicia, whose presence in the house was tangible, even if it was merely the odor of her cooking, was nowhere around.

"Sam," she called. There was no answer, only an odd echo. Perhaps the strangeness in the house was merely the effect of her own resolution.

Today was the day, the moment she had chosen to put herself finally and irrevocably in the hands of fate. She wondered if she was going against the grain. Had she received a sign that this was the moment? She wasn't sure. Certainly the evidence that both Jackie and the evil Darryl knew her secret was an absolute sign that she had to go through with her confession. Admittedly, their knowledge had forced her decision.

"Where are you, Sam?" she cried, walking to the rear of the house. Even if he were outside, she would not be able to see him. The fog blocked all vision. Seeing no sign of him, she walked up the stairs.

"Sam," she called again, coming into the bedroom. It, too, was deserted, but as she was about to leave, she saw him sitting on the balcony, barely visible in the mist.

"There you are," she said cheerily, coming closer so that she could see his face, which was unshaven, an uncommon occurrence in itself. She noted his dark mood instantly. He was dressed in slacks and a polo shirt, not shorts and a T-shirt, his usual attire for their beach walk.

On his lap was the framed photograph of Anne that he kept on the night table next to his bed. Despite the mist, he wore sunglasses, and it was difficult to see where his eyes were focused. Observing him sapped her courage. Perhaps she had better postpone her confession, she told herself. Something was obviously bothering him.

"Is there something wrong, Sam?" Grace asked.

She waited a long time for him to respond.

"Everything," he muttered, turning his face toward her. Although she could not see his eyes, his expression, his aura, seemed to reflect anger and hostility, which startled her. Her instant reaction was that Darryl had taken his revenge and told him the truth about her.

"Something concerning me?" she asked with alarm and trepidation.

"All about you," he croaked, making it clear, beyond a shadow of a doubt.

"You know then?" she asked. It was hardly a necessary question.

"Yes," he hissed. "I know."

The game was up. His words and demeanor confirmed that fact. The truth of her treachery was exposed. Any opportunity for an explanation from her had been usurped. How he came by the information was hardly relevant at this juncture. He knew.

Yet despite the sick feeling in her heart, she felt oddly relieved. The burden of keeping obscene secrets, of dispensing lies and mentally cross-indexing them, had finally been lifted.

"Well, then, you must think I'm a monster," she sighed.

He nodded, confirming her speculation. There was no ambivalence about his reaction. Even through the mist, his expression of utter contempt and profound disgust were clearly visible.

"Oh, God, I'm so sorry, Sam. I know you won't believe me now," she said. "But I was going to tell you today, the whole awful story. I'm so ashamed."

"There's no need," Sam said, looking into the cloud of invisibility that hid the pounding surf. "No matter how one tries, the indefensible can't be defended. Bottom line: I was a gullible old fool."

She understood his anguish and observed him for a long moment before speaking. As if trying to ignore her presence, he did not turn his face in her direction.

"I know how you must hate me, Sam. All I ask is that you respect my need to explain. I can't hold it in any longer. I hadn't expected to have to do it under these circumstances. . . . I . . ." She swallowed hard, determined to find her voice.

"It's pointless."

He lifted the picture of Anne and studied it. Grace noted that it was beaded with moisture. At that moment she was strongly tempted to lash out, to reveal the ultimate secret that would explode the myth of Anne's saintliness. Ironically, the evidence, the letters, were still in the bag that hung from her shoulder.

"What goes around comes around," he sighed. "I got my comeuppance. I would appreciate your leaving as soon as possible."

She felt both the pain and the anger of his dismissal. Her fingers reached for the clasp of her handbag. But they went no further. To inflict such additional pain on someone she loved so deeply would only make her detest herself even more.

"All right, Sam, I'll leave if you want me to, but first I'd appreciate it if I could tell my side of it."

He shrugged, which she interpreted as a kind of grudging consent. She paused, gathering her thoughts, forgetting how she had originally planned to begin. Above all, she decided, she must find the discipline not to show him tears. Not tears. In her state, tears would cheapen her motives, make her an object to be pitied.

It's over, she told herself. *What does it matter? Whatever I say,* she vowed, *will be the complete, uncensored, unvarnished truth.* She owed him that.

"I was financially desperate and I set out to find a rich man," Grace began, her voice wispy at first, growing stronger as she continued. "I know the means I chose were cynical and beyond forgiveness. But it did work. I found what I was looking for, a rich, grieving widower, and I took full advantage of him. My objective was, pure and simple, marriage, and all that went with it, to rescue me from the hole I had slid into."

"All that crap about not wanting anything," Sam muttered. "Then selling Anne's clothes. It makes me want to puke."

"Who can blame you?" Grace said, groping for some more palatable way to explain what she had done. Unfortunately the little speeches she had concocted in her mind earlier seemed inadequate and bumbling.

"Why don't you just leave?"

"Sam, please. Let me unburden myself. Give me that. I know we're finished. Just give me the courtesy . . ."

"Courtesy? Good God."

He appeared suddenly old, depleted. It was a condition she knew she had caused, and it broke her heart. He shook his head and turned away from her to peer toward the unseen ocean.

"Just let me explain, Sam," she said, turning to face him.

He did not reply.

"All I ask is that you listen. I know it won't redeem me in your eyes, but I need to say it. Grant me that."

He remained silent and immobile, shifting his glance now to Anne's image in the photograph. Again she assumed his silence meant a kind of consent, more like sufferance.

Grace hesitated for a moment, losing her train of thought. She was sure she knew what was going through Sam's mind. The verdict had already been handed down: guilty as charged. What she needed to do was explain the extenuating circumstances.

"I don't know how much you know, Sam, so I guess I have to start from the beginning." She took a deep breath and walked the short distance to the edge of the balcony. Not seeing the ocean, she felt constricted, imprisoned by the fog. Then she turned again and stood before him, confronting the blankness of his dark lenses.

"I just got tired of the struggle, Sam," she began. "I wish I could convey to you what it means to be desperate, financially desperate, not in control of your own destiny, lonely, defeated, totally down on your luck. It is a very horrible feeling. You feel useless, left out, cast aside like garbage, always at the mercy of others. It kills your spirit. It makes you crazy, willing to do anything to regain your dignity. You feel deprived. You see others prospering, in good shape, not scratching around just to survive." She paused and sucked in a deep breath. "You know you're a loser. Everybody around you knows you're a loser. Here you are, a single mother with a teenage daughter going bad, and you just feel powerless, helpless, lost. Why me? you wonder. Why have I been left out? You're a loser, so you have nothing more to lose. I know I'm whining, Sam, but for me life has been one long self-pitying whine. It takes its toll, Sam, makes you do things that never crossed your mind before. Anything to climb out of the hole."

She discovered that she could barely hear the sound of her voice, only that continuing inner whine.

"So here it is, Sam. Warts and all."

She took him through her actions from the moment she was fired by Mrs. Burns. Deliberately, she did not look at his face as she spoke. She wanted nothing to inhibit the fidelity of her revelation. She wanted to give him the whole truth. Nothing but.

She told him how she had haunted funeral parlors, looking for the right target, preferably Jewish. Why Jewish? She tried to explain that as well, citing Mrs. Burns's various dictums and distortions. She told him how she had adopted the disgusting but apparently clever ploy of suggesting to the bereaved widower that she dispose of the deceased's clothes. Could anything have been more cruel, taking advantage of someone's vulnerability in his moment of grief? Worst of all, she confessed that she had never known Anne, had never heard of her, had made it all up from beginning to end.

As both judge and jury listening to her own testimony, she could barely sustain the pain of her own awful revelation and the terrible deception she had perpetrated on this good man, knowing that her story had to be making Sam confirm his foolishness and sheer gullibility and increase his sense of violation and betrayal.

Still she pressed on. She recounted the story of Millicent Farmer in all its appalling detail. "Ring around your finger, dummy," she cried, as if in punctuation.

Then came her justification for the sale of Anne's clothes, which brought her to recount the long, dreary story of Jackie and her involvement with Darryl, the frightening Nazi skinhead, and the episode with the yellow Honda. She spared no detail, telling him about Jackie's flirtation with prostitution. She assumed it was Darryl who had provided him with the information that condemned her, but she did not refer to that. What did it matter how he discovered her deception?

He remained unmoved, frozen. She had no idea if he was absorbing anything she was saying. To her, the important thing was that she was saying it, emptying herself, cutting through the tissue of lies.

She spared no detail of her early life as well, growing up poor in Baltimore, living over the barbershop with her immigrant Italian parents, telling him about her paltry schooling, her foolish marriage, her husband's true background and her unhappy life with him. Of course he wasn't a lawyer in Washington, just a stupid dreamer with more ambition than brains, a bum with impossible dreams. Nor was he gay, another absurd premise that had jumped madly into her head.

She admitted having little knowledge of politics, current events or culture. By his standard, she told him, she was ignorant and unschooled. Not that she was without ambition to learn. She believed she had the capacity to better herself. She knew she was not mentally inferior, but luck and opportunity to advance and grow simply had not come her way. There was shame in it, she admitted. To be ignorant and uninformed was not a virtue. She had only herself to blame.

She hoped he was listening, but if he wasn't, she told herself, it didn't matter. It had to be said out loud. Had she left a single lie unexplained? She was determined to correct the record as accurately as possible. Throughout her confession Sam remained immobile.

She corrected the chronology. She had lied about that as well. Lies, she tried to explain, take on a life of their own. Embark on such a path, you lose all context about yourself. It becomes less a lie, which is such a brutal term, than a fiction. She had created a fiction about herself and the people around her.

"I wanted to make myself appear better in your eyes, Sam," she told him. "I wanted to lift myself into your world."

Lift herself from where? From her level, it was easy to believe that people who had wealth were different, better in every way, smarter, cultured, educated, well-spoken, polished, socially practiced, mannerly, and, above all, more in control of their lives. She knew she could never match that. To compete, she had to recast herself, make herself over, copy others and lie like hell. As she spoke, it amazed her how deeply and honestly she was portraying herself, all portals open, down and dirty, the whole skinny.

"You might not ever understand where I'm coming from or why I did this. Unfortunately, I know why. Having failed at every venture tried, marriage, parenting, job, life itself, I could gamble everything on one last desperate move. Do you understand that, Sam?"

Still he did not reply. She watched his hands, frozen it seemed, around the picture of Anne, the unblemished Anne that lay exalted in his memory.

Was this the moment? she asked herself. Anne's letters were in her purse. What would be the consequences to her now? So what if he

would hate her forever? It seemed obvious to her that all hope of re-
claiming their relationship was gone.

Again her fingers moved to the clasp of her purse. She had nothing to lose now. At the very least he would learn that Grace wasn't the
only fraud in his life, that his beloved sainted Anne betrayed him
with far more evil intent for most of the years of his marriage. What
could be worse than her disloyalty and unfaithfulness? Let him know
that he had been an unloved husband, a victim of a cheating wife
who had led a double life and betrayed him at every turn. Let him
know that all the agony of his guilt feelings over the years had been
based on a false premise.

She had continued to cling to the notion that the revelation of
Anne's infidelity would shock him into seeing that even the most
revered of human beings were fallible, and that the most blatant acts
of dishonesty and betrayal might not be what they seemed.

If Grace was ever to act on this, it was now. She paused and observed him. He refused her even the most casual glance. She
reached out for the clasp. He continued to look at Anne's picture. In
his mind, Grace supposed, Anne was still safe to worship and revere.
In death she could no longer betray him.

Again her fingers stopped moving. No, she could not bring herself
to do this. She had hurt him enough. Her gift to him would be this
act of non-revelation. This would be her own special act of love, allowing him to preserve forever his illusion of Anne's fidelity and devotion.

"How was I to know, Sam," she cried, suddenly, "that I was to get
entangled emotionally?" She wanted to say "fall in love with you," but
she couldn't utter the words, knowing that they would sound phony,
hollow, self-serving. More than ever she was certain that she loved
him, loved him completely, truly. She wanted, needed to reach out
and embrace him. But her fear of rejection was too powerful for her
to attempt such an act.

"I know I don't deserve forgiveness. I betrayed you. I made myself
out to be something I wasn't. I lied. I cheated you."

From his reaction thus far she had no idea what he was thinking.

"Don't you have anything to say, Sam?" she asked finally in frustration, waiting through a long silence, hoping for a reply. Finally he
stirred and shook his head.

"Please go, Grace," he whispered. "Don't put me through any
more of this."

She studied him for a moment. He didn't lift his eyes toward her. Finally she turned and started to the door of the balcony; then she turned again to face him.

"All I really wanted, Sam," she whispered, "was protection for me and my daughter. My falling in love with you was an unexpected gift."

The words had erupted beyond her will to stop them. He offered no reaction. It wasn't money. Not money alone that she sought, she told herself. Love and protection! That's what it was. Was that so much to ask?

With effort, her legs unsteady, she began to move through the door that led to the bedroom. She stopped for a moment and glanced again toward Sam. He did not lift his head to meet her gaze. Instead he continued to look at the photograph of his late wife.

Then she moved quickly through the patio door, her eyes glazed with tears. She could let them come now.

But as she descended the stairs, she recognized a familiar and frightening sound. It held a strong imprint in her mind. Unmistakably, it was the ominous purr of Darryl's "hog."

Confused by its proximity, especially since she believed that he had already accomplished his objective, had made good on his threat to destroy Grace's relationship with Sam, she abruptly stopped crying and ran down the stairs.

The fog was lifting, although a brightening haze continued to inhibit visibility. Through it, she saw the vague outline of her own car, and beside it Darryl's bike. He was lifting his leg over the seat and removing his helmet. Behind him on the bike, on the so-called "bitch pad," also removing her helmet, was Jackie. Jackie! She couldn't believe what she saw, Jackie in matching biker's clothes and helmet.

Grace was completely bewildered and, for the moment, paralyzed by the sight. She felt blind anger festering inside her as Darryl and Jackie approached, two swaggering apparitions bent on evil intent. In her mind they had become the devil's messengers, and she girded herself to resist them.

Peripherally, she caught a glimpse of Sam standing and watching them from the balcony. The sound of the oncoming motorcycle so close to the house had apparently caught his attention.

"Surprise, Mama," Darryl said, lumbering toward her in his biker's uniform, the leather jacket with its metal swastikas jingling as he walked, the tight jeans showing his arrogant genital bulge and his black high-heeled cowboy boots reminding her of the goose-stepping Nazis she had seen in old movies. Behind him, doing a kind of female imitation of the swagger, was Jackie, unsmiling and mean-faced, aping her mentor.

"What the hell is happening here?" Grace shouted angrily, although the sight she was witnessing left no room for doubt.

"You should never have threatened Darryl, Mom," Jackie said, acting the part of a tough broad, glancing toward Darryl for approval. "I got a clue for you, Mom: That car belongs to him. I saw his registration. He had every right to sell it to me. And we've come for the money. In cash."

Grace studied her daughter. It was obvious to her that she had, whatever the fine points and legalities, lost the last vestige of parental control over Jackie. The issue of the car was hardly worth refuting. Even if Darryl did own the car, he was exploiting Jackie for money. If she was too stupid to see it, then so be it. At that moment she had no mental energy left for argument.

"That's it, then?" Grace said, with an air of finality.

"Figured we'd pick you up, and if we couldn't get your consent to come with us to the bank, we might get Sammy Jew boy up there to come up with the bread."

Darryl looked up at Sam and waved. It was a familiar wave, complete with an uplifted finger.

"Face it, Mom. I'm tired of the bullshit. I know you tried your best. But your best just won't hack it with me. I've moved in with Darryl."

Grace sighed. She saw in her daughter's hard face no remorse, no contrition, no regrets. So be it, she thought again.

"How does that grab you, Mama?" Darryl said, cupping his crotch as if to underline the statement. "You got visiting rights, though."

"Guess we'll just have to have a nice little talk with old cut prick up there. I'm sure he'd love to know about how you got the dough, selling his poor dead bitch's threads. Maybe there's even more to tell about you he don't know. Maybe you got lots more to hide from the kike."

Grace felt a strange sensation, an odd sense of vindication. She had assumed that Darryl had been the informer, which only proved how misguided assumptions were more the rule than the exception. It wasn't Darryl at all. Maybe Sam himself had her investigated. What did it matter now? she told herself. She looked up at Sam, shook her head, then turned to Darryl and Jackie and shrugged, showing her indifference to their threat.

"Be my guest," Grace said, watching their faces as they exchanged confused glances. Then she turned and moved quickly toward her car. The ironic sense of victory passed quickly and she felt herself engulfed by a rising tide of explosive rage. She felt compelled to act, do something, anything.

It was only when she drew nearer to her car and saw Darryl's bike parked beside it, his vaunted Evo, his miraculous hog with its pulled back buckhorns and bitch pad glistening in the moist and eerie light of the fog, that an idea of action struck her. In this light the bike looked like an evil, arrogant monster. Here was her epiphany. She had, at last, come face-to-face with her destiny. It was a compulsion beyond logic or reason, her appointment with the enemy. There could be no retreat. She must wrestle this evil force to the death.

Mounting the monster, she forced herself to remember the mechanics of the "kicker." Jason had taught her that years ago. It came to her in a flash of memory, and she turned the ignition key and placed her foot on the kicker and jumped, hearing the telltale gasp. She jumped again, then again. Finally she hit it right and it burst into life.

She heard Darryl's angry curses and Jackie's screams as the bike shot forward across the driveway onto the strip of shrubs that separated the property from the beach. Looking up as she sped past the house, she saw Sam's vague outline as he stood on the balcony. She couldn't see his face.

As she sped into the fog, navigating by instinct parallel to the ocean, she sensed that she was taming the beast, controlling it at last. She felt free, unshackled, liberated, sailing effortlessly through time and space, hurtling to an ending.

The wind and saltwater bit her face and soaked her hair as she revved up the accelerator, hoping that the greater speed would crush the monster and release her mind of its ghosts and terrors, unburden her heart, chase the demons that had conspired against her and, by some miracle, propel her to another less painful dimension.

After a few minutes, she made a sharp U-turn and headed into the fog, sensing that she was moving again toward Sam's house. She peered into the brightening mist but saw only a white slate of nothingness. That, she assured herself, was where she needed to be, hurtling into the blankness of oblivion.

Slowing, she stopped the bike, let it idle and listened to the pounding of the surf. In the distance she could see the enemy now. Jackie and Darryl, gripped by their fantasies of anger and greed. And Sam, dear Sam, unable or unwilling to distinguish between real truth and betrayal.

They were all there now, flaying their arms. Vaguely, she heard their voices but could not make out what they were saying. Nor did it matter.

In the end it all came down to misconceptions, distorted ideas, inaccurate perceptions, misinterpreted words, phony expectations, conflicting desires, competing game plans, bloated optimism, miscalculations, misunderstandings, inadequate explanations and the mysterious intrusions of luck and chance. People were maddeningly imperfect. Was the battle really worth it in the end?

She revved up the bike, hearing the angry growl and cough of the engine, then headed forward, certain now that she was moving toward her nothingness, her real destiny.

CHAPTER TWENTY-NINE

Sam had listened to Grace's confession with every fiber of his being, his outer persona frozen into immobility while his insides, the core of himself, burned with the heat of his agony. Until then he had never understood the meaning of heartbreak. Now he discovered that it was even more painful than loss, more torturing than guilt.

Her words, assaulting him in an endless stream, bit into his brain with laserlike power, illustrating how deadly words could be, how they could create false realities, manipulate the mind's images, foster illusions, induce empty hopes.

Before her incredible outpouring, he had convinced himself of his own failed judgment. His antennae, which had once detected fraud and chicanery with remarkable accuracy, had simply shut down. His libido had pumped up his ego and blinded him to the ravages that age had wrought on his perception. That was the only credible explanation for his naive stupidity.

But when she explained the machinations of her effort to insinuate herself into his life, he felt less and less to blame. It was, he decided, although he would not reveal to her any hint of admiration, a masterpiece of planning and dissimulation. As she had admitted, desperation makes one powerfully creative and cunning, especially when survival was at stake.

He had deliberately steeled himself against any show of emotion, any engagement of her attention that might reveal a softening of resolve. She had suckered him once and he was determined not to be suckered again.

But he did listen with rapt attention, fighting off any desire for forgiveness. He knew he was at war with himself. If anything, her words provided enlightenment as to the terrible price one paid for purveying lies. He had paid it in spades. Secrecy had forced him to overcompensate in his display of affection and generosity toward Anne. It had distorted his marriage, given him not a single day of peace of mind, of contentment, of openness.

What hurt him most was that he had truly believed that with Grace he had found trust, that illusive ingredient that melted barriers between human beings that opened the way for total communication. Nothing would be hidden, not the darkest desires, not the deepest motives. No emotion was exempt. The criteria between them would be truth, truth in the absolute, truth in its purest form.

Now this. He had been on the verge of a lifetime commitment to her in every way, a full partnership, a pledge to the end of his life, the end of time and consciousness. Love had come to him late, but with all its latent power intact. It had been the greatest thrill in his life. His body's reaction had only been the tip of the iceberg. Its depth defied all measurement.

Indeed, the whole idea of his accumulated wealth and its preservation paled beside the power and glory of love. Beyond creature comforts and the little vanities, what more was needed to satisfy their future needs? Surplus seemed an absurdity at his stage in life. What he detested most was the greed of his children. They had not earned any of his fortune, yet they felt entitled to every dime.

But this thing with Grace: He had really believed that their relationship was beyond money, that his wealth hadn't been a motivating factor for her. He had felt it in his bones. How could he have been so far off the mark? It was true, he supposed, that if she had revealed her real history, he might have rejected any idea of future commitment.

She was below him in education and accomplishment and far, far lower on the economic ladder. Her perception of herself was accurate. She was, indeed, a luckless waif, a loser. She had no special social skills or connections to the protocol of his world. Her knowledge or interest in cultural pursuits, current events and politics were limited.

But what had any of that to do with the chemistry of attraction, with the mystery of love, with the sincerity of her soul? What counted for more? Achievement or wisdom, however acquired? Where was the true measure of success? Who made the final judgments on the worth of a life lived?

When she had said that she loved him, he felt his rage begin to dissipate, but he distrusted his own judgment. He wanted to respond. He wanted it, desperately, to be true. With all his being he wanted to join her in the cleansing process of her confession, to forgive, to believe in her sincerity. Still, he held back. Her lies, her dissembling, had been too formidable, too cunning. And he had let the moment pass. He would tough it out, get beyond it, be more wary of predators. The thought brought him back to his son, who had exploited his self-appointed role of guardian angel. He felt no filial gratitude in the revelation, none at all.

And then Grace had left him and he was bereft. He was marooned now. All bridges burnt, surrounded by an infinite, impenetrable swamp.

In the split second of her leave-taking, he had seen the bleakness of his own future and the long, hot desert of regrets he would walk for the rest of his life. It was then, as he wavered on the razor's edge of decision, that he had heard the grating sound of the motorcycle.

He stood up and peered over the railing. At an angle below him, through the fine mist, he could see Grace talking with two strangers, vaguely seen and oddly dressed. He had no idea who they were.

He stood up, peered through the fog, watched Grace move toward her car, then disappear into the mist. He felt assailed by his own reticence. *Go, bring her back,* his heart told him, while his mind berated his judgment. *Go. Act.*

Then, suddenly, he saw, as if the mist opened briefly just to give him this clear snapshot, Grace mounted on the motorcycle, crouched on the seat, her hair flowing in the wind. He saw the machine shoot through the green edge of his property onto the beach.

The ominous sight panicked him.

"No," he shouted, flailing his arms, certain that she was deliberately headed for her own destruction. Below him, he could hear a man's voice shouting curses into the wind.

"Bitch," the voice cried, loudly, repetitively, inciting Sam to anger. He heard the girl also scream a word. It sounded like "Mom." Mom? A stab of fear shot through him.

He ran down the stairs and cut out the back door to the beach, his heart pounding, banging against his chest. He saw nothing, but he could hear the sound of the bike's motor, growing fainter as it headed farther away.

Coming up behind him was a man in black leather. He saw silver swastikas dangling on metal hooks. The man was shouting obscenely, "That bitch stole my bike. I'm gonna kill that fucking bitch."

Beside the young man was a girl in a similar outfit, almost a child.

"M-o-m," she was shouting into the dense mist. "You come back."

"I'll kill that fucking bitch," the man in black screamed again.

Beside him, the young man and the girl looked like ghosts, floating into emptiness, their shouts muffled as if coming from a far distance.

"Where the fuck is she?" the man in the black outfit screamed.

In the distance they heard the motor's growl, fading away. Sam noted that the mist was rising, clearing from the ground up.

"She's up ahead," Sam said.

The man in the black outfit turned and saw him.

"You make her come back, you Jew son-of-a-bitch. She stole my bike."

The phrases of hate stunned him. Suddenly his glance caught that of the girl. Her face was ashen, and her expression showed the familiar grimace of abject fear.

"Darryl, stop," the girl cried.

"I'm gonna slit her fuckin' throat," the man shouted.

Frightened, Sam peered forward into the rising mist. In the distance he could hear the motor's angry growl, growing louder now. Straining, Sam could see the outline in the distance, a figure on a motorcycle, drawing closer. Then, suddenly, there was no movement, only the persistent, rhythmic growl of the motor, moving from loud and frenetic to soft and steady. She was revving it up and down, taunting him.

"There she is. Crazy bitch," the young man shouted, pointing.

She looked like a still photograph, its image slowly emerging in a development bath.

Sam stood beside the young man and the girl, frozen figures in stunned contemplation.

"You bring that bike back, bitch," the young man shouted through cupped hands. Despite the makeshift sound tunnel, his voice sounded reedy and hysterical.

"M-o-m," the girl whined.

The response was a revved-up motor, still alternating between a soft purr and a hard, angry growl. He could detect only the sounds, no movement.

"Bitch is playin' with us," the young man said, turning to Sam. "Make her come, Jew boy."

Sam looked at the man, his anger rising. He shook his head and turned away in disgust.

"Go on and call your cunt, Jew boy," the young man prodded.

Sam remained silent, shaking his head, hoping the man would note his disgust and contempt.

"You hear what I'm sayin'?"

"Hear?" Sam shot back. "I hear. You offend my ears and I can smell the stink of you," he hissed, freezing the man out of his perception, concentrating his gaze through the rising mist to Grace perched on the motorcycle, watching them, revving the motor in teasing insult.

"She fucks up my bike, I'll waste her ass," the young man cried across the distance between them. Above the din of the pounding surf, his voice carried. Sitting on the motorcycle, Grace didn't respond except to rev the motor into an angry, guttural squawk.

"I'll cut your fuckin' heart out."

Suddenly he pulled a knife from behind him and brandished it in a menacing manner, slicing it through the air. The blade glistened, catching brief sparks from the quickening sunlight emerging swiftly from the mist.

Sam looked at the young man and spat into the sand.

"Stop being an idiot," he said.

"Want me to stick it in you, Jew boy?"

"What hole have you crawled out of?" Sam muttered despite himself, refusing to show the man his fear.

"Darryl, stop," the girl whined.

"Your mama is dead meat," the young man shouted at the girl, who winced; then, to her mother, "You trash that, I'll trash you."

Again the answer was a revved-up motor.

"She's not afraid of you either," Sam chuckled, admiring Grace's bravery. She was ridiculing him.

The young man moved suddenly, grabbing the girl by the hair. He laid the blade of the knife flat across her throat. The girl screamed. He pulled the girl's hair sharply upward, lifting her head, pressing the knife harder against her neck.

"You better move, bitch. I'll cut her fuckin' throat."

Grace's response was another loud, repetitive growl of the motor.

"You better move it," the young man shouted, "or this little pussy is dead meat."

"No need for that," Sam said calmly.

"Keep out of this, kike," the young man screamed, pulling harder at the girl's hair. Her panicked scream cut through the air. As if in counterpoint, like some weird concert, the motor responded with its angry, rhythmic beat.

"She don't mean shit to me, bitch," the young man shouted. "You don't bring that bike back, she's gone."

Suddenly there was nothing but silence. The mist was quickly disappearing. Sam could see Grace's face, clearer now but impassive, strangely calm. All four of them were frozen in a deadly tableau, like silent figures in a desert. Even the ocean was unruffled, as if pausing between waves, waiting for life to begin again.

In the silence Sam found his moment to act. He sprang forward and, gathering his energy into his arm and fist, he smashed it into the young's man's arm, a hard, glancing blow that stunned him momentarily, forcing him to release his hold on the girl. She slipped like a stone into the sand.

Before the young man could recover his equilibrium, Sam hit him again, a pounding blow directly into his face. The force of the blow threw him backward like a fallen plank. The knife slipped out of his grip and fell into the sand.

Stunned, the young man sat up, shook himself, then turned and crawled wildly, like a spinning top, his hands groping into the sand in an effort to recover the knife. Sam kicked sand in his eyes. Darryl screamed in pain.

In the distance he could hear the motor growl angrily. The calibration of the sound had changed. Suddenly the bike, like an oncoming missile, was moving toward them with accelerating speed.

Reaching for the girl, who lay whimpering on the beach, Sam pulled her away and threw his body over her, watching the bike come at full speed toward the kneeling young man. By then he had found the knife, and he was making an effort to rise and get out of the way of the bike, which was still coming at him.

By a split second he managed to evade the oncoming vehicle.

There was no question of Grace's intent. She was deliberately coming at the man, determined to hit him. She circled the bike, paused for a moment, then headed back in the young man's direction. Sam watched her, mesmerized, struck by her focus and determination.

As the bike moved forward again, the man danced away, side-stepped, then, as the bike missed him by inches, jumped on the seat behind her as she passed, gripping Grace with his thighs. Grace revved the motor, and the bike shot forward. As it pulled away swiftly, heading like a speeding bullet toward the ocean, he saw a glint of light as the man's arm went up, then down again, then again.

Sam tried to shout, but panic prevented his voice from coming.

Again the young man's arm shot up, then down again, sunlight spangling on the blade in his hand. The bike continued to shoot ahead, Grace still in control. It moved headlong into the ocean, now at full high tide, roaring into the oncoming surf, cutting through the foam and slicing madly into the waves, which swallowed it up with one greedy gulp.

For the moment the sight stunned Sam into silence, paralyzing his will. Then, panicked into movement, he ran to the water's edge, his mind numbed by fear as he scanned the surface for some sign of life. He saw nothing but the undulating ocean, heard no sound except that made by the surf slapping the shoreline.

"There. There."

He looked toward the young girl. She was pointing to something bobbing in the distance. Shielding his eyes from the now bright sun, he squinted across the water and saw what seemed like a human head, bobbing like a floating beach ball.

Moving quickly into the surf, he was toppled by the undertow, then found himself struggling to reach the object, still moving above the surface. Adrenaline charged him now. Was it Grace? Dear Grace? Sweet Grace? *What have I done?* All of his energy was focused on his mission. Please God, let it be Grace.

CHAPTER THIRTY

It came as a burst of light, an explosion of sudden discovery, an epiphany, as if she had awakened from a long slumber in the moist darkness of a tomb . . . or a womb.

Her mind groped for words, a sentence to describe what was happening. This is the end of expectations. This is the death of all dreams. This is the end of the future. This is the murder of hope.

Before, when she had, in that moment of insanity, jumped on Darryl's hateful icon, bounced her foot on the ignition pedal, sped blindly away into the sanctuary of the mist, she had felt only the prospect of ending, of shutting down, of getting out.

All her faculties seemed acute. She felt no sense of hysteria or panic. After all, she had chosen to take this ride into the beyond. Beyond what? Beyond where?

Then suddenly, for no apparent reason, she had turned back, let the motor slow, then idle. In the rising mist, she saw the three figures emerging, heard voices whose words did not register except as blasts of anger, which she returned in kind, working the motor's growl in response.

Desperation, she decided, had given her permission to do this. Perched on the bike, she watched the three figures emerge more clearly, but still she couldn't hear their voices, only the anger. Then they were fully developed, visually whole. Her child devil, harvest of her bad seed, the beast of hatred with the twisted cross of hate glinting in the sunbeams and the man, that piece of flotsam, her last potential lifesaver, the ring-around-the-finger man.

All nails in her coffin, she saw, feeling her lips curl in what could pass for a smile, but which she knew was contrived as the last look people might see, a frozen death mask of a smile. Then she saw the beast rise, seize the child devil and, as she believed, slash the knife across her throat.

Well, then, she thought, here was the moment, the license she had been seeking to kill the beast with his own weapon of choice. Desperation had given her permission. Despair, after all, offered no options. She had lost all the battles. What was one more to lose?

Then she had moved the monster forward, took dead aim. Her first pass was a miss. Turning, she tried again, missed again. There were voices, shouts, but she heard nothing except the sound of her own purpose. *It's all over; what does it matter?*

Suddenly he was behind her. She felt his weight on the seat, and she was now aiming the monsters, both of them, directly into the sea. She felt the first cut as she crossed the mudflat along the edge, then another and another as she shot into the sea.

It toppled her swiftly and she was flopping in the angry water, swallowing the salt sea. She felt something move beside her, a hand grasping at her blouse, and when she opened her eyes she saw the metal-punched swastikas still shiny and luminous, like tiny tropical fish, in the sun-drenched silence of the water. She was moving downward, pulled by the weight of his hand.

Why downward? Then her mind interpreted the reality; the bike was sinking like a rock, settling in the mud of the ocean bottom. Above her, she could see the sunlight above the water's surface. His hand still grasped her blouse. She flailed at his closed fist, but the water inhibited any power. Then she noted that the bike held him, a metal protrusion caught on the buckle of his Nazi belt. He had grasped her to save himself.

She fought his grasp and tried to find the mystery of the buckle, the undoing of it. But it held fast. Her fingers seemed useless. As she worked, she could see his face, a desperate child's face now, his eyes pleading, a fountain of bubbles spewing from his lips, his fist still tight around her clothes.

Marshaling the last vestige of strength, she ripped apart the buttons and slid out of the blouse, floating upward with bursting lungs, punching into the sunlit air.

Sucking in air, she felt her chest lurch; then she gagged, vomiting water. Disoriented, she imagined she noted that for some reason she was floating in a pool of red. Sharp pains shot through her body as she forced her head to stay above the surface, her eyes unfocused. Nausea and dizziness assailed her, and soon she felt herself slipping, going down, then bobbing upward just barely.

"Easy," a voice said. She felt hands pillow her. "Relax, float. Let me. . . ."

Her first thought was that someone was guiding her to oblivion, a watery grave.

"I tried . . ." she whispered, engulfed by a sudden blackness, a void.

"Just float," the voice said. "You're needed here." Suddenly she was trembling with cold.

CHAPTER THIRTY-ONE

When consciousness seeped back into her mind she opened her eyes to Sam's face.

"I'm here," Sam said, smiling. He patted her arm. Looking toward it, she saw the IV plugged into a vein at the back of her hand. She inspected her surroundings, her eyelids fluttering. Her gaze caught masses of color. Flowers.

"Where's 'here'?" she asked.

"Hospital," Sam said.

Memory was returning in tiny tendrils. As she moved, her back ached and pain shot through her. She saw Sam's face descend, then it was out of focus, but she did feel a cool sudden weight on her forehead. A kiss.

"Close call, my darling," Sam said.

"Him?" she asked.

"Drowned," Sam said.

She shrugged, feeling a vague remorse, despite the memory of her contempt.

"Jackie?"

"Waiting in the lounge. She's been here, staying at my place."

She felt herself being plugged back into events. *Is this where I want to be?* she wondered, then went blank again. But she could hear his voice.

"You rest, Grace. Be back later."

When she awoke nice people in white came. A nurse moved her bed up and she saw the room from a new angle. It was filled with flowers.

"Who from?" she whispered.

"'Love, Sam,'" the nurse said, her kindly face very black against the white of the uniform. Then a doctor came by, checked her pulse and put a cool hand on her cheek.

"Welcome back," he said.

"Back?"

"Palm Beach Memorial Hospital actually."

She tried to move, but the pain stopped her.

"Stitches," the doctor said. "Pain bad?"

"Bearable," she said, remembering finally.

"The cuts were nasty, but nothing sliced beyond repair. We put you together nicely. Call yourself lucky, lady." He chuckled. "Mr. Goodwin here pulled you out. Saved you. He can fill you in."

Again Sam's face came close, moved downward, and she felt his cool lips on her forehead.

Later she felt stronger. A purpling in the sky told her the sun was setting. With her eyes closed, she recalled the events in detail: the madness on the beach, the motorcycle, the race into the sea. And before that, what she had said to Sam, and the worst part, his reaction.

"Can you ever forgive me?" Sam said.

"Forgive you?"

They had brought in a tray and placed it before her—soup, toast, tea. "You've been pretty out of it for three days. They say you'll be okay."

"Do they? Then why do I feel still under the water?" She felt a sudden urge to giggle, which she did. She winced with pain. "He stabbed me."

"That he did. A number of times."

"He caught his belt buckle on his bike. I couldn't get him loose." She remembered his face, his eyes pleading, the trail of bubbles, the swastikas glistening.

"That part's over, Grace. And Jackie is confused, but contrite. She's too embarrassed to come in now that you're feeling better. She's ashamed. She seems to be comfortable at my place. I gave her my daughter's old room."

"Beware of generosity, Sam. It can be unhealthy," Grace protested. It was all registering now, coming back fast.

"I know," Sam said.

"In a few days I'll be out of your hair. Get back to my place. Find a job."

"I have one for you."

"Sorry, Sam. I can handle things on my own," Grace said. Her IV was out now and he was gently holding her hand. She felt his grip tighten, but she made no move to extricate herself.

"Sorry, I'm taking charge," Sam said.

"No way."

"We'll talk later," Sam said.

"Now."

"You're still weak."

"I'm strong enough," Grace said, feeling her anger begin. Then she crashed and closed her eyes again. Later, she warned herself. She needed a clearer mind. Logic had disappeared.

Later was the next day when she was stronger, much stronger. She had managed to sit up in bed when he came in first thing in the morning. She had been thinking about things all night. It was inexplicable to her, but the episode, her brush with death, had made her braver than before. What more could happen?

He came in holding a bouquet of yellow roses and wearing a big smile. His tan face looked handsome, his teeth white. He wore a kelly green silk shirt and brought with him a happy, festive air.

She smiled at him and shook her head. "It's nice, but it's not going to work."

"Is this another role you're playing?" he said.

"Everything about this was a role," she said. "I spelled it all out. Were you listening?"

"I heard every word. Your deceit was very effective. I was completely taken in. You fooled the hell out of me, Grace. I was stunned. It was my son Bruce who blew the whistle. He had you investigated."

"Sorry, Sam. Guilty as charged. I was after your money."

"Join the crowd," he said.

She shifted in the bed, wincing slightly.

"Shall I get the nurse?" he asked, concerned.

She shook her head.

"Jackie, then? She's been waiting in the hall outside. We tried talking last night. This Darryl thing, what he did and said, has stunned her. And nearly losing you. I'd say she needs professional help, Grace. But now she needs you most of all. Shall I call her?"

Grace contemplated the answer. Not yet, she decided, shaking her head.

"Is there any hope there, Sam?" Grace asked.

"There's always hope."

"I'm not optimistic," Grace sighed. She wasn't. "People don't change."

"People change all the time."

"You're no expert, Sam."

"As you very powerfully illustrated."

She was quiet for a long moment, watching his eyes, inspecting her.

"There were certain aspects that were sincere, Sam."

"I have no doubt about that."

"The way to a man's heart is not always through his stomach."

"Almost never." He smiled. "Message received."

He continued to look into her eyes.

"And what is the way to a woman's heart?"

She let the question hang in the air.

"I want you to marry me, Grace," Sam said.

Her reaction was a pointed harrumph.

"After hearing my story? You've lost your mind."

"Yes or no?"

"No," she said, shaking her head to emphasize her decision.

He looked puzzled.

"Are you still playing with my head?"

"You want honest. You're getting honest."

"But you said . . . that stuff about protection. Well, here I am, Sam Goodwin on his white steed come to rescue the maiden in distress. You're joking, right?"

"No. I'm rejecting your offer."

"I love you. You said . . . you loved me."

"You sound like a teenager."

"I feel like one. And I hate being rejected."

She saw that he was pouting, a real pout. He had discovered that what he had mistaken for banter was dead serious. She had seen her course clearly, although he was right about protection.

"Am I too old?"

"When you're eighty I'll still be nearly ten years younger than you are now."

"You have a point. If I make eighty."

"What about the baggage I carry? A dysfunctional daughter. And your kids. Obviously I will not be welcome with open arms. Who, after all, put a private eye on my tail? Will your fancy friends accept me? I doubt it. You'll be a laughingstock. Who is that treasure-hunting little, ignorant, uneducated, rough lady Sam has on his arm? Look at the rock on her finger. He's in his second childhood. He's gone senile. If she was a spectacular beauty, well, maybe. He's entitled to a trophy wife. . . ."

"Stop it, Grace," he said, raising his voice, then softening. "Stop it, please. I'm not a total fool."

"You're too much of a romantic, Sam," she said. "It makes you vulnerable, an easy mark. You need to be more hard-edged, more on your guard."

"I have other priorities."

"Like what?"

"Quality time," he whispered. He watched her through a long pause. "Love."

"You may be reading it wrong, Sam, putting too much stress on the physical."

"Better than not enough." He shrugged, smiled and winked.

"The comparisons will kill it, Sam. Your friends. Your kids . . ."

"Anne is dead," he said, interrupting.

Anne again, Grace sighed, suddenly panicked by the memory of the letters.

"Oh, my God," she cried, sitting higher in the bed. She felt the stitches stretch. "My pocketbook."

He opened a drawer, pulled it out and gave it to her.

"I found it in my driveway."

With shaking fingers, she took it from him, opening it quickly, then snapping it shut. She had glimpsed the letters.

"It's all there," he said.

"All?"

"Your wallet and keys. Some letters. It could only be yours. I picked it up, checked the ID and brought it here."

"Did you . . ." She cleared her throat, felt words forming on the tip of her tongue. Then she bit down on it, hard. "Thanks," she said.

He continued to hold her hand.

"About the matter at hand," he said. "You think I'm too much the romantic, then I'll talk turkey and make you an offer you can't refuse. Here's the deal: Ring around your finger. No prenup. What's mine is yours, what's yours is mine."

"Mine? I have nothing, Sam, but a screwed up teenager."

"You're the real thing," Sam said, after a long pause.

"The real thing?"

"It's about time," he said. His statement confused her. What did he mean?

He bent over and kissed her gently on the lips. "It all balances out, Grace. Think of our arrangement as a depletion allowance." When she frowned he said, "Oil. The devil is in the details."

She felt herself fading again.

"You rest," he said. "I'll be outside."

He started for the door, stopped.

"I'm selling as hard as I can, Grace," Sam said before leaving the room.

She nodded and closed her eyes. Then quickly opened them again. Reaching for her pocketbook, she opened the clasp and took out the letters, inspected them. There were no signs of their being tampered with. She arranged them chronologically again, then opened the first letter.

"Darling," it began. "My mind can barely accept this . . ."

She checked the envelope again. This was the last letter. It was placed in the envelope of the first one. *Thinks he's the clever one,* she thought. Now she understood what he meant by "the real thing." Compared to Anne.

She lay for a while, her eyes closed, then felt a sudden surge of energy. She pressed the nurse's button. The nurse's voice responded.

"Tell Mr. Goodwin I'm ready to see him again. And yes, he can bring in my daughter."

Ring around her finger, she whispered to herself, laughing. The stitches hurt, but she didn't care.

W24
LC 2012
ADD'D
25

DISCARD

03-01

F   Adler, Warren
            Mourning glory.